In Full BLOOM

JIM HOOKER

Publishing Coordinator – Sharon Kizziah-Holmes

Paperback-Press
an imprint of A & S Publishing
Paperback Press, LLC

ISBN -13: 978-1-960499-22-6

DEDICATION

This book is dedicated to those who are suffering or have suffered from mental health issues. It is also dedicated to the many families who have felt the impact of a loved one dealing with it, and who have chosen to support and nurture that loved one, even when the road at times became difficult.

My heartfelt condolences to those who have tragically lost a loved one from suicide, due to mental health issues, including PTSD.

CHAPTER 1

'My life for the last two years has been a struggle.
I have refused to let one pleasant thought touch my soul.'

April 30, 1959.

I anticipated the day ahead of me. I heard the alarm clock go off in the bedroom at the far end of the hall. It was not unusual for me to be up before the alarm, a habit I inherited from my dad, who never set a clock in his entire life. I had been up long enough to be on my second cup of coffee.

Last night was the last night I would spend in this house. We sold our home six weeks ago. The new owners would take possession today. I said *we* sold it, but I should have said I sold it. My wife, Karen, is no longer with me.

Karen was tragically killed in a car accident February 12, 1957, along with our beloved little boy Randy. He would have turned seven years old this June 17th.

I loaded the last few things from the house into Dad's Ford station wagon. Larry, my brother, who is eighteen months older, wanted me to drive the wagon to Decatur, Illinois where he lived. Mom always wanted a girl, but Larry and I were the only kids they ever had.

I made one more trip through the house, double checking to make sure everything was in good shape before I left. I stopped briefly in the back bedroom where Karen and I made so many memories and dreams – dreams that would never have a chance to come true. I made my way over to the bedroom window and stared at the sandbox I built for Randy. God, how I love that boy still. To say the last two years have been a painful nightmare would be an understatement. My life has been mired down in total grief.

My dad passed away from a sudden heart attack in May of 1955. Dad's passing was hard on all of us, especially Mom. I was still in the Marine Corp. Karen and I put our house up for rent, and she and Randy moved into the farmhouse with Mom. It was a good move for all of us. Mom, Karen, and Randy became very close during those months. The accident and loss of Karen and Randy crushed Mom. Everyone agreed Mom would have lived longer if not for the loss of the two of them.

We thought Mom's breast cancer was in total remission, but not so. It came back in a fury, and rapidly spread to her liver. She succumbed to cancer nine months after the accident. Thank God I was able to be home with her at the time.

I checked my watch. I didn't want to get over to Mom and Dad's farmhouse too early. My cousin, Donna, and her husband had a lease on the old farm and the house. Donna, a cook at the high school, didn't leave for work until 8:30. We had an agreement with her that we could use one of the four bedrooms to store the last of Mom and Karen's personal belongings.

Larry's wife, Martha, asked me to get an old vase of Mom's. Larry wanted an old box that held Mom's diary, some old personal notes, plus cards, and keepsakes. I wanted Mom's Bible. She had so many mementos in it and had underlined her favorite verses.

I glanced at my watch one more time. I wanted Donna to have left for work when I got there. I had said goodbye to her a couple days before. I wanted some time by myself to reminisce about all of the good times I had growing up on the old farm.

I deliberately drove by the school, and like I expected, Donna's car was there. I drove the long way out of town. I didn't want to go past where the accident occurred. It hurt too much.

When I pulled up the long driveway to the old home place, I recalled so many memories. Larry and I had spent our entire lives growing up on this old Kansas farm. We caught the bus every day at the end of the long drive until Larry was old enough to drive. His driving made it so much easier for Mom and Dad because we were both active in sports.

I went into the back bedroom, where Mom's belongings were stored, and retrieved the items Larry and Martha requested. After I placed them in the back of the old station wagon, I went to the porch and sat on the swing that faced the road. The farmhouse and the homestead sat on one-hundred-twenty acres of mostly pasture, with only a few wooded areas and grown-up water ways. Across the road my folks owned another three-hundred-eighty, acres of fertile crop ground. Dad and Mom had worked hard to make sure the farm, and everything they owned, was paid for. Although Dad wasn't a well-educated man, he certainly mastered the curriculum of how to accumulate assets.

I sat in the swing for what seemed like five minutes but was closer to twenty. I decided to walk around to the back of the house where Mom's clothesline remained. Larry and I helped Dad set those posts so many years ago. No matter what direction I looked, nothing but wonderful times flew through my mind. I didn't realize then how blessed we were to have such loving parents.

Mom was a Christian lady. She never missed church and tried so hard, in her words, "To please the Lord". Dad, on the other hand, never went to church except on Easter Sunday and to watch the Christmas programs. Dad loved kids and truly enjoyed watching the small one's blunder through their parts and sing the little songs, mostly out of key. Mom often joked the only reason Dad went to the program was to get the little brown bag of candy, nuts, and a big red apple. Dad usually smiled and agreed.

I could stay here and drive up and down Reminisce Road and Recall Avenue until the sun went down, but if I am going to baby this old station wagon, take my time, and get to Decatur, Illinois by Sunday, I need to leave Memory Ville. I started to walk back to the old '42 Ford Super Deluxe Woody Station Wagon. Larry asked me to sell my vehicle and said he would help me buy a new one when I got to Decatur. I still can't believe he wanted, and expected, me to drive this old beat-up vehicle that far. I'd spent my entire life on the premise that if Larry wanted me to do something, it was what I did. I replaced all of the belts, installed new plugs and put in a new battery. The tires seemed okay to me, but he demanded I put all new ones on.

Our old Ford wagon was turquoise blue with wood grain down each side. Our dad bought it used. He was a conservative man and never bought anything new.

I remembered how proud we were when he brought the car home, but the wagon had been sitting in the barn since Dad passed away. During the last few years, he owned it, the outside cosmetics had deteriorated badly. His eyesight and judgment of distance started to diminish toward the end. He constantly got too close to a tree, a fence, or even a parked car. The Ford looked pretty darn rough on the outside, but inside it was in remarkably good shape. We named it, "Ole Limpie", after an old cow that had a bad foot. Dad sold the cow to help pay for the wagon.

I couldn't wait to get the thing to Larry. He assured me a friend of his, a member of their church, who owned an Oldsmobile dealership, would get me a fantastic deal on a new Oldsmobile.

I looked at the roadmap a few days ago and decided to just follow my nose. I figured as long as I headed east-northeast, I could take small paved country roads and not rush the old Ford. Besides, I was looking forward to seeing the country. I had been told about the Ozark Mountains in southern Missouri and wanted to enjoy them. I also wanted to see the vast row crops in the bootheel of Missouri, and in Northeast Arkansas.

My first inclination was to cross the big Mississippi River at Cairo, Illinois, east of Charleston, Missouri. Once in Illinois, I would head north to Decatur where Larry and Martha lived. Larry was dead set on me getting to Decatur sometime Saturday so I could go to church with him on Sunday. Amazing as it is he has become involved in his church. When we were growing up, he simply hated church. When he got to high school, he refused to go. I didn't want to disappoint Mom, so I always went with her and proudly admitted I enjoyed church.

Larry was the rebel. He always dreamed he would get a Harley Davidson motorcycle and cruise around the U.S. living in the moment. He didn't think we could have a good time unless we had a six-pack of beer and two packs of cigarettes. I hated the taste of beer, but I always drank one with him and his buddies so they would not call me a sissy. It would have killed Mom if she had known about the beer. In her Christian belief, if you held a can of beer, you could go to hell, and if you drank just one can, you would surely become the devil's right-hand man.

I filled the gas tank on the station wagon. I would soon see

Wellington, Kansas in my rearview mirror. I planned to drive to Winfield, Kansas, which was approximately twenty-five miles, and wing it from there. My plan was to take my time since I didn't want to get to Decatur until Sunday around noon.

The way Larry wound up in Illinois was really pretty simple. He received a scholarship to play football for Southern Illinois. That's where he met Martha. He dreamed of playing professional football. However, like I had done with baseball, he came to realize he didn't have the talent to make that happen. Martha's uncle, who lived in Decatur and worked in management for the Caterpillar Company, promised Larry a good job if he was willing to move. He accepted the offer, and as usual, he excelled and advanced rapidly in the new factory in Decatur.

It was a beautiful and sunny day. I quickly put the miles behind me and enjoyed the new life that began in every plant, tree and wildflower. Farmers on tractors plowed fertile fields, built new fences–did all things country. That was me, 'country', it was who I was. That's where my heart was and has always been. Larry was confident I would love working at Caterpillar just as he had. I was not so sure. I did agree a change might do me good.

My life for the last two years had been a terrible struggle. I refused to let one pleasant thought touch my soul. I blamed myself for the loss of Karen and Randy. She tried so hard to talk me out of re-enlisting in the Marine Corps. They offered me, what I thought at the time, was a deal I could not refuse. Karen had been right. I should have been home to help raise Randy and take care of Mom.

CHAPTER 2

'I remember something my mom often said,
"You never get a second chance to make a good first impression."'

M y wristwatch confirmed what my stomach had been saying for miles. It was way past lunchtime. Those two fried pies Donna had left for me were long gone. I most certainly was ready for some protein. I hoped to find a nice little country cafe along the way, but no such luck. The next decent sized town was Lamar, Missouri, which was only a few miles ahead, and about twenty miles from the Kansas line. I also needed a place to fill up the old Ford.

Just as I hoped, one of the businesses at the edge of Lamar was my long-awaited oasis. A big sign out front said, "Mary's Café" with a footnote at the bottom of the sign that read: "Just Wonderful Country Food". I had a gut feeling, no pun intended, that I had found what I was looking for. The next business on the same side of the highway was a well-kept service station. Gas was a little more than I was used to paying back in Kansas. Our price in Willington was .31 cents a gallon, it was .34 cents here.

After my meal, I planned to fill up and try to put several miles behind me before dark. I didn't trust my luck with the old wagon after the sun went down. Hopefully, I could find a motel somewhere. My back-up plan, in case I couldn't find a room, was to sleep in the wagon. The weather was perfect, not too hot or too cold. I pulled Ole Limpie up to the front of the café. As soon as I walked in the door, I smelled the aroma of fried foods. The country decor that hung on every wall made me feel welcome. I also noticed how empty the place was. Considering the time, two-fifteen, was good news for me since I had avoided the noon rush, I wouldn't have to wait long for my meal.

In the far corner of the café, I noticed an elderly couple. I nodded my head and politely spoke to them, and they both said hello. In the opposite corner from the couple, next to the front and close to where I parked my wagon, sat two young men who looked like they were just out of high school, or perhaps were dropouts. The boys stared at my old wagon.

The larger of the two looked at me, and I immediately said, "How are you fellas?"

They ignored my greeting, and the smaller one sneered. "Man, you aren't too far from walking are 'ya?" Both let out loud, obnoxious laughs.

"Yep," I smiled. "She looks pretty rough but seems to run okay."

"I noticed you have Kansas plates, are you from Kansas?"

"Yes, sir," I said, but before I could say anything further, the bigger boy said, "Well, that explains everything. Most people from Kansas don't have 'nuff sense to drive without runnin' into something."

After both of them laughed again, I felt my blood pressure rise. I told myself to keep my cool.

I chose the table as far away from the smart-alecky boys as possible. The elderly couple got up from their table and went to the cash register to pay. I'm sure they sensed possible trouble and just wanted to exit as soon as possible.

I picked up the menu that was on the table and directed my full attention to looking over the choices. I still heard the 'want-to-be tough' boys make short, sarcastic remarks and laugh. Part of me wanted desperately to invite them outside and give them what they needed, 'a good old country ass-kicking'. I surmised neither one of them had ever been in a real fight in their life. I kept in good shape. I lifted weights and ran for the last two years. I found physical exercise to be a good escape. Before I joined the Marine Corps, I was the Kansas Golden Glove Champion in my weight division. The last nine months I was in the Marine Corps, I was a hand-to-hand combat instructor. I also had my black belt in karate.

As much as I would have enjoyed calling these young men's

bluff, there were three reasons I didn't go down that path. First, I was hungry and wanted to enjoy my meal. Second, I was having a good day and didn't want something as stupid as a confrontation with a couple of wet-behind-the-ears teenage boys to ruin it. Third, and perhaps the most important of all, was this beautiful blonde waitress that smiled at me as she headed to my table.

Uninvited, she politely sat down straight across from me. She leaned across the table and softly whispered, "I thought you might need someone to rescue you. However, I must admit, it doesn't look as though you need any help at all."

She leaned back and sat straight in her chair, took out her order pad from her checkered apron, and without losing her beautiful smile, asked, "Have you decided what you want to order?"

I stared at her, and without thinking I said, "Well, I did before you sat down. Now I'm thinkin' it might very well be you."

Realizing how inappropriate that statement was, I quickly added, "I am so sorry, I shouldn't have said that." We both nervously chuckled. "Is the special of the day still available?"

"Yes sir, it is." She took my meal order and politely asked, "What do you want to drink?"

At that very instant, the phone on the wall behind the counter rang. She hastily said, "I'll have your order out shortly." She rushed toward the phone. Before she could get that far, a middle-aged lady from the kitchen area quickly stepped out and answered the phone. She paused for a little while, then said, "Okay, I will tell them, Ruby." She looked across the room toward the want-to-be tough boys.

"Rex, that was your mama on the phone. She needs help putin' the garden out. She said if you want a place to sleep tonight and breakfast in the mornin', you best be gettin' your lazy butt's home."

The two quickly got up from their chairs and hastily started toward the door. The younger of the two turned to the lady behind the counter and said, "Put the Cokes and ice cream on Mom's bill."

"I got you covered boys. Thanks, and tell 'yer mama, hi'fer me."

Still by the phone, she looked at me, and with a very warm smile said, "Thanks for choosin' to eat with us," before proceeding to apologize for the two rude boys.

"Here in Lamar, we pride ourselves in having warm, friendly people, and those two most certainly are not that."

I replied, "Oh, that's ok. I suppose every town has a few like that."

"My name is Mary. The bank and I own this place."

I assured her I could totally relate to that type of business arrangement and said, "You have a nice place here." I smiled, "My name is Leon Wilson."

About that time the aforementioned gorgeous waitress appeared from the kitchen carrying my meal. Mary turned and looked at Miss Beautiful and said, "Leon Wilson, I would like for you to meet my sweet little sister, Brenda."

While never once losing her warm smile, she said, "So pleased to meet you, Leon-from-somewhere-in-Kansas."

Mary was summoned to the kitchen by a man I assumed was the cook. Brenda placed my meal on the table and told me to enjoy it. I began to chow down. My first impression was correct. Everything on my plate was just like when I sat at Mom's table when I was a teenage boy.

Brenda was gone for a short time then came back out with a pitcher of tea.

"I hope sweet tea is okay. I assumed that is what you wanted?"

"Absolutely! That is exactly what I wanted, the sweeter the better."

Brenda carefully filled my glass with the sweet tea and politely asked me, "Do you live just over the state line?"

"No," I replied. "I was actually born and raised in south central Kansas, in a small town called Wellington."

She set the pitcher of tea on the table next to my glass and went back into the kitchen and returned with two large salt and pepper containers and began to refill the small salt and pepper shakers on each table. She worked her way across the dining room, occasionally looking my way. She always wore that beautiful smile. Mother nature had been extremely kind to her. Her smile was not the only thing I admired. Not only was she simply gorgeous, but everything was in perfect proportion from the top of her head to the bottom of her feet and everywhere in between. You see, I am a thirty-year-old red-blooded American male. Yes, I promise you, I noticed her perfect derriere, and how she filled out that white, tight-fitting blouse.

I had almost finished my wonderful meal, and Brenda noticed. She came across the floor to my table and asked, "Do you care for a piece of pie?"

Out of nowhere, I opened my mouth without having my brain totally engaged. I readily replied, "The only way I want pie is if you would let me buy you a piece, and you sit down at this table, and we eat together."

I didn't think her smile could be any warmer, but all of a sudden, her expression lit up the whole room. Her smile quickly faded when she stared directly into my eyes and firmly asked, "You aren't married, are you?"

I answered with a question of my own, "Are you?"

She defensively replied with a stronger voice. "No, but you haven't answered my question. Are you married?"

I hesitated, why do I hate telling my story? Was it that I didn't want the sympathy that came with it? Or because of the sting I felt every time I retold it? I proceeded to inform her I had lost my wonderful wife along with our precious five-year-old son in a terrible car wreck a couple of years ago.

Brenda looked shocked and embarrassed. "Gosh, I'm so sorry."

It was obvious Mary had been eavesdropping on our conversation. She said, "Mr. Handsome from Kansas. We close in eight minutes. May I make a suggestion? It is a beautiful day. Why don't you guys go to the park and eat your pie there?"

I looked at Brenda and said, "That's fine with me."

Mary proceeded to ask me if I liked President Truman.

"Well," I replied. "Sure, as a matter of fact, I have always admired President Truman. For goodness-sake why are you asking me a question like that?"

Brenda giggled and intervened by saying, "Lamar is the birthplace of Harry S. Truman, thirty-third President of the United States. We have a Harry S. Truman Museum here, in Lamar."

I paid for my meal that included two pieces of apple pie. I proudly laid a dollar on the table for Brenda's tip, about four times what I normally tipped for a lunch meal.

I wasn't sure she would want to be seen riding around in Ole Limpie, so I asked, "Are you okay being seen in this old wagon?"

She laughed, "Oh, it's not that bad. You wouldn't believe some of the vehicles I've owned."

I politely opened the passenger door for her and she softly said, "Well, thank 'ya, sir."

On the drive to the park, I took the opportunity to explain why I was driving the wagon to my brother in Decatur, IL. I told her the story of how the Ford got its nickname, Ole Limpie.

She seemed to enjoy the story and slowly began to ask questions about my area of the country in Kansas. I could tell she was very curious about me. I, as well, had many things I wanted to know about her.

She asked, "Do you want to eat our pie first or visit the museum first?"

I replied, "I'm okay with what you choose."

She said, "Let's go to the museum first."

I carefully followed Brenda's directions to President Truman's Museum. We clearly enjoyed each other's company. She told me the next exit to my right would be the museum. The first thing we noticed were several construction trucks, then the sign that read, 'Closed'. A worker in front of the building told us there was a water leak in one of the bathrooms that caused a considerable amount of damage.

I quickly assured her, "Somehow I think I might enjoy sitting at a picnic table and eating pie with you more than looking through a museum anyway."

"So, are you a democrat?" Brenda asked with a smile.

"No, not necessarily," I replied. "I do pretty much like my dad always did. I vote for the man and what I think is best for our country, regardless of party."

"To be honest with you," Brenda said, "I don't understand politics enough to have an educated opinion. I usually vote for whoever Mary, my twin sister, Linda, and their husbands think is the best."

Our conversation bounced back and forth, mostly small talk, while both of us repeated nervous chuckles.

We found a table at the end of the park shaded with several large trees. Brenda had brought a dish towel from the café to clean off the table. She was also thoughtful enough to bring a quart of tea, sweet of course, with ice and a couple of plastic cups. We retrieved the pie from the back seat, then sat across from each other at the picnic table. Somehow, I knew this would be the best little mini picnic ever. A part of me was anxious and nervous, and a part of me felt so comfortable in Brenda's presence.

I remember something my mom often said, "You never get a second chance at a good first impression."

I knew I needed to be myself. I so much wanted Brenda to like me–I mean really like me.

We both downed our apple pie and it was delicious.

I asked, "Who made the pie?", and jokingly added, "I bet it was you."

She laughed, "We actually have a good cook at the café, but Mary has always been in charge of the pie making."

"How long have you worked there?"

"I started a couple of months after my divorce, about two years now. I was working at a bank in the bookkeeping department. The vice president of the bank, a married man with two kids, kept coming on to me and making it very difficult and uncomfortable working there. At that time, I wanted nothing to do with any man, let alone a married man."

She began her story about the big mistake she made when she married Eddie Ray. "Eddie Ray is good looking, has always been. He has always known it! Looking back, I guess that was the main thing that attracted me to him. But I can assure you, that is the only thing he had going for him."

She continued to speak negatively about Eddie Ray, at times, almost angrily. I sat there and listened to her. I felt her pain while she continued to talk about him. I think I was the sounding board she so desperately needed.

Brenda had not mentioned if she had children. I very much wanted to know if she did, so I had to ask, "Do you have any kids, Brenda?"

Her face turned to a look of pure jubilation, "Yes, I do!" she replied. "I have a sweet little girl named Sheila. She is the joy of my life."

"Do you have full custody of Sheila?"

"Yes, thank God, I do. Eddie Ray never wanted a baby. In fact, he became very angry and pissed at me when I became pregnant. The physical and mental abuse, which was most certainly bad before the baby, only got worse after she was born. As Sheila got older, he became very physical with her."

"My folks never liked Eddie Ray, especially my dad. If he had known only ten percent of the abuse and certain things Eddie Ray did to me and Sheila, he probably would be in prison now, because he would have seriously harmed Eddie Ray. Dad and Mom gave us five acres of land on the far side of their eighty-acre farm to build a new house on. Eddie Ray and I had absolutely no money. He couldn't hold a job at one place for more than a couple of months."

She paused momentarily and looked down at her empty paper plate. "I'm so glad Dad and Mom were smart enough to see through him. They borrowed all the money for the house from the bank solely in their names, including the deed to the five acres. We made payments to them, and they in turn paid the bank. Looking back, I'm sure the bank didn't want anything to do with Eddie Ray. We borrowed enough money to purchase all new furniture including the appliances. That too, was in Mom and Dad's name. So, when we divorced, he couldn't claim any of it. Dad gave him $500.00 and asked him to please stay out of our lives."

"That pleased him, because he didn't care one thing about me or Sheila. He left shortly after the divorce. I heard he went up north somewhere in Michigan to work in construction with his cousins. That was about two years ago and I haven't heard one word from him. I can assure you, that is fine with me."

Brenda looked at me and took a deep breath. I was quite sure she was going to ask me something. But before she could, I quickly, and intentionally asked about Sheila. Brenda once again burst into that beautiful smile, and a sparkling glow danced in her eyes.

"Sheila is my reason for living."

I smiled back at her, "How old is she?"

"She's five years old. I had her almost exactly a year after Eddie Ray and I got married. I'm so fortunate Linda, that's my twin sister, loves Sheila almost as much as I do, and keeps her while I work. Linda and Daryl, her husband, have never been able to have kids, so Linda loves to spoil her. Daryl is an attorney here in town, so Linda doesn't have to work. That works really well for me to have such a good babysitter for her."

"Oh, that's great," I said, "Do you have any other siblings

besides Linda and Mary?"

She shook her head, "Nope, it's just the three of us girls. We've been so blessed to have had such wonderful loving parents."

Without hesitation, I replied, "I most certainly can relate to that. My brother and I were also blessed to have had great parents."

I truly felt the seriousness in her voice when she said, "Bless your heart, Leon. I can't imagine the pain you have gone through these last few years. Would I be out of line to ask how the accident happened?"

"No, it's nice you care to know." I proceeded to tell her. "I was on active duty with the Marines, and Karen was a school teacher. The day was no different than any other. Their route to school crossed a busy state highway which had a signal light. According to the investigators and an eye witness, Karen had a green light and was proceeding through the intersection when a large ten-wheel dump truck, loaded with chat, ran the light and hit her car broadside."

"To this day, I still become emotional when I replay that awful day." I knew my voice broke since I choked on my words. "In that instant my life forever changed." I tried hard to pull myself out of this pity trip. "I do have some comfort knowing that neither suffered, they were killed instantly. The Marine Corps gave me a hard-ship honorable discharge."

We both sat there, swapping little tidbits about ourselves. It had been a long time since I had enjoyed an afternoon like this one with Brenda. I somehow felt the same was true with her. As it often does when you really enjoy yourself, time flies. I looked at my watch and couldn't believe what time it was. At that second, we both turned our heads toward the far end of the park, where a police car approached in our direction. I realized it was coming straight toward our table, which was at the end of the road. I glanced at Brenda and realized her smile had turned into a chuckle.

She pointed, "That's Harold." Brenda chuckled a little louder. "Big sister is checking on me."

Before I could question her to figure out what was taking place, she proceeded to let me know Harold was Mary's husband, and he was the deputy sheriff of Barton County.

Harold pulled up behind Ole Limpie, opened the car door, and slowly crawled out of the patrol car. Harold was a very large man, with quite a sizable mid-section. He looked towards us then headed our way. When he came closer, a big smile appeared and he spoke in a deep southern drawl.

"Y'all ain't got any pie left, have you? I'm kinda hungry."

"Are you kidding?" Brenda said, "We were hoping you were bringing us some more."

He stared in my direction, so Brenda introduced us. I quickly slid out of the picnic bench and took a couple steps toward him. We both latched our hands and gave a meaningful shake.

Harold asked, "Where are you from in Kansas?"

"South-central."

That didn't seem to be quite what he was searching for. He asked, very directly, "What town?"

"Wellington."

"That country is very flat, ain't it?" he asked.

"Kinda' rolling, it is wheat country," I replied.

Harold said he was born and raised in southern Arkansas. I thought that explained the southern accent. Before I could comment, he added, "I grew up on a damn old cotton farm. Did 'ya ever pick cotton?" he asked.

"No, I can't say I have."

Don't," he said, "There ain't nothin' any harder than working on a damn ole cotton farm. Trust me, I know."

It was obvious Harold was somewhat different, but I liked him. He came across as a 'what you see is what you get' kind of guy. He didn't have a need to impress anyone. He looked at Brenda. "Mary told me to tell you that Linda came by with Sheila, and for you to enjoy your evening. She's taking Sheila home with her to spend the night. She'll drop her off at your house sometime in the morning."

Harold and I both acknowledged it was nice to meet one another. We said goodbye and he headed back to his patrol car. He stared at my Kansas license plate on Ole Limpie. We observed him writing the number down on a small pad. Brenda and I both agreed he would probably be calling Kansas within the next five minutes. I told Brenda I totally understood, and quite frankly, respected him for it.

I again looked at my watch and simply couldn't believe how late it was. I told Brenda, "I best get you back to the café to get your car."

I was going to have to say goodbye and head toward the next town east. Brenda stared off across the park. I could tell she was deep in thought. She looked back at me. "You know, we have a nice hotel here in Lamar, and you know you're going to need to eat supper sometime."

I agreed, then asked, "Is there somewhere here to get a hamburger and Pepsi later?"

"Sure, we have a little drive-in about four blocks from here." She paused, "Let me run this by you. I am not much on fixing big meals, but I make a great ham sandwich, and my specialty is Pecan Brownies."

"Well Ma'am," I said, in a fake western drawl, "I think I might just be plum delighted to eat one of your ham sandwiches."

She smiled from ear to ear.

On our way back to the café, we decided I would drop her off to get her car, then I'd go to the hotel and check in before driving to her house.

She looked at me with a sly grin. "That will give me a chance to straighten up the place before you get there."

I must admit I truly loved her down-to-earth honesty. I assured her I vividly remembered Karen saying it is a losing battle to pick up behind a five-year-old. When we got back to the café, Brenda went directly to her car and wrote down directions to her house.

"When you turn off the highway onto the gravel road, my house will be the second one on your right. My folks' house will be the first house on your right." Then she added, "Mom and Dad built their house when Linda and I were in the ninth grade. I remember it being so cool because we each had our own room."

Just as Brenda got into her car, I politely asked if there was anything I could pick-up at a grocery store and bring.

"Well, as a matter of fact there is, but you won't need to stop at the store."

I quickly asked, "What?"

She smiled, looked directly into my eyes. "I only need you and that sweet grin of yours."

I felt my grin get bigger and I shook my head. "You got it girl. See you in a little bit." I made sure Brenda's car started before I got into mine.

I gingerly drove Ole Limpie across town to the hotel. I checked into my room and freshened up. I was ready to drive to Brenda's. I looked at my watch, not sure how long I had been here. I wanted to get to Brenda's as soon as possible, but I also wanted to give her a little time. I decided to just sit and chill for ten minutes. I looked at my watch again, only five minutes had passed, but it seemed like thirty. Ah, what the heck, I thought, she's had plenty of time.

I carefully followed Brenda's detailed directions, and before long I was looking for the big Baptist church on my left. The next gravel road to the right was closer than I had expected. I drove about a quarter mile and there it was, Brenda's childhood home. I could just picture her, Linda, and Mary getting on the bus. I slowed down and carefully looked everything over. I hoped one or both of her parents would be outside. I didn't see them, but I couldn't help noticing how much their yard resembled my folks' yard. Mom loved flowers and it was obvious Brenda's mom did too. A couple of red rose bushes were 'in full bloom' along with some bright yellow lilies. Everything was neat as a pin.

Just as she described it, Brenda's house was white with green shutters, and had a purple hat, adorned with flowers, that hung on the front door. It had two bedrooms and a large carport. She said her dad insisted on a large carport so she could get in and out of her car without getting wet from the blowing rain or snow. I drove into the driveway and pulled Ole Limpie close to the house.

Before I could get out of the car, Brenda came out onto the front porch. She wore her big, friendly smile that I loved.

"I see you found it!"

"Yep, you give great directions, young lady."

Brenda looked like an angel. It was apparent she had changed clothes, fixed her hair and applied new make-up, including fresh lipstick. I walked up to the porch, stopped before going up the steps, and slowly looked over the yard and house.

"Brenda, what a nice place you have."

"Thank you," she replied. "I am very proud of it. It makes a wonderful place for me to raise Sheila. I have my folks to thank for that. I am not throwing my money away paying rent. I'm far enough from them to have privacy, but close enough to be there for them in case of an emergency, or if I need help with Sheila."

"Absolutely," I replied. "It's just perfect."

Brenda turned and opened the door, "come on in."

When I passed her, I smelled her sweet perfume. Then the aroma of brownies baking in the oven overpowered her sweet perfume as I walked inside. "Wow, are those brownies I smell?"

"Yes sir, I hope you like pecans in them. That is usually the way I make them."

"I love any kind of nut," I replied.

Brenda let out a big laugh. "Boy, you would love my twin sister. She's always been a big nut."

She pointed to the table. "Are you ready for that sandwich I promised?"

"Yes, I most certainly am."

Brenda gave me a paper plate. "The fixings are on the table. If you don't mind, you can just build your own."

I said, "Oh, yes, I almost forgot, I stopped at that little store at the edge of town and got some sodas and potato chips."

"Well, how thoughtful."

I quickly jogged out of the house and returned carrying the chips and six sodas, three Pepsi's and three Orange Crush. Brenda looked at the sodas, then at me. I smiled and said, "Somewhere in our conversion in the park you mentioned you liked Pepsi and Sheila liked Orange Crush."

Her big smile turned into a full-blown glow. "You are just too darn sweet." She retrieved two glasses with ice from the refrigerator and set them on the table.

While she filled the glasses, I opened the bag of chips.

We sat across from each other at her kitchen table. I could not have enjoyed a meal more if I was sipping fine wine and eating a filet mignon. Somehow, I wanted to think Brenda felt the same. We were sitting at the table making small talk when all of a sudden, without any warning, Brenda let out a loud yell. I about jumped out of my pants. She flew out of her chair and made a mad dash for the stove. Grabbing a dish towel, she jerked open the oven door and quickly looked at the brownies and pulled them out. I was afraid of the worst, but hoped for the best. They looked perfect and could not have been any better if she had been checking on them every thirty seconds. Brenda gave a big sigh of relief, her face red with embarrassment.

"Thank God," she muttered to herself. She set the pan of brownies on top of the stove. The aroma filled every nook of her little kitchen.

"If they taste as good as they smell, I think I could eat the whole pan."

She laughed. "I'll take a couple out for Sheila, and you can have the whole pan."

"Oh, I was just joking." I laughed at her.

We sat at the table for a few minutes and caught our breath from the excitement of the brownie rescue. She suggested we go to the living room where we would be more comfortable. The subjects of our conversation bounced all over the place, from things we liked and disliked to our activities in high school.

I told her what a wonderful wife Karen had been, and how I felt so guilty for staying in the Marine Corps. She shared things about Sheila, and I talked a lot about Randy. Her sympathy about my loss seemed so sincere. I gradually became more comfortable with her.

I had to ask, "I just don't understand how someone as attractive as you can still be single after being divorced for over two years."

"Well," she began, "it took me a few months after my disaster with Eddie Ray before I wanted to have anything to do with a man. Linda fixed me up with a guy her husband had represented in a divorce case. He was nice looking and actually was a nice guy. We just simply didn't click. I've been asked out several times at the café and dated a few times. Most of them were losers and pretty much all they wanted was to take me to bed."

"One time, on a first date, mind you, I had made a nice meal, he came in, gave me a kiss, then before I knew what was happening, he started to grope me all over. It seemed he had more hands than an octopus has legs. All of them were desperately trying to explore forbidden places. I tried hard to calm him down, but nothing worked. I got pissed and told him to leave. He did and I laid across my bed and just cried."

"A couple of months passed. and this new guy came into the café. He was from Oklahoma." She hesitated for a few seconds and stared at the floor. She looked back at me then continued her story.

"The guy told me he had been divorced for a couple years. He didn't have kids, but said he had always wanted some. Sheila

19

thought he hung the moon. He was so polite and had a great sense of humor. It was apparent he was interested in me. He was a salesman for a company that sold dairy supplies, milking equipment and other supplies to dairy farmers."

"Anyway," she continued, "we went out on a few dates. He was really nice and seemed to always say the right thing. I was definitely falling for him. Looking back, there were so many signs I was just too dumb to see. He told me I couldn't call him because he took out his phone. He claimed his ex-wife and her new boyfriend were harassing him. I mentioned more than once I would drive there for a weekend, but he always had some excuse. So many signs, so many lies."

"Boy, he was Mr. Slick. I must admit, he got what he wanted. After a few dates, we became intimate. I even spent a weekend in Kansas City with him. I fell, and I mean fell hard. I got up in the morning thinking about him and went to bed every night thinking about him. I can't believe I was so blind."

"Brenda," I began, "there is an old saying. *'The easiest thing in the world is to convince someone of something if that is what they want to believe'."*

"Maybe," she admitted, "one day Mary's walk-in cooler went on the blink. She called a company out of Joplin, Missouri to fix it. Mary was visiting with the repairman and asked him if he enjoyed living in Joplin. 'Well," he said, 'my wife and I moved to Miami, Oklahoma, a few years ago, and we really like it there' When I heard Miami, Oklahoma my ears perked up. I went over to him and asked if by any chance he knew Wilbur Tate. 'Oh goodness yes,' he said, 'my wife and I go to church with him and his wife, and his two boys are good friends with our two boys.' I almost passed out. My knees got weak, and I immediately got sick to my stomach."

I felt extreme hurt in her voice. "Oh Brenda, I am so sorry."

She continued, "I got in my car, went home and cried. Mary said the repairman asked why I had reacted that way. She told him the whole story. The guy was floored and he couldn't believe it. Mary asked him, 'Are you sure we are talking about the same guy?' She proceeded to tell him that Wilbur Tate sold dairy farm supplies. He said, 'That's the same guy!' I am sure word got back to him. He never came back into the café or called, or anything. I never heard one word from him again. A part of me would like to see him just one more time, to tell him what a sorry bastard he is."

"I think all of us would love to see you do that, Brenda."

Brenda looked at me and worked hard to show me a smile. This one was not as natural, but sweet, nonetheless.

"I'm sorry I have been forcing you to ride along on all my pity trips, Leon."

"Oh, I don't feel that way at all. Trust me, I can totally relate to your need to vent." I started to comment further, but Brenda interrupted me.

"Hey! We've got brownies to eat!"

She headed to the kitchen. I asked if I could use her bathroom to get rid of a little Pepsi. She pointed to the bath and said, "Don't pay any attention to the leaking faucet."

"No problem," I replied. I entered the bathroom and soon realized the drip she referred to was more of a stream. I looked over the fixture, and it was much like the one we had at home. I had replaced washers many times. I was hoping she might have washers or what some call O-rings. If she did, I could get the drip fixed before I left.

I exited the bathroom and went down the short hall. Brenda was by the kitchen table with two pieces of brownies on small plates, accompanied by table forks and two empty glasses. She said, "Would you like a glass of cold milk with these?"

"You bet! That would be great. The drip is kinda' bad, isn't it?" She explained that her dad always fixed all the maintenance problems around the house. However, they had left that Monday, along with her dad's brother and her mom's sister, for a ten-day trip to Colorado.

I said, "Wait, your mom's sister married your dad's brother? How cool is that?"

"Yeah, it is! They do everything together, from going to church, to going fishing to going to ball games. You name it and they do it together. The faucet has been leaking for a while, but I didn't want to bother Dad. They have been so busy the last few days trying to get everything organized before leaving on their trip."

I asked Brenda if she knew if she had any O-rings.

She chuckled. "I don't have a clue what an O-ring is." Before I could explain, she told me her dad had an old wooden box full of stuff in the storage room.

"Do you mind getting it for me?" I asked.

She went into the storage room and returned with a rather large wooden box filled with a few tools, some light bulbs, fuses and an assortment of household repair items, including O-rings.

Taking it out of the box, I closed the lid and said, "We'll have that leak fixed in a jiffy."

Brenda pointed to a large clock hanging on the living room wall. It read 25 minutes after midnight.

"Oh my gosh, I didn't realize it was that late," I said.

"Leon, I would love for you to meet my sister, Linda, and I would love for you to meet Sheila too," she continued. "Linda has a hair appointment at 8:00 in the morning. She'll be bringing Sheila by here before she goes to the hairdresser. Why don't we do some trading? I'll fix you breakfast for you fixin' my leaking faucet in the morning."

I hesitated for a moment. I had planned to be on the road by 6:00 am. I could tell how much she wanted me to meet Sheila, and to tell the truth, I wanted to meet her myself. I agreed with Brenda's trade. I thanked her for the great sandwich and brownies. We both acknowledged that we had truly enjoyed our afternoon and evening. I got to the door, then turned and looked at Brenda. We both stared at each other. I wanted so much to grab her and lock lips, but my better judgment told me not to. I was so afraid that if I lit that fire, it might get totally out of control.

Brenda had been shoved, pushed, battered and abused. I wanted so much to restore her faith in my gender. We gave each other a gentle hug and said good night. I exited through the door and walked straight to the car.

I looked back and said, "I'll see you in the morning."

She waved, "Scrambled eggs and sausage, okay?"

"That'll be perfect," I replied.

I started up Ole Limpie and headed for the hotel. When I got there, I was so sure I would be ready to hit the sack, but found I was still wound-up from the day. Wow, I thought, while I reflected on everything that had happened from the moment I walked into Mary's Café. I undressed, showered and crawled into bed.

I set my alarm clock and headed to Snooze-Ville. I turned and tossed for a few minutes still trying to absorb the day. All of a sudden, I heard a loud clatter. What in the world was that? I tried to get my wits about myself when I realized it was my alarm clock. Surely there is a mistake, it couldn't possibly be six in the morning, but it was.

CHAPTER 3

'Remember boys, women love getting flowers. It doesn't matter what kind of flowers or what kind of vase. It is the thought that touches their hearts.'

I went to the front desk and checked out, desperately hoping I would find fresh brewed coffee. I got my wish, and unlike some hotels, the coffee was quite good. I checked my time. I didn't want to be late, but I also didn't want to be too early. I remembered seeing flowers in Brenda's folk's yard. I felt sure it would be okay with them if I picked a bouquet for their daughter. I had the perfect vase, an empty Pepsi bottle on the floorboard of Ole Limpie. In no time at all I was on the gravel road to Brenda's house. I drove up the driveway to her folk's place and took a few moments to admire it.

I remembered often, usually in the spring, Dad picked flowers for Mom, sometimes wildflowers. He put them in every type of container you could imagine. He would say, "Remember boys, women love getting flowers. It doesn't matter what kind of flowers, or what kind of vase. It is the thought that touches their hearts."

Somehow, it just seemed to me, it would be better if I placed the flowers somewhere in Brenda's house and let her find them after I left. In order to get them in the house without her seeing them, I needed a sack or box. I remembered I had sacked up Randy's toys to take to Decatur. After Randy's death, Mom cleaned all his toys. She thought Randy would have wanted his cousins, Larry's kids, to have them.

I located the extra-large bag of toys and decided to dump them on the floorboard in the back seat of the old wagon. As if it was meant to be, a big yellow plastic horse, Roy Rogers' Trigger to be exact, lay at the top of the pile. A light went off in my head. I remembered Brenda telling me Sheila liked horses, and her dad and mom planned to get her a pony for Christmas this year. I rummaged through the pile of toys until I located other pieces that were in the set we bought for Randy. It included plastic figures of Roy Rogers, his horse, Trigger, Dale Evans, her horse Buttermilk and their dog Bullet. I was sure Sheila would love them.

A look at my watch revealed the time ten to seven. Perfect, I thought. I drove to Brenda's house, got out the bag with the toys, Brenda's flowers, and a Phillips and standard screwdriver I had in the ole wagon. It's all I would to need to work on the faucet.

I walked up the steps and knocked on the door.

"Come on in," Brenda called out. "Have a seat. I'm not going to leave these biscuits. I don't want them to burn."

"That's fine." I grabbed the O-ring that was still lying on the kitchen table. "I'll go fix your faucet while you finish breakfast."

I was sure she didn't notice the size of the bag. I quickly closed the bathroom door, got out the Pepsi bottle and flowers, then rearranged the towels in the linen closet to make room for the flowers. A perfect place for now.

I headed into the kitchen with the bag of toys. I set them on the kitchen counter and began to pull them out carefully, one piece at a time. Brenda looked quite surprised. "Do you think Sheila would like these?"

She squealed, "Oh my gosh, she will love them, Leon. How sweet of you."

I explained the full story as to why I had them as I returned each piece to the sack.

She said, "That's so special, thank you so much, Leon." She pointed to the table. "Your breakfast is ready, sir."

"Boy, this looks good, and by the way, your faucet is fixed."

"Bless your heart, I appreciate it so much."

I remarked, "Well, from the looks of this food, I would say I made the best trade."

We sat down at the table, and I can assure you, I was ready to dive in. I commented several times how great everything was, and repeated it was one of the best trades I had ever made. We nearly had everything cleaned up. I was brave enough to give her a kiss. I knew anything would be short lived, since Linda would pull into the driveway any minute.

We both wound up at the sink at the same time. Standing side by side with our bodies literally touching, we each turned, faced one another, and our eyes met. Then we heard the sound of a car door slamming. Darn, I thought. I hoped she was disappointed in the timing also. We gave each other a pleasant smile, shrugged our shoulders, and headed to the living room.

The door flew open. It was Sheila holding a closed quart jar with what appeared to be a crawdad. She had been so excited to show her mom the crawdad, she hadn't noticed I was in the room. Brenda took the jar from her and took a second to admire her prized possession.

She said, "Sheila, I want you to meet someone."

Sheila turned her head in my direction, and before her mother could say a word, she blared out, "Who are you?"

I gave her a big smile and said, "Well, my name is Leon."

She said, "What are you doing here?"

I searched every nook in my brain to come up with the right answer, and I knew I needed to do it in a hurry. "Well, your mother told me she would make me breakfast if I would fix the leak in the bathroom faucet."

"Uh, okay," she said, "you wanna' see my crawdad?" She quickly took it out of her mother's hand.

Before I got caught up in the crawdad tale, I felt it best to show Linda some respect and introduce myself. I walked toward her, she took a step or two in my direction, and I offered her my hand. She readily accepted and we shook hands.

"Hi, I am Linda, Brenda's sister."

They were pretty much spitting images of each other. Wanting to inject some humor into this, I said, "Let me guess, I bet you girls are twins?"

Linda was just as Brenda had said, full of wit. She quickly replied, "Wow, not only are you good looking, you're a genius." We both laughed.

"I most certainly wouldn't go that far. So nice to meet you Linda, my name is Leon." Not wanting Linda to outwit me, I looked toward Brenda then back at Linda. "I don't think she is nearly as ugly as you said she was." They both let out a big laugh.

Linda looked straight toward me, "I like you a lot."

Sheila was dead determined I was going to pay some attention to her and her crawdad. I asked her if it had a name. She answered no and wondered what she should name it.

"Funny Legs." She giggled.

"That's the perfect name," I smiled at the cute little girl.

I happened to remember Roy and Dale and their horses. I grabbed the big bag and asked, "Do you like horses?"

"Yep," she replied, "they're my favorite animals."

I lifted each one from the sack and told her what their names were. Her eyes lit up like a Christmas tree. I got out of my chair and dropped down on my knees to be eye level with Sheila. We started playing. She was Dale Evans on Buttermilk and I was Roy Rogers on Trigger. I can honestly say, I don't know who enjoyed it more, me or Sheila.

Linda bluntly said, "Brenda, I think you best go pinch him and make sure he is real."

While I continued to play horses with Sheila, I overheard them whispering. Brenda told her sister about some small things that happened at the park, and about my loss of Karen and Randy. I overheard Linda ask if I had spent the night. She assured her nothing had happened, but Linda didn't buy it.

They debated back and forth. I spontaneously, as I often do, said, "Linda, I can get my receipt from the car if you like. It will show I spent last night in room number twenty-four at the Travelers Hotel in Lamar, Missouri."

She shook her head. "Okay, okay, I believe you. I just like giving Brenda crap." She glanced at her wristwatch and said, "I've got to get out of here or I'm going to be late for my hair appointment."

I rose to my feet and we once again repeated the ritual. "It was nice to meet you." Brenda walked outside with Linda, and they talked briefly. She came back in and joined the Roy Rogers and Dale Evans show Sheila and I were deep into. Then out of nowhere, as five-year-olds often do, Sheila looked at me while she held one of the toys. "Are these your toys?"

I hesitated for a moment. "Well, actually they are yours now."

Her eyes grew big, and her mouth dropped open. I told her I once had a little boy who was hurt really badly, and God took him to heaven to fix him up and make him better. I told her he was just like new now, and he lived in heaven with Jesus. "I know he would like for me to give them to a little kid like you." Like little minds so often do, she asked questions from the heart. "Will God let him come back to your house?"

"No, but someday I plan to go see him in heaven," I said.

She seemed to be pleased about that, and quickly began to play with the toys again. Brenda and I stood up from the floor and looked at each other. I saw emotion and grief on her face while she took a tissue and wiped tears.

Somehow, at that moment, I felt a special bond with Brenda, a feeling I couldn't quite describe. I felt torn, wanting to stay longer, and also realizing I desperately needed to put some miles behind me if I was ever going to get to Decatur. I walked over to the kitchen table and picked up the big brown bag that contained my two screwdrivers.

I looked down at Shelia playing with the new toys. "Hey, Dale Evans, this cowboy has to hit the trail."

Brenda looked disappointed when she said, "I don't suppose I could talk you into staying just one more day, could I?"

A part of me wanted to say yes, but I knew I had to go. Just then, I remembered the flowers. I politely asked if I could use the bathroom one more time. I retrieved the flowers from the linen closet, then placed the vase on top of the vanity. I took the note I wrote early this morning from my shirt pocket and placed it under the vase. I threw a little water on my face and dried off good. Then I went back to the living room and made my way to the door.

Brenda reached down, picked up Sheila and turned to me. "Sheila, tell Mr. Leon, thank you for the toys."

Sheila, affectionately, gave me a hug and said, "Thank your little boy, and I sure hope he doesn't hurt anymore."

"I sure will sweetie, and I'm so happy you like the toys."

Brenda set Sheila down and told her to go play.

She picked up a small brown bag and placed it in the big brown bag I held. She looked at me with her awesome smile. It completely melted me to a puddle.

"I thought you might want a brownie in a couple of hours."

I graciously thanked her and stepped out onto the front porch while she followed me out. We faced each other, and I felt I knew what she wanted. I wanted the same. I knew I didn't want this to heat up and become too hot. We stood there and read each other. I eased my arm around her and pulled her closer to me.

Her body surrendered, then our lips met. Soft and gentle at first, then more passionate the longer we continued. Reality and my maturity set in. Ease up I thought. She followed my lead and we both slowly pulled away. I stepped back, one small step, then another. I gave her a big smile. Thank God my wits kicked in. This lady was different. Special. She gave me a feeling I hadn't allowed myself to feel in such a long time. I smiled, then said, "The folks in Lamar need to install a large sign with Eddie Ray's picture on it and a quote that reads, 'Barton County's Dumbest Man.'"

Brenda smiled. I turned and quickly went down the steps and straight to my car. I opened the door, turned and looked back up at Brenda who studied me from the porch. The light of the sun filtered through the trees and the brightness went directly to her. She looked like a movie star, or a performer on stage. My gosh, 'how beautiful you are', I thought.

I threw her a kiss. "Take care of yourself now."

Then, as though she had forgotten, she hurriedly said, "I wrote down Mary's Café phone number on a piece of paper in the brown sack. Please call me when you get to Decatur."

"Okay, I will."

"Promise?" she asked.

"Yes, I promise." I got in my old car, backed out of the drive and headed toward the highway.

CHAPTER 4

'I knew this situation had only one way to go.
Dad wasn't much on stump speeches and neither was Larry.'

I mapped out my trip across Missouri, taking small, curvy state roads. The scenery, at times, was so pretty I wanted to stay and enjoy what was around me. There were also several dairy farms and cattle ranches. I was now on the outskirts of West Plains, Missouri. A sign at the edge of town recognized that this was the home of Preacher Roe. I remembered him pitching in the 1952 World Series for the Brooklyn Dodgers. Before long I arrived at the Missouri-Arkansas line. I enjoyed the big spring at Mammoth Springs, Arkansas. It was obvious why they named it Mammoth.

The big breakfast Brenda made for me was totally gone. I hoped I could find a café but wasn't having much luck. Ole Limpie was doing great but was running low on fuel. I drove a few more miles, and when I was really nervous about running out of gas, I found the answer to my prayers. A small country store that sold gas. When I pulled up to the pump, a middle-aged man promptly rushed out to my side of the car.

Before I could speak, he bluntly grunted out, "How much do ya' want?"

I would have loved to have said, "With an attitude like yours I don't want anything," and then quickly drove off. But I knew I wasn't going to take a chance on running out of gas. "Fill her up."

While he gassed Ole Limpie, he intently studied all of her scars.

He said, "Looks like you like driving really close to trees."

Being confident my wit would make him let out a big laugh, I said, "No, grasshoppers were really bad back home in Kansas last year."

I looked at Ole' Grumpy-Grump-Stoneface, but did not see the slightest hint of a grin. I thought to myself his mommy and daddy must have whipped him when he was a little boy if he dared smile. I made my way inside the store, walked to the soda cooler in the corner, put in a dime, and pulled out my Pepsi through the little trap doors. I noticed a sign saying 'Sandwiches'. About that time Old Grump arrived.

"I see you make sandwiches?"

"Yep."

"What are my choices?"

"Only got two," he replied, "bologna and cheese, or cheese and bologna."

"I will have the bologna and cheese."

Old Grump got out two ingredients from the see-through cooler. I thought surely, he would wash his hands, but no. When he was about halfway into making my sandwich, I decided to try my luck one more time to inject a little humor into Old Stoneface's day.

I cleared my throat, then loudly said, "Hold it. I changed my mind I think I'll have the cheese and bologna."

He stopped, looked up, and gave me a go to thunder look. I realized right there I must surrender to old Stoneface, because not only did he not smile, I actually put a frown on his face. It took a lot of effort not to laugh at the thought.

After paying for the gas and sandwich, I knew I wasn't ready to get back in the wagon. I noticed a chair in the front corner of the store. I politely asked if it would be ok to sit in the chair and eat my sandwich. Well, Old Stoneface hesitated for a second, then said, "If Oscar doesn't want it, you can have it."

I thought who the heck is Oscar? I hadn't seen anyone outside, and there sure wasn't anyone in the store. About that time, this gosh-awful looking dog came from behind the counter. I supposed he heard Stoneface use his name. This dog was like an alien from another planet. I had never seen anything that looked like that in my entire life. He must have weighed around one-hundred twenty pounds, with long, dirty, shaggy hair. Math never was my strong suit, and I was exceptionally weak in fractions. However, I believe this dog was half Bulldog, half German Shepherd, half Pitbull, half Great Pyrenees and half Great Dane. His ears were short, his eyes pooched out, and his front teeth hung out over the bottom of his jaw.

I don't know much about inbreeding, but if I were a betting man, I would put good money on his mother and daddy being litter mates. My dad had a saying about something he thought was extremely unattractive. He would say 'it's as ugly as a tub full of eyeballs and noses'. I think this dog might have been uglier than that. I stood there in disbelief while I watched Oscar slowly meander over to the chair and climb into it.

Well, so much for using the chair. I didn't say a word. I just turned and left the store. About the time I got to my car, Old Stoneface Grumpy-Grump, owner of the world's ugliest dog, stuck his head out the door and hollered at me. "There's a roadside picnic table about two miles down the road."

"Okay, thanks."

I pointed Ole Limpie in that direction. I didn't go more than a half-mile, and sure enough, there it was. Three picnic tables, and two outside toilets were nestled in a cluster of large red oak trees. I parked Ole Limpie in the nice gravel parking area, and immediately knew this was much better than Oscar's chair. I got out of the old wagon and chose the table that was completely shaded. I got out my sandwich, Pepsi, and the brown bag that held Brenda's brownies. I chowed down on my sandwich, looked around, and felt so calm and peaceful. My mind went back to Brenda's front porch and that wonderful kiss.

How could I be missing someone that I had met two days ago? I felt so at home with her. I wished I had the nerve to tell Larry I was going to be a week late. I could go back to Lamar, stay at Travelers Hotel for three or four days, and see how things might go with Brenda. Larry had always controlled me, and I guess now wasn't any different. However, I was also taught to honor your commitments. Larry and his superiors at Caterpillar were expecting me on Monday.

I finished my Grumpy-Grump Stoneface's sandwich, which was better than I anticipated, when a car pulled into the picnic area. The back car door opened as fast as starting gates on the stalls at a horse race. A young boy jumped out, instantly followed by a big yellow dog that appeared to be a well-bred, Labrador retriever.

A man and woman, who I assumed to be the boy's parents, exited the car. It was obvious the woman had one thing on her mind, and that was getting to the ladies' toilet as soon as possible. The man headed toward the men's toilet, but at a slower pace.

A couple of minutes later, the boy and the dog ran around the picnic area and released what appeared to be an excessive amount of energy. Then the dog made a straight line for the further corner of the freshly mowed picnic area, found the perfect place and peed for what seemed like five minutes. The young boy looked around, saw me, and headed toward my table.

"What's your name?"

"Leon, and what's your name?"

"Kenny," he said.

"Boy, you sure have a fine-looking dog."

"He's the very best dog in the world."

"Does the best dog in the world have a name?"

"Burt, we named him after the man we got him from."

The lady looked my way and smiled at us. "You best go to the potty Kenny."

Kenny did as he was told, and when he came out of the toilet his dad said, "Let's go. Oh, has Burt done his business?"

Kenny replied, "Yep, both."

About that time the lady looked up my way, smiled, then waved. The man also waved and said, "Have a good day."

They all got back in their car and pulled out onto the highway. Kenny waved one more time.

I sat there for a few moments and thought about how I had always planned to get Randy a dog. A dog of his own. Randy had adopted Dad's farm dog, Rusty, and they bonded very well. However, I wanted to buy Randy a puppy and let them grow up together. That was like so many things that would never be. It seems all I did was recall and relive things regarding Karen and Randy. My thoughts always concluded with the fact that all the 'what if's' and 'if only' would never bring them back.

I finished my sandwich, then opened the little brown bag that contained Brenda's brownies. I quickly consumed one of them and reached into the little bag to retrieve the second one when I noticed a folded paper inside. Oh, I thought, it's the phone number to

Mary's Café. I knew I needed to place the number in my wallet or glove box so I wouldn't lose it. Without even thinking about it, I opened it up. Brenda had also written a note I was certainly anxious to read.

Dear Leon,

Oh my, what a gentleman you are. It's been a long time since I enjoyed myself as much as I have these last couple of days. You are simply a breath of fresh air. Thanks for sharing your story about the loss of Karen and Randy. I can't imagine the pain you must have gone through. I hope God blesses you with love and happiness. Please take care of yourself and please call.

Love, Brenda

Mary's Café ph.# 417-258-3131

I sat there and stared across the field where cattle grazed. I felt a tug at my heartstring. The heck with Larry, I thought, I needed to follow my heart, and I most certainly needed to be my own man. He was not in control of my life, I was.

I made sure I cleaned up around my table, then headed to the old wagon. I thought I would drive hard and check in at the Travelers Hotel. I would surprise Brenda at the café. Perhaps we could go to the Barco Starvue Drive-in Theater I had noticed at the edge of Lamar. My thoughts about going back to Lamar were all over the place. I soon realized I was back at Old Stoneface's place. As fate would have it, Old Grump was out gassing up a truck. I honked my horn and gave him a big wave. He didn't respond. He stood there looking surprised it was me. I drove for about fifteen minutes and asked myself, "What the heck am I doing?'

I knew how disappointed Larry and Martha would be, and the job at Caterpillar might not be available for me at a later time, even though I wasn't sure I would like it. There was a gravel road on my right about two-hundred fifty yards away, with a large approach to the highway. I could easily turn around there. I was still having mixed emotions about my decision, but I quickly turned Ole Limpie around and headed back south and east.

I still debated my decision when I realized I was going to pass Old Stoneface's place once more. I was happy to see a car parked at the gasoline pump. My wish came true when I saw Old Stoneface was out pumping gas. I couldn't wait to honk my horn and wave one more time. A part of me wanted to give him a one finger salute, but my mama's good Christian raisin' kept me in line as she would expect. Once again, I laid on Ole Limpie's horn and waved as though I were saying goodbye to an old friend. I chuckled to myself when he slowly turned his head and watched me drive away.

I soon passed the little roadside tables and anticipated getting into the flat cotton country. I was traveling through what the people from here refer to as 'the ridge'. Crowley Ridge is a unique geographic area where the rich flat delta farmland is on both sides of a large ridge, which is several miles wide. On this ridge, a lot of folks owned homesteads with farms that contained both flat ground and hilly areas, suitable only for livestock and home sites. I passed what appeared to be a father with two teenage boys working on a fence. The three of them working on that fence triggered a memory of a time when my brother and I were in school. Larry was a senior and I was a junior.

~ ~ ~ ~

It was in the fall of the year. We both played football. As a matter of fact, Larry was a star linebacker and several colleges had offered him scholarships. Most were mid-major size schools. One Friday night we had finished playing a school in our conference. It was something of a ritual after home games, several of the high school kids, mostly football players, their girlfriends and cheerleaders, would go back to the football field parking lot and hang out. The guys from vo-ag had made a cooler with a false bottom. We could get several cans of beer under the wooden bottom and a lot of ice and Cokes on top. It was common for the police to pull up to check everybody out and check the cooler. We were all expected to pitch in to help pay for the drinks. It was pretty much on an honor system. Don Perry, one of the guys from the vo-ag class, was in charge and you were expected to put money into the C.B. Fund, (cold beverage, or cold beer) however you chose to view it.

Most of the kids were honest and contributed their fair share. However, there were a few that didn't follow the rules, especially Tony 'Stubby' Hall. He would have been a senior, but he dropped out of school in his sophomore year. He had two cousins, the

Simpson brothers, from a town about twenty miles away. They would always be there. Not one of the three of them would ever put in a dime. They were not very well liked by the kids from Wellington. The two cousins of Stubby Hall were in their early twenties, they were big and downright mean. No one wanted to have a confrontation with them, including Larry and me. So, everyone turned a blind eye and let them have their free beer.

That particular night, Coach Johnson was waiting for us when we walked out of the locker room. There was an assistant coach from a small college in north-west Kansas who wanted to talk to Larry. Larry took a few minutes and was very gracious, even though he wasn't interested in playing there at all. The little party at the football field parking lot was in full swing by the time we got there. A few cars were leaving when we pulled in, which seemed a little strange. When we got out of our car, two girls were getting in their car to leave. We vaguely knew them I think they were freshmen. I looked over and one of the girls shook her head and said, "That's not right, that's just not right." They backed out and left.

Larry said, "What was that all about?" Then it all started to come into focus.

It seems Stubby Hall and his two bully cousins were having a hay day poking fun at Freddy Joe Barnes. Freddy Joe was a boy who had Tourette Syndrome, a debilitating condition he'd had since birth. It wasn't too bad when we were in grade school, but as Freddy Joe got older it got worse. Freddy was much liked by all the kids in school. He wanted to fit in, and wanted to be everyone's friend and buddy. He wanted to play sports but didn't have the physical ability to make any of the ball teams. The coaches appointed him equipment manager, a role Freddy Joe enjoyed.

There had only been one time that I could remember anyone making fun of him. We were all in the lunchroom. The ball players usually sat together and Freddy Joe would sit as close as he could to them. Freddy Joe was a freshman. Carl Newton was a senior, who was an outstanding athlete. He was by far the best athlete that had ever walked the halls of Wellington High School. He was about six-foot-five inches tall, big and strong. He had numerous colleges offer him scholarships in both basketball and football, including K-State. Carl ended up turning down all scholarships and followed his passion to join the U.S. Army shortly after graduation. The last I heard he was a Sergeant Major and had every intention to make the Army a career.

Well, this particular day in the lunchroom, Freddy Joe was sitting at his regular spot. Big Carl was sitting at the end of the table, five or six spaces from Freddy Joe. Two small-built freshman boys sitting across from Freddy began making fun of him, blinking his eyes and shaking his heads. One of them, it was reported, laughed and asked, "Are you trying to shake the dandruff out of your hair?"

Me and my buddies were a table over, and from my vantage point, I clearly saw the whole thing unfold. It was apparent Big Carl had also heard them, and there was no question, he saw nothing funny about it. He slid off the bench and walked over to these two dudes. Pointing his finger about twelve inches from their faces, and in a deep, demanding voice, he said, "I dare you." The lunchroom was as loud as a grain elevator at the peak of harvest, but in a second it became as quiet as an empty church on Monday morning. Big Carl continued blasting those guys. Even to this day, I can almost repeat his speech verbatim.

"You shallow-minded scum bags." He pointed to Freddy Joe. "He has more character in his little finger than you do in your entire body."

One of the boys, perhaps both, had a grin on their face. Carl said, "Wipe that cheesy smile off your face before I slap it off." Carl pointed to a table in the back of the room that was seldom used. He said, "Both of you get your low life asses over there at that table. Neither one of you have high enough standards to have the honor to sit by Freddy Joe," he repeated. "Get your sorry ass over there, now."

That was the only time I could ever remember anyone poking fun at Freddy Joe, except for this scene that unfolded in front of us.

We walked across the football parking lot and worked our way to the inside edge of the circle of students, close enough to hear the horrible remarks being thrown toward Freddy Joe. Freddy Joe looked like a little puppy being scolded for peeing on the living room floor. His symptoms always got worse when he became nervous. He would clear his throat, one time after another, and often stuttered if he tried to speak.

One of the Simpson boys said, "Doesn't matter what you ask him...he shakes his head no." Then he said, "Do you like pretty girls?" Freddy of course was uncontrollably, blinking his eyes, and rapidly shook his head back and forth. "See, he doesn't even like girls!"

Freddy Joe, all but in tears, pleaded, "Please stop it."

Little Stubby Hall and his two smartass cousins each gave out a big laugh. I looked over at Larry. Rage and sheer anger danced in his eyes. Without warning, he loudly demanded, "Stop that right now."

The two Simpson boys, along with Stubby Hall, took a few steps in our direction. Both of the brothers were big, but one was bigger than the other. The smaller of the two walked straight up to Larry and said, "Well, mister football star, what are you going to do if we don't?"

I looked at Larry and knew this situation had only one way to go, and it wasn't going to be good. Larry was so much like Dad in a lot of ways. Dad wasn't much on stump speeches and neither was Larry.

Larry had fired one shot across their bow, and I can assure you, there wasn't going to be another. Without warning, and quicker than a cat can wink, Larry thrust his strong body into a furious football tackle and jammed into the midsection of Simpson. He went down like he had been hit by a Mack Truck. Larry was on top of him in a split second, and just as quickly, got his right arm behind his back. As luck would have it, I wound up going against the larger of the Simpson brothers. Wrestling wasn't my thing, but boxing was since I was nine years old. A thousand thoughts went through my head. Don't let him connect on one of those haymakers he was throwing at me. So far, I was amazed by how slow this guy was compared to sparring with Dad and Larry. I easily kept ducking and dodging his every swing. I waited for my opportunity to land my first blow. I remembered very clearly what Dad had said about never hitting a man in his nose. "Take your target six-inches behind his head but, go through his nose to get there."

Then my opportunity presented itself, he dropped his guard. I unleashed a big right hand with the speed and force of a mama cow kicking a wild coyote. It landed directly on his nose, I don't know how far behind his head it landed, but Mr. Simpson was hurt, and I knew it.

Lesson Number Two was about to be tested. If you see a man is hurt, don't make the mistake of taking a premature victory lap. I unleashed a barrage of left, right, left, right blows. I could tell he was going down. I knew enough to not let him get back up. Time for putting lesson Number Three into action. Dad's Flying Torpedo. I had practiced this maneuver at least a hundred times on a burlap bag of wheat, but this was my first time to use it in a real fight situation.

The Flying Torpedo, as Dad called it, was a maneuver you took when you had your man down. You would take your right knee, bend it out in front of you, then launch it into the midsection-belly of your opponent. I went airborne, knee out in front, and jumped much like a frog jumping from a pond bank. Simpson laid flat on his back, the perfect position for the Flying Torpedo. Dad said, "If you hit your target dead on with all your weight behind your thrust, the fight probably would be over." I missed my target, but not by much, slightly off center, but most certainly good enough to completely knock the air out of this hunk of mud. He let out a growl that sounded like a mama cow calling for her baby calf.

Dad would say, "It still isn't time to take the victory lap. Get on top of him as quickly as possible and unleash one more barrage of lefts and rights into his face or jaws." If he managed to get to his feet, it would be time for lesson Number Four.

I remember I was puzzled at the possibility of needing a lesson Number Four. A big grin would consume Dad's face and he would say, "If he gets up from lesson one, two and three, then run like the devil is after you, cause if he has survived that, there is a darn good chance he 'is' the devil."

The kids that witnessed the whole thing said when little Stubby Hall realized his two big cousins were getting the crap beat out of them, he left in a hurry. They said he ran across the football field and out the far side. It was all the talk around school for the next few days. Rumor had it that little Stubby had been seen, still running south, somewhere in central Oklahoma. We found out later that both the Simpson brothers were taken to the hospital that night.

Dad had found out about the fight before Larry and I got home that night. As I said before, Dad wasn't much on stump speeches.

He just told us to get to bed and wasn't interested in hearing our side of the story. He had us up before daylight and darn near worked us to an early grave that Saturday building a fence. He found out the next Monday at work what the fight was all about.

That afternoon when he came home from work, he told Larry and me to go to the workshop. Dad told us he was proud of us for standing up to the Simpson brothers and for taking a stand for little Freddy Barnes. He apologized for assuming we were at least partially at fault.

"However," he said, "I'm not apologizing for the workday. A good hard day of work never hurts anybody."

We would have loved to debate his position on that subject, however, we both knew not to go down that path.

CHAPTER 5

'Leon, Leon Wilson, oh my Sweet Jesus, Sweet Jesus, he yelled so loud you could have heard him for five miles.'

I slowly and steadily kept the old Ford rolling, putting more miles behind me. I was amazed at the amount of open farm ground. Tractors worked in each and every field.

I had planned to try and see an old Marine buddy, Bill Johnson, on my road trip. We met in boot camp and became friends. We seemed to always have each other's back. Bill was a devout Christian with a high standard of morals I admired. We both agreed to always stay in touch. As things often seem to do, we simply didn't. Bill didn't re-enlist as I had, and we each went our separate ways.

Bill was born and raised in the cotton country around Neelyville, Missouri. He would often talk about picking cotton. More than once he remarked to me how it seemed strange to him that he could fight for our freedom on a world stage, but had to pick cotton with his people, the blacks. He told me that when they all came in to weigh their cotton sacks, his people had to wait and let the whites go first. His great grandfather had actually been a slave for a large landowner in the county where he lived.

I agreed with Bill, it most certainly wasn't right back in the days of slavery, and it's not right today. Unfortunately, racial tension and discrimination still strongly exists in our country.

Me and Ole Limpie were scooting across the countryside when I noticed a road sign: Neelyville 12 miles. I thought I would stop at some type of business, perhaps a gasoline station, to ask if anyone knew the Johnson family. It wasn't uncommon for the first business at the edge of town to be a gas station, and Neelyville was no different. The first place on my left was a Gulf Oil station. I pulled in and a young, friendly black man quickly came to my car.

"Fill 'er up?" he asked.

We chatted a while before I inquired, "Do you live around here?"

"Yep, I've lived here all my life. I see your license plate has Kansas on it. You from Kansas?"

"Yes, I was born and raised in Kansas. I don't suppose you would know a fella named Bill Johnson, would you?"

He looked shocked that I asked that question. He replied, "Yes, I sure do, as a matter of fact, I am kinda' kin to him. My wife and his wife are cousins. I've known Bill Johnson all my life."

"Does he still live around here?"

"Well, no. Not really. His momma still does."

"So, is his dad gone?" I asked.

"Yep, he died 'bout a couple-years ago. His momma lives at the farmhouse where Bill grew up, just south of town. How do you know Bill Johnson anyway?" he asked.

I proceeded to tell him Bill and I were in the Marine Corps together, and that I had always considered him one of my best friends.

He said, "Bill lives around St. Louis somewhere."

"Oh shoot," I said, "I was hoping he still lived around here. I was really wanting to see him. It has been several years."

"Well," he said, "today might be your lucky day, cuz' if he ain't left yet, he's at his momma's house, about eight miles from here." Then just out of the blue he said, "He got him a brand-new shiny car. Stopped in here yesterday and filled it up with gas. Boy, it sure is a fine-lookin' car."

I immediately said, "I bet it's a dark blue Buick."

Surprised, he asked me, "How in the world did you know that?"

"Bill commented numerous times, "I am going to buy myself a brand-new dark-blue Buick someday. Do you mind giving me directions to his mom's place?"

"You bet," he readily said, "better yet, I'll draw you out directions."

He also told me how to get there while he put the directions on paper. It seemed simple enough. I thanked him.

He said, "I sure hope he's there. I think that's great…you wantin' to see him an' all."

I thanked him again and told him to have a good day.

He again repeated, "I sure hope Bill hasn't left."

I pulled out onto the highway and looked at my odometer. I needed to go about four miles. There would be an old rickety barn. I drove a little over three miles, the land was as flat as a kitchen floor. I saw the old barn Jess had told me about. I turned on a gravel road to my right at the first crossroads. The rocks loudly crunched under my tires. I turned left and went about a mile and a half.

There it was, Big Bill Johnson's home, where he grew up. The house was smaller than I expected, but what a beautiful setting. It was nestled in a group of large sycamore and oak trees. I actually felt my heart race. Oh my, I thought, because just as Jess had said, maybe it would be my lucky day. Well, it surely was, there sat that dark-blue Buick! The trunk lid of the new Buick stood wide open.

Bill was loading suitcases. There were three kids running around the yard, one boy, who looked to be about four years old, and two girls. One I would guess was around six and the oldest looked to be eight years old. When I slowed Ole Limpie to a crawl and started to pull into the driveway, everyone, including Bill, stopped what they were doing and stared at me.

I stopped Ole Limpie rather close to the back of Bill's new Buick, shut off the engine, and got out. "I'm looking for a fella named Leon Wilson. You wouldn't know him would ya?"

Bill's mouth flew open and he looked at me as if trying to get his eyes focused. I couldn't hold my smile any longer. It was so good just to see him standing there. I felt my face almost explode in jubilation. It was obvious Bill recognized who he was looking at.

"Oh' my sweet Jesus, sweet Jesus," he yelled so loud you could have heard him for five-miles. "Leon, Leon Wilson," he kept repeating with an occasional, "paise the Lord, praise the Lord."

We walked swiftly toward each other. I stuck my hand out and he instantly grabbed it with a grip that could have crushed a coconut. He pulled me in toward him and opened his arms. We both hugged, backed away, then hugged again.

"How in the world are ya, my dear friend?" Bill asked.

"I'm good Bill, how are you?"

Bill's mouth was wide open. "Well, I was just good a couple minutes ago, but now I am fantastic!"

Bill looked at the oldest girl and said, "Go in the house and get your momma." Bill pointed at the smallest girl and said, "Leon, this is my daughter Janice."

I spoke and she smiled. Bill picked up his little boy who was as cute as a bug's ear. He had a big grin that matched his daddy's and seemed to have a personality from here to the Mississippi River. Bill said, "Leon Wilson, this boy right here is going to be the best shortstop the St. Louis Cardinals will ever have."

I readily agreed. "I bet you're right about that, Bill."

"What in God's creation has you in this neck of the woods?" he asked.

Before I could answer, the little girl came running out of the house and shortly after, an attractive lady appeared in the doorway.

"Come here, honey," Bill said. "I want you to meet someone."

She had a very pleasant, but puzzled look on her face. She stepped off the porch and walked toward us.

Bill pointed at me. "You've heard me talk about this guy often. Honey, this is Leon Wilson." Her puzzled look turned into a warm smile. Bill said, "Leon, this is my wife, Wanda."

"It is so nice to meet you, Wanda." I nodded at her and smiled broadly.

"Likewise," she replied.

Wanda did something I wasn't expecting. She bluntly asked me to turn around. When I hesitated, she said, "No please, turn around."

Bill was as confused as I was. We had no idea where this was going. Her smile had turned into a chuckle and somehow, I felt comfortable complying with her wish. I turned my entire body around. She took her hand and patted across my back.

"Okay," she barked out, "you can turn back around."

I was simply flabbergasted, and by the look on Bill's face, so was he.

She explained. "Bill has said so many nice things about you. I was sure you were an angel, and I wanted to see if you had wings."

During my excitement seeing Bill and meeting his kids and

wife, I had been oblivious to a sweet little lady just sitting in a rocking chair on the far end of the porch. We both made eye contact and I started walking across the porch toward her. Before I could say a word, Bill loudly said, "Oh yes, Leon, I want you to meet the world's best momma."

"Well, if my mom were still alive, I might say that could be debated, but since she is in heaven, I'm sure you're right." Then I gave her a big smile. "I am so pleased to meet the world's greatest mom." There was no doubt where Bill got his big, contagious smile.

Bill put his hand on the lady's shoulder. "Leon, this is my mother, Mable Johnson. Momma, this is my dear friend, Leon Wilson."

I hadn't had the opportunity to answer Bill's question as to why I was, as he put it, in this neck of the woods. So, he once again asked, "What brings you to Neelyville?"

"Well, actually I am on my way to Decatur, Illinois. You remember me talking about my brother, Larry?"

"I sure do," he replied.

"Well, Larry met a lady from that area when he was in college and wound up getting a job at Caterpillar in Decatur. I have a job waiting for me at Caterpillar when I get there. So, when I looked at the map, I decided to head this way, hoping you still lived here. I understand you live up north in St. Louis now?"

"Yes," Bill said, "I work in the Chrysler factory just outside St. Louis. I also pastor a small Baptist Church in the community where we live." Bill simply gleamed when he talked about his church.

"When I became the pastor, we had about thirty who attended Sunday Services. I've been there for a little over two years, and we are now getting close to one-hundred. We had ninety-two this past Sunday."

"That's wonderful, Bill. That says a lot about you."

"No Leon, it's not me. Number one, we have been blessed by the Lord. Number two, I've been blessed to have such a good hard-working bunch of people in our congregation." He continued. "We do things a lot different than most churches do. We put more emphasis on helping people in the community than trying to fill up a church house. As a matter of fact, we don't have a Wednesday night service at the church. We all gather in work clothes, pray, then spread out in the community, helping as many people in need as possible."

"We've been blessed with so many diverse, professional people, including carpenters, electricians, mechanics, people with lawn mowers, and of course, good cooks. We have youth groups who get involved on Saturdays. It has absolutely been a joy and a heart-warming experience."

I was happy to see Bill so satisfied with his church and life in general. The kids were all wanting a little attention and Bill just couldn't hold in his pride when he talked about each of them. Wanda returned from the house with more items to load in the car. She unloaded her big arm full of stuff, then walked up the steps to the porch.

Bill asked me, possibly after noticing I didn't have a wedding ring on, "Have you ever married, Leon?"

Wanda immediately stopped, apparently wanting to hear my answer.

I had to tell my friend. "Yes, I got married about eight years ago. I married as good a woman as a man could ever hope to find, much more than I deserved. We had a little boy about a year after." I once again had to hesitate. I needed time to get my composure. It's still hard to talk about this part of my life.

"There was a really bad accident a couple years back, I lost them both." Wanda placed her hand over her mouth. I heard a soft gasp. I looked at Bill, who stepped toward me, those big arms reaching wide. We shared a meaningful hug.

Bill said, "Oh my, Leon, I am so sorry."

I looked at Wanda, she too walked toward me, arms stretched out, and gave me a big, genuine, loving embrace.

I didn't want this little reunion with Bill to become bogged down with sadness. I wanted it to be a joyous time. The way I was positioned on the porch I was looking directly at Bill's new Buick.

I broke from Wanda's hug and walked off the porch toward Bill's car. "I want to look at this new car of yours. A real beauty, my friend."

Wanda and Bill sensed my desire not to talk any more about the accident. Wanda went back into the house and Bill followed me out to their new car. He was very proud of it, and was more than eager to give me the full tour. He explained and demonstrated all the new features and gadgets.

I, of course, commented how beautiful it was and how happy I was for him. Then jokingly I said, "I don't suppose you would be interested in a straight across trade with my old station wagon, would you?"

Bill had a great sense of humor and was a very modest man. He replied, "I might be if you take over my payments." He laughed and slapped me on the back.

Miss Mable had gone back inside the house. Bill and I returned to the porch and sat in a couple of chairs. I was truly enjoying my visit with Bill. We reminisced and swapped old boot camp stories and shared little bits about our lives.

Wanda made a few more trips to the Buick and barked at the kids to clean up and go to the bathroom. She stepped out on the porch and announced, "I would rather take a whoopin' than to say this Bill, but we really need to be on the road. I don't know if he told ya or not Leon, but Bill is a line foreman at the plant, and he has fourteen men under him." She looked at Bill and I saw and felt her pride.

I smiled. "Well, that's super, but that does not surprise me. Give him a few more years and he'll be the general manager."

Bill laughed loudly. "That ain't going to happen, I most certainly am not qualified, and I wouldn't want that headache if I was."

Wanda once again looked at her watch, looked at Bill and said, "We do have to go honey."

Bill explained he worked the third shift and was scheduled to be at work at eleven o'clock tonight, however, this shift he was required to be at work earlier for a foreman's meeting.

I spoke up. "Hey Wanda, I understand, and quite frankly, I need to be heading toward the Mississippi River. I want to find a hotel somewhere around Sikeston, Missouri."

I got Bill's phone number and address, and gave them Larry's phone number and address. We all three agreed to do a far better job of staying in touch with each other.

Bill said, "You know Leon, when you get settled in Decatur, it's only about three hours to St. Louis. You must come to see us."

Wanda spoke up and said, "Plan to spend the night, we can put the kids on the floor and you'll have a bed, no problem at all."

Before I could thank her or say a word, Bill jumped in. "Hey, we could go to a Cardinal's game and you could go to church with us on Sunday."

I smiled. "You know guys, that sounds fantastic! Let's make that work."

I thought it would be best if I left first, so I started saying goodbye. Bill stuck his head inside the door and called for his momma. Miss Mable stepped out onto the porch, which made it obvious that Bill got his size from his dad. Miss Mable was a very short, small-built lady, and just as sweet as a bowl of sugar. After receiving hugs from everyone, including the kids, I said my final goodbye, climbed back into Ole Limpie and headed back to Neelyville. The image of Bill's mom sitting on the porch just seemed to linger in my mind. I thought about how I would love for her and my mom to have had the opportunity to know one another.

CHAPTER 6

'Miss Mable, as far as I am concerned there is
only one Angel on this porch and I am looking at her.'

After leaving Bill's mom's place, I drove a few miles when I realized how thirsty I was. I remembered my thermos of cold ice water in the back seat of the old wagon. I pulled over to the shoulder of the road and opened the back door. There were Randy's toys laying on the floor. It was as though a light went on in my mind. I was disappointed I hadn't given the toys to Bill and Wanda's kids, or perhaps Bill's church could have used them for some worthwhile cause. I got me a much-needed drink of water, got back under the wheel of the old wagon, and was ready to put more miles behind me.

~ ~ ~ ~

I thought of something Mom requested Larry and I do. Before she became extremely ill, she told both of us boys, "You're going to receive mine and your dad's inheritance. It will be as the 'will' states, exactly fifty-fifty, do you understand?" We both said, "Yes, Mom we do."

"I will be looking down from heaven, and it will break my heart if you disagree on one single thing." She continued, "My personal bank account has approximately $790.00. I would like both of you to have your names added to that account. I have already made arrangements with the bank for you to do this. What I'd like for you to do is not close that account, but use it as you see appropriate for some worthwhile charity. Not for your own personal gain, but perhaps use it for a needy family, purchasing pies at a pie supper, or maybe buying shoes for needy kids." She hesitated for a moment then continued, "Even something as simple as buying someone a bouquet to cheer them up. Use the money in that account for things like that until it is used up." She looked at both of us and said, "Can I trust you both to do that?"

"We'll not take one penny out of that account for ourselves," we both replied. She seemed very pleased.

Larry told me he took $200.00 out in cash to take home with him so he could have it handy if a worthy need arose. I told him that was a great idea. I took out $25.00 and used it to purchase pies at a pie supper fundraiser for a family whose house had burned in our community.

~ ~ ~ ~

Well, somehow, while I drove down this lonely road, it seemed Mom was strongly suggesting I turn the wagon around and take the toys back and leave them with Miss Mable. Larry's two kids have way more toys than they need, and are too old for Randy's toys anyway. I felt in my heart Mom suggesting I take $20.00 out of that account and give Miss Mable $10.00 for her to purchase something for herself, and give $10.00 to Bill for his church.

I'm sure by the time I returned to her house, Bill and Wanda would be long gone. I could sit on her front porch and just visit for a few minutes. I would still have plenty of time to get to Sikeston, find a room, and get Ole Limpie off the road before dark.

I headed back to Miss Mable's as fast as I dared push 'Ole Limpie'. In a few minutes I once again pulled into Miss Mable's driveway. She was sitting on the porch, reading her Bible, which didn't surprise me whatsoever. I got out of the car, waved, and gave her a big 'hello'. I opened the rear car door, placed the toys into the big brown paper sack, and walked toward the porch.

"I knew Bill would be gone, but I have a big sack of my little boy Randy's toys. Would it be okay if I left them with you to give to the kids later?"

"Oh, yes sir," she replied. "How nice of you."

I walked up on the porch, set the toys down near the door, then sat in the chair next to her. I had folded two $10.00 bills and put them in my front shirt pocket. I took them out and began to tell her the story of Mom's wishes for how she wanted Larry and me to use the money in her bank account.

I said, "There's no doubt Mom spoke to me and insisted I give you one bill to spend on yourself." I handed her the bill just as she reached out her hand and took it. I handed her the other bill and said, "She also told me to give this one to Bill for his church."

She looked at me with that big warm smile. "Thank you so much, Mr. Leon."

"You're so very welcome, Miss Mable." A warm feeling consumed me. There wasn't a doubt in my mind Mom was present on this porch and very happy I came back.

Miss Mable looked straight at me. "Bill is so lucky to have you as a good friend."

I reached out and patted the back of her hand. "Well, Miss Mable, I think I am the one who has been blessed to have Bill as a dear friend." Then I quickly added, "You sure did a fine job raising him."

She had a glow on her wrinkled face as she started talking about Bill. She described each one of her kids and how blessed she was. She was thrilled that each one of them turned out to be, as she said in her own words, good servants of the Lord.

"You know Leon, I saw Wanda patting your back looking for angel wings. I think we have many angels here on this earth that don't have wings, but walk among us, and I think you are one."

I smiled at her. "Miss Mable, as far as I am concerned, there is only one angel on this porch, and I am looking at her."

As it always seems to happen, the time flew by because Mable and I were enjoying ourselves. I was most certainly glad I came back to sit on this porch with her, but it was time I got on the road. I rose to my feet and told her I had to leave.

"You have certainly made my day, Leon." We gave each other a big hug and just as I was getting into the car I looked toward the porch. Miss Mable waved and said, "God bless you, my son," never once losing that big smile. I will take that scene with me to my grave.

I boogied down the highway, taking in the different scenery, mostly big open-row crop fields, dotted with occasional farmsteads. Many tractors were visible working in the large fields. I began thinking about Bill's church, and his philosophy of putting the emphasis on helping people in the community. Dad didn't go to church, and I never exactly knew why. However, he was always one of the first to help someone in need. I certainly could have seen him going to Bill's church.

Several years ago, a retired couple, Charley and Sharon Parker, originally from Nebraska, moved into my parent's neighborhood. They built a new home on a small piece of property just down the road from my folks. Mom and Dad worked at being friendly with them, even going as far as inviting them to their home for a dinner meal. The Parkers were faithful, church going people.

When Mom was first diagnosed with cancer, the onset was breast cancer. The news quickly spread through our little community. There was an outpouring of people reaching out to help in various ways. However, the Parkers, Mom and Dad's closest neighbors, never helped in any way. I heard Dad tell others not one meal, not one phone call, not one visit, not one card. Absolutely not one thing, he would say. But every Sunday morning, every Sunday night, and every Wednesday night you would hear their car start up and they would head to church, driving past our driveway.

Dad loved to write poems, little one liners and short songs, or as he called them jingles. He wrote a jingle about the Parkers. It went like this.

"He will sit on the front row
and from the good book he will read.
But Charley just passed a man in need.
You can call it, judge it, for what it is worth.
But Charley is too busy going to church."

CHAPTER 7

*'It's okay, Bo. The dog's demeanor quickly changed.
His name is Bo. He is my bestest, bestest friend in the whole
world.'*

All of a sudden, completely without warning, steam started to appear from under the hood of the old wagon. I immediately looked down at the thermostat gauge on the dashboard. The needle was all the way in the red, over two-hundred degrees, and the steam was increasing. My military training instantly kicked in, "keep your cool, keep your cool," I kept reminding myself. My mind raced in every direction. What could be the problem, a broken belt, a split water hose, a hole in the radiator? There basically wasn't any shoulder on the road to pull off. I saw a gravel road approximately a half-mile on the right side of the highway.

My first assessment of the situation was to get to the gravel road. There was a nice wide approach onto the highway. In less than a minute I pulled the old wagon off the highway. I unlocked the latch and lifted the hood, and desperately looked for the problem. The fan belt seemed okay, and the radiator hose appeared to be all right. I took a good look at the engine in general. There was no doubt it was the water system and not the engine itself. That was good news, actually great news. Water dripped from under the front of the wagon, possibly a hole in the radiator, I thought.

After seeing no traffic on the small country road, I looked down the road where, to my relief, I saw a homestead in the distance, probably less than half-a-mile away. I could make out two large barns, a metal grain bin, and a large white house, all shaded by several large trees. I searched the road ditches, hoping for a small puddle of water, no such luck.

I remembered the gallon jug I had filled up at Brenda's folks. I only drank a small amount from it. I carefully removed the radiator cap. Even though the engine had cooled quite a bit, it was still very hot. I slowly poured the cool water as carefully as I could into the radiator. I was able to start up Ole Limpie, get her out of the lower gears, and putter slowly toward the house. I made it to the driveway of the homestead before the engine became dangerously hot.

The homestead wasn't the oasis I had hoped for. The yard and barn lots were completely grown-up in large vegetation. The old house was in bad shape, so were both barns. It appeared no one had lived here for a few years.

The condition of the gravel road showed a reasonable amount of traffic. That was a good thing. At the rear of the house, I saw an old hand pump barely protruding from the weeds. It was the type of hand pump that had to be primed. I didn't have any priming water. I wasn't confident that water was my answer anyway. I once again looked under the hood of the old wagon and tried to determine where the problem was located.

I leaned back on the rear section of the wagon. I certainly began to question my decision to agree to drive this hunk of junk all the way to Decatur. A part of me began to get totally pissed at Larry. I finally came to my senses and took a deep breath. I decided pointing fingers or blaming myself or Larry wasn't going to help this situation one bit. The gravel road was flat for a good distance before it rose straight up onto the ridge. I stared down the road and wondered how far it might be to an occupied house.

Out of nowhere, I saw what first appeared to be a black dog. I worked desperately to focus my eyes. I knew it was too small for a vehicle, and when it came closer, I saw a small puff of dust. I finally made out that it was a black dog trotting alongside a person on a dark colored bicycle. When it got closer, I saw the rider was a young boy wearing a St. Louis Cardinal baseball cap. I kept my position leaning back on the old wagon while he came closer and closer. He finally got up even with me, stopped, and looked at the raised hood on the car.

He asked, "You got troubles?" He remained sitting on his bike on the far side of the road. The dog didn't appear to be too fond of me. He positioned himself between me and his buddy and growled a warning.

"He won't bite, will he?" I asked.

The young boy shook his head. "Not unless you try to hurt me. My daddy has to put him in the corn crib every time he whips me."

He looked at the dog and said, "It's okay, Bo." The dog's demeanor quickly changed and he laid on the road at the boy's feet.

"Did I hear you call him Bo?"

"Yep. His name is Bo. He is my bestest, bestest friend in the whole world."

"Boy, he sure is a beautiful dog."

"Yep, and he is very, very smart, too." The boy once again looked at the open car hood. "So, you got trouble?"

"Yes, my radiator is getting hot." I paused for a moment. "Do you live around here?" I asked, knowing full well he did.

"Yep, I live up on the ridge about a-mile-and-a half down that way," he said, pointing in the direction he had come. "You don't live around here, do ya?"

"No, I live in Kansas."

"Man," he said, "that's like a thousand miles from here, ain't it?"

"Well, not quite that far, but it is a long way." I smiled at him.

"My dad can help you get your car fixed. He's a very good mechanic. I'm going to the store to get my mom a bag of sugar. When I get back to the house, I'll tell Dad you've got troubles. He'll help you. I know he will."

"How far is it to the store?" I asked him.

He tapped his chin. "About when you get on the blacktop around that big curve. You can't see it from here, but it isn't very far. Well, I gotta get going, I'll see you in a little while."

Before he could get his bicycle going, I asked, "What is Bo's bestest, bestest friend's name?"

It took him a couple of seconds to get my drift.

He smiled, "Donnie, Donnie Roy Hopkins, and ask,

"What's your name?"

"Leon Wilson."

"Okay, Mr. Wilson, I'll be back pretty quick."

I could tell he had been raised with manners by calling me Mr. Wilson. I didn't like to be called Mr. Wilson, so I said, "I would prefer you just call me Leon."

"Okay," he quickly replied.

I had only met this boy for a few minutes, but I already liked him. "Donnie, do they sell soda pops at that store?"

"Oh yes, all kinds."

"What kind do you like?" I asked.

"I like them all, but Dr. Pepper is my favorite."

I reached into my pocket and pulled out a handful of change. "How much do they cost?"

"Ten cents," he replied.

"If I bought you a Dr. Pepper, do you think you could bring me back a Pepsi?"

"Sure. That would be great!"

I gave him a quarter. "You can keep the change."

He said, "I'll get me and Mary Beth and Alice a tootsie roll pop. They're two cents each, but you can get three for a nickel."

I was concerned about possible tax and that he wouldn't have enough. I had another dime in my pocket, so I gave it to him. "Just wanting to be sure you have enough,"

"Thanks man, thanks a lot."

There wasn't any doubt in Donnie's mind he had made a very good deal, and I really looked forward to my Pepsi.

Donnie pedaled toward the highway on his bike, and Bo trotted by his side. I couldn't help myself. When I interact with a young boy, I think of Randy. What would Randy have been like at Donnie's age? I wished I wouldn't do that, but somehow that is what always happened. I took another look at Ole Limpie and examined the radiator again. I couldn't see where there was a hole or split. It could possibly be the water pump. I was lucky the road was near when the old wagon got too hot to drive. However, I sure wished I had been farther down the road, closer to that country store. Perhaps this was just as well if Donnie's dad could fix the old thing.

I looked down the highway, anticipating Donnie would be heading in my direction soon. Sure enough, I saw the two of them coming, Donnie burning up the road, peddling as if he were in a race, and Bo right there by his side. He had an extra-large basket mounted on his handlebars. When he came closer, I saw the sugar and my Pepsi, lying on its side, in the basket. I was glad Dad had put a small bottle opener on his key chain. I also was aware I would probably lose half of my shook-up Pepsi when I opened it. As dry as I was, half is better than none. Donnie, out of breath, rode his bike close to the wagon, took the Pepsi out of the basket and gave it to me. I saw the three tootsie pops in his shirt pocket, but I didn't see his Dr. Pepper.

"Did you get a Dr. Pepper?" I asked.

"Oh yeah. I chug-a-lugged it at the store. I couldn't hold it and ride the bike. Thanks for the soda, Leon."

"You're welcome. Thank you for bringing me the Pepsi."

"No problem," he replied. "Well, I best get this sugar to my mom, and I'll tell Dad about your car trouble."

Once again, he left, burning up the gravel road. Bo was in a fast pace trying to keep-up with his bestest, bestest friend.

CHAPTER 8

*'Just about the time I was so sure I didn't
like this guy, his whole demeanor changed.'*

I looked at my watch, it was ten till five. There was no way
Limpie would be repaired today, regardless of the problem. All
of the auto parts stores would be closed, and I knew I would
need something, a water pump, hose, belt, radiator repair, or
something. I was in deep thought as to how I could solve this
problem.

I was sure I had a solution. Larry could borrow, or rent a truck
and trailer and drive down tomorrow, load the old wagon, then
drive back to Decatur. Then I remembered him mentioning in our
telephone conversation Sunday night, that he and Danny would be
out of town Saturday. He was Danny's little league baseball coach.
So, scrap that plan. I knew Larry wouldn't miss Danny's game. I
didn't know what my next move was. I suppose I should remember
what Mom always said, "This too shall pass."

I sat and searched for options. An immense feeling of loneliness
fell over me. I heard tractors in the distance working the fields and
an occasional car out on the highway. A vehicle had just dropped
off the ridge and kicked up dust while it headed toward me. I was
sure it would be Donnie's dad. I wasn't expecting him to be
driving a car. When it slowed down, I saw two females in the front
seat, young teenage girls that looked to be sixteen or seventeen
years old.

They stopped, and the girl who was driving said, "It looks like
you are having problems."

"Yes, I certainly am," I replied.

"Would you like for us to send someone to help you?" she asked.

"No, thank you, I have help on the way." At least I hoped I did. "A boy, I would say 10 or 11 years old, name is Donnie, is supposed to be getting his dad to help me."

The girl who wasn't driving spoke up, "Did the boy have a black dog with him?"

"Yep, he sure did."

She said, "That would be Donnie Hopkins. We don't live too far from them. They're good people, don't worry, they will help you."

I thanked them for offering to help. The girl who drove said, "I hope it isn't too big of a deal." Then she drove off. I felt a little more comfortable and confident this was going to have a better outcome. The dust from the girl's car had barely settled when once again, a vehicle approached from the direction I expected Donnie's dad.

This time it was a pick-up truck. I was all but certain it was them, especially when Donnie's St. Louis Cardinal baseball cap came into focus. A medium built man stepped out of the truck and very confidently walked toward me. I spoke and offered him my hand. He took it, gave it a quick shake, and turned it loose.

I said, "My name is Leon." He didn't reply, just went straight to the old wagon.

The man briskly started examining different things. I could tell he was eliminating one thing after the other. Without looking in my direction he said, "Start her up." I quickly slid onto the front seat and turned the ignition, the engine started rather quickly. It ran for no more than fifteen seconds when he barked, "Shut it off."

"Water pump," he said.

"I was afraid of that," I replied.

"Well," he began, "I was too. I was hoping for a hose or belt. We could have had you back on the road pretty quick." He looked at me. "Have you ever driven a vehicle being towed?"

"Yes, I have."

"We gotta get your rig back to the house. The parts stores are all closed now. You're going to be lucky if they have that water pump anyway."

I'm sure I had a grimace look on my face.

"They can probably order it out of Memphis or St. Louis, if they don't have it," he said.

Without another word, he jumped into the pickup truck, turned it around, then backed up to the old Ford. I wanted to help somehow. However, he was in full control. He grabbed a chain out of the back of the truck and secured it to his bumper. I picked up the other end of the very long chain and was going to hook it to my old wagon. He reached his hand out and basically took it from me.

He remarked, "The chain is going to need to be tied right. I'd rather do it myself, if you don't mind."

"Sure, that's fine." He tied the chain around my front axle and told Donnie to get in, pointing to the front seat of his truck. He turned to me and said, "Leave the engine off."

I said, "Okay."

"Let off your brakes when you need to, and ride them when necessary."

He made it very clear my main job was not to run into the back of his truck. I was very confident that would not happen. I helped Dad numerous times pull our tractors and 2-ton truck. I understood exactly what I needed to do.

In no time at all we arrived at the ridge. I could tell Donnie's dad was trying to pick up some speed. We booked it up the hill, the old 'International' truck's rear tires throwing rocks from time to time. We only went a short distance before going around an almost 90-degree curve. We crossed a small bridge over a shallow creek. I saw what I thought to be the Hopkins' place just up ahead. Sure enough, the truck's right turn signal flashed. Donnie's dad worked his way off the right edge of the drive to the intended resting place for Ole Limpie. He jumped out of the truck, looked in my direction and said, "We're going to leave her here."

I put Ole Limpie in gear and set the parking brake. In no time at all he had the long chain unhooked from both vehicles and gave it to Donnie. He looked at his son. "You know where that goes, put it up."

Donnie quickly replied, "Yes, sir!", and headed to what appeared to be an equipment shed.

Just about the time I was so sure I didn't like this guy, his whole demeanor changed. He seemed very relaxed, then confidently said, "We will get you fixed up, don't worry."

"You don't know how much I appreciate you helping me, Mr. Hopkins," I said, while we walked toward the house.

CHAPTER 9

*'Nope, you don't owe me anything,
that's what Christian people do.'*

It was an older looking house with no paint, but appeared to be in good shape. It had a long front porch that ran all the way across the front of the house. Just when we got to the steps, Donnie's dad stopped and said, "My name is Orville Hopkins."

I once again stuck my hand out and said, "Nice to meet you."

He said, "Now, what did you say 'yer name was?"

"Leon Wilson," I replied.

"Well, it's nice to meet you."

Without hesitation, he called out, "Katie Jean come here."

Almost instantly a young girl bolted out of the house and onto the porch, followed by an older girl. I would guess the young one to be around six, and the older to be twelve, maybe thirteen-years-old. Then an attractive lady stepped out onto the porch. She looked in my direction, gave me a smile and a little wave.

Orville said, "Katie Jean, this is Leon Wilson."

Katie said, "Nice to meet you, Leon."

"Likewise, it's nice to meet you, Katie Jean." She looked at the girls, pointed to the older one and said, "This is Alice Ann," and before she could say another word, the younger one spoke up and said, "My name is Mary Beth."

I commented how pretty they both were.

Orville spoke up and asked, "Is supper ready, Katie?"

"Yep, give me about fifteen minutes."

She looked in my direction. "I sure hope you like fried

chicken."

"Oh yes, I love fried chicken."

"Me too," Mary Beth said.

Orville sat down in one of the several chairs on the front porch and said, "Have a seat."

"Thank you so much for your help. I most certainly plan to pay you for your time and trouble, whatever you deem fair." I greatly appreciated their help and hospitality.

"Nope, you don't owe me anything," he replied. "That's what Christian people should do, help each other."

Then he shocked me with his question. "Are you a Christian?"

"Yes, I have my mom to thank for that." My reply seemed to please him, exactly as I anticipated.

"Well, I've been sittin' here thinking about your situation," Orville said. "I'd bet this farm, none of the local parts stores are going to have that water pump. Tomorrow is Saturday, most likely it will be Monday before they can order it. I say your best hope is maybe Wednesday, even Thursday before we can get it installed. Orville paused for a moment, "Can you drive a tractor?" Before I could answer, he asked, "I mean, have you ever pulled a plow or disk?"

"Well, actually I have pulled a disk hundreds of miles. I was raised on a wheat farm in south-central Kansas."

"That's good. Really good," he said. "Maybe it wasn't just a coincidence your water pump went out at the same time Donnie was going to the store."

I had a bit of trouble following his reasoning.

"You see," he began, "we have a neighbor who's down on his luck. He had a bad accident. He does farm repairs for farmers all around here. He was working on a breaking plow, tow type, two bottom, and the plow was hooked up to the farmer's tractor. The hydraulics on this old tractor would leak off. So, Buzz, that's his name, Buzz Overtree, placed blocks under the plow frame as a safety measure. Well, the pressure leaked off and put too much pressure on the blocks. Somehow, he isn't sure how, but they kicked out. The plow fell and pinned him down with all the weight of the plow on his leg. He laid there for 'bout forty-five minutes to an hour before someone found him. He broke his leg in two different places.

Buzz is kinda' a jack-of-all trades. He cuts hair, that is if you want a buzz cut. I guess that's how he got his nickname. He also farms on a small scale. He has a twelve-acre cotton allotment, about four or five acres of corn, and approximately thirty acres of soybeans. Buzz and his wife, Hazel, only have one child, a girl about Donnie's age. Hazel works in town at the five and dime store. Well, Buzz can't even stand on that leg, he's in a blasted wheelchair now.

The neighbors, and several from our church, are going to surprise him and Hazel about daylight in the morning. We should have over ten tractors pulling into his driveway shortly after sunup. We plan to get his crop in the ground tomorrow. At least his cotton and corn, and hopefully his soybeans."

We sat there on the porch for what seemed like thirty minutes just visiting. He was very inquisitive about why I was driving in this area of the country.

I explained why I was driving the old wagon, the job waiting for me at Caterpillar, and being out of the Marine Corps for a couple years. I asked him questions about his farming operation and how long he had lived in this part of the country. I didn't mention Karen and Randy. I was really hopeful one of the part stores would have the water pump and I could be on the road come Sunday.

The windows of the house were open. The aroma of fried chicken and pastry baking filtered out onto the porch. I was getting hungrier by the minute. Without warning, Mary Beth pushed open the screen door, and bolted out onto the porch.

"Mama said y'all might want to wash up, supper is 'bout ready."

We both washed our hands at a wash basin on the back porch.

Katie said, "Leon, you can sit at the end of the table if you want."

Orville sat at the other end. When we were all seated, it was obvious the kids knew not to start eating. They sat and looked at me. I was afraid Orville or Katie Jean would ask me to give thanks. I was comfortable enough, but I haven't prayed in public for a long time. However, without warning everyone bowed their heads and Orville recited what seemed like a rehearsed prayer.

Katie said, "Sorry it took longer than I thought. I decided to bake a cake."

Donnie immediately asked, "What kind?"

"Your favorite, coconut!"

Very cheerfully Donnie replied, "Boy, today has been a good day. I got a Dr. Pepper and now coconut cake."

Mary Beth said, "Where did you get a Dr. Pepper?"

Donnie looked at his sister and said, "I have a surprise for you Mary Beth, I'll give it to you after supper."

It was Friday, but the meal in front of me had Sunday written all over it. Fried chicken and all the fixin's, and I mean all, including homemade biscuits. We finished our meal, had a piece of the coconut cake, then went into the living room.

Orville looked at Donnie. "Got your chores done?"

"No, sir."

"Well, you best get out and get 'em done right now."

"Yes, sir," Donnie replied, then hurried out the front door.

Orville pointed at a chair. "Have a seat." Orville then sat down himself.

Before I took my seat, I stepped into the edge of the kitchen. Katie Jean glanced up from the table, where she was gathering dishes to take to the sink.

"Could you use some help?" I politely asked.

"No thanks."

I once again thanked her for the meal and repeated what a wonderful cook she was. I went back into the living room.

Orville looked at me and said, "I have a plan."

"Okay, what's your plan?"

"I know this guy that runs the Auto Parts store. I have done a lot of business with him over the years. If you'll help us out by driving one of my tractors in the morning, I'll call him as soon as he is open. If he doesn't have the pump, I know he will call other auto parts stores, even from other towns, and see if he can find one for you. One of us can go get it before they close. We can put it on early Sunday morning."

"Sounds fantastic." I told him how much I appreciated his help. He reiterated the fact that the probability of us getting it tomorrow was very slim, and of course I understood.

It was obvious Orville was experienced in handling break downs and situations like mine. One could almost hear the cogs turning in his head as he developed a plan of action.

"Do you think you could help Donnie prepare the tractors and plows for our workday tomorrow?"

"Sure, what do we need to do?"

"Grease the plows, fuel up the tractors, and check the oil and water on both. If you'll help him, I'll take your water pump off the wagon. It's pretty much a one-man job. I won't need any help."

Just when we walked off the porch, Donnie ran across the yard from the barn. Orville asked him if he had all his chores done.

"Yes sir, I do."

Orville explained to Donnie what the plan was. He seemed eager to work with me while we both headed toward the tractors.

Orville raised the hood on the old wagon, then assembled the tools he would need while we prepared the tractors and equipment for tomorrow's workday. I was eager to get to the wagon and see if I could possibly help. When I finally got in view of the wagon, I noticed the hood was down and Orville held the water pump in his hand. He pointed to the tools lying on the ground and instructed Donnie to put them up.

I was surprised. "You got it off already?"

"Yep, it wasn't difficult at all," he answered, then started to walk toward an outside water hydrant. There was a small table with a wash basin, a bar of lava soap, and a towel that hung off the corner. We both washed our hands and began to walk back to the house.

Orville asked, "Y'all got the tractors and plows ready for in the morning?"

"Yup," I replied.

We walked up the steps to the porch and sat down. He began to tell me the full plan for tomorrow's big day.

"We are going to roll out very early in the morning." He clarified by saying, "You and Donnie will drive the tractors down to the crossroads, Katie and I will be in the truck. We'll meet three other men with tractors and plows. We will all proceed to the highway and hook up with four more tractors with plows. The nine of us will motor down the highway to the Crossroad General store. That's where the rest of the work party will be waiting for us. We'll all drive down the gravel road to Buzz's farm. There should be twelve, possibly thirteen tractors total. The women are going to prepare a big meal come noon. Some of 'em will be in the convoy, in cars or trucks of course. They want to be there to witness the look on Buzz and Hazel's faces when all the men on tractors pull into their drive."

"Randal Cox, a big cotton farmer, owns several hundred acres, all of it in the delta. He suggested to the John Deere dealer over in Malden, to bring one, or perhaps, two of his new 730 John Deere diesels to demonstrate for the farmers. I think he's convinced him to leave it all day. We all plan to take turns driving the big diesel with the five-bottom plow. We hope to have most of Buzz's cotton and corn land ready to plant by noon. Hopefully we will be able to get his complete crop in by dark, including his soybeans."

There was no doubt you could hear and feel the pride in Orville's voice while he explained how the day was expected to play out.

"What you people are doing is wonderful, and to tell you the truth, I am very happy to be part of it."

Orville added, "Well, that's what good neighbors and friends should do. Buzz is a very good man and has carried credit on most of the farmers he has worked for. On more than one occasion, I've seen him work past midnight just to get that farmer back in his field, knowing he wasn't going to get paid till harvest time."

I agreed with him about Buzz being a good man. I was about ready to remark how my dad would have loved to be a part of tomorrow's workday when Katie stepped out on the front porch.

CHAPTER 10

*'I couldn't help but think of Brenda. The what-
if's keep resurfacing over and over in my mind.'*

Katie had a smile on her face, looked at me, and said, "Leon, you are in luck, you're going to have your own motel room." She glanced over at Orville. "The Mex house."

I didn't have a clue what she was talking about. I very quickly let her know that I had sheets, blankets, and my own pillow, and I would be fine sleeping in the station wagon.

She emphatically said, "No, there's absolutely no reason for you to sleep in your wagon."

She explained that they sometimes use Mexicans in the fall to help pick their cotton. I had only vaguely heard of this labor partnership between the U.S. Department of Agriculture and the Mexican Government, whereas farmers from the U.S. would contract to house a certain number of Mexican laborers to help harvest their crops, primarily cotton of course, in this area.

Katie once again said, "You're in luck."

She explained her sister's daughter had a wedding a couple of weeks back. "We cleaned up the Mex house for her family to stay in when they attended the wedding. They cleaned it up and left it 'spic-and-span'. Plus, there is an old hot water heater mounted above the outside shower. The water will not be hot, but the sun heats it enough for one to take a luke-cool shower."

She suggested I go to the wagon and get my personal things, including my pillow and sheets. She said there were several blankets I could use, if needed. Katie started walking off the porch, but paused and addressed Orville. "The girls and I will go make sure everything, is in working order, and there are clean towels."

I quickly exited the porch and went to the old wagon to retrieve my suitcase and bedding. Katie and the girls were already inside the Mex house when I got to the door.

Katie smiled. "Come on in." She pointed to the bed. "Did you bring your sheets?"

I could tell she planned to put them on for me. I assured her I could put the sheets on myself. I thanked her, but told her I may not have learned a lot of things during my time in the Marine Corps, but I most certainly knew how to put sheets on a bed.

Katie laughed. "I am sure you do and probably better than I can."

Katie instructed Alice to check the cabinet on the back porch for clean towels. Alice started out of the room and Katie shouted to her. "Check for soap in the shower also!" Shortly, Alice returned and confirmed there were plenty of both. About that time, Orville stuck his head in the front door and asked if everything's a-go.

Katie said, "Yep, he is set for the night."

Orville told me he would wake me up around 5 am.

Katie spoke up, "I'll have breakfast ready as soon as you make it to the house." She only walked a couple of steps toward the house when she quickly turned and asked me, "What is your favorite pie?"

"I like any pie, but to answer your question, my favorite is Coconut Cream," which prompted another smile.

We all said good-night. I walked over to the front door and said, "I'll see you folks in the morning." Mary Beth turned and said, "I hope you sleep well, Mr. Leon." I told her I was sure I would, and once again thanked them for their warm hospitality.

I opened the rear door of the Mex house and was very pleased. There was a rough sawed-lumber sidewalk running a considerable distance to the shower, and a few feet further down the wooden walk was a rather new outdoor toilet. I closed the door on the Mex house and plopped down on the one, and only, full-size bed. The rest were cots.

I did not dare to be late tomorrow. I knew I should take a shower and shave tonight. I grabbed a clean towel and headed to the outside shower. I hoped Alice was right and there was soap and plenty of water. The shower had a wooden floor, and four posts that held it up. The old water heater and the shower head had a shut off valve. The only pressure was, of course, gravity-fed. For privacy there was a double wrap of burlap feed sacks that circled the four posts, leaving two feet completely open at the bottom of the shower. Katie's description of a luke-cool shower was dead on. Quite frankly, it was downright cold at first. However, it was amazing how refreshing and wonderful it became the longer I adjusted to the temperature. I dried off, wrapped the towel around me and headed back inside. I checked the old gas range and was pleasantly surprised to find a clear blue blaze. With a pan from the cabinet, I heated up some water to shave.

There were only two windows in the Mex house. The sun had totally gone down, and before you could think about it, the natural light in the house began to fade quickly. I flipped the light switch in each room to make sure they worked, and was happy to find all in working condition. I turned out the lights, and from the window in the front room, I saw the back of the Hopkins' house. I couldn't see any lights on at the house at all. I was sure they had all retired for the night and knew it was in my best interest to set my alarm clock and do the same.

The bed and mattress were comfortable enough, especially after a day like today. While I laid on my back and stared at the ceiling, a thousand thoughts rushed through my mind. I couldn't help but think of Brenda. The 'what if's' kept resurfacing over and over. I also thought about how I could see Randy in every movement Donnie made. I knew if I didn't get the water pump tomorrow, I was going to need to inform Larry about my situation.

CHAPTER 11

'Brother Sloan had no more than said Amen, when the gestures of love, jokes, and laughter filled the air at the outside dining hall at Buzz and Hazel Overtree's yard.'

I turned and tossed for what seemed like an hour before finally drifting off. My deep sleep was suddenly interrupted by the alarm clock. I knew I needed to roll out of my nice, cozy bed and start preparing for the day ahead. I was completely dressed and ready when Orville yelled from the yard that breakfast was ready. I was greeted by the wonderful aroma coming from Katie's kitchen several feet from the porch.

The moment I stepped into the kitchen, I was welcomed by a warm smile and a very heartfelt "good morning, sir," from Katie Jean.

"Good morning indeed, ma'am."

I was surprised how awake Donnie seemed to be. He looked in my direction and asked, "Which tractor do you want to drive? The Big G or the 60?"

I looked at Orville, but before I could speak, he answered, "The G probably would be the better choice."

"I am okay with either," I answered.

Orville pointed at the far end of the table and said, "You can sit at the end, Leon." I sat down and took inventory of the breakfast spread before me. Homemade biscuits, sausage-gravy, scrambled eggs, sausage patties, fried potatoes, and an assortment of jams and jellies.

Orville poured me a cup of hot coffee and asked, "Do you use sugar or cream?"

"No, just black," I replied.

Katie sat a large glass of milk down by my plate, then said, "I am sure a country man like you, like's milk."

"Yes ma'am, sure do," I said.

Donnie quickly added, "Me too!" We all made small talk while eating a wonderful breakfast.

Orville told Donnie to go wake the girls. He looked at Katie and questioned her about the list of chores she had written down for them to do. She assured him they would get all the things done and do a good job of it.

Orville looked over at me and Donnie and said, "Well, if we are going to get ole Buzz's crop in, we best be heading in that direction."

Donnie and I cranked up both of the big green John Deere's. Orville pointed for Donnie to take the lead and I followed. I was amazed by how he seemed so much older than he was, how Orville relied on him, and how quickly he responded to his father's sharp commands.

Katie and Orville quickly drove the pickup truck up behind me, then we all headed down the gravel road. The sun was slowly climbing above the horizon. It didn't take any time at all before the cross road came into focus. Just like Orville said, there were three men sitting on tractors waiting for us.

Orville sounded the horn on the pickup. I turned back to see what he wanted. Katie had her arm out the window and pointed for Donnie and me to pull over to the right side out of the road. They pulled along-side of us, and Katie said, "You guys stay back and bring up the rear."

We all began driving toward the highway. Just as Orville had said, four more tractors were assembled where the gravel road joined up with the highway. There were two older fellas in a pick-up truck and some women in a car. He quickly moved the pickup to the front and pulled onto the highway. I knew our next stop would be the store where Donnie had purchased the sugar and my Pepsi. One tractor after another pulled onto the highway, a total of nine. Some pulled wheel-type disk plows, others had three-point breaking plows, and two with four row planters. A warm feeling consumed my soul as I looked to the front of me, then to the rear.

This, I knew, was going to be a day I would never forget. We made a sharp ninety-degree turn onto the highway. A short distance away, we clearly saw the Crossroad store. There were three or four vehicles, and at least four, maybe five, tractors with attached equipment that waited for us.

Orville and Katie were already at the store. The waiting tractors started repositioning to make room for our convoy. Soon we were all parked around the store and in an open field next to the store grounds. Everyone began to dismount from their tractors, including Donnie and me. Much like a general assembling his troops, Orville directed everyone to come closer to his location.

Orville gratefully thanked everyone for coming to be a part of this very blessed day. Everyone who had chosen to participate in this worthwhile event felt the pride and love that invaded everyone's soul.

The owners of the store, a couple who looked like they were in their mid-forties, thanked each and every person. The lady often wiped tears from her eyes. Katie spoke up and told the group that she had called Hazel, Buzz's wife, and apologized for calling so early. She explained to Hazel that she had a very busy day planned and wanted to bring her and Buzz, a pot roast for lunch. She wanted to be sure they would expect her early.

Someone in the crowd spoke up and said, "So this is a complete surprise to them?"

Several in the group answered, "Yes, a total surprise!"

Orville abruptly spoke in a loud controlling voice, "Okay guys, let's get this man's crop in the ground."

Men scattered in every direction to get on their tractors. Orville and Katie pulled out first, followed by the other vehicles, and the tractors took turns getting into formation. Donnie and I, just by total circumstance, found our way once again, to the middle of the pack. I, of course, had never met Buzz and his wife, but I was anxiously looking forward to seeing the looks on their faces when this convoy of fourteen tractors with equipment pulled into their driveway.

I had overheard Katie telling one of the ladies in the car to get behind them. We want to hurry ahead of the tractors and have Buzz and Hazel out in the front yard when the tractors begin to arrive. We headed straight east from the store on a gravel road. The warm glow of the morning sun just crested the horizon. I saw the dust from Orville's pickup and the car full of women way out in front of us. They soon faded out of view. Once again, I thought of how much my dad would have loved to be part of this, this type of thing was his church.

We passed a couple of houses, then I saw an older couple in a yard, each holding a sign. One read 'Thank you so much,' the other read 'God Bless each of you.' I would learn later they were Hazel's parents. The next house came into view and I noticed a large farm shop. That had to be where Buzz worked on the farmers' equipment. The tractors ahead of us started to slow down and pull into a large parking area around the workshop and filled the long driveway to the barn. Orville and the women folk had rolled Buzz out to the edge of the parking area. Smiles were on everyone's face and, yes, there was more than one person wiping tears, including some men. Like turtles bailing off of a log on a farm pond, men crawled off tractors and walked briskly toward Buzz and Hazel. You could tell by the look on Buzz and Hazel's faces they were in total shock. The men who had driven the tractors went over to both of them and assured them their crops would be in the ground by sundown. Buzz tried to thank them, but he was overwhelmed by sheer emotion. Hazel tried to do the same, but she barely said a word or two, then choked up in emotional tears.

Orville spoke up and said, "Buzz, you have helped everyone here so many times over the years. This is not a hand out, this is a payback."

A very large man, who stood at the back of the crowd, spoke up. "Are we going to talk all morning, or are we going to get this man's crop in the ground?"

Several seconded his statement, but before anyone else could speak up, one of the two men who were in the pickup truck announced, "I would like to take a couple minutes to ask God's blessing on all the workers, if that is okay."

Katie Jean quickly said, "Absolutely, Brother Herb."

He asked everyone to bow their heads and he began to pray a very appropriate prayer that ended with a very loud Amen. Numerous amens echoed through the crowd.

Then everyone turned toward the big truck that just pulled up in front of Buzz and Hazel's house. The truck was painted in John Deere green, with yellow letters that boldly read Malden Equipment. Sitting on top of the flatbed two-ton truck was the Big 730 John Deere Diesel.

Luther Copeland, a church member and neighbor to Buzz, had only one tractor, but had a twenty-year-old son who had never married and still lived at home with Luther and his wife. He would be the first to drive the big 730, then would trade tractors with anyone who might want to try out the new 730.

Once again, Orville took control and directed each tractor and its equipment to different fields. The tractors went in every direction and began to turn up the fertile delta soil that was as black as the diesel smoke rolling up from the exhaust of the big John Deere 730 in a field a short distance from where Donnie and I worked.

I was enthralled by the feeling I was experiencing. It was a spiritual feeling stronger than any church sermon. A feeling I must admit, I hadn't felt for a very long time. I had turned away from God, and quite frankly, almost everything Christianity stood for. I blamed God for taking my beloved Karen and Randy. For the last two years I have begun and ended each day with bitter feelings deep within my saddened heart.

The morning moved quickly. I was in awe at the amount of all the work we had accomplished. The majority of Buzz's crop land was like most of the farms along the ridge. The homestead was on the ridge and the crop land was across the road. From the field where I worked, I watched the women folk arrive at the house.

The activity was as busy as a hive of bees, people setting up tables and carrying food. Shortly after noon, two pickups left their parking place in front of the house and picked up men from their tractors. In no time at all the back of the trucks were loaded and back at the house.

Under a large shade tree, the women set up wash pans with buckets of hot water, with plenty of soap and towels. I looked over the large smorgasbord of food on the long table. It looked like a meal fit for a king. There was a large assortment of meat dishes and numerous bowls of vegetables. On another long rectangle table were desserts and assortments of drinks including iced tea, kool-aid and lemonade. The fellow Katie Jean had earlier called Brother

Herb, asked everyone to gather close to the food. He looked at the gentleman who had been his companion in the truck all morning. "Brother Sloan, would you care to ask the blessing?"

Brother Sloan had no more than said Amen, when the gestures of love, jokes and laughter filled the air of the outside dining hall at Buzz and Hazel Overtree's yard.

There were a large number of folding chairs under the big oak shade tree in the yard. I found one that set off by itself. Everyone was very friendly, most making an effort to speak to me and add some small gesture about the event of the day, or remark about the food we all enjoyed. I looked up and made eye contact with Katie, who then walked in my direction. I remember thinking how attractive she was this morning at breakfast, but it was obvious she had put on make-up and fixed her hair. She was very stunning. It was amazing how some women could have three kids and still keep a youthful figure.

Katie walked up to my chair, placed her hand on my neck and whispered gently, "When you are ready for dessert give me a wink." She explained, "I put back a piece of my coconut cream pie for you. It's in the refrigerator in the house."

The sweet aroma of her perfume lingered around my chair when I once again made eye contact with her. I was most certainly ready for my coconut pie, and I did exactly as she suggested. I gave her a subtle wink. She returned a wink and gave me a very warm smile. It did not take her long to return from the house with my coconut cream pie.

I thanked her, and I must admit, her early flirtation, and her natural beauty, ignited a spark of lust and desire. I reminded myself to direct my thoughts in another direction. She was a married woman, and I had no business having such thoughts about her. I hadn't quite finished my coconut cream pie when I saw Orville exit the house and walk rather quickly toward me.

He said, "Well, I have good news and bad news."

"Okay," I said, "let's hear it."

"Well, the bad news, as we both expected, no parts store within forty-miles of here has your water pump. The good news is, Joe Loveland at the auto parts store assured me the water pump would either be in a warehouse in Memphis or St, Louis and could be shipped Monday."

Shortly after we had all finished our meal, several suggested we head back to the fields to complete what we had set out to do. I admired how the community was devoted to achieve the goal of getting Buzz's crops in the ground. Brother Herb and Brother Sloan were busy going from tractor to tractor, making sure everyone had a fresh drink of cold water and giving updates on the progress. Everyone was pleased to learn that the cotton and corn were in the ground. Only soybeans were left to plant.

The sun was beginning to get low when Orville told Donnie and me to take the two Johnnies back home before it got dark.

He told Donnie, "Be sure and get all the afternoon chores done as soon as you get the tractors home."

I let Orville know that I would help Donnie. Orville told us he and the remaining workers were going to work past dark if necessary to get all the soybeans planted.

I saw a noticeable gleam in his eyes as he remarked, "We are going to get it done."

CHAPTER 12

*'"Do you have children Leon?" She stared into my eyes.
I could sense she was curious as to what my answer would be.'*

Donnie and I had no more than got home with the two tractors and disk plows when a car pulled into the drive. It was one of the ladies who had helped with the noon meal bringing Katie home. Katie stepped out of the car with several containers and they each said goodbye. Katie walked across the yard, in my direction. The yellow blouse she wore was very dirty, and both knees of her blue jeans were covered in dirt. She had a satisfying glow on her face. She pointed to her dirty jeans.

"Brother Herb, Brother Sloan and I, along with a couple of women from our church, helped Hazel get her garden planted this afternoon. What a blessed day this has been," she said.

"I couldn't agree with you more, Katie."

Katie looked at Donnie and me as she started walking toward the house.

She said, "Come on guys, I think all three of us deserve a glass of iced tea."

When we stepped up onto the back porch, Donnie spoke up, "Where is Mary Beth and Alice?"

"They are still at the Melford girl's house. They are going to spend the night and go to church with them tomorrow. We'll bring them home after church." Katie looked at Donnie. "You best finish your tea and start getting your chores done."

Without hesitation Donnie said, "Yes, ma'am," and gulped the last bit of his tea, then bolted toward the door.

I quickly stood up from the table and said, "Wait, Donnie, I'll help you."

I no more than got that statement out of my mouth when Katie said, "No, he won't need any help."

Donnie looked at me then back at his mother, then back at me and replied, "I can get things done by myself."

"All right then." I watched him exit the house. I remarked to Katie what a fine young boy Donnie was.

"Do you have any children, Leon?"

She stared into my eyes, and I sensed she was curious as to what my answer would be. I looked at the floor and hesitated for a moment.

When I looked up, our eyes met, and I once again felt that awful feeling. I began telling the story of how I had a little boy, and how Donnie reminded me a lot of him. I again found myself forced to crawl through the muddy fields of my mind and recall that awful day one more time. Katie wasn't any different than anyone else I had shared that day with. She had a look and genuine words of sympathy for me.

We both stood in the kitchen and faced each other.

"Bless your heart," she said and started to move in my direction.

She opened her arms to hug me. We both hugged for a few seconds, then backed away. Katie did something I wasn't expecting. She opened up her arms again and reached out to me. We again embraced, this time it was different. Nature had been good to Katie in regard to her breasts. She was certainly well endowed, and as we hugged this time, it was obvious Katie had every intention of pressing her large breasts into my chest. We both backed away from the hug and looked into each other's eyes. I felt ashamed, but there was also a part of me that wanted to grab her and take it farther. That's when my better judgment kicked into overdrive.

CHAPTER 13

*'The screams were coming from Donnie.
He and his dad were across the road at the pig pens.'*

I quickly asked Katie if I could use the phone to make a long distance collect phone call to my brother Larry in Decatur. I explained to her I needed to let him know the water pump situation.

"Of course, the phone is in the living room."

I called Larry. He felt guilty for the problem I had with the old wagon. He apologized more than once. I told him not to worry about it, then briefly told him about my day.

I no more than hung the phone up when I noticed out the living room window that Donnie carried two large buckets of feed, and headed toward the hog pen across the road. I thanked Katie for the use of the phone and rushed out of the house to help him with the heavy buckets. I called Donnie's name and he stopped to set the buckets on the ground. His dog, Bo, seemed startled, and the hairs on his back bristled up, and he growled while he looked in my direction. Bo and Donnie were inseparable. Wherever Donnie was, Bo wasn't far from his side.

He said, "It's okay, Bo, it's my new friend, Leon."

Somehow his referring to me as his new friend touched my heart. We finished feeding the hogs and were crossing the road, walking back to the house, when we heard a vehicle approach from down the road.

Just as we both thought, it was Orville in the pickup. When he pulled into the drive, Katie Jean opened the front door and walked out onto the porch. Orville climbed out of the truck and Katie called out, "Did you get it all in?"

Orville gave us a thumbs-up. "We got it done! Every seed of Buzz's crop is in the ground."

Katie let out a big, "Praise the Lord, Praise the Lord." Then she said, "I'm warming up leftovers from lunch. I hope that is okay."

Exhausted from the blessed day, we all went into the house, washed up and ate supper.

"We normally attend Sunday School, but we're just going to church services in the morning," Katie Jean said. "We sure would be honored if you would go with us."

To be honest, I didn't want to go, but I knew it was the appropriate thing to do. "Sure. I'd love to go with you."

Orville pushed his empty plate away. "I think the best thing all of us could do is take showers and get to bed as soon as possible."

I was getting ready to remark what a great idea that was, when all of a sudden, a flash of lightning in the distance lit up the dark night sky, followed shortly by a large rumble of thunder.

Katie looked at me and said, "I'll have breakfast around 8:30 in the morning since we often sleep in on Sundays."

I replied, "Thanks, that sounds great."

The wind began to blow stronger, then another flash of lightning. The roar of the thunder was much closer and much louder. Orville and Katie commented about how fortunate we were to have Buzz and Hazel's crop planted before this rain storm. We all said good night and I headed to the Mex house.

"See ya in the morning," Donnie said.

"Yep, see ya in the morning."

I rushed into the Mex house. It dawned on me that the ceiling to my shower house was open to the sky and there were no lights. Realizing it would probably be raining shortly, I pulled the shades over the windows that faced the Hopkins' house and quickly began to undress. The sound of large raindrops began to pepper down on the metal roof. I retrieved my flashlight from my duffle bag and headed outside. I stepped into the shower and noticed the rain had become much heavier. The shower water, combined with the steady rain, felt absolutely heavenly. If I hadn't been concerned about the lightning, I think I could have stayed in that shower for an hour.

I headed back inside the Mex house, dried off and slipped into my Marine-issued shorts. I laid on the bed, stretched out flat on my back and stared at the ceiling. I was mesmerized by the pitter-patter rhythm of rain that steadily fell on the metal roof. The events of the day faded while my mind slowly drove through the streets of Snooze Ville. I don't think I moved until my full bladder woke me up. I crawled out of bed and stumbled to the back door. The rain had stopped and I noticed a few stars scattered in the night sky.

I looked at my watch. It read 4:10 am, so I crawled back into bed. Suddenly, I was awakened by a strange noise. I had laid in bed longer than I thought since the room was completely consumed with sunlight. I looked at the alarm clock that read 7:10 am. Once again, I heard a strange noise. It was a definite scream. I quickly ran and opened the front door.

The blood curdling scream belonged to Donnie. He and his dad were across the road at the pig pens. Orville had his belt off and was pounding him with one lash after another. Donnie screamed in excruciating pain from each blow of the heavy, wide belt. Then, out of nowhere, Bo raced toward the commotion. Every hair on his back was turned up and he growled, as if to say, "stop and I mean stop right now!" Orville did just that. He abruptly stopped and backed away.

Bo positioned himself between the two of them and looked Orville straight in the eye. With every hair still bristled on his back, Bo continued his deep, meaningful growl. Orville's professed Christianity quickly faded in the early morning wind. He pointed his finger at Donnie and said, "If I had a gun right now, I'd kill that sorry, son-of-a-bitch, excuse of a dog."

Donnie didn't say a word. He stood stone still with fear all over his face. I walked out on the steps of the Mex house and looked in that direction. I think Orville caught my movement in his peripheral vision. He turned and looked in my direction, then barked out something in a low voice to Donnie. Donnie went back to finish whatever he had to do in the pig pen. It looked as though he held a water hose over to fill a big trough for the hogs. About that time, I heard the front door of the farmhouse slam shut. I was certain Katie had walked out on the porch and witnessed the whole thing.

I went back inside the Mex house, then turned and looked out the window toward Donnie. A part of me wanted to go give him a hug. I knew there couldn't have been anything that would have merited a whooping like that. My goodness, I thought, that boy worked side by side all day long with grown men yesterday. I admired how he never complained or talked back to Orville. It was 'yes sir,' 'no sir,' 'okay,' and 'I will sir'. I knew I didn't want to be around Orville. I shaved, put on clean work clothes then prepared my church clothes. Katie had told me that everyone dressed very casual.

While I waited in the Mex house, I used this time to work on a song I had begun to write. I was consumed in my song when Donnie knocked on my door.

I had barely opened the door when he said, "Mom said breakfast is ready."

He didn't give me a chance to say one word before he quickly turned and walked back to the house.

When I opened the door to the back porch, Katie spoke in a very cheerful voice. "Good morning."

She had once again prepared a large breakfast. "Go ahead and sit down. Orville has already eaten. He's going to check cattle in the back pasture."

I tried numerous times to start a conversation with Donnie, but I could tell he was embarrassed from the situation that had occurred this morning with his dad.

I made an effort to inject something positive into his day. I said, "Boy, I was so impressed at how you handled that tractor and disk plow in the fields yesterday."

He looked up at me and the redness in his eyes from crying this morning was very obvious. He tried hard to force a smile, but it simply wasn't in him at the moment.

Katie spoke up. "Donnie has been driving the tractor since he was nine years old. The last two years, during times when we are trying to get the crops planted, he has driven the tractor ten to twelve hours a day."

Donnie finished his breakfast and immediately got up from the table and rushed out of the house.

CHAPTER 14

'You don't know how many times I've heard one of those planes fly over and desperately wished I had my three kids with me on that plane.'

I thanked Katie Jean for a wonderful breakfast and asked if I could help with the dishes. She readily accepted my offer. We both worked at making small talk while we took care of the kitchen chores. She was very inquisitive about my life, going as far as asking if I was romantically serious with anyone since the loss of Karen.

Katie glanced up at the clock on the kitchen wall. "Oh my, it's later than I thought. I need to get ready for church. We'll need to be ready in about thirty-five minutes."

Katie looked across the kitchen table at me, and with a very sweet tone in her voice said, "Thank you so much for helping me with the dishes."

"Well, you're so welcome." I smiled at her. "Orville is very lucky to have such a wonderful life's partner." She once again surprised me. She walked around to my side of the table, reached out and took my hand.

With very flirtatious eyes, she said, "You're a very gentle, kind, and good-looking man. I promise you, the woman who winds up with *you* is the one who is lucky."

I found myself in a place I am not too familiar with...speechless. I frantically searched every nook of my mind trying to come up with the perfect come back. The only thing I could think of was, "That's a sweet thing to say."

We stood for a few seconds smiling at each other. I quickly turned and said, "We best get ready for church."

I walked toward the Mex house and noticed Donnie in the yard out by the garden. He sat on his butt, legs out straight and leaned against a large oak tree. Bo laid next to him with his head in Donnie's lap. I heard Donnie talking to Bo, as if he were a human. He muttered words to Bo and continued to pet his head. Bo's tail wagged back and forth in complete contentment. There's absolutely no doubt Donnie loved Bo and Bo loved Donnie.

I no more than got into the Mex house when I saw Orville entering the back porch. Shortly after he went into the house, Katie stuck her head out the door and told Donnie to get ready for church. He had his church clothes on in nothing flat and made his way over to the Mex house. I assumed he came just to get away from his dad. I invited him in and we both laughed and joked with one another until we heard Katie Jean yell, "Let's go guys."

Orville and Katie's family car was a four-door 1952 Pontiac, very clean and in good shape. They only used it for church and social events. The church was only fifteen minutes from the Hopkins' farmstead.

The church wasn't big, but was well kept. It was white with light blue trim and nestled in a scenic setting. The church property was large, and included a baseball field with a back stop. Among the large trees that were scattered on the property were different types of playground equipment. There was a big swing, teeter totter, and several picnic tables. It also had a beautiful and well-cared-for cemetery. I commented how attractive the church was while we pulled into the large parking area. They both made comments about how they were proud of their church and their church family. Their remarks reminded me of the many times I had heard my mom say the same thing about her church.

When we walked into the building, many people greeted us. Mary Beth and Alice waved at me with big friendly smiles. I recognized several people from yesterday's workday at Buzz and Hazel's, including Brother Herb and Brother Sloan. The church services were much like Mom's church. Songs were sung, the pastor gave his message, and special prayers were requested. Just like our church, the pastor asked someone from the congregation to dismiss while he made his way to the back of the church to greet each person as they exited.

Just as the gentleman the pastor designated to dismiss uttered his last word of the prayer, including Amen, the congregation began a cheerful reunion of handshakes and laughter, at times getting rather loud. Katie and Orville seemed excited to introduce me to different people in the church. More than one made a noticeable attempt to greet me and make me feel very welcome. It took quite a while to make our way to the back of the church.

Orville spoke up and said, "Pastor Blackmore, we'd like for you to meet our new friend, Leon Wilson. He's from Kansas."

We gave each other a meaningful handshake, each repeating the usual, 'nice to meet you' ritual. Orville briefly explained my situation with the car and how I had participated in the workday yesterday. Brother Blackmore commented on how proud he was that we got all the crops planted. He said if it had not been for the funeral of an old school friend, he most certainly would have been there.

While we pulled out of the church parking lot, I recalled how I really had not wanted to go to church this morning. However, I really enjoyed myself and was glad I made the effort. Donnie sat in the backseat with his sisters. He stared out the window, seemingly daydreaming in his own world. Mary Beth and Alice were in competition trying to tell their mother about the sleepover with their two friends. Orville, Katie, and I listened to the chatter from the front seat. It was as if the warmth of the noon sun, along with the church service, dismissed the event of Donnie's whooping this morning. Everyone seemed so happy.

In no time at all we were back at the Hopkins' farm. Katie Jean told the girls to change out of their church clothes because she needed help getting dinner ready. I was impressed by how quickly Katie and the girls had the Sunday meal on the table. Shortly after dinner, we all, with the exception of Orville, helped clean the table and put away the leftover food.

I made my way out to the front porch to visit with Orville. I only sat there a minute or two when Donnie approached us with his baseball glove and bat.

"Could y'all hit me some grounders and fly balls?" he asked.

Orville looked at me and said, "Have you ever played baseball?"

A part of me wanted to say 'yes, as a matter of fact, I received a scholarship to play college baseball.' Instead, I just replied, "Yes, I love playing."

Donnie had two gloves. He tossed me one and headed to the far end of the yard not far from the road. Orville hit one ground ball after another. I was very impressed by Donnie's skills. I realized Orville never once praised his son. It was one criticism after another. I decided I would praise him the next time he made a good catch. The next ground ball hit was to Donnie's left. He sprinted after it and very smoothly gobbled up the ground ball. Then in one motion, he took the ball out of his glove and made a perfect throw I easily caught.

I immediately said, "Wow, good play!"

Orville not only didn't second my comment, but rather he said, "You should've charged that ball more, Donnie."

He caught one ground ball after another. Orville never said a word unless it was to criticize him. The next hit was a sizzling ground ball to Donnie's right. He once again sprinted to it and made a beautiful, backhanded catch, then stopped, and made another perfect throw.

I quickly let out an enthusiastic praise, "Great play Donnie!" He had a smile that showed every tooth in his head.

Orville said, "You should've planted your right foot more solid before you released the ball. You would've gotten more on your throw."

I began to feel my blood pressure rise. I wanted to respect Orville, so I felt the best thing was just to get the heck away from him. I wasn't in dire need to go to the toilet, but I excused myself and headed to the Mex house.

I thought I might visit with Alice and Mary Beth, but when I left the Mex house, I saw them walk across the road. I made my way back to the porch and watched Donnie practice his baseball skills. I only sat on the porch for a couple minutes before Katie stepped out of the house and offered to keep me company.

Katie and I made small talk and were occasionally interrupted by Orville's criticism toward Donnie's performance of catching the baseball. She was in the middle of making a point on the subject we were discussing, when Orville's tone became harsh and loud.

Katie didn't attempt to finish her thought on the subject we were talking about. She said, "I don't know how that boy can take one criticism after another without even one word of praise."

"You know, I must be honest, I was thinking the very same thing."

Katie looked at me with a very saddened face. She looked toward the pig pens across the road, then slowly turned toward me and our eyes met.

"I'm so sorry you had to witness what took place across the road this morning."

I really didn't know what to say, but I desperately wanted to know what the awful whooping was about, so I just asked. "What did Donnie do that was so wrong?"

"He didn't run enough water in the hogs watering trough."

"A whooping like that for not running enough water in the hog trough?"

Katie had a mixed look of anger and sadness on her face. "Donnie gets way too many whoopings like that." She continued. "I want desperately to intervene, but I know it only gets worse for Donnie. Then Orville becomes very angry with me, and sometimes becomes physical with me."

We were at such a distance from Orville and Donnie, they couldn't have heard a word she spoke. She was comfortable talking about Orville, and began to tell me about his dark side. I listened to her speak one negative thing after another about him and realized I was her sounding board. I knew she had no one to vent to. She certainly couldn't talk to the neighbors, or the women at church.

She had a need to unload her built up anxiety, and I was the perfect candidate. I would soon be driving away from this farm, and it was apparent she didn't feel threatened that I would reveal her secret. Katie paused for a moment, then glanced up at the sky over the flat delta fields that lay across the road from us. She pointed upward to the large commercial jet plane that was roaring overhead.

"You don't know how many times I've heard one of those planes fly over and so desperately wished I had my three kids with me on that plane."

She continued, "I actually fantasize about landing on a small island thousands of miles from this damn old cotton farm. Then some attractive man greets me with outstretched arms, holds me, and assures me my new life will be different."

I wanted to say something that would brighten her day. But as hard as I searched through my mind for the right words, they simply didn't appear. I could not think of one thing. Even if I would have thought of something, I probably would not have had a chance to express myself.

Orville and Donnie were quickly walking back to the house. Orville looked up at us and said, "I think a good long nap sounds good. How do y'all feel about that?"

Katie and I both remarked we couldn't agree more.

Before I started walking to the Mex house, I made a point to tell Donnie what a fine baseball player he was, and once again that big smile consumed his face.

He said, "I am going to play for the St. Louis Cardinals someday."

Even knowing full well, the possibility of that was extremely low, I would not dampen Donnie's dreams. "Well, I can't wait to see that happen."

He added, "Me and B.J. are both going to play for the Cardinals."

I said, "Who is B.J.?"

"He's my best friend." He pointed down the road and said, "He lives down that way."

CHAPTER 15

*'On the far side of sunshine there's a dark cloud of rain and
on the front side of love there's a back door to pain.'*

Tired and ready for a nap, I laid on the bed and expected to
doze off to sleep. Katie's remarks about the airplane would
not leave my head. As I often do, I hear one phrase
someone says and it triggers a reaction in my brain. A voice
seemed to be saying, 'go write, go write.' I usually surrender, grab
a pen and paper, and jot down my thoughts. I kept thinking about
her fantasy and wrote this.

*"I would like to book a wild flight out of nowhere,
headed to anywhere, just as long as I know I would be gone,
straight to the arms of someone who would hold me
and assure me what I am doing is not wrong."*

I laid back down on the bed and thought how we often don't see
the forest for the trees. How we have the ability to mask our true
feelings. How love is so often associated with pain. It shouldn't be
that way, but it is.

I thought about my love for both Karen and Randy and how
much pain I have endured these last two years. I thought about
Brenda, her marriage to Eddie Ray, her ordeal with the married
dude from Oklahoma. I recalled an event that occurred in our
community in Wellington.

~ ~ ~ ~

There was this girl, Francis was her name, she was about two years older than me. Francis and her mother attended the same church as Mom and me. However, Francis didn't go to the school I attended. She was very pretty, had a very nice figure, and was always somewhat flirty. I liked her a lot. I guess you could say I had a crush on her. She always seemed to have an older boyfriend, so we really never became boyfriend and girlfriend.

Our mothers were very close friends. I remember Mom crying so hard when she heard the awful news. I was only sixteen, but I understood the meaning of pregnancy. However, I was somewhat confused about what she did. It seems that much like Brenda, Francis, too, was hoodooed by a married man. However, unlike Brenda, Francis became pregnant from the older married man. Francis' mom told my mom that Francis had come to terms with being pregnant, accepted it, and had become quite excited about it.

But when she found out about his true age, and the fact he was married, it was just more than she could handle. Francis did the unthinkable. There was a dry creek that wasn't too far from her folks' home. It would have very little water in it most of the time. But during heavy rains it rose rather quickly and the water became deep and very swift.

Francis went missing, she hadn't been seen all afternoon. Word soon got out in the neighborhood, and people started looking for her. Her car was found on an old logging road, not far from the raging creek, but no Francis. Later that night, a couple of men, who had braved the swift water in a boat, found her lifeless body about two miles downstream, hung up in a farmer's fence that crossed the creek. In a couple of days, the creek water receded and they located her dad's 38 caliber pistol. It was lodged and laid under a large rock in the creek bed downstream from where the logging road crossed the creek.

I so vividly remember the pain my mom showed while we drove home from church that Sunday morning. I felt so sorry for her. Mom sat in the front seat and was looking out the window, lost in thought, while I drove. She spoke to me in a low, hurtful voice, never turning her head away from the window. "See how beautiful and sunny this day is?"

I softly answered, "Yes, Ma'am."

"Well over that horizon there is a dark cloud of rain." She hesitated for a couple of seconds. "It seems so many times love is overshadowed by pain." She continued. "Just as we have sunny days and cloudy days, so do we have love and laughter in our lives. But somehow, and way too often, the love and laughter turn to pain." Although I was only sixteen-years-old, I had a passion for putting words on paper, often turning them into songs.

When I got in my room later that Sunday afternoon, I wrote this song.

~ ~ ~ ~

FAR SIDE OF SUNSHINE

Verse
"He was two years shy of thirty, still in his prime.
He strummed her a tune he had played a hundred times.
She was eighteen and pretty, on the mild side of wild.
Caught up in a romance now she carries a child."

Chorus
"On the far side of sunshine, there's a dark cloud of rain.
And on the front side of love, there's a back door to pain.
Something so precious, Lord what a shame.
But on the front side of love, there's a back door to pain."

Verse
"Blinded by the passion, she believed every lie.
Should have seen the look on her face when she heard of his wife.
Now she walks down by the river where the swift water flows,
Her final destination, only God in heaven knows."

Chorus
"On the far side of sunshine, there's a dark cloud of rain.
and on the front side of love, there's a back door to pain.
Something so precious, Lord what a shame,
but on the front side of love, there's a back door to pain."

CHAPTER 16

'Leon, Leon, stop. You don't own this anymore than I do.'

I eventually dozed off into a good nap, only to be awakened by the sound of one of the John Deere tractors. Orville was driving it down by the shop building. I got out of my comfortable bed and slipped on my boots. Donnie was doing his late afternoon chores.

The sun quickly dropped behind the ridge. We had all the chores done, then finished our leftovers from our Sunday noon meal. After Sunday night supper, Orville summoned me to the front porch.

He said, "I need to talk to you."

"Sure, what do you have on your mind?" For some reason, this made me nervous.

"I was wondering if you'd help me for the next few days until your water pump comes in." Before I could reply, he said, "I'd pay you 50 cents an hour, just as I would any farm hand." He said, "Joe Loveland down at the parts store was pretty sure your water pump wouldn't get to him until the delivery truck ran on Wednesday."

"Orville, I'd be happy to help you, but you don't need to pay me a penny."

He said, "No, you just work for me as a hired hand and I'll pay you."

I could tell that was what he really wanted, so I politely agreed. He seemed pleased and began to explain tomorrow's workday. "The fields will be too wet to work in the morning. I need to replace worn blades on the disk plow. I will go into town and get the disk blades and check on the status of your water pump. You can take the old disk blades off the plow while I am in town."

I replied, "I can do that!"

He thanked me and told me he appreciated my help. I reiterated how much I appreciated his hospitality.

"We will roll out very early in the morning. I'll call you when breakfast is ready."

He said good night and remarked that he and the family would be going to bed rather soon. I returned to my quarters, laid on the bed once again and recalled today's events, and those of the last several days. I often think about Brenda and Sheila. Somehow, I just can't get them off my mind. I finally felt myself drift off to sleep. I had set my alarm. Once again, I was awakened before it went off. I looked over at the farmhouse. and as I expected, lights were on in every room.

Orville soon called out that breakfast was ready. All the Hopkins kids were busy getting ready for school. Soon after breakfast, the big yellow bus stopped for the kids. I looked down toward the bus just in time to see Donnie drop on his knees and give Bo a big goodbye hug. What an unwavering love between that boy and his dog.

I convinced Orville I wouldn't have any problems getting the disk blades off. Shortly after he left, Katie Jean came out of the house with a basket full of washed clothes. I looked up toward the clothes line, just in time to see her hang the last piece of wet clothes on the line.

She stood there and looked in my direction. Then she shouted out, "If you need any help let me know."

"Okay," I was sure she would be going back into the house, but instead, she set the clothes basket on the ground and headed my way. She walked over and stood a few feet from where I was working.

"I hate to say this, but I must be honest. I'm glad you had trouble with your car at the very time Donnie was going to the store. If not, we would have never met you. By the way, I want you to know that several of the women at church commented to me how handsome you are."

I smile, "Well, if that water pump was going to go out, I feel blessed for it to have gone out when it did. If not, I'd never have met a wonderful family like yours, and I would have missed out on meeting you. You've been so kind, and you're also pretty dang easy on the eyes."

Our eyes locked, and we had a moment. Katie's face lit up in a warm, glowing smile. Her smile quickly disappeared and her facial expression changed to a very serious look.

"I'm going to tell you something I have never told anyone, except my sister and my best friend." Once again, I was shocked as she proceeded to unveil her well-kept secret. "I haven't loved Orville for years. To tell you the truth, I'm not sure I ever truly loved him.

"I met him when I was fifteen, he was twenty. My folks were friends and neighbors with his folks. My folks thought he was a nice, church going, young man, and they were okay with me dating him. We only dated a few months, and he wanted to get married. I was only sixteen, but I thought I was mature. Of course, I said yes. I was very concerned we might let things go too far, and I would wind up pregnant. I found out later from my mom, that she and Dad were also concerned about that, so they were all for the marriage.

"I've never dated or been with another man except Orville. The marriage wasn't so bad at first. I had Alice about a year after the wedding, and I quickly started noticing drastic changes in him. He began to be abusive, and at times, even physical. He has a need to control me and the kids. He is never going to let me learn to drive. If I could drive and had my driver's license, I think I might very well load up the kids and leave. Maybe go to Wisconsin. I have a sister up there. I probably wouldn't go, I'd be too afraid he would find me, and it would turn worse for both me and the kids."

I knew I needed to continue to work on the plow. Orville would expect me to have it disassembled and ready for the new blades. I kept on working as she continued to express her feelings about her life with Orville. The large nut on the axle of the plow was frozen and stuck.

I pulled on it with all my strength when suddenly the wrench slipped off the nut and my hand crashed down on the steel frame of the plow. I let out a loud groan, turned, and slung my hand in excruciating pain. I looked down at my injury. I had busted my right index finger. I held my hand still long enough to assess all the damage. It wasn't serious at all, but it needed a bandage, at least a large Band-Aid.

By Katie's first reaction, she thought it was much worse than it was. Even though I tried to convince her it wasn't bad, we both knew I needed to wash it with alcohol and stop the bleeding. Katie suggested we go to the house where she could attend to my finger. She had me stand over the kitchen sink while she went to the bathroom. She returned with alcohol, some gauze and medical tape. In a couple of minutes, she had my finger bandaged and the bleeding stopped.

I looked at my wrapped finger then looked at Katie Jean and said, "Thank you so much, Nurse Lovely Lady. What do I owe you?"

"A big hug would be payment in full," Katie said.

Once again, we faced each other. Our eyes met in a deep gaze, as if we both were trying to look deep into the other's soul. Our arms invited the other to engage in a meaningful embrace. Katie once again squeezed her large breasts against my chest. My heart nearly stopped. There was no doubt this was certainly more than just a warm hug. It had lust and desire written all over it. If I said I didn't enjoy it, I would be lying. We released our hug and looked at each other. It was as though Katie looked through my eyes straight to my heart. I felt my heart beat faster. Her short, deep breathing steadily increased. Then it happened. It just happened...our lips met. This kiss from Katie Jean wasn't from some young inexperienced teenage girl. The kiss she gave me was from a loved starved, mature woman.

I was suddenly struck by a jolt of common sense. It was as though a voice deep within my soul screamed, 'No! No, you can't, she is a married woman.' I abruptly turned. "I'm sorry, I'm so sorry!" I rushed out of the house.

While I walked across the yard, my mind spun in circles trying to figure out what just happened, I heard Katie call my name, "Leon, Leon, *stop!*"

I instantly halted.

"Don't be sorry, please don't be sorry. You don't own this any more than I do, and I don't feel the need to apologize to anyone, including God." Katie continued, "For years I have endured the wrath of this man's abuse, not only to me, but also my sweet kids."

I stood and listened to the anger and sadness in every word she spoke.

"He never has a kind word for me or the kids, we are no more than tools in his toolbox." She pointed to the plow I was working on. "He loves me like he loves that plow. He hasn't told me he loves me in years, even when we make love. No, I should say, 'when he makes love.' It is all about him, not me. I don't know how long it has been since he has kissed me. Even a little peck on the cheek would be nice."

Katie had a need to vent, an understandable need most would agree. She continued to blast Orville and her miserable life. She choked up, her words overpowered by the sheer frustration of her feelings. She broke down in an outburst of tears, then quickly turned and ran back to the house.

A part of me desperately wanted to go to the house, wrap my arms around her, and make mad, passionate love to her. Thank God, my better judgment said to work on this plow, and work on the plow is exactly what I did. I finally got the frozen nut off and had the plow ready for the new blades. Shortly, Orville returned from town. He was happy I had the plow ready for the new blades. He told me that Joe Loveland at the parts store assured him the water pump was ordered and was in stock in St. Louis. It would arrive at his store late Wednesday afternoon.

Orville and I got the disk plow put back together. He gave me instructions on where to start plowing the cotton field. It was quite boring riding the tractor, going up one set of rows, turning and plowing up another set of cotton rows. My mind constantly turned to Katie. I had to work hard not to become totally aroused. I wondered where that kiss might have led to this morning.

CHAPTER 17

*'What color of towel will she hang at
the east end of the clothes line.'*

The early May sun was straight overhead. Time for lunch. I was constantly looking toward the farmhouse. I was sure I would soon see a signal from someone telling me to come in for lunch. However, I was surprised when I saw Orville on the other tractor heading straight down the field road in my direction. When I made it to the end of the cotton row, Orville waved. I could tell he wanted me to stop my tractor. In his hands he held a brown sack and a quart jar of tea.

"Katie made some sandwiches for your lunch. If you don't mind, we won't take a normal lunch break. Eat your lunch, then go back to the plowing."

I glanced at Orville. "That's fine, no problem."

Orville dropped his breaking plow and rapidly went to work, turning up the rich delta soil.

The day was warm and sunny, not a cloud in the sky. I thought of the comment Mom had made about, 'over that horizon there's a dark cloud of rain.' I couldn't help but wonder where the pain lay. Was I heading for it?

The afternoon quickly disappeared. The cotton rows ran straight toward the house. I looked forward to turning the tractor toward the homestead. I hoped to get a glimpse of Katie out in the yard removing clothes from the line, or cleaning around the many flower beds. I turned once again and plowed toward the house. I saw Bo walk across the yard and lay next to the road. At first, I was puzzled as to why, then it came to me. He was waiting to greet the kids, especially Donnie. I caught the sight of the approaching bus. Bo's tail wagged about a hundred-miles-per-hour in anticipation. Alice and Mary Beth stepped off the bus first.

They didn't pay much attention to Bo, and it was very apparent that Bo wasn't too interested in them. However, things quickly changed when Donnie bounded off the bus. The bus lunged forward and was soon going down the road. He laid his books in the yard, dropped to his knees, and gave Bo a big hug. I don't know who was the most excited, Bo or Donnie. It was a sight that sent a surge of warmth through my entire body. Now that I had witnessed and heard the stories of how Orville treated Donnie, seeing him with Bo, his bestest friend, took on new meaning. Donnie needed Bo. The afternoon sun rapidly began to set, and this day would soon be over. What a day. What a day indeed.

Things were pretty uneventful at supper. Katie and I both, of course, acted as if nothing ever happened. I went straight from the kitchen table to the Mex house and took a shower. I only had to close my eyes to envision her just before we kissed. Katie Jean had a look so different from any other women I had been with. There was a hunger in her eyes. I believe what I witnessed was what I've heard men refer to as 'bedroom eyes.'

Daybreak, Tuesday morning, found a thin layer of fog hanging over the flat bottom ground across the road. Orville and I finished breakfast and were soon in the field. When I turned the big G at the end of the field, I faced straight toward the homestead once more. I was confused when I realized Orville had left. He was on the field road headed toward the house. I noticed an excessive amount of black smoke coming from the exhaust of the tractor.

In no time, Orville had the tractor parked next to the machine shed. I watched while he walked to the house. A moment later he waved his hat, and I knew he wanted me to come to the house. I looked at my watch, it was 11:35. He met me at my tractor with a concerned look of deep disappointment.

He looked up at me and said, "Broken ring, there is also a knock, possibly a rod bearing."

I shook my head, "Oh man, that's not good."

"It's worse than not good, it's absolutely horrible," Orville said. "Wash up, lunch is ready. Just as soon as we eat, I am going to the

John Deere dealership to see about getting parts."

Orville gobbled down his lunch faster than a hungry dog. Katie mentioned she had fresh strawberries and shortcakes. He turned it down and told her he didn't have time and swiftly headed to the door.

He stopped, looked at me and said, "You should have plenty of plowing in the field you are working in."

I heard the old pickup roar while Orville was driving away from the farm. Katie turned toward me. "Well, handsome, are you going to turn down my strawberry shortcake?"

"I would absolutely love a piece of that shortcake."

Katie cut me a piece of cake, loaded it down with ripe, sliced strawberries, and placed it in front of me, then sat down straight across from me at the table.

"I'm sorry I lost my composure and started crying yesterday."

Just when I was about to tell her it was okay, she interrupted me.

"I'm not in any way apologizing for what we did." She looked me straight in the eyes. "I hope you understand."

"I do understand. You're a very good woman, caught in a hard, unbelievable place. Trust me, I have all the respect in the world for you."

She gave me one of those beautiful smiles. "Thank you." She walked out of the kitchen when I was on my last couple of bites of the strawberry cake. I took my time to finish those bites. She returned to the kitchen, and it was obvious she had put on fresh makeup and brushed her hair. It was also very apparent that she had removed her bra and had unbuttoned the first few buttons on her front button denim dress. I immediately became very aroused. I felt myself pitch-a-tent, a ripple of anxiety consumed my entire body. I stood up from the chair and turned toward her when she casually walked in my direction. I was completely caught up in the moment. I knew this had but one way to go, and I was more than willing to fan the blaze of the fire we both were getting ready to light. Katie and I met in the middle of the kitchen.

I saw a gleam dancing in her eyes, a look of uncontrollable desire. We engaged in a beautiful sensual kiss. My hands were rapidly exploring what normally would be forbidden places. My clumsy hands desperately tried to unbutton that faded denim dress.

I don't have a clue how we made it to the bedroom, but there we were, lying on the bed.

Katie had a need like no other woman I had ever held. She wilted each time I touched sensitive areas of her warm, willing body. Her breath came in short bursts. I wanted so much for this to be good for Katie. I reminded myself to climb that mountain slowly, and to pick her a few wildflowers on the way to the top. It then became apparent she didn't need me to pick any more wildflowers. We were at the top of this lovely mountain, where a large field of beautiful wildflowers grew. All of the flowers, including the smallest bulb, suddenly burst into '*full bloom.*' We both simultaneously enjoyed the awesome sunset on this peaceful mountain.

We both laid there in an effort to catch our breath. I gently squeezed her hand. Then I turned to her with full intentions of giving her a gentle kiss, but quickly raised straight up in bed. I was so sure I had heard something. I knew it was a noise from outside. Then it became very clear, without a doubt, it was the sound of a vehicle in the driveway. I heard tires roll over the gravel to the house. 'Oh, my word! Could it be Orville'? Had he forgotten something? What if it was one of the neighbors? I shouldn't be in this house. I threw my clothes on faster than a fireman responding to a five-alarm fire. I was shocked by how unconcerned Katie seemed. She slipped out of bed and methodically walked to the window, still only wearing her birthday suit.

She barely cracked open the window shade. She looked at me and said, "It's okay. Just as I thought, it's Carol Hughes, the mail lady."

The mail route ends at the Hopkins' house. Carol would always turn around in their drive and go back the way she came. I'll admit to anyone, that mail lady scared the living crap out of me. I wanted out of this house, and I wanted out as soon as my physical abilities would let me escape. I literally had my clothes on, including my boots, in mere seconds.

I rushed out the door when Katie called out, "Hold up, wait a minute."

I stopped a few feet from the back door, double checked to make sure my clothes were on properly. Katie too had rushed to get her clothes on. She began walking in my direction.

I listened for any sound of a vehicle. With the exception of a few songbirds, it was as quiet as a church house on Tuesday morning. I looked at Katie, and she had that smile, the one that could tame the Devil, and somehow, I was sure the Devil had a big smile on his face.

I couldn't keep from feeling a measurable amount of guilt. We were once again engaged in a lustful lip lock, and the heat of all that passion rapidly burned away the guilt. I couldn't help but wonder how she would feel in an hour or so. We had crossed that forbidden line, the one you can't erase. I gave Katie a concerned look.

"Are you sure you're okay with this?"

"I'm okay, trust me, I am fine."

"I noticed you had wet clothes ready to be hung out on the line." She seemed puzzled. "Do you have any white towels in that basket?" I asked. The puzzled look on her face only increased when she afformed, she did, "I desperately need to be on that tractor working," I reminded her. "Give yourself some time to think things through. If you are having second thoughts, or you wish this to go no further, trust me, I will understand."

I pointed to the east end of the clothes lines. "If you decide you want this to stop, hang a dark color towel at the east end of that clothesline. If you decide you want this to continue, then hang a white towel at the east end of the clothesline."

She smiled and said, "Okay, I understand."

I knew I must get that tractor rolling before Orville returned from town. However, when Katie asked for another hug, we opened our arms and embraced.

Katie whispered in my ear. "I didn't know it could be that good."

I smiled at her. "The feeling is mutual." We both smiled at each other for a moment, then I turned and swiftly walked toward the tractor.

I was back in the cotton field in no time at all, pushing the Johnnie as fast as the big engine would let me run. While I sat on the tractor, a thousand thoughts raced through my mind. What will she choose to do? My emotions, along with my judgment, spiraled. I know for a fact this thing could most certainly get out of hand. A raging wildfire always starts from a small blaze.

A part of me almost hoped I would see a dark towel. Today was Tuesday. By Friday morning I could possibly have the water pump in the old wagon and be on my way to Decatur. This might just be a one-time thing, and I could get out of here.

There also was a part of me that hoped the towel would be white. It had been a long time since I was with a woman in a passionate way. Katie wasn't just an ordinary woman. She had a natural beauty that would catch any man's eye. When it came to making love, she had all the right tools and right moves to make a man feel like a king.

CHAPTER 18

'Donnie had his arms wrapped around Bo's neck,
bawling, pleading, and begging his dad not to shoot.'

I had been in the field for nearly an hour and was surprised I hadn't seen Katie at the clothesline. This time when I looked toward the house, I saw what I had waited for. Katie carried the basket of wet clothes to the line and walked straight to the east end. The mixed feelings I had felt earlier soon faded. I was desperately hoping to see a white towel.

A big smile came over my face when I saw a bright white towel hanging there in the warm afternoon sun. I was completely surprised by another white towel, followed by another white towel. Not one but three bright white towels gently basked in the afternoon sun, all three hung at the east end of the line. Katie walked toward the road and out in the open yard. She gave me a big 'ole wave. The smile on my face turned into a loud chuckle. Voices began to battle in my head. I heard, 'What on God's green earth are you doing?' Then another voice told me, 'Go with it, it will be just fine.'

I can't keep from feeling a certain amount of shame and guilt. I desperately searched for a justifiable answer. I have not been involved sexually with a woman since I lost Karen. God should know a man of my age shouldn't be expected to be that strong.

I kept driving the big John Deere, desperately trying to take my mind off the events with Katie. No matter how hard I worked, I just couldn't. I looked down the gravel road and saw dust boiling up. Just as I suspected, it was Orville returning from town. I hoped he had the tractor engine parts. He had been in town a long time and was back only a few minutes before the school bus came.

Orville and Katie were in the freshly plowed garden. I knew she was anxious to get her seeds planted. I turned toward the house and saw Bo laying out by the road. No doubt this was the best part of Bo's-day, getting ready to greet his best buddy. The big yellow bus appeared, and the same events from yesterday once again unfolded. Donnie dropped his books, dropped to his knees and gave Bo a big hug.

Soon, all three Hopkins' kids had changed clothes and were helping in the garden. I could tell there was something taking place. Then all of a sudden, the scene came into focus. Orville had a rather large stick or pole, and was whipping away at the back side of Mary Beth. I gradually got closer to the unbelievable scene I was witnessing. I wanted to scream, 'Stop man, *stop*! You are going to seriously hurt that little girl.'

Then the unthinkable happened. Donnie had a garden hoe and was heading over to rescue his little sister. He took his hoe and knocked the pole out of his daddy's hand. Mary Beth started running to the house with a noticeable limp in her gait. Katie Jean was slinging and flailing her arms noticeably, while yelling at Orville. Alice ran toward her mother and stood by her side. Orville turned and pointed his finger at Donnie, motioning for him to come to him. It was obvious he was reluctant to go, but out of pure fear Donnie did as he was told. Orville unbuckled his belt and started taking his anger out on Donnie, one lash after another. Just as he had done with the altercation at the pig pen, Bo came running from around the house. Every bristle on his back raised. Bo growled, then lunged at Orville, who turned and ran to the pickup truck he had parked close by.

I made my way to the end of the cotton rows, stopped the tractor and was in total shock. I couldn't believe what I was witnessing. Orville retrieved his shotgun from the pickup. Donnie had his arms wrapped around Bo's neck begging his dad not to shoot. He was bawling and pleading in merciful cries. Katie rushed toward Orville, also pleading for him not to shoot. Orville pushed Katie to the ground.

My blood began to boil. I began to climb off of the tractor to stop the madness. Then I froze. It was an act of God, a vehicle pulled into the driveway. Donnie, Alice, and Katie quickly scurried to the house. Bo trailed close to Donnie's side. Orville quickly slipped his belt back on and walked toward the pickup truck that just stopped in the driveway. He greeted the man with a very cheerful, 'Hello.' Orville turned and walked toward his pickup truck, and retrieved the shotgun he had laid on the ground when he heard the truck. He got in his truck and followed the man while they quickly drove down the dusty road.

I knew the cotton field needed to be plowed. I also knew I couldn't continue to work till I knew everybody was okay. I shut the tractor off and walked to the house. Katie met me in the backyard and started crying uncontrollably. We hugged and she told me how the whole thing unfolded. It seemed Mary Beth wasn't laying the green bean seeds into the seed bed exactly the way Orville had told her to do. He got mad when she started crying and said she didn't understand what he wanted her to do. He picked up an old wooden tomato stake and started hitting her.

"When he starts to whoop one of these kids, he becomes so angry and won't stop." She added, "I have seen it a hundred times."

I was at a loss. I had no idea what to do to solve these problems. I looked at Katie. "What can I do?"

She replied with pain evident in her voice. "What do you mean, what can you do? You don't seem to get it, there is nothing any of us can do. I have no options. I can't take these kids and leave him. I promise, he would track me down, and it would be worse for me and the kids. I can't go to the authorities, they are more apt to believe him than me, and at best just talk to him for a bit. It would be much worse on me and the kids. The best thing you can do is get back on that tractor." Katie pointed across the road. "Just plow that damn old cotton ground."

Catching her breath, she continued, "He's gone to help Dean Basham, the man who drove up a while ago. His tractor won't start. He'll probably come home and act as if nothing ever happened, especially if you are here. I'm going to have Alice and Donnie help me get the garden planted. If Donnie has all the chores done, most likely everything will be okay. Trust me, I know him. You best get back on the tractor and be working when he returns."

I didn't want to disappoint or argue with Katie, and I was sure she knew best. However, the way I felt at this moment, there was nothing I would have liked better than to take that tomato stake and beat the living shit out of that sorry bastard, whom some people called, Orville Hopkins. This thing with him had consumed every ounce of my resistance. I looked at Katie in stunned disbelief. I thought when will it become equal to what is being taken from Katie and the kids? Perhaps never?

I did as Katie requested, got on the tractor and started working. I was still reeling in disbelief from what I witnessed in the garden. I kept looking toward the house. I wanted so much to be there when Orville returned. I noticed the fuel gauge on the tractor was close to empty. The sun was also sinking in the west, so I knew when I got to the end of the cotton field, I needed to go straight to the house. I had no more than shut off the tractor when he pulled up in the pickup. Just as Katie had said, his demeanor was as though nothing had ever happened.

I had only known Orville for a few days, but it was apparent he had a need to brag. He said, "I got Dean Bassham's tractor going, his fuel line was stopped up. A very simple thing if you know what you are doing and have an understanding of engines like I do."

I wanted to say, 'Too bad you don't have an understanding of how to be a good father and husband'. Instead, I replied, "That's good, the neighbors around here are very fortunate to have a good mechanic like you in the neighborhood."

"Yes, they are," he replied, "and I don't charge them anything, that's what good neighbors do."

I desperately wanted to know the status of the engine parts for the tractor. "Did you get your overhaul kit for the tractor?"

"Hell no, Leon. I am the unluckiest man in the world. They normally keep an inventory of two of these kits on hand. They sold 'em both last-week. The parts are on order, the manager was sure they would be in Malden, possibly as early as next Monday or Tuesday."

Orville continued. "I've been thinking that I might drive the tractor at night, and you could drive during the day. We could work twelve hours a shift, keeping the Johnnie going twenty-four hours straight, never shutting it off. There isn't as big a rush on the soybeans as there is with the cotton. I need to have that cotton in the ground in the next few days. This time of year, we normally get rain, so the first rainy day we get would be a good day to work on the tractor engine."

He added, "Your water pump is due tomorrow afternoon, we could possibly get it on your wagon Sunday afternoon." He looked at me as if to ask if that was okay.

A part of me wanted to say, 'Orville, I can put it on myself Thursday. I need to be in Decatur by Sunday', but I didn't. I simply replied, "Sure, whatever it takes."

He groaned. "I'm going to the house, grab a quick bite and fill my thermos. I'll plow until 1:00 am, then sleep till around 8:00 in the morning. My plan is to start working on the tractor engine tomorrow. I can relieve you at noon so you can take a lunch break, then work till 7:00 pm. I'll rest for a few hours in the afternoon. Then we'll work twelve-hour shifts, from seven to seven. How do you feel about that?"

"Sure," I said. "I think that's a good plan."

I no more than got the tractor fueled up, when Orville walked across the yard. I could tell he wasn't interested in small talk. He wanted to turn some soil. He thanked me, and told me again he appreciated my help.

He said, "I'll park the tractor next to the fuel tank when I quit at 1:00 a.m. That way it'll be ready for you at 7:00 in the morning." He added, "Be sure to check the oil and water and grease the plow."

I replied, "I understand the plan." I then told him to have a safe night.

CHAPTER 19

*'Does Mary Beth need medical attention? No, that's the beautiful
thing about a child, they repair themselves very fast.'*

I helped Donnie with his chores. Supper was ready. Everyone
was at the table except Mary Beth. I let it slide like everyone
else appeared to do. Katie filled a plate of food and went to
Mary Beth's room. Alice, Donnie, and I cleaned up the kitchen and
washed the dishes. Both had homework. Katie returned from Mary
Beth's room, then she and I went out on the front porch.

Katie let out a deep breath. "Mary Beth won't be going to
school for a few days. His whooping with the tomato stake bruised
the back of her legs and busted open the hide. It looks awful. He
also hit the back of her heel and she has trouble standing and
walking on her foot."

I sat there on the porch, thinking what a horrible situation this
was for Katie and her daughter. "There must be someone who can
help you. Surely there is some type of authority that would object
to this abuse to these kids."

The light from the inside of the house projected onto the porch
enough to see the frustration and hurt in her eyes.

"Please stay and help us get this crop planted. Usually, once we
get the crop planted, the stress is not so much on Orville. He
always seems to be more tolerant with all of us once the crop is in
the ground. However, anything can upset him at any time, and he
becomes angry at the world. The kids and I, especially Donnie,
have to pay the price. We call them mad fits. He can be that way
for days, then someone can visit, or he can just go to town, and

when he returns, everything is back to normal."

She turned to me and took my hand in hers. "Please, please, stay and help us get the crop planted."

I did not want to get any more involved than I already was. "Katie, isn't there someone local you could get to help you?"

She shook her head. "It's difficult to get farm help these days. Young men who graduate from high school, and are not going to college, are going to the large cities and getting good paying jobs in the factories. We had this young man, Jesse, a neighbor boy who was recently discharged from the Army. His mother called and wanted to know if possibly Orville could use some farm help. The young man told Orville he had a job in St. Louis at some factory where they were opening a new assembly line, and he wouldn't be hired until July sixth. He said he could help us until July 1st. We thought he was a Godsend. We both liked the young man. He worked for three days, then on the Wednesday before your car broke down on Friday," she hesitated for a second, "Orville fired him."

My reaction was spontaneous. "What for?"

She continued. "He had seen Orville whoop Donnie really bad two times. The second time he confronted Orville, he told him the whooping was way too hard and he didn't merit a whooping at all. Orville got mad at him and told him he needed to mind his own business, and that these were his kids, and the way he whooped his kids wasn't any of his business, and to keep his mouth shut about it. Jesse then got mad at Orville. He was a strong built young man. Jesse told him, 'Why don't you try to whoop me the way you whooped that boy?' They both squared off for a couple of seconds. I was at the clothesline and witnessed the whole thing. Orville looked at me and told me to write him a check. He told Jesse he was fired while he stomped back to the machine shed. Jesse got his check and started to get in his car, then all of a sudden, he headed into the machine shed where Orville was. Orville saw him coming toward him, jumped in his truck and sped out of the driveway. Jesse left and we haven't heard a word from him since."

"I can assure you I know how Jesse felt. If I hadn't been on that tractor across the road, and if Dean Basham had not arrived when he did, things could have gotten awfully ugly."

Katie replied, "I have all the respect in the world for you, and you would have been justified in whatever you did to that man. However, please trust me when I say, it wouldn't help me and the kids any. It would only make it worse. I know the man."

Feeling defeated, we sat on the porch, both of us, obviously having difficulty finding the right words. The stillness of the night was interrupted only by a lone cricket calling for a mate, and the distant sound of the tractor working in the furthest field across the road. I heard a little sniffle come from Katie Jean.

She spoke in a whisper. "I hope you haven't lost respect for me for what happened today." Not giving me a chance to say a word, she continued. "I've been completely faithful to Orville. You are the only man I've ever been involved with. Please believe me. There is an old saying that 'what is good for the gander is good for the goose'," she paused for a second.

"Yes, I've heard that."

She continued. "We sell eggs to a single lady that lives in Malden. She is about forty-years-old and has a couple of kids in high school. Orville is always ready to volunteer to take her eggs when he goes to town. He always takes Donnie when he goes, so I would have never suspected a thing. However, I have a dear friend, Bonnie, who lives on the same street in Malden as this lady. Bonnie lives on the opposite side of the street just a couple of houses down. We've been close friends all our lives and were inseparable when we were in high school. We still visit often on the phone. We also cook extra desserts and different dishes and share them with each other from time to time. One day she called and said she made a peach cobbler for my family. We sat at the kitchen table that afternoon and she shocked me out of my pants. It seems when Orville delivers the eggs, Donnie never gets out of the truck, and Orville is in the house for a long amount of time. That is, if her kids are gone. If the kids are at the house, Orville is in the house for only a couple of minutes.

"My friend Bonnie is the only person, with the exception of my sister, that I have ever told, about Orville's abuse. She feels I should divorce him. However, I don't have any solid proof of his affair, it's just my word against his. I'm too scared to take a chance of making it worse for me and the kids, so I just turn a blind eye to it and live with it, but it has hurt me a lot. I'm not saying what he's doing makes it okay for what we did today. I am saying I don't care. I hope you understand."

"Of course. I understand and I can't even imagine what it would be like to be forced to live the life you are living." I leaned over and took her hand. Her sniffles had turned into a heartfelt cry. Neither of us said a word, we just sat there. I broke the silence by asking how Mary Beth was. "Does she need medical attention?"

"No, I don't think so. I've disinfected the cut on her leg and foot. It'll heal rather quickly. That's the beautiful thing about a child, they repair themselves very fast."

I knew we both needed a good night's rest. I remarked to Katie, "I am going to take a shower and turn in for the night." She followed me off the porch, and as soon as we were in the dark shadow of the house, I felt her touch my shoulder. I turned toward her. We both got lost in each other's eyes. We didn't have to worry about Orville, we could still see the dim glow from the headlights on his tractor in the distant cotton field.

I wasn't concerned about Donnie or Mary Beth suspecting something between their mother and me. Alice was different, however. Alice was thirteen, sharp as a tack, and might read into something more quickly. We knew we must be careful. My eyes had adjusted to the darkness of the night so I clearly saw Katie's beautiful face in the moonlight. The heat of the passion quickly burned away the guilt. We once again were in a luscious kiss, our hands gently caressing each other's faces.

I spoke low and softly into her ear. "Goodnight beautiful." She, in turn, softly said, "Good night, sweetie."

I felt Katie locating both my hands with hers. She squeezed them, then with a merciful plea said, "Please stay and help us get this crop planted, please." Before I could answer yes or no, she said, "I know coconut cream pie is your favorite and you love fried chicken. I've been known to cook both on consecutive days, and you must not forget there are fringe benefits to this job, if you get my drift."

I spoke to her with a deliberate fake western draw. "I'll give this offer deep consideration, Ma'am." We once again said goodnight.

I walked into the Mex house and started to undress. A part of me wanted to crawl in bed because I was exhausted to the bone. I retrieved my flashlight and made my way to the shower. When my head finally hit the pillow, my thoughts were spinning, trying to dissect all of the day's happenings.

Katie's plea still danced in every nook of my mind. How could I not help her? I didn't want Donnie, or the girls, to go through any more abuse. I would tell everyone tomorrow I was going to stay. I felt I didn't have a choice. I couldn't turn my back on them.

I set my alarm for 6:00 a.m. and somehow fell asleep. Orville's tractor engine had awakened me at 1:00 a.m. when he came in from the fields. A few minutes later, I was awakened once more to the blasting alarm clock. Well, it seemed like only a few minutes. I dressed and greeted everyone at the house. Then I helped Donnie with some of his early morning chores, and was on the tractor in the field before 7:00. Shortly after that, the big yellow bus, barely visible in thick morning fog, stopped to pick up the kids.

CHAPTER 20

'Training dogs and lemonade, either is made sweeter, by adding more sugar, not more lemons.'

I could remember back home how much time there was to think when I would disk ground. I've written many poems and songs while sitting on a tractor seat and thinking about life. At this moment, I couldn't help but think about Donnie and his faithful dog Bo. I also kept thinking of the events of the past few days and even months. Actually, for the last eighteen months.

It's funny how events can seem like too much of a coincidence. I've seen things happen that only God could have orchestrated. Sitting on this tractor with time to reflect, I thought about how Donnie and his dog reminded me so strongly of a gentleman I became friends with several months ago. I want to think that…this is also not a coincidence, but something from God.

One day, while I was working on the house, I heard over the radio that the Wellington baseball team would be playing in the district tournament. The game would be in Wellington. I thought, 'What the heck. I think I'll go watch that ballgame.' I made it over to the ballfield and found a suitable seat in the bleachers. An older gentleman was sitting a few feet down from me on the same bench. A particular call was made concerning the strike zone. He and I both disagreed with the umpire. Eventually, we closed the distance between us and now sat next to each other.

His name was Johnny Hooper, from Sumner County Kansas. It was like there was a voice speaking to my heart, telling me this man needs a friend, or perhaps it was his ability to constantly make me laugh. There was most certainly a warm, friendly vibe I felt when talking with him. As the game played on, we dove more and more into each other's personal life.

Johnny asked me if I liked dogs. "Oh yeah, I love dogs," I replied.

He said, "I have a kennel, and I also train dogs." He invited me out to his farm.

We quickly became friends. I even started working part time for him at his kennel. Johnny had a passion for dogs. It was apparent he enjoyed teaching me how to train the dogs. It didn't take long before he shared his life experiences with me. Many things mimicked Donnie to a tee. Johnny was also abused as a little boy, and like Donnie, he had grown up on a cotton farm with an abusive father. He also had a black dog that was his anchor in the rough waters of his abusive life.

Johnny and his wife, Margaret, were simply the breath of fresh air I needed at the time. Margaret was kind to me. There is no telling how many meals I ate at their home. She was an excellent cook. They both showed me so much love and sympathy for the loss of Karen and Randy. Johnny had a sign at his kennels that read,

"Training dogs and lemonade, either is made sweeter,
by adding more sugar, not more lemons"

While I sit here on this tractor and recall that sign, I think how great it would be if Orville would use Johnny's psychology of training dogs to love and care for his wife and kids. Why can't he understand they need more sugar, not more lemons?

Was it simply by chance that I met Johnny Hooper when I needed support, and he needed a friend to vent to about his PTSD (Post Traumatic Stress Disorder)? Was it just by chance that the old station wagon's water pump went out on the gravel road at the same time Donnie was riding his bike to the store?

There is something else I thought about the other night. It was during my second year at Wichita State. I looked over classes I thought I might be interested in taking. I found myself going back more than once to a certain psychology class, something I never thought I would be interested in. I did enroll in that class and was surprised by how much I enjoyed that class, especially when the effects of childhood development were discussed. The topic of how child abuse had a lasting impact on a person, even when they become adults was of great interest to me, even then.

I was sure when I got out of the Marine Corps I would go back to college. I could use my G.I. bill and the government would pay for my degree. I set my sights on becoming a high school baseball coach. However, now when I think of furthering my education, I find myself seriously considering a career in social work. I can't keep from wondering, could there be a divine intervention in all of this?

There are so many more 'little Donnie's' out there being abused. They very well will become adults with severe PTSD like Johnny Hooper. I thought of how gratifying it would be to know I could be the light of hope at the end of their dark tunnel.

In no time at all the morning has passed. The warm spring sun was at high noon, time for lunch. I drove the tractor toward the fuel tank and saw Orville over at the machine shed. He raised up from the tractor engine. "Well, how did your morning go?" he asked.

"Great," I replied. "How is the engine repair going?"

"Real good. I've pretty much got the engine ready for the new parts."

We both made our way to the outside wash station, then went into the house for lunch. Katie, once again, had a wonderful meal sitting on the kitchen table. She looked so pretty we both smiled and spoke to each other. Orville gave me an update on the status of the water pump and tractor parts.

"They both will be ready to pick up tomorrow afternoon. I'll go in and get the parts, along with the cotton seeds.

"If the rain holds off, hopefully we can get the cotton planted Monday." He laid out his entire plan. "We could stay with the same seven to seven day and night rotation until Saturday." He continued. "Donnie can drive the tractor Saturday. We can get your water pump on and start getting the tractor engine back to running."

I knew Katie anticipated my decision on helping get the crop in, so I spoke up. "If you want me to, I could stay a few more days and help you get your crop in."

Orville quickly replied, "Oh man, yes, that would be a tremendous help."

I glanced at Katie Jean. She lit up like a Christmas tree, then discreetly wiped a tear of joy from her eye. There was no doubt, I had made both of them very happy, especially Katie. Just as soon as lunch was over, Orville wanted me to help him with the tractor engine. The two-man chore only took about five minutes, then I headed back to the field.

While I sat on the tractor, my mind drifted back to the bedroom scene with Katie Jean. I desperately tried to justify both of our actions. I know most would say, 'in the eyes of God it was wrong.' If Orville wasn't abusive to Katie and showed her love and respect, she wouldn't have done what she did. If God hadn't taken my Karen, I wouldn't have had a desire for another woman. As a matter of fact, I wouldn't have been in that old wagon for it to break down and caused me to, as Katie would say, 'be on this damn-old cotton farm.'

CHAPTER 21

'The Hatfield's and McCoy's were all in the middle of the church aisle.
I never witnessed as much crying and hugging in all my life.'

I wish I could allow the hands of time to unwind back to when my life was simple. I would love to be back home, say, when I was fourteen years old. I would be home with Mom and Dad, dreaming of playing professional baseball with the St. Louis Cardinals, going to church with Mom on Sunday mornings and shooting hoops at that old basketball goal with Larry.

Mom was a very Christian lady, and I know what she would say about my actions with Katie, a married woman, and that makes me feel extremely guilty. I also know she would be so disappointed in me.

Thinking about Mom and her love for her church made me think about the time the little church almost split. It all started during a period when the church had finally accumulated enough money in the building fund to add a couple of Sunday school classrooms. There were several members of the church who were good carpenters, so to save money, they didn't hire professional carpenters from outside the church. They had workdays and slowly finished the project.

Brother Jerry Dobbs was one of the workers. He accused Brother Gordon Burkhart of stealing his hammer and tool bar. What started out as a disagreement escalated into a feud as bad as the Hatfield's and McCoy's. Mom went to her grave totally convinced it was the work of the Devil. She would say, 'the Devil has split us almost fifty-fifty.' One side of the church was for Brother Burkhart, the other side for Brother Dobbs. The pastor and the deacons knew they had to act and act fast. They were quickly losing the congregation and decided to call in a special speaker.

They encouraged all the members to attend. Actually, they begged each and every one to attend. We didn't have Sunday school that Sunday Morning, we all met at 10:30. The pastor and the special speaker were in the basement. At 10:30 they appeared at the side door. One carried a folding table, the other a cardboard box. Pastor Neal unfolded the table and set it in the middle of the aisle, just in front of the pulpit. Brother Walker, the so-called 'special speaker' placed the box he carried behind the pulpit.

Pastor Neal opened the service by praising everyone who attended. Then he promptly turned the service over to Brother Walker. He opened his sermon by reiterating much of Mom's feelings about this being the work of the Devil. He said, "I can assure each and every one of you, the 'ol Devil is dancing in the aisles of this church as I speak to you this morning."

He spoke a few more words, and when I say a few, I mean *very* few. His next actions shocked the living dickens out of all of us. He picked up that cardboard box behind him and walked out in front of the pulpit. He placed it on the folding table, took a red marking pen, and in large letters wrote 'L O V E' across the small, printed shipping label on the box.

He walked back to the pulpit, picked up his Bible and said, "You have to have love in your heart when you pray. That is all I have to say." Without uttering another word, he walked out the back door of the church. Everyone in attendance that morning just sat in awkward silence.

I sat in the back near the window. I looked toward the gravel road. Dust rolled up behind Brother Walker's, 1939 Studebaker, black, two door coupe, Brother Walker was not coming back.

Pastor Neal sat frozen on one of the chairs behind the pulpit. He never said a word, nor did he move from his seat. Everyone sat, stunned, ashamed, embarrassed, and some even guilty. Eventually the right side of the congregation started to look toward the left side, and the left side looked to the right. Brother Jerry Dobbs added more drama to the already unbelievable morning. The very large man was the one who had accused Brother Gordan of stealing his hammer and tool bar.

Well, I suppose you could say the Lord's Spirit touched Brother

Jerry, or perhaps the word, '*love*' on that cardboard box did. Brother Jerry stood up and walked straight over to Brother Gordon. He looked him straight in the eyes and stuck out his hand. Brother Gordon quickly rose to his feet, latched on to Brother Jerry's hand and they engaged in a big, long-lasting hug, both shedding tears. Before long, the Hatfield's and McCoy's were all in the middle of the church aisle. I never witnessed as much crying and hugging in all my life. Later-on that week, I wrote this little poem.

BROTHER WALKER

The little church was getting weaker, the deacons called a special speaker, just to hear what he might have to say.

He said my name is Brother Walker and with a cardboard box and a magic marker, he shocked the congregation that day.

He spoke of brothers not loving brothers, members not speaking to each other and how you gotta have love in your heart before you pray.

Then he placed the box upon the table wrote LOVE across the small shipping label.

He said, "that's all I have to say," picked up his Bible and slowly walked away.

Mom would tell Dad later that morning when we returned home. "George, you should have been there. Brother Jerry stepped out in that aisle and just kicked that Old Devil right out the back door." I can assure you, that was one of the happiest days of my mom's life.

Dad had a half-sarcastic, half-serious tone in his voice. He said, "Do you suppose congress could get that Walker fella to talk to both the Democrats and Republicans? It's got to where they are more like the Hatfield's and McCoy's every year. They don't care about the hardworking American people. It's all about their political party." He wrote this little jingle. I always got a kick out of it.

"I wish we didn't have Democrats and we didn't have Republicans.
And what we had were country loving Americans.
Ones that care about me and care about you.

IN FULL BLOOM

And all the things we are trying to do,
But all they want to do is to fuss and argue.
The only thing they care about is their own political party"

CHAPTER 22

'Margaret would say Johnny doesn't have the patience to let the coffee brew, but he has the patience of 'Job' when it comes to training a dog.'

I turned the tractor and faced the house. I knew without looking at my watch exactly what time it was. Bo had walked out by the road and laid down. That school bus would soon bring home his bestest, bestest, buddy in the world. What an amazing love and bond Bo and Donnie had for each other.

I think about my friend, Johnny Hooper, back in Sumner County Kansas. It is almost scary how his life story, and what I have witnessed with Donnie, parallel each other. Johnny told me he had an old dog that came into his life when he was a little boy. He said he named the dog Boomer. So, Boomer walked up to him in his folk's yard, wagged his tail, and gave Johnny a few kisses. They couldn't find anyone he belonged to, so his folks let him stay. Johnny often talked about Boomer and would become emotional. He said, "He was my rock. We clung to each other like a magnet to steel."

Johnny and I would sit and talk. Frankly, he did most of the talking. It was gratifying for me to hear his wife tell me how appreciative she was for my visits with him. She knew that helped his PTSD. Johnny told me it was tough when he was a little boy growing up on a cotton farm in Northeast Arkansas. The abuse went as far back as he could remember. He said he was five years old, sound asleep in bed early one morning before daybreak. He felt someone grab him and lift him straight out of bed. The only thing he had on was a pair of shorts, no shirt. He suddenly felt a belt whipping across his back. He had no idea who was whipping him, or for what reason. The man he didn't recognize, of course, was his dad. Johnny explained that he was pulled by his arm through the house to the front porch and received one blow after another. His dad screamed and yelled while he continued to whip him.

This is where the story becomes unreal. Just as I have seen Bo come to the rescue of Donnie, so did Johnny's dog, Boomer, come to rescue him. Although he lived in northeast Arkansas, and Donnie lives in the bootheel of Missouri, both were on cotton farms, and both on the edge of Crowley's Ridge. It was unbelievable they both were forced to live with abusive fathers, and both had a black dog that was their rock. It seemed Johnny's beating was because he had failed to open a gate to let the cattle out to another pasture.

Johnny said it was always bad, and it became far worse after his dad bought a large farm near Jonesboro, Arkansas. The soil was very hard to work, and the family was over their head in debt. The first year the crop was a disaster because of too much rain. He shared endless stories of abuse at the hands of his father.

I was very thankful that Johnny and I became close friends. His way of talking and communicating with a dog simply amazed me. Margaret would say, 'He doesn't have the patience to let the coffee brew, but he has the patience of Job when it comes to training a dog.'

CHAPTER 23

'Larry and I had been taught by Queen Christian Mama Doris Wilson not to say one dirty word.'

It was now late afternoon and I was certainly ready to get off this tractor. I mentioned the best way for me to pass the time while sitting on a bouncy ole' tractor was to write songs in my head or simply think about the past. I thought about that when I helped Donnie feed the pigs this morning. He had to dump buckets of feed into the trough. The ground corn was in the feed room in burlap bags. Donnie would use a small can to fill up the 5-gallon buckets.

Just when he had the small can full and prepared to dump it into the larger bucket, his elbow bumped the back of the wall, which caused him to spill the entire small bucket on the floor. Spontaneously, without thinking, he blurted out, "Oh shit." He looked at me in fright, and realized in that second, he had taken the safety off his loaded mouth and had fired the awful dirty word.

He immediately began to pick up the ground corn and put it back into the five-gallon bucket. Donnie glanced up at me and waited for my reaction. He seemed sure I perceived that saying that word was an unforgivable sin. My thought was to ignore it, let it go. I most certainly didn't think it was that bad, and it wasn't my place to address it anyway. Donnie didn't address it either. We just went on, as if that word was never spoken.

Later that day, I began to think about how wonderful it was that God gave us the ability to have recall. I vividly remember when Larry and I were about eight to ten-years-old. Most of the boys at school would curse some. Larry and I had been taught by 'Queen

Christian Mama' Doris Wilson, not to say one dirty word. Larry was much braver than me. One day he just flat out asked Dad if we could curse. Dad seemed surprised, and I think he felt honored that we trusted him with such a subject.

He thought for a minute or so. "Yes, you can say one curse word." We were excited to know what word we would have the liberty to say.

Larry asked, "What word is it, Dad?"

"You can say crap."

Larry looked somewhat surprised, and a little disappointed. "Crap?"

Dad nodded. "Yes, you can say crap."

He looked at our dad quietly for a moment. "How bad a word is that?" The tone of Larry's voice reeked of disappointment.

Dad said with a slight grin, "Well, it's just pretty darn bad."

Larry seemed okay with the word. "How many times can we say crap?"

"There's no limit. You can say crap as much as you wish."

Larry and I quickly hurried out of the house. We were really excited to exercise our new freedom to curse. We quickly started to use the word crap. For the next few days, there was no telling how many hundreds-of-times we used the word. Mom was not pleased about the whole thing, especially since we had no limits.

We used the word in every possible way you would use it in the English language. We used it as an adjective, a noun, a pronoun, even an adverb. You name it, we used it. We even added prefixes and postfixes to the word crap. If we dropped a fork at the table, 'Oh crap, I dropped my crappy fork,' or perhaps, 'pass me the crap out of the green beans,' or 'I just drank the crap right out of my milk.'

One night at the dinner table, Larry and I were both rolling the crap out of the word crap. Mom gave Dad a go-to-thunder look, then looked at Larry and me, then back at Dad. Mom did something I had never seen her do before. She gave Mr. George 'Dad' Wilson an ultimatum. She slapped her hand down on the kitchen table, much like a judge hits his gavel. The law was then laid down.

"No more!" she barked. "Enough is enough. George Wilson, if you don't reel these boys in from using that word, you can expect this to be the last meal I cook for you. You can cook for yourself and these boys whatever you wish, but I am done. Do you understand?"

Mom had hit Dad where it would hurt him the most. Square dab in his breadbasket. Dad was a big eater, and Mom was a darn good cook. You never saw a man surrender as quickly as he did that day. "Yes Doris, I totally understand."

He looked straight at me and Larry. "Boys, consider the word crap off limits. Don't say crap anymore."

It was a sad moment at the dinner table for both of us. It struck the core of our very existence. Our freedom to curse was gone. Dad would later tell us we could say crap, but never around Mom.

CHAPTER 24

*'Katie looked at me and winked. Do you still think those sheets will
need to be looked at around midnight? "Oh yes," I replied.'*

The rest of the afternoon went quickly. I noticed a car in the
driveway around 4:30. It was Vera Eagleman, a lady who
attended Katie's church. She picked up Katie and Alice, so
she could give Alice a permanent curl in her hair. Alice's eighth-
grade graduation was approaching pretty soon. Donnie informed
me that his mom had left supper on the table. She wasn't sure
when they would return. I had the tractor ready for Orville's night
shift. I showered and went to bed.

Thursday morning was the same old repeat, getting the ground
ready to plant cotton. Just before noon, I was surprised to see the
pickup truck headed in my direction. I was even more surprised to
see it was Katie. Orville never let her get her driver's license, but
she could drive the pickup around the farm fairly well. She drove
the truck in behind some large willow trees along the drainage
ditch, somewhat in the shade.

When I approached the end of the field, she held up what I
perceived to be my lunch. I drove the tractor over to where she was
parked. She had a pop bottle full of warm water and some soap. I
washed my hands and rinsed them off. She began to tell me why
she had brought my lunch.

"Orville doesn't want you to stop the tractor too long," she
continued, "rain could be on its way.

I simply looked at Katie. "Sure. I understand, no problem."

We sat in the cab of the truck while I ate my sandwich. We

were completely concealed from the house. I was sure it was not by chance Katie parked the truck where she did. I no more than finished my last bite of pie, when we both were wrapped in each other's arms. It was like I stepped back in time, and it was me and my first girlfriend at the Chisholm Trail Drive-In Theater in Wellington, Kansas.

We were all over the seat. There was no doubt I was aroused. Katie wisely brought both of us down to planet earth.

"Hey, I'll be bringing Orville his late-night supper around 11:30 tonight." She smiled. "Do you think I might need to check your bed sheets to see if they need to be laundered?"

"Umm, I most certainly think they need to be looked at."

We both knew the tractor needed to be in sight of the house, just in case Orville woke up. We shared a meaningful kiss. Then I climbed back on the tractor. She threw me a kiss as I turned and dropped the plow. I couldn't keep from smiling when I read her lips, 'I love you.' I pointed at her and threw her a kiss.

I spent the afternoon with my mind more on the midnight rendezvous with Katie than I did my work. Katie told me that Orville was going to Malden around 2:30. He was going to get my water pump, his tractor parts, and the cotton seed I needed to keep the tractor rolling so I could get as much land ready as possible before the rain came. I was surprised by how quickly the heavy clouds had rolled in. The sky became darker and darker. I saw lightning in the distance.

The school bus dropped the kids off just when the first large drops began to splatter on the hood of the tractor. I was glad I was not at the far end of the field. The wind began to blow dust from the freshly plowed ground. It was time to head to the house. I quickly parked the tractor under of the equipment shed. The heavy rain pounded down hard on the metal roof.

I heard a vehicle coming down the road. It was Orville. I quickly moved an empty 55-gallon drum out of the way in the stall next to the tractor so Orville would have a covered parking place. I knew he would have cotton seeds. I looked in the bed of the truck, no cotton seeds.

Orville remarked, "I forgot to take the tarp with me. It was pouring down in Malden."

Before I could ask about my water pump, he said, "Well, I do have some good news. I got your pump all of the tractor engine parts and brake shoes for the truck."

"Great." That news was the best I had heard in a very long time. I couldn't wipe the smile from my face. Just as fast as the rain had come in, it left even quicker. The sun came out and put a bright glow on everything.

Orville looked around the yard. "There's no need for you to go back to the field, I'll change my clothes and we can get your water pump on."

"Man, that would be wonderful."

Donnie was absolutely right about his dad being a good mechanic. He had my water pump on in just a matter of a few minutes. He requested I fill the radiator with water.

Orville tapped his fingers on the hood. "We'll see if she'll start."

I slid onto the seat inside Ole Limpie and turned the ignition. Crank, crank, crank, and just as I hoped, she started right up. Orville checked for any possible leaks. About that time, Donnie skipped up.

Orville spoke in satisfaction. "Looks like you're in business."

I gratefully thanked him.

"Leon," he said, "you might want to take a short trip just to make sure everything is okay."

Donnie spoke up. "Can I go with him? Please," he begged.

"Do you have all your chores done?"

Donnie dropped his head and looked disappointed. "No sir."

"Well, no. You can't go. You need to finish your chores," Orville commanded.

"Donnie, I'll help you get your chores done so you can go with me. How would that be with you, Orville?"

"That's fine." He barked at Donnie in an unnecessarily harsh voice, "You had better not screw up boy, you hear me?"

"Yes sir," Donnie politely said.

Orville said, "I plan to start plow tonight around eight o'clock. I'm going to the house and eat a bite, then sleep for a few hours. Leon, could you get the tractor ready for me?"

I questioned Orville about the ground being to wet to plow. He explained, "I deliberately plant my cotton on a sandy-loam plot of ground that drains and dries very fast. It will be ready to plow by eight o'clock."

I replied, "that's great, I will have the tractor ready for you."

Katie sent Mary Beth to let us know supper was a little early, so Orville could eat before going to bed. Katie cooked a wonderful supper as usual. As soon as Donnie and I had the chores finished, we took off in Ole Limpie.

Orville said I should drive long enough to get the engine warm. I suggested we go to the Crossroads General Store and get a soda. I remembered when I was his age how a soda was a special treat. There was no question it was just as big a treat for Donnie, too. We made our way to the store and bought our sodas. Donnie suggested we not drive back the same way.

"Let's take that gravel road." Donnie pointed to the right. "That's the road that'll go by B.J.'s house."

"Sure! That sounds like a great plan."

We drove up the highway to the first gravel road to our right. Donnie's voice had a certain amount of anxiety when he asked, "Do you like black folks?" So many times, he shocked me with things he asked or said. This question was not any different.

"Sure, I don't think black people are any different than white people, except the color of their skin."

Donnie seemed very pleased with my answer. "My best friend B.J. is a black boy."

I smiled at him. "That's great! One of my very best friends is also black."

Donnie got a big grin on his face. "All of us Hopkins' like B.J. and his mom and dad. Well, everyone except Daddy. He calls them dumb ass niggers. He'll let me go in B.J.'s house, but won't let B.J. come in my house. I don't know why he calls B.J. dumb. He can spell words I can't spell. And he knows way more about history than I do."

We had driven a considerable distance down the gravel road when Donnie blurted out, "B.J.'s house is just around this next curve." He excitedly asked, "Would you like to stop and meet B.J., Leon?"

"Sure. I would love that!"

Ole Limpie's tires had barely stopped rolling when Donnie opened the door and flew out of the car. B.J. and his mom were walking back from the garden. It was clear that the two boys were over the moon excited to see each other. B.J.'s mom was a very petite little lady. She walked up to the car with an infectious, pleasant smile.

"I couldn't figure out who in the world you all were."

I introduced myself, briefly telling her about my car trouble and explaining I was helping Orville and Katie get their crops planted.

"Well, I am so glad to meet 'ya, Mr. Leon. My name is Norvella." She pointed to B.J. "And this here is our son, B.J."

It was obvious that B.J. had been taught good manners. He walked up to me, looked me straight in the eyes, stuck out his hand and said, "I'm very pleased to meet you, sir."

Our hands grasped together. Even at his age and size, I felt a strong affectionate squeeze on my hand.

Donnie asked in a pleading tone, "Can me and B.J. go play catch?"

"Sure, but we'll need to go pretty soon."

Miss Norvella asked me to have a seat on the front porch with her. I no more than sat down when she asked if I would like a glass of water. I thanked her, but said I was good. B.J. and Donnie were at the far end of the yard, where B.J.'s dad had made a backstop screen.

"Donnie has told me so many good things about your son. It's great to have a best friend like that."

"Well, I can assure you the feeling is mutual with B.J. He thinks Donnie hung the moon. Robert and I are so very lucky to have B.J. Ya see, my husband, Robert and I, always wanted a bunch of kids. But after a couple of years of being married, we soon realized I wasn't getting pregnant. We went to see a doctor. He questioned Robert if he had ever had the mumps. Robert of course, said yes. The doctor told us that was most likely our problem. We both were heartbroken since it seemed we would never have a child." Miss Norvella looked toward me. "Do you believe in God, Mr. Leon?"

"Well, yes I do."

She smiled. "So do Robert and I, and we think God sent us B.J. My oldest sister's daughter got pregnant when she was in high school. She had B.J., and she didn't want him. My sister thought Robert and I would possibly want him, and of course, we were all in. We got him when he was six days old. He doesn't know that Robert and I are not his blood Momma and Pappa. I know we'll have to tell him the truth someday. I just hope he'll still love us as he does now."

I looked into her eyes. "B.J. is clearly a very bright young man. He'll appreciate and respect you and Robert, and his love will not diminish, whatsoever." She appeared very happy I said that.

The sun rapidly began to go down. Miss Norvella asked, "Do the Hopkins have their cotton planted yet?"

I shook my head. "No, but we have most of the ground ready."

She said, "Robert has been on that tractor since daylight every day this week. He got rained out this afternoon."

I knew I needed to get Donnie home, and I was very much ready for a shower and bed.

I called out to Donnie. "We best be going."

About that time Robert walked up to the porch. Miss Norvella introduced us. Robert was a small, but strong built man. We made small talk for a few short minutes before Donnie and I said goodbye.

I hadn't driven two-hundred feet when Donnie began his questions.

"How do you like my friend B.J.?"

"He sure seems like a very nice young man."

"Oh yeah, he is, and he is a really good baseball player, too. You want to know how he got his name B.J.?"

"Sure."

Donnie began to give me the full details. "Well, you see, the B stands for Booker. That is for a man his mommy likes a whole lot. His full name was Booker T. Washington. He was like a very smart black man. He died a long time ago. The J stands for Jackie. Have you ever heard of Jackie Robinson?"

"Sure have." I gave him a big smile. "Most everyone knows Jackie Robinson."

"Yep." Donnie grinned. "B J. said his dad likes baseball, and his hero is Jackie Robinson. So, his mommy and daddy named him Booker Jack, but they call him B.J. I think that's a cool name, don't you?"

"Absolutely. That's a great name."

When we pulled into the drive, I saw Katie Jean removing clothes from the clothes line.

"Let's go help your mom," I suggested. Donnie and I began to grab the clothes and towels from the line. We had the big basket full, and all the items off in a short time. Katie told Donnie to take the basket to the back porch.

Katie picked up one sock that was on the ground. "How was your drive?"

"Good." I told her about meeting B.J. and his mom and dad.

Katie changed the subject. "Orville decided to rest until about nine o'clock tonight before he gets back on the tractor. He is going to drive all night till around six, or six-thirty in the morning." She looked at me and winked. "Do you still think those sheets will need to be looked at around midnight?"

"Oh yes." I gave her a big smile and a wink.

We both said goodnight.

I looked under the hood of Ole Limpie one more time. Dry as a bone. It felt so good to have a drivable car once again. I showered and set my alarm for eleven. I was eagerly anticipating my meeting with Katie later tonight, and I wanted to be alert and ready.

CHAPTER 25

'I like that song too, Momma. We both have dreams, dreams to be off this ole farm, don't we, Momma?'

I checked my suitcase. I still had a few more birth control protections. I absolutely could not take a chance of getting Katie pregnant. She started the pickup the moment my alarm went off. They were almost simultaneous. I stepped out of the Mex house just in time to see the tail lights from the truck head to where Orville worked.

I washed my face and refreshed my entire body. What a breathtaking sight. That big 'ole southern moon filtered through the window. Moon beams cast their light on the bed, like a beam from a bright flashlight. The headlight beams from the pickup danced across the yard. Katie turned the truck toward the equipment shed and turned the engine off.

The truck may be off, but I swear, my motor was revved up to a thousand RPM's. Katie eased the Mex house door open. Before she shut it, she looked toward the house. It was dark, not one light anywhere. We both stood behind the door and engaged in a luscious kiss.

The next few moments were a blur. It was as though the room was spinning. We both were undressed and lying across the bed. A ripple of anxiety shot down my spine. I felt my heart beat faster in anticipation. I kissed her gently and tenderly at first, then the moment became more passionate. The big southern moon shined its light on us through the open window and cast a perfect glow on Katie's face. She was simply breathtaking. We both began to take the journey to the top of the mountain. Things went much slower this time, and we took time to explore the scenery. I often thought if heaven was anything like foreplay, I would never sin again. We each picked windflowers for the other to enjoy while we worked our way to the summit. Simultaneously, we reached the top of the beautiful mountain. Colorful, bright, radiant flowers, once again burst into '*full bloom.*'

I nuzzled my face against her. The sweet smell of Katie's perfume lingered in the air. I gave her another soft, gentle kiss. She whispered when our lips separated, "I love you so much." It was as though she talked straight to my heart. Her warm kiss still burned on my lips. I felt the need to say, 'I love you too', but my heart simply would not go there. Katie's warm, tender, sexy body pressed against mine and was something a lot of men only dreamed about. We remained in each other's arms and stared at the ceiling.

Katie said, "I didn't know love could feel like this." I gently squeezed her hand, since I was unable to say the words, she was wanting. She remained quiet beside me for a few minutes before she really surprised me with what she said next.

"I'm thinking seriously about asking Orville for a divorce. School will be letting out in two weeks. I have a sister, Wilma, that lives in Wisconsin. She and her husband, Chester, have a small cabin on a lake about sixty miles from their home.

"She knows about the abuse the kids and I have endured from Orville. They have deliberately not told anyone in our family, including our other sibling, about the cabin. My sister and her husband have kept my secret for a long time, but she has wanted me to divorce Orville for years. She said we could hide out there, away from Orville, and she and Chester would help me file for a divorce.

"So...I've been thinking, as soon as school is out, if you would let us ride with you to Decatur, Wilma could meet us there and take us on to Wisconsin. Orville wouldn't have a clue where we had ended up."

I laid there and tried to absorb every word she said. Then we both heard what sounded like the slamming of a door. Katie quickly raised up in bed.

"Oh no," she said. "It's Alice. She's in the backyard next to the back porch."

Katie's reaction was so different from the reaction she had with the mail lady. She was visibly beginning to panic. I racked my brain, trying to think how we should handle this. Katie grabbed her clothes and crawled to the far side of the room. The bright moon had not lit that area. She quickly dressed, then spoke to me in a nervous voice.

"Don't get up. I'm going out the back. I can go past the shower and toilet and make it to the machine shed without her seeing me. I need to get to the pickup." She quickly exited the Mex house.

I stretched my neck to try to see where Alice was and was shocked to see her halfway down to the road. She appeared to be looking toward the field where Orville was working. BAM, I heard the truck door slam. Katie had made it to the truck and deliberately slammed the door loudly to make it appear she had been in the truck. Smart, Katie, smart.

Alice yelled out, "Mom, are you okay?"

I saw Katie walk toward Alice. "Yes, I am fine honey, what are you doing?"

"I heard the truck and saw your lights when you came back from the field. I kept thinking you would come into the house. I got worried," Alice replied.

"Oh, bless your heart, sweetie."

I was very curious about what Katie was going to tell Alice. "Your daddy wanted me to turn on the radio and get the weather forecast. I had to sit and wait for the forecast. To tell you the truth, the DJ said he was going to play the Everly Brothers' song 'Dream'. I love that song, so I was waiting to listen to it."

"I like that song too, Momma. We both have dreams, dreams to be off this ole farm. Don't we, Momma?"

Katie and Alice walked toward the house, but both just stopped, and they faced each other. Katie reached her arms out and they hugged each other. Then Katie said, "Yes baby, and maybe someday soon you'll be away from this farm." They both walked to the house.

I sat up in bed and looked at the house. A couple of lights came on, but just for a few minutes. The house then went completely dark, except for the bright reflective glow of the big full moon. I laid back on the bed and took a very familiar position looking up to the ceiling. I reflected on many things Katie said. Would her plan work to get away from Orville? Should I go along with it? I searched for reasons not to believe it would work. But, why would I not go along with it? It might very well be the one, perhaps the only way, she could get herself and the kids away from the monster.

Katie's words echoed in the back chambers of my mind. 'I love you so much.' I couldn't help but wonder if she could actually know and feel real love? I had deep feelings for her, but I must be honest, I questioned it all myself. Am I feeling real love for her? Or did I just feel sorry for her and the kids? Am I confusing lust, and the craving to hold a beautiful woman like Katie, with true love? When I weigh everything out, I feel I know the correct answer.

Katie came onto me full throttle. She knew her time to make her move was short. I was her 'knight in shining armor' on the big white horse, who came to rescue her from the awful villain. This was most certainly not her fault. I was more than willing to be her knight in shining armor. Those twenty minutes with Katie in this bed, with that big southern moon glowing on her face was heavenly.

CHAPTER 26

*'Orville's yelling and Donnie's screaming made
me sick to my stomach.'*

The night was short. The sound of Orville driving the tractor up to the fuel tank woke me from a nice sleep. I looked at my watch and it was five-thirty a.m. Another day of riding that noisy, rough, bouncing tractor lay ahead of me. I helped Donnie with his morning chores. I liked to take as much off of him as possible. I don't know how a little boy can handle such continued abuse, both physical and mental. Harsh words can be almost as hurtful and devastating as physical abuse.

I was very concerned about Donnie. Broken kids so often grow up to be broken adults. He most likely would find himself battling demons, and facing the onslaught of acute PTSD like Johnny Hooper.

Saturday morning found the Hopkins' bunch busy as a hive of bees. Orville was overly anxious to get the engine back in the John Deere, and so was I. Donnie may only be twelve-years-old, but he let out on the tractor as if he was twenty. Katie and the girls had a busy day of laundry, cleaning house and mowing the yard.

Orville and I got the engine ready for the test. The big green machine cranked right up and ran like a new one. At least for now, there would be a little less stress on Orville, which was good for everyone.

It was three o'clock Saturday afternoon. I got up enough nerve to ask Orville if I could have the rest of the afternoon off. He said he was actually going to suggest I do exactly that. Orville got in the truck and headed down to the field where Donnie worked.

I thought it might be good to just remove myself from the family for a while. About the time I was ready to climb into the shower, I heard Orville's deep yell. My first thought was he must be hurt, perhaps he needed help. I slipped my pants on and ran out to the edge of the yard. I heard an awful scream from Donnie. Scream after blood curdling scream turned into agonizing cries.

Orville's yelling and Donnie's screaming made me sick to my stomach. I desperately wanted to go down to that field and beat the living hell out of this so-called '*man*', but I knew I couldn't. Katie's plan to get away would vanish in a heartbeat.

I dropped my head, turned, and went back to the Mex house, while sadness for Donnie gripped my heart. Out of sight, out of mind, I decided. Donnie drove the tractor up to the fuel tank with Orville trailing behind him in the truck. Orville went straight to the house. Donnie started fueling up the tractor. When I walked over to Donnie, he was sad and embarrassed. His tears had mixed with dust from plowing. Under his eyes was a light coat of mud. He looked pitiful. I wanted to scream at the top of my lungs, 'It's just not fair! God, where are you?'

Orville exited the house with what appeared to be meds and syringes. He looked my way.

I quickly spoke-up and asked, "I'm going into Malden, do you need anything?"

He replied, "No thanks." Then barked out to Donnie. "As soon as you get that tractor fueled up, come down to the pig barn and help me vaccinate some pigs."

Donnie politely said, "Yes sir."

I really could not wait to have some freedom from Orville and this farm. My plan was to go to town, maybe get a hamburger and a pepsi. A lot of guys would be wanting a cold beer. Beer is just not my beverage of choice. It isn't that I think drinking a beer or two is bad, I simply don't care for the taste.

I drove down the gravel road a half-mile or so, when that image of Donnie with that sad, dirty face and red eyes came into my mind. I needed to go back. That message played over and over in my head. I impulsively made a big U-turn and drove back to the farm. I parked Ole Limpie and walked straight for the pig barn. I felt if I were there maybe Orville wouldn't be as hard on Donnie. I walked up to the barn. There wasn't much noise coming from the pigs, which seemed strange, so I opened the door. To say I was shocked and stunned would be an understatement. Orville had his back to me with his pants completely down below his knees, his bare butt shining. Donnie sat on a bale of hay, directly in front of his dad. I couldn't make sense of the sight before me. Orville grabbed his pants and quickly pulled them up. He stepped off to the side a bit, but kept his back-side to me.

When he stepped off to the side, Donnie and I looked directly at each other. Donnie was shocked and frightened. Orville quickly spoke up. "Sorry about that. I had a tick on my privates and was getting Donnie to pull it off."

It was certainly embarrassing for me and I didn't know how to react.

"Do you guys need any help with the vaccinations?"

Orville quickly said, "No, not at all. We are about through here."

I turned and walked back to the wagon.

While I drove to Malden, I thought about what Orville had Donnie doing with the tick. I would have never expected Randy to do such a thing. If I couldn't have done it myself, I would have gotten Karen to help.

Still puzzled about my encounter, I went on to enjoy driving around Malden and sightseeing. There was a nice little drive-in eating spot that caught my eye. Carhops were everywhere. I decided to eat my supper there. I pulled in and placed my order. It felt so much like home.

My days back home flooded my mind. I didn't realize at the time, what a stress-free world I had lived in. I then thought about Johnny Hooper and how he was afraid to get out and do much when he was a young boy. He was always afraid of his dad. I wonder what it will be like for Donnie in a few years?

I stopped at a pay phone and called Katie to let her know I wouldn't be in till later and not to be concerned about my supper. Malden was very similar to Wellington. Not much to see.

I drove by the baseball field where a game was going on. I again thought of Johnny and the day we met. It made me hurt to think how depressed one must get to take their own life. My concern now was for Donnie. Will he be strong enough to handle the inevitable? The onslaught of PTSD would most certainly affect Donnie, just as it had Johnny. He didn't sink into alcohol abuse like most PTSD sufferers did. Johnny's coping mechanism was his remarkable love for dogs, and their unbelievable attraction to him.

I decided I had taken in all Malden offered. It certainly was a nice small town with a lot of very friendly people. While I drove into the Hopkins' place, I remembered Katie had mentioned to me when I called her that they were going to an ice-cream-social at the neighbors and probably wouldn't be home until late. The freedom of having the old wagon running again made me feel more like myself. I parked Ole Limpie and was in bed in a matter of minutes.

CHAPTER 27

'Hopkins, you best tell your plowboy to mind his own business.
Donnie is my business and no one is going to whoop him
over that dog.'

Sunday morning came way too soon. A part of me didn't want to go to church, but as hard as I tried, I did not have a viable excuse. I went along with the normal Sunday morning ritual. This Sunday was somewhat different, it was Mother's Day. Much of the church service was centered around celebrating the special day. This is the third Mother's Day I have not been able to celebrate with Karen and Randy. This day could be so different for me. Instead, it's a sad day, spent thinking about what could have been.

Church was over, and the Sunday noon meal was about the same as before. Katie and the girls prepared a wonderful spread. Orville recited the same prayer, never once mentioning the fact that it was Mother's Day. He could have so easily given Katie a sweet and kind compliment, but true to form for Orville, not one word. It became more and more apparent to me just how self-centered he was.

Once we finished our meal, Orville asked if I would help him work on the pick-up truck. He had replaced the wheel cylinders and added brake fluid to the master cylinder, but needed help to bleed the air out of the brake lines. I replied, "Sure."

My job was very simple. All I had to do was pump up the brakes and hold my foot on the brake pedal while Orville crawled under the truck and released the air on each wheel. We only had one more wheel to go when a truck pulled into the driveway.

It was the large man I had seen down at the Crossroad store. I remember Orville called him Alfred Taylor. He farmed quite a bit of land about five miles south of the store. I remembered Orville saying he was a tough, bully-type guy. He slowly crawled out of his truck, then walked over to where we were working.

Orville slid out from under the truck and quickly spoke. "Hello Alfred, how are you?"

Alfred barely grunted, then very loudly said, "You ain't seen one of my foxhounds have ya?"

Without hesitation Orville answered, "No, I sure haven't seen any foxhounds around here."

"Well, I am going to ask you again. Are you damn sure about that?"

Orville seemed confused and nervous. "No, I haven't seen one of your dogs around here, Alfred. I'm sure."

Alfred moved a little closer to Orville, "Your neighbors, the Hicks boys, said they were over there checkin' you-all's border fence, and up there where that old half falling-down barn is, they seen your boy feedin' a dog. Now I'm missin' one of my foxhounds exactly like the dog they described to me."

All three of us turned and looked at Donnie. Donnie had a guilty look all over his face.

Orville barked at Donnie. "Do you know anything about his dog?" Donnie looked stunned and scared.

He said, "Yes sir, I might."

"You might? Hell," Orville yelled at him, "you either do, or you don't. Now you tell me. right now. What do you know about this?"

Taylor said, "I can tell 'ya what he knows 'bout it. He's trying to steal my dog."

Donnie spoke up. "No, I'm not trying to steal your dog, Mr. Taylor. A couple of days ago I was driving the milk cows to the barn. I saw this skinny dog who looked really hungry so I took him some table scraps. He was still at the old barn yesterday so I took him some more food. I wasn't trying to steal your dog, Mr. Taylor, I promise. I just didn't want him to be hungry."

Orville yelled at Donnie. "Get your ass up there and bring this man his dog." Donnie started to walk off, and Orville said, "Go by the barn and get a rope."

Big Alfred Taylor said, "Orville, you 'oughta be ashamed to have a boy who'd steal 'nother man's dog."

Orville didn't say a word. I wanted so much to tell this excuse of a man how wrong he was to accuse Donnie of stealing his dog, but thought it was best I keep my two cents out of it. In no time at all, Donnie led the hound into the front yard.

Just as soon as Donnie turned over the dog. Mr. Taylor said, "I 'wanna see you tan that boy's hide right now, Orville Hopkins."

Orville started to unbuckle his belt. My anger burned hotter. I couldn't keep my mouth shut any longer. I looked at big Alfred Taylor and said, "Donnie was not trying to steal your dog, Taylor. He was doing exactly what he said. He thought the dog was starving, and all he did was keep him alive by giving him something to eat."

Taylor looked at Orville, then back at me. "Hopkins, you best tell your plow boy to mind his own damn business."

I was beginning to get very pissed at Mr. Alfred Taylor.

"Donnie is my business," I said, "and no one is going to whip Donnie over that dog."

I believe Taylor wasn't use to someone standing up to him. His wide eyes showed a look of surprise and total shock.

Taylor once again looked at Orville and said, "Ya best tell your plow boy to shut up his smart ass mouth or he is gettin' ready to get his ass kicked." Anger came over me like a sudden storm.

I had all I could handle from Taylor. There wasn't one drop of blood in my entire body scared of him. I slid out of that truck seat faster than a frog's tongue could snatch a fly. I whipped my tee shirt off and tossed it, along with my sunglasses, on the hood of Orville's pick-up. I glanced over at Orville who had turned white as a bed sheet. I then looked at Big Taylor, who resembled a fresh Kansas snow bank.

I walked straight up to Taylor, who drew a breath deep enough to be heard. I was close enough to see the nasty, tobacco crusted in the corner of his mouth, barely showing through his four-day beard. There was a strong smell of whiskey coming from his nasty breath. Taylor was a big man, probably six-foot-six-inches and three-hundred-plus pounds. A lot of that weight was obvious in his extremely large gut. There was not one ounce of fat on my entire body, and I can assure you Alfred Taylor knew it.

I looked him straight in the eye. "You just breezed right through the easy part, Taylor, talking about it. Now, when you get ready to take on the hard part, you just feel free to jump right in."

He stood there and stared into my confident eyes for what seemed like five minutes, but probably was more like thirty seconds. He turned and gave Orville a go-to-hell look, then quickly got back in his truck. He left out of the driveway, the motor roaring while he sped away in a cloud of dust.

I didn't realize Katie and the girls were out on the porch and witnessed the whole thing. The girls were giggling while they went back into the house. Katie gave me a tender look that instantly turned into a pleasant smile, then she returned into the house. Orville immediately started in on Donnie. I had always shown Orville respect, not once had I questioned, or confronted him about anything. That was about to change right here and right now. I loudly spoke up in a strong voice.

"Orville, for God's sake man. You know Donnie was only feeding that dog because he felt sorry for him. He wasn't trying to steal that dog, and you know it." I continued. "Today is Sunday and we have a hard week of work ahead of us. Why don't we get these brakes finished on the truck and relax a little before tomorrow?"

Orville didn't say a word, just crawled back under the truck. We had the brakes done in less than 5 minutes. Orville picked up his tools and was walking to the tool shield.

I spoke up again and said, "I'm going to take a little drive, I'll be back in a couple of hours." I looked over toward Donnie, and it hit me. I best not leave Donnie here with Orville.

"Hey, Orville, Donnie is going with me. Is that okay?"

He never turned, just barked out a loud, "Yeah."

I knew Donnie would be thrilled to be getting away from his dad and he certainly was.

We both headed to Ole Limpie, of course Bo was right by Donnie's side.

"Do you want Bo to go with us?"

Donnie lit up like a morning sunrise. "Are you serious?" he asked.

"Yep, I sure am."

Donnie looked toward the tool shed. "Do you think I should ask

Dad if it is okay?"

"No, I'll tell your dad it was my idea."

"Okay," Donnie replied.

Donnie first had to convince Bo it was okay for him to get in the car. We were ready to travel. I was behind the wheel, Donnie rode shotgun, and Bo sat between the two of us, happy as a pig in a mudhole.

Donnie was happier than I had ever seen him. He had dodged a run-in with his abusive dad, and who knows what might have happened if that Taylor-idiot had gotten his way. Donnie's arm was around his bestest, bestest buddy in the whole world, riding in a car with his new best friend. He needed more of these happy afternoons in his young, stressed, and abused life. Donnie always worked hard to be happy and make everybody else laugh. There's an old saying, *'A light seems to shine so much brighter in a dark place.'*

It was obvious Donnie had a need to bring up the altercation I had with Alfred Taylor.

"Boy, I bet you could have punched that mean 'ole-Taylor guy right in the nose so hard it would have bled!"

I was determined to throw cold water on this conversation as quickly as possible.

"Well Donnie, as far as I am concerned, Alfred Taylor doesn't deserve us taking our time to talk about him. Let's talk about something else."

"So, what do you want to talk about, Leon?" Donnie asked.

"What do *you* want to talk about Donnie?"

"Does the radio work in this car?"

"I think so."

"I guess we could listen to the Cardinal game."

Smiling, I reached over, turned the radio on, and fumbled with the knob until I found the Cardinal game.

After taking one new road after another, I was thankful I had a full tank of gas. We reached a rough gravel road full of potholes, and I wasn't doing a good job of missing them. All of a sudden, I slammed on my brakes and started to back up. Donnie was about in shock.

"What the heck are you doing?"

I looked at Donnie. "I missed one of those potholes. I don't like to miss any of them."

Donnie let out a big belly laugh. "You are so funny."

It made me feel good to see and hear Donnie laughing. We occasionally turned the game off so we could just talk. Before we realized it, we entered the peach country around Campbell, Missouri. There was one big peach orchard after another. I told Donnie it's too bad they aren't ripe so we could buy some to take home to his mom. We had made a big circle and were now headed back toward Malden. I noticed a big general store with several cars in front of it. "How would you like a Dr. Pepper and a candy bar?" I asked.

"Oh man, yeah, that would be great!" Donnie looked down at Bo. "But what about Bo?"

"He'll be okay. Just keep him close to you."

It was obvious he was very pleased that Bo got to go into the store with us. I paid for our sodas and two big Babe Ruth candy bars. Then we spent some time just walking around in the store. Donnie looked up at me with wide eyes.

"Boy, they've got lots of stuff in here." He pointed up on the wall where some hula hoops hung. "That's what Mary Beth and Alice want for their birthday."

"When are their birthdays?"

Donnie hesitated then said, "I think in just a few days. They are just two days apart. Momma usually makes a coconut cake for Alice, a chocolate cake for Mary Beth and we celebrate their birthdays on the same day. Sometimes we have homemade ice cream. Momma said that she might get one hula hoop for them to share, but we can't afford to buy two."

Suddenly a thought rushed through my mind. I could buy each one of the girls a hula hoop for their birthday and have a party. Katie Jean almost always cooks three meals a day every day, and since it was Mother's Day, she should get the afternoon off.

"Hey Donnie, what do you think about us getting some hotdogs and buns and have a weenie roast for supper tonight?"

His eyes got wide. "Are you kidding me? Are you serious?"

We immediately began to gather items for our late Sunday afternoon Mother's Day party. We got sodas, hotdogs and buns, mustard and relish, and a big bag of marshmallows. We also picked up two bags of potato chips, and got everyone a big king size candy bar. Donnie was simply beside himself when he saw me retrieve two hula hoops from the rack on the wall, I had to say, his excitement truly made my day. Then it quickly became even better.

"You're the best man in the whole world, and I am so proud you are my new best friend."

We loaded up the party goods, including the two hula hoops. When we exited the store, I noticed a sign that read, 'Mother's Day Special.' It was above a rack of kitchen aprons. I knew Orville hadn't done one thing for Katie for Mother's Day.

"Donnie, do you think your mom would like one of these aprons?"

"Oh my, yes, I know she would,"

The regular price was $.99, but was marked down to $.79. "I'm going to buy this for you and the girls to give to her for Mother's Day."

Donnie was over the top thrilled. In no time at all, we had finished our business at the store and found ourselves back in the Hopkins' farm driveway.

CHAPTER 28

'Those cold winds were blowing, the storm clouds got bigger.
But it was them Johnny, not you, who pulled on that trigger.'

Everyone, including Orville, was sitting on the front porch. I barely got the car stopped when Donnie opened the door and jumped out, followed by Bo. Donnie's excitement hadn't eased up any. He started broadcasting the upcoming event of the afternoon.

"Mama, you ain't going to have to cook supper tonight!" he yelled out. "We're going to have ourselves a party." Katie and the girls were very excited also.

Katie smiled. "Oh, how nice is this!"

I wondered what Orville's demeanor would be like after the earlier event of the day. Katie always said he can go from one mood to another in the drop of a hat. He was all smiles and seemed just as excited as everyone else that we were going to have sodas and hotdogs, and as Donnie called it, a party in the backyard.

Katie suggested we eat right now. She cleaned off the big picnic table in the backyard. Alice and Mary Beth helped their mother put the food on the table. Orville, Donnie and I went to the workshop, and each got a big arm load of scrap wood. Shortly, we had a fire going and everybody roasted their hotdog to perfection. We all chowed down on hotdogs and chips, and everyone enjoyed their favorite soda. When we finished, out came the big king size candy bars. I made my way back to the car and returned with the two hula hoops.

Alice's birthday will be this Thursday and Mary Beth's will be

Saturday. But I had made the decision to give my presents to them today. They were each getting a hula hoop. One dark blue and the other a bright red. Donnie made the girls turn their backs so it would be a surprise. Their faces spoke volumes and they let out a joyful cheer. We all watched them illustrate their skills at keeping the hoops up while they twisted and twisted. Everyone took a turn trying to keep the hoops up, including Orville and me. My favorite performer, of course, was Katie. I would be lying if I didn't say I truly enjoyed every twist and every move.

Katie was busy showing off her skills with the hoop. I whispered to Donnie, "Get Mary Beth and Alice to go with you to the car, and the three of you give your mom her Mother's Day gift."

He lit up like a bright midnight star. The three retrieved the brown sack that held the apron. Alice gave a beautiful, heartfelt little acknowledgment of what a great Mom they had, Mary Beth gave her mother a kiss, and Donnie gave her a big hug, then handed her the gift.

Katie was very surprised, and smiled broadly while she opened the bag and pulled out her gift. "I love it very much! I will treasure it forever." Katie wiped a tear of pure joy.

A Sunday afternoon that started off very rough, had turned into a wonderful, joyous time for everyone. In no time at all the sun had gone down, the afternoon chores were done, and we were all in bed anticipating the day ahead of us.

Once again, I desperately tried to get Johnny Hooper off my mind. Staring at the ceiling of the Mex house, I thought about the fact he will never enjoy another family get-together like the Hopkins enjoyed this afternoon. I thought about his family and wondered if they could not see past the laughter and feel his pain. I got up and retrieved a couple of poems I wrote about Johnny after his passing. I, too, felt as though I had let him down, enormous feelings of guilt always consumed me. When I looked back, I realized, Johnny, in his own way, telegraphed his intentions. The first poem goes like this.

RUN JOHNNY RUN

"He would have swum the coldest river for any one of you. No, not somebody's hero,
Just a brother, a father, a friend you never knew. No, you never knew his heartache, no you never felt his pain. You left him outside your door in a down-pouring rain.
So run Johnny, run. Run as fast as you can, for they will never understand this broken and wounded man. You have been stabbed by a father, abandoned by a mother and felt the bitter hate of so many others. Those cold winds were blowing, the storm clouds got bigger. But it was them Johnny, not you, who pulled on that trigger."

I remember one day he began telling me how much he loved his family and how he felt so bad. He knew he had hurt each of them in some way.

He said, "I wish I had a magic switch that I could turn off, so I wouldn't hurt my family. But there is no magic switch. The only thing I can do is just keep pushing on." Later that day I wrote this.

SPECIAL WISH

"I wish I had a Genie with a special wish. I would ask that Genie for a magic switch. One that I could turn off and I could turn on. When it comes to hurting my family, I would never turn it on. But there is no Genie, there is no magic switch. So, the only thing I can do is just keep on, pushing on, pushing on."

CHAPTER 29

'Don't be the thread that comes unwound.'

Oh my gosh, it's Monday morning already. Orville was up much earlier than normal. The day was overcast and cloudy. I knew Orville desperately wanted, and needed to get the cotton planted before the rain that was forecasted rolled in. If the rain would hold off until late Friday, and everything went well, we should have the cotton and corn planted. Once we ate breakfast, he and I were in the field, preparing the ground to plant.

The morning flew by, Katie brought us lunch. Orville motioned for me to drive toward him. There was a large shade tree along the edge of the drainage ditch at the end of the cotton field. We all three sat on the tailgate of the truck and ate.

Katie explained to Orville that her friend, Bonnie, would be picking her up around two-thirty this afternoon. She said Alice and Mary Beth were going home with her two daughters after school. Bonnie's daughter, Julie, would be graduating from the 8th grade with Alice. Mary Beth and Ola Mae, Bonnie's youngest daughter, were in the same grade, and were also very good friends. Bonnie was a good seamstress and had made many of the girls' clothes. She and Katie were going to make the two oldest girls dresses for their graduation.

Orville no more than swallowed his last bite of lunch when he headed toward his tractor, and I followed his lead. There's an old saying, 'You gotta make hay when the sun is shining.' I could totally understand him needing to roll these tractors.

I saw the homestead each time I drove in that direction. I

watched when Katie's friend picked her up. I was so happy Katie had a dear, long-time friend like Bonnie. What a blessing for her.

An hour or so after Katie and Bonnie had left, Orville raised his disk plow and exited the field we were in and drove to the field behind the grown-up drainage ditch. The large willow trees prevented him from having a view of the house or me working the field I was in. It made for a perfect situation for me to address something I had been wanting to check out for myself.

I noticed each afternoon, after Donnie came home from school, he would go to the house for a bit and then make his way to the tater shed. Of course, Bo would be right by his side. They would go into the tater shed and close the door. After a short time, they would leave, and either go help his dad, or start doing afternoon chores.

I was deeply concerned Donnie was smoking. That wasn't uncommon for boys his age to do. They would pick-up cigarette butts, collect them and hide them somewhere to smoke later. I suspected that was going on in the tater shed. I also knew if his dad caught him, it would not be a normal discipline of a young boy, it would be a severe beating. I knew this would be my best chance to catch Donnie in the tater shed smoking. I had to be careful not to lose his trust in me. However, I most certainly didn't want Orville to catch him with a cigarette in that shed.

I soon saw Bo out by the road waiting for his bestest, bestest buddy in the whole world. The bus stopped and the same ole ritual began, boy glad to see dog, dog glad to see boy. I deliberately slowed the John Deere to be close to the road when Donnie went into the house. I stopped the tractor, left it running, and quickly sprinted to the barn. From behind the barn, I moved in behind an old broken-down combine and some other abandoned equipment. Weeds were grown up nearly over my head. I made it to the tater shed and found a hole in one of the rough sawed oak boards that made a perfect spy hole. I was sure I was going to catch Donnie uncovering his stash of cigarette butts.

He soon entered the building with Bo near his side. Orville and Katie were no different than my mom and dad, or any farm family. Come winter, they would cover their potatoes with hay. Orville had left a couple of bales of hay in the shed. Donnie sat on one of the bales with Bo by his side. Donnie put his arm around Bo, and then shocked the dickens out of me. He closed his eyes and bowed his head. Oh my God, he is going to pray.

Donnie started praying out loud, softly and quietly, but thankfully loud enough I could make out what he said. He prayed meaningfully;

> *"God thank you for this day, and God thank you for Bo.*
> *Please let Bo live for a long long time.*
> *God thank you for Mama, and Alice and Mary Beth, and*
> *my new best friend, Leon.*
> *God, please don't let Daddy take me to that old pig barn*
> *and make me do those old nasty things down there.*
> *I don't like that, and please God, don't let him whoop me*
> *today."*
>
> *Thank you for loving me and Bo.*
> *Amen*

My dad had always encouraged me and Larry not to cry. He would say big boys don't cry. I was determined I wasn't going to cry while I watched this little boy pray that he wouldn't have to face the abuse of his father. That being said, someone needs to tell me what this warm thing is, running down my cheek.

I turned and ran as fast as I could back to the old combine, then quickly to the barn. I didn't want Donnie to know I was anywhere near that tater shed. I reached the tractor, got on, and turned toward the back of the field. I was an emotional wreck. A million thoughts rushed through my brain. The words of Donnie's prayer echoed in every corner of my twisted mind. It was obvious now, something I just couldn't let my mind believe at the time. There never was a tick. Anger arose inside me. It was very clear to me now.

I felt my skin crawl with sheer, uncontrollable anger. Somebody had to do something for this family, especially Donnie, and that somebody had to be me. I'm going to plow to the backside of this field, then I am going to drive this tractor over to where Orville is working. I'm going to pull him off his tractor, and I am going to kick the living shit outta' that SOB.

I know I have the skills and physical ability to do it my way. My blood boiled hotter the closer I got to the end of the field. I planned to sock him one blow after another. This one for Donnie, this one for the girls, and this one for Katie Jean. I would let him catch his breath, then I would shove him up against the tractor and tell him what a sorry excuse for a human being he was. I felt panic work its way through my body.

Before I got to the end of the field, I once again heard that voice. I don't know if it was Dad's spirit or just common sense trying to speak to me. I kept hearing, 'Don't be the thread that comes unwound, don't be the thread that comes unwound'. As mad and angry as I am right now, I know I could seriously hurt, or even kill Orville.

I remember something that happened a few years back. It was just days after the fight at the ballfield with the Simpson Brothers. Word got out how bad it ended for the brothers. It seems one of them had a broken arm, broken nose and a broken jaw. The other had two broken ribs and three teeth knocked out. We had no idea it was that bad. Dad somehow heard that news.

He had a talk with the two of us. We could tell the concern and seriousness in his voice when he explained how one's life can quickly be changed and ruined forever. He said, "Just keep that in mind." The next morning, when we got in the car to go to school, Dad had left us a note taped to the steering wheel. He had written one of his little jingles. It read;

"Family is a fabric, you are a thread,
don't ever stray from the way you have been led.
That fabric is woven, that fabric is bound,
don't be the thread that comes unwound.
Sometimes let it slide, sometimes hold your ground,
But never be the thread that comes unwound"

I had plowed to the far end of the field. It was decision time. I have never been this mad and angry in my life. There was nothing I wanted more than to go over and beat Orville's brains out. Quite frankly, that was what I was concerned about. *'Don't be the thread that comes unwound'*. Those words echoed in my mind. My better judgment took control, or perhaps the spirit of Dad. I vividly recall him saying, *'A split second in your life can forever change every second you have for the rest of your life'*.

I turned the tractor and plowed back toward the homestead. I slowly began to cool down. I was pleased with my decision. Not only would it have been wrong in so many ways, but Katie's plan for her and the kids to leave would no doubt be blown completely out of the water. When I got closer to the homestead, I looked at that tater shed. The image and words of Donnie praying will forever be etched in my mind.

"God, where are you? Please God, where are you?"

CHAPTER 30

'Donnie had one thing and one thing only on his mind, his precious Bo. Bo was Donnie's beacon of light, his beacon of hope.'

We kept driving tractors hard into the late afternoon. The glow of the sunset was rapidly fading. Thank God this day was over. I needed supper, a shower, and a comfortable bed. When we approached the equipment shed, a man pulled into the yard driving a pickup. He walked toward Orville and I heard Orville say he would get his tools and be over to his place as soon as possible.

Orville looked in my direction. "Tell Katie I will be home as soon as I get Thurlo Bates' two-ton truck started."

I was very relieved Orville would not be at the supper table with me. I knew I would have trouble carrying on a conversation with him after what I had witnessed and heard from Donnie's prayer in the tater shed.

I washed up and went to the house. Katie had supper on the table. I relayed the message Orville had given me. She said, "Sometimes I wish he wasn't so quick to help everybody with their mechanical needs."

Katie instructed the kids to wash the dishes and clean up the kitchen. She followed me out to the back porch and we walked toward the Mex house.

Katie informed me of her escape plan. She called her sister Wilma, in Wisconsin, and she said she would be happy to meet us in Decatur. Wilma said any day or any time would work for her. Katie gave me the full details on how the next two weeks would play out.

"We should be able to get the cotton and corn planted this week. Alice's graduation would be next Tuesday morning, the nineteenth. School would let out next Wednesday, the twentieth. My brother William, who lives in Belleville, Illinois, has a daughter that is getting married on Saturday the 23rd. We're all planning to go, and will leave early Saturday morning. The wedding starts at two in the afternoon. We're going to spend the night with my youngest sister, who also lives in Belleville. We will return home Sunday afternoon.

"The local cattle auction is held on the fourth Monday of each month. The next auction will be the Monday following the wedding. The Petroleum Co. has informed us we cannot purchase any more tractor fuel until we make a sizable payment on our charge account. Orvillle is going to sell three cows on Monday, the 25th."

Katie kept laying out her full plan. "Orville will leave early Monday morning with the cows. He will stay until he gets the check. I want to have everything packed and ready for you, me, and the three kids to head north just as quickly as we can after Orville leaves."

Katie looked at me, and I knew she wanted me to give her my response to her plan.

"What do you think? Are you sure you're okay with this?"

I assured her I was. I wanted to say, if you could have witnessed what I did this afternoon in the tater shed, you wouldn't be second guessing your decision. But I knew it was best not to say a word about that. We said good night. I was sound asleep in a few short minutes. I don't think I turned over all night.

The next morning, I sensed an urgency, both from Orville and Katie. Orville spoke up at the breakfast table. "We have a bit of bad news." He proceeded to tell me that Thurlo Bates, the man who had truck trouble last night, had told him the seed company in Malden was out of cotton seeds.

"Now I'll have to drive all the way to Poplar Bluff to get seed. I'm going to work until about 2:00 this afternoon, then go to Poplar Bluff and pick it up."

Katie told us she would bring lunch around noon. "Bonnie is coming to get me around one o'clock today. We are going to try to get the girls' dresses finished this afternoon." She had a sparkle in her eyes when she described how beautiful she thought the dresses were.

I looked at her. "Oh, I bet they're pretty, and I know Alice will be one of the prettiest girls at the graduation." Orville, of course, said nothing, par to course for him.

The morning in the fields went smoothly and fast. We were definitely getting ground ready to plant. Shortly after lunch, I watched Katie and Bonnie leave the farmhouse. The Hopkins' girls were going to ride the bus home with Bonnie's daughters.

While driving the tractor away from the house, I turned at the far end of the field just in time to see Orville leave. I continued pushing the tractor to get as much finished as possible. If the rain held off, and we had no breakdowns, we could have the cotton and corn planted before Friday night.

From my vantage point in the field, I saw the big yellow bus come into view. Donnie would soon be hugging his rock, his life support, his beloved dog, Bo. I looked toward the yard next to the road and looked for Bo, who would be faithfully waiting for Donnie. I was shocked. I didn't see Bo. What? No Bo? I quickly scanned every foot of the yard. Bo was nowhere in sight. This had bad news written all over it.

The bus soon drove on down the road. I saw Donnie standing on the edge of the road. Even at the considerable distance I was from him, I watched his mannerisms and body language. I knew he couldn't believe his eyes. Where was Bo? I watched when Donnie quickly went to the house and put away his books.

He returned to the yard and ran to the big barn. I saw him frantically search every building, including the tater shed, behind the outdoor toilet, and the back of the house again. I knew I needed to keep the tractor rolling. I also knew Donnie needed consoling. I stopped the tractor and shut the engine off. Donnie crossed the road and went toward the pig barn. Perhaps Bo had gone into the barn and the wind had blown the door shut behind him so he couldn't get out. Please Dear God, let that be the answer. Donnie walked out of the barn alone. With the tractor engine shut off, I could hear Donnie, mercifully calling, "Bo, Bo, Bo, come here, Bo."

Donnie looked in my direction. It was obvious he noticed I had stopped. He began sprinting toward me while I still sat on the tractor.

With a frightened and worried look on his face Donnie stared at me. "Have you seen Bo? I can't find him anywhere."

"No Buddy," I said. "I don't have a clue where he might be."

I wanted desperately to believe he would show up, but my gut feeling said differently. "I can't help you look for him now. I have to keep working, but if Bo hasn't shown up by quitting time, I'll help you look for him." I felt it necessary to remind Donnie he must get his afternoon chores done. His dad would be very upset if he didn't, no matter the reason.

"Bo will probably show up before dark," I told him. Once again, I reminded him to do a good job with his chores. Donnie had one thing, and one thing only on his mind, his precious Bo. I started up the engine on the big John Deere and went back to preparing the ground for planting. I can't imagine Donnie's life without Bo. Bo was Donnie's beacon of light, his beacon of hope, his everything, and now that's gone?

While I kept the tractor rolling, my mind did the same. I tried to think of a probable possibility as to where Bo could be. My mind replayed seeing Orville pulling the truck strangely close to the house before he left for Poplar Bluff.

I also know how much Orville hated Bo. Had that truck not pulled into the driveway the afternoon he beat Mary Beth with the tomato stake, I believe Bo wouldn't have survived that day. Orville didn't get his gun out of the truck to scare Bo. He had every intention of killing him, right there in front of Donnie and the rest of the family.

Orville had the perfect window of opportunity this afternoon. Everyone was gone and he could have loaded Bo into the truck and driven near Poplar Bluff. He could have gone down some uninhabited field road and dropped Bo off, or worse yet, took his gun and killed him. I had trouble convincing my mind a father would do that to his twelve-year-old son's dog. However, I know Orville, and that might be exactly what happened.

CHAPTER 31

'Damn you Orville. Donnie doesn't want just a dog.
He wants his rock, his best friend, his precious, Bo.'

I worked for an hour or so when I saw Orville, park his truck with the cotton seed under the equipment shed. Donnie met his dad out in front of the barn. I was sure he was explaining Bo's disappearance. Orville only talked to Donnie for a few seconds then went into the house. He returned shortly and climbed on the other tractor and headed to the field next to the one I was working.

Shortly after Orville entered the field, I saw Bonnie's car at the house. Donnie ran to the car. Everyone was locked in on every word he said. Katie dropped down on her knees and hugged him. Bonnie soon left and the girls went out in the yard to help Donnie look for Bo. They went into the out-buildings and looked in places Donnie had already looked. I would bet big money Bo was not on this farm.

Seeing Katie hug and hold Donnie made me wish that Orville was half the father that Katie was a mother. Orville and I worked till dark. Katie had supper ready. Donnie didn't eat three bites before he went back looking for Bo. Orville desperately worked to convince everyone Bo was stolen out of the yard by someone just driving by. I didn't know how Katie felt, but I promise I wasn't buying one word of it. It didn't make any sense whatsoever.

After supper was over, I told Katie and Orville, Donnie and I would take the old wagon and drive to different neighbors to see if anyone had seen Bo. I was ninety-nine percent sure we weren't going to find him. It wouldn't be in vain. It would at least give

Donnie some hope. We drove to several of the neighbors. No one had seen Bo. We returned home, feeling defeated. I told Donnie perhaps Bo would return in the night. I dropped to my knees and gave Donnie a big hug and told him to just pray, and maybe God would send Bo home. My intention was to give him any kind of hope possible. I knew what my bedtime prayer would be focused on tonight. God, please.

Wednesday morning found everyone at the breakfast table sad. But none were as sad as Donnie. My heart ached for him.

Katie drove the truck to the field and helped Orville with the cotton seeds each time the planter needed filling. The day went fast and very-good. Orville and Katie were quickly getting the cotton planted. If all went as well tomorrow, the cotton would all be in the ground. I kept looking at my watch then to the edge of the road where Bo should be laying, waiting for his bestest buddy, Donnie. Sadly, no Bo in sight.

The big yellow bus stopped and let the kids off. Oh my, I thought, how sad Donnie must be. I knew Katie's plan to leave was only twelve days away. I can't imagine how Donnie would feel driving away from this farm without Bo. 'Please God, send Bo home, please.'

Sadness settled over the supper table. Just to look into Donnie's devastated eyes would break your heart. After supper, everyone went their own way. I knew by the looks of Katie and Orville they were as tired as I was.

Daybreak Thursday morning came way too soon. Thankfully things went smoothly. I couldn't believe it when it was midafternoon. Thank God the cotton was planted. I kept the tractor rolling, getting more and more ground ready for planting corn now. I was in a field behind a drainage ditch, so I didn't get to see the bus when it dropped the kids off. My heart was simply broken for Donnie. I knew he missed Bo terribly. We worked till dark. Katie and Orville desperately wanted to get all the corn planted before the predicted rainstorm due Friday night.

Alice and Mary Beth made a simple, but very good supper. I was getting ready to get in bed when I heard Orville yelling at Donnie. He was on the back porch, so I got close to the open window. Orville was yelling at Donnie to stop crying about that dog.

He said, "I'll get you another dog, now shut up."

I literally ached for Donnie. Damn you, Orville, Donnie doesn't want just a dog. He wants his rock, his best friend, his precious Bo.

Friday morning arrived, and I was up before daybreak. The predicted rainstorm for tonight was only hours away. If all went okay, the corn would be planted. Orville and Katie were going in a dead run. They knew how important it would be to have the corn planted before the rain. All the corn ground was ready. I was now plowing the soybean ground.

It takes a special breed of people to farm. I wished Orville could love and respect Katie and these kids for all the hard work they put forth on this farm. Honestly, he did not, and had proved time after time, he was not capable. They were, as Katie had said, just tools to help him with this farm.

Sundown found us all back at the house. All three of us were completely exhausted, but so relieved that the cotton and corn was now in the ground. A much-needed good night of rest was anticipated by all.

CHAPTER 32

*'I put my arms around Donnie, I could hear his sniffles.
I knew his little heart was breaking.'*

***B**oom!* A large clap of thunder shook the windows of the Mex house. I grabbed the flashlight I always have near my bed and checked my watch, ten minutes after two. The thunderstorm the weatherman predicted had begun to roll in. The rain slowly peppered down on the tin roof above me. I rolled over, ready to catch a few more hours of shut eye. Then I heard a voice. Was it Donnie? I heard the words, "No...no...no." Oh my gosh, in fact it was Donnie. It sounded like he was on the porch. Orville must be whooping him on the porch at two in the morning! The only reason I could think of, Donnie is crying about Bo, and Orville was mad at him.

I am not going to let that happen. No way. Right is right and wrong is wrong and this is over the top wrong. Again, I heard Donnie cry out the words, "No...no...no." I quickly had my clothes on. I didn't feel the need to rehearse a speech. I'm simply going to let Orville know how I feel and put a stop to it.

I stepped out of the Mex house and looked toward the back porch. I was shocked to see there were no lights on at the Hopkins' house. Not one light. Was I dreaming? I was so confused. Then I heard it again. It was coming from down the road toward the old bridge. A bright bolt of lightning lit up the night sky. Then I saw Donnie. The flashlight he carried cast a dim light. The rumbling roar of thunder was closer, and the rain was coming down harder. I heard the sound coming from Donnie's direction. This time the words were clearer. "Bo...Bo...Bo." He wasn't saying 'no' at all. He was calling out for the love of his life, his precious Bo.

With the loss of Bo, Donnie had lost everything. His bestest, bestest buddy in the world. His rock, his water when he was thirsty. Bo was the reason Donnie could cope with the stress and abuse he had to endure in his young life.

I heard the heavens unleash a volley of thunder, and bolt after bolt of lightning danced across the night sky. By the time I reached Donnie, I was at a full run. He seemed surprised, but happy that I was out on the road with him. I shined my flashlight into his little face. Even though the rain came down, I saw hurtful tears in Donnie's eyes. He choked back sniffles and began to explain.

"I had a dream that Bo was under the bridge, caught on a piece of barbed wire. I tried to look under the bridge, but my flashlight didn't shine very far." He looked up. "Could you use your flashlight and look under the bridge?"

I was positive Bo wasn't under that bridge, but I would not disappoint Donnie.

"Sure." I stepped down the embankment near the bridge and aimed my light underneath. I made sure I didn't miss one single inch under that bridge. Donnie was right by my side, and his eyes followed every movement of the light. We searched every nook and cranny.

As I feared, there was no sign of Bo. I put my arm around Donnie. I heard his sniffles. I knew his little heart was breaking again. The continuous thunder and lightning put on a show. The wind began to blow even stronger and the rain hammered down.

"We best get back to the house," I said.

"I know."

"I sure was hoping Bo was under that bridge."

"Me too, Donnie."

We rushed back toward the house. I told Donnie to come with me, so we both made our way to the Mex house. I was concerned about Katie and Orville. I could see Orville getting upset with Donnie. I decided to pull one of the cots over near my bed and put the extra sheets Katie had left for me on the cot. I got some paper and wrote Katie and Orville a note explaining the situation, and why Donnie was in the Mex house with me. I knew I had seen some folded clothes on a table on the back porch. Hopefully

Donnie would have clean shorts and a tee shirt in that basket of clothes. I got him one of my clean towels and suggested he dry off and wrap the towel around him until I got back from the house.

I grabbed my poncho and carefully protected the note. I made it to the back porch and found I was in luck. The clothes still sat on the table. I retrieved Donnie a pair of shorts, a t-shirt, and clean socks. I left the note on the kitchen table and hurried back to the Mex house. Donnie quickly got his clothes on and we were ready for a few hours of sleep before morning.

Donnie's cot was only five or six feet from my bed, close enough we could talk to each other in a soft low voice. He soon spoke up, "Do you think God can really hear you pray?"

I didn't have a lot of parenting skills, but I remember something my mom often did. She would often answer a question with a question.

"I do. What do you think?"

Donnie replied, "Well, I've been praying and praying and praying for God to send Bo back home to me. But so far, God hasn't sent him home. I'm afraid God doesn't want Bo to come back home. Or maybe God just can't hear me pray."

I desperately wanted to tell him Bo would come back home. Honestly, I was beginning to have my doubts. "Well, buddy, I'm not going to give up on God just yet. So why don't we both say a silent prayer for Bo right now. Then let's try to get some sleep."

Donnie agreed. The Mex house became silent, with the exception of a steady rhythm of rain pounding down on the metal roof. In a few minutes I could tell Donnie was sound asleep.

CHAPTER 33

*'Sunday morning found me physically in pretty good shape,
mentally I was a wreck. This whole thing has
turned into a nightmare.'*

Saturday morning was much different than all the other early
mornings this week. Everyone actually slept in until 7:00.
The rain had stopped and the sun was out. I decided I would
go to town this afternoon, just to get away.

Orville told Donnie he needed him to help fix the cattle pasture
fence. He instructed Alice and Mary Beth to wash the family car.
Both girls took off out of the house with a bucket and cleaning
supplies. I heard a commotion and stepped out of the Mex house. It
was Mary Beth and Alice, engaged in an all-out water fight. Each
laughed hard when they chased each other with small cans of
water. I got the biggest kick out of it. It was refreshing to hear
laughter and see them having such fun.

About that time, Orville yelled from the top of his lungs. "I told
you girls to wash that car and that is exactly what I meant for you
to do. Do you understand me?"

Both girls immediately said, "Yes sir."

When they got back to the car, Mary Beth couldn't resist
throwing her full can of water on Alice when she bent over to wash
the car. Orville saw her. He screamed out in anger and walked
briskly toward her.

Orville unbuckled his large belt, whipped it out of his pant
loops as fast as a snake striking its prey. He quickly made his way
over to Mary Beth, grabbed her by the arm, and started whaling

away across her backside. Alice desperately pleaded with her dad to stop.

She pleaded with him, "I'm sorry, Dad, it's my fault. I started it."

Orville turned on Alice. "Don't think for one second you are too big for some of this."

Orville yelled at Alice while he boiled with anger. "You won't talk back to me!" He never let up on his onslaught of lick after lick. It was appalling. It made me physically sick. You never think you'll witness something like this until you do.

I could not handle this anymore. I hesitated for a moment, then headed in their direction. Katie had stepped out on the front porch. Orville saw me coming toward them. He abruptly stopped and headed to the pasture gate behind the house. He yelled for Donnie to come with him. Katie and I made it to Alice about the same time. Katie held out her arms and hugged her. I looked in Orville's direction. He had his back to us while he walked briskly toward the back of the field. Donnie walked with him, both of them carried fencing tools.

Katie dropped to her knees and looked at Alice's legs. Alice and Mary Beth both had on shorts, and both had noticeable swollen red welts across their upper and lower legs. Alice had one welt that was actually bleeding.

Katie looked at me and said, "Thank goodness she'll be wearing a long dress for graduation."

I stared into Katie's eyes. I was totally pissed and told Katie that I didn't know if I could keep myself in check much longer.

"You can't get involved. Remember, we are too close to the plan."

Alice stopped crying, looked at her mother and asked, "What's the plan Momma?"

Katie and I quickly made eye contact. I was curious about Katie's answer. She finally responded, "I'll tell you in a few days. Just keep this between us."

Alice replied, "Okay, I will."

I told Katie, "I must leave, I need to be off this farm because I just know I can't safely be around him. Me not standing up for the kids consumes every ounce of my resistance."

Katie understood that. I told her not to expect me for supper. I was going to Malden and I didn't need to be back on this farm until late tonight.

"I understand, and I think that's a wise choice. Please be careful, we need you."

I went to the Mex house, freshened up a bit, then headed to Malden. I went by the baseball field, and sure enough, there was a game going on. I sat and watched the game for quite a long time. I decided to just drive and try to take my mind off Orville Hopkins. I made a large circle outside of Malden in an area of the country I had not seen before. The sun was going down while I made my way back into town. I took my time, stopped at the little drive-in, ate a couple of hamburgers, and of course, drank a Pepsi. I drove around town for a few minutes, then turned the old wagon toward the Hopkins' farm.

I drove into the farm's driveway and parked close to the Mex house. I didn't want to interact with any of the Hopkins. When I turned the light on there was a large piece of paper on my bed. It was a note from Katie.

Leon,

I am sorry about today. Orville came in from working on the fence, and as he often does, you wouldn't have known anything had ever taken place this morning. Please go to church with us in the morning. Donnie has become physically sick over the loss of Bo. I know you are his hero, please be there for him tomorrow. I hope you had a good afternoon. See you in the morning,

Katie

Sunday morning found me in pretty good shape physically, mentally I was a wreck. It seemed like the mental and emotional stress I tried to put behind me when I left Wellington had gotten far worse. This whole situation had turned into a nightmare.

I certainly was looking forward to the day, Katie and the kids were in Ole Limpie with me heading to Decatur. I was ready to see this damn old cotton farm and Orville Hopkins in my rearview mirror.

I got out and helped Donnie with the chores. We all sat at the breakfast table and tried hard to make things seem normal. Honestly, it was anything but normal. Except for Orville, the rest of us were hurt by Donnie's loss of Bo. I sensed nervousness in Katie's demeanor, knowing in just a few days she would be leaving the man she had shared her life with for the last fifteen years.

We all loaded into the car for the trip to church. The drive had an eerie feeling. It felt as though the tension could be cut with a knife. Perhaps it was just the sad vibes from Donnie. All I was sure of, the atmosphere definitely felt different.

I sat near the front, on the outside of the pew, near the center aisle. Katie was to my right and Orville was next to Katie. The girls sat with their friends somewhere toward the back of the church. Donnie also sat at the back with some of his friends. The Pastor had finished his sermon, gave the usual invitation, but not one person stepped forward. Just like our church back home, this was also the time for any special prayer requests.

I enjoyed the sweet aroma from Katie Jean's perfume and anticipated Sunday dinner once we returned to the house. I was very surprised to see Donnie had made his way up to the front and stood in the aisle to my left. He didn't say a word, but it was obvious he wanted to sit on the pew between his mother and me. Politely, I turned my legs to give him a free passage. Just as Donnie settled in, Brother Blackmore asked if anyone had any prayer requests. You were expected to stand and speak loudly when requesting a prayer for someone. A couple of people had requests, and after he addressed their needs, Brother Blackmore asked again if there were any more requests.

When no more prayer requests were made, Brother Blackmore prepared to ask someone in the congregation to dismiss service. Donnie began to squirm in his seat. Then he stood up. Brother Blackmore seemed as surprised as the rest of us. It was now clear why Donnie had a need to sit between us. I'm sure he felt somewhat intimidated amongst his friends at the back of the church.

Brother Blackmore looked at Donnie, smiled, then called him by his name. "Yes Donnie, do you have a need for a special prayer?"

Donnie tried to speak. The nervous dryness of his mouth made his words hard to understand.

Brother Blackmore walked down from the pulpit and got closer to Donnie. He graciously said in a kind, loving voice. "It's okay, just take your time and tell us your request."

Donnie swallowed hard, cleared his throat, and miraculously spoke loud and clear. "I lost my dog, Bo. He is my bestest, bestest buddy in the whole world. Somebody took him out of our yard. We haven't seen him for five days. I've prayed to God a lot. I mean like lots and lots. God must not hear my prayers 'cause he hasn't sent Bo back to me yet. Momma said she believed when lots of people pray together in a church, God can hear them better. So, I was hoping maybe we could all pray that God will send Bo back home."

Donnie abruptly sat down, dropped his head, and stared at the floor. The sounds of sniffling could be heard in every corner of the little church. I slowly turned and looked across and back at the congregation. So many eyes were being wiped of tears including several men. It was obvious everyone felt his sad and depressed feelings when he spoke.

Brother Blackmore moved slowly and walked to the center of the church in front of the pulpit. He too choked back sheer emotions. He said, "I've had the privilege to visit the Hopkins' home on several occasions. I have witnessed the love Donnie has for his beloved dog, Bo. It's truly a bond like no other I have ever seen. I am going to dismiss service today. Please give me time to go to the back of the church before you leave. I want to greet each of you as you depart. I'm going to ask each of you to pray for Donnie's beloved friend, Bo. Pray silently from your heart while I pray out loud."

Brother Blackmore asked the congregation to please rise. When I looked over at Katie, she wiped tears from her eyes. I stared in Orville's direction. He looked my way without one sign of emotion, but I did see a look of guilt. A part of me wanted to step out in the aisle and point my finger at him. I would so much like to shout out that no one walked in the backyard at the Hopkins' house and stole Bo. That hypocrite right there took Bo, Donnie's precious dog, and either shot him or dropped him off far away from home.

As much as I wanted to do that, I knew I couldn't. I dropped my head and prayed harder than I have ever prayed in my life. Donnie didn't stand. He sat with his head bowed and stared at the floor. Brother Blackmore had no more than spoken the last word of his heartfelt prayer when Donnie bolted past me and basically sprinted to the side door and quickly ran out of the church.

I walked over to that side and looked for Donnie. I saw him already in the car, sitting in the back seat, staring out the window across the adjacent plowed field. I, too, avoided the crowd at the back of the church and exited out the side door. I wanted to get to Donnie as soon as possible. The Hopkins' bunch were in the car much quicker than normal, and in no time at all, we were driving the dusty gravel road home.

The first couple of miles going home were quite eerie. Katie broke the silence by commenting on the pastor's sermon. Then Mary Beth had one of her talking spells, blasting one of her friends for making fun of her shoes and rambled on and on about it. Donnie stared out the window in a trance.

I remember something Sergeant Jack Padgett, one of my Marine instructors in basic training, would often say. *'Bravery isn't something you feel, bravery is something you choose.'* It took sheer courage to do what Donnie did back there in that church building. Although, I'm not so sure it was so much bravery as it was pure love for the anchor in his life, a dog named Bo.

CHAPTER 34

'Donnie was throwing one hard throw after another up against the
wall, harsh sadness consumed his entire body.'

K atie and the girls preparing Sunday dinner wasn't any
different than any other Sunday. However, everything else
had a sad air about it. Donnie went straight to his room.
Katie tried desperately to make everyone feel as though everything
was normal, but it just wasn't. Donnie hardly touched his meal,
including the peach cobbler dessert.

When Orville finished his meal, he got up from the table and
said he was going to the bedroom to take a nap. I helped do the
kitchen chores. I felt blessed to be around Katie. I also got a big
kick out of teasing Mary Beth and Alice. I stepped out on the front
porch. Donnie threw a hard rubber ball, about the same size of a
baseball, off the concrete block garage building. One-hard throw
after another, up against the wall, harsh sadness consumed his
entire body.

I stepped off the porch toward Donnie. I thought I would go see
if I could possibly cheer him up, but decided perhaps the best thing
was for him to be by himself, taking his frustrations out on that
concrete wall. Feeling a need to also be alone, I decided to take a
long walk and do some soul searching. I made my way out to the
road and headed in the direction of the old bridge when something
caught my eye. I couldn't decide if it was moving or perhaps a
piece of litter blowing in the wind.

It was over to the edge of the road, near the ditch. It was black.
My first thought was, could this be Bo? However, it was too small

to be him, in fact I could not tell if it was an animal at all. Suddenly it moved toward the center of the road. There was no doubt it was some type of animal. It must be a large cat, or perhaps a dark colored coon. It was still too far away to make out exactly what it was. I walked toward the bridge, never once taking my eye off of the mysterious animal that slowly walked in my direction. When it came closer, it was obvious it had a broken gate, actually a very distinct limp.

To my surprise, while it moved closer, I could tell it wasn't a coon or a house cat. The only thing it could be was a dog, a black dog. Dear God, please let this be Bo. It seemed too small and skinny for Bo. There was no doubt this dog was hurt and was most certainly skin and bones. The dog would stop momentarily then limp on. While watching it get closer and closer, I decided it could very well be Bo. He looked so different.

The dog stopped, held his head up, and looked straight in my direction. When we walked closer to each other, his tail began to wag back and forth. I was sure at that moment it was indeed Bo! I wanted to yell at the top of my lungs to tell Donnie, but I was still cautious, desperately trying to absorb the fact that it was him.

When I got a direct look straight into Bo's eyes, all doubt left me and my heart flipped with relief. It was in fact Bo! 'Thank you, Lord, thank you Lord, thank you Lord' was all I could think to say. Donnie was behind the concrete block garage and couldn't see me or Bo. I dropped to my knees. Bo's tail wagged even harder. I could tell by the dullness in his sunken eyes that he was in bad shape. But thank God he was alive and was home.

Unknown to me, Mary Beth had come out of the house and saw what was going on with me and Bo. I told her to go get Donnie. Bo and I started walking slowly toward the house. Mary Beth turned and sprinted to the front yard, screaming from the top of her lungs, "Donnie, Bo came home. Donnie, come quickly, Bo came home!" Mary Beth was so excited and happy for Donnie. Her happy screams became louder and louder. You could have heard her all the way to Malden.

Bo and I slowly came into the yard. Alice and Katie rushed out of the house. I was sure Katie was concerned that Mary Beth was hurt. Donnie came running from around the garage. The look in Donnie's eyes was worth a million dollars. He ran toward Bo then dropped to his knees. He cried out, "Bo, Bo, my Bo, my Bo."

The pain Bo endured must have been excruciating, but he left my side. His slow walk turned into more like a slow trot. Bo almost pushed Donnie over when he shoved his head against the sides of Donnie's face. He rapidly licked every inch of Donnie's face, and his tail still wagged a mile a minute. Just when I thought he was going to stop, Bo repeated the same scene over and over again. The sight of that reunion will forever be embedded in my brain and soul.

Katie and Alice ran from the house to the corner of the yard. Katie was visibly ecstatic. 'Praise the Lord, thank you dear Jesus,' was coming from her emotional voice while she wiped away tears of sheer joy.

Donnie looked up at his mother, and said, "Momma, the Lord heard us all praying at church this morning. There is a God, and He does answer prayers!"

Donnie hugged Bo so hard that he pulled him to one side. Bo let out a painful yep. That was the first time Donnie realized Bo was hurt.

He patted Bo on the head and said, "Oh no, Bo. I'm so sorry. I didn't know you were hurt." Donnie looked up at me. "How bad is it? Can you tell?"

"I noticed the wounds earlier. It looks like he's been shot with a shotgun. See all of those pellets? Dang. Some of them look deep, and definitely infected."

Katie Jean spoke up, "Let's get him to the house and give him some food."

Mary Beth blurted out, "He has to be hungry, look how skinny he is."

"I wouldn't have recognized him with all those cockleburs and thistles embedded in his hair." Alice shook her head. "He looks awful."

Alice was right, Bo looked bad in every sense of the word. But at the same time, we all thought he was the best-looking thing we had ever seen in our lives.

Katie told Alice to go in the house and get the leftover fried chicken pieces that were in the refrigerator. She told Mary Beth to go with her and get some biscuits and a big bowl of milk. I remember something Johnny Hooper told me, be careful and don't over feed a sick dog, give small portions at first, then increase their feed slowly. I shared that information with Katie.

"That makes perfect sense." Katie nodded several times. "You're right."

We all surrounded Bo at the far end of the porch. I guess the commotion and Mary Beth's loud screams woke Orville. He opened the door and walked out on the porch. Mary Beth looked toward him and with great excitement said, "Look, Daddy, Bo has come home!"

Orville appeared as though he just saw a ghost. He was as white as a sheet, and without any emotion at all, uttered in a low voice, "Well that's great."

Alice spoke up and said, "He's been shot."

I spoke directly to Orville. "We need to get him to a vet."

Orville looked over at Katie as she stared back at him. Katie said, "We'll need to wait till tomorrow. Dr. Barton will charge an after-hours fee if we take him in today, and we simply don't have the money."

I boldly said, "He doesn't need to wait till tomorrow. Bo needs attention as soon as possible. Trust me, that wound and infection is bad. He needs antibiotics now."

Donnie had a look of concern and worry on his face. I thought to myself how extremely blessed we were to have Bo alive and in this yard. The goal line was just a few yards away and we could not fumble the ball now.

I announced, "I'll pay to get Bo to the vet today if you can get in touch with him."

Katie looked at Orville. Orville said, "Are you willing to foot the whole bill?"

I said, "Absolutely, including any medications."

Katie rushed to the door. "I'll go call Dr. Barton right now."

Donnie squeezed Bo's head and said, "It's going to be okay, Bo. God brought you home to us, and Mr. Leon is going to pay to get you all fixed up."

We fed Bo a small portion of the milk and biscuits and chunks of chicken. The poor thing was so hungry. Donnie and Mary Beth combed Bo's hair and slowly removed the cockleburs. Cockleburs are an indigenous weed in this part of Missouri. Their seed is a sharp sticky burr that latches onto anything it comes in contact with. Normally they mature during the late summer and fall and are all gone by this time of year. But no doubt, Bo had traveled down the drainage ditch which had a lot of last year's crop. Bo's hair was totally matted with these nasty things.

Katie returned to the front porch with a big smile on her face. "I got a hold of Dr Barton. He'll meet you at his office in forty-five minutes."

Orville hadn't said a half dozen words from the time he appeared on the porch. I'm sure he couldn't believe that dog had made it back home.

I turned Ole Limpie around and helped Katie get Donnie and Bo in the back seat. Katie placed a blanket on the seat. We carefully laid Bo on the blanket. Donnie sat with Bo's head in his lap. What a heart-wrenching scene. Donnie continually patted Bo's head and verbally repeated sweet things to him, much like a mother to her newborn baby. I muttered under my breath, "Thank you Lord, thank you."

Donnie was familiar with Malden and knew exactly where Dr. Barton's Vet Clinic was. I was relieved to see his car in front of the building. Bo's injuries were soon going to get the attention they desperately deserved.

Dr. Barton was a pleasant man. His primary concern was giving Bo his full professional focus. Bo was somewhat apprehensive, but followed every command Donnie and Dr. Barton asked of him. Dr. Barton spoke to Donnie and me without ever taking his attention from Bo.

He said, "You definitely did the right thing by getting him in here today. The infection in these wounds, are ready to become very, very serious."

Bo lay there like a trooper, never once flinching while Dr. Barton performed one procedure after another. Dr. Barton said, "He's one lucky dog." He was getting ready to explain his reasoning behind that statement when Donnie said, with a very questionable tone, "Why do you think he's lucky when he has been shot with a shotgun?"

Dr. Barton looked at Donnie and with a light chuckle said, "Well, Donnie, your point is well taken. My point is this, he was shot straight from the rear. In other words, Bo was running away from the shooter."

Dr. Barton pointed to Bo's wounds and said, "Most of the pellets went into the heavy muscle of his back leg, off to one side. Had the bulk of the pellets hit him a little higher and closer to the center of his body, the outcome would have been much different. The pellets could have, and actually would have, hit him in his spine. Bo would have been instantly paralyzed, and would have laid and died a slow painful death."

Dr. Barton had finished working on Bo and was washing his hands. He looked at me and said, "I've given him an extra dose of penicillin and these capsules are a high penicillin-based antibiotic."

He retrieved a jar of ointment, handed it to me and continued to give me instructions on what to do when we got him home. "Be sure to keep the wounds clean, and if he has any trouble, be sure and get him back in here as quickly as possible."

I repeatedly told him how grateful we were that he took the time to help us on his day off. He politely said, "That's what I'm here for. I'm just glad I was home."

I gladly paid the bill, and we got Bo loaded in the old wagon, then headed back to the Hopkins' farm.

We were about halfway home when I remembered something Donnie told Dr. Barton. It hit me like a ton of bricks and made my stomach roll. I had trouble keeping my mind on driving. Dr. Barton had asked Donnie if he got Bo as a puppy. Donnie said, "Nope. He just walked into our backyard on July 4th last year. I remember because we had a 4th of July get together at our house, and all of my cousins were there. They all left, and I went to do my chores, and Bo just walked up to me with his tail wagging. He's been my bestest, bestest buddy ever since."

I remember very well the time and date Johnny Hooper committed suicide. It was late afternoon, July 4th, last year. I had written this poem about his death, a couple of days after his funeral. I can recite verbatim every song and poem I have written. The last paragraph of this poem says,

"Only sunshine in heaven, there won't be any rain,
And for the first time in years, he will feel no pain.
Perhaps he will return as an ole dog sent from above,
To walk beside some little boy and deliver God's much needed Love."

My head spun in circles. Was the timing of the events just by chance, or was this a paranormal thing? Or was it an act of divine power, or was the whole thing just a set of circumstances? There had been numerous times during the last few days I felt as though I was in some mysterious dream.

I was in deep thought about everything when Donnie blared out, "Hey, you just passed our road." I made some joke about it and turned around and proceeded on the gravel road to the farm. I no more than shut the switch off on the ole wagon when Mary Beth flew off the porch quickly followed by Alice and Katie Jean.

I was all but certain Orville wasn't going to let Donnie keep Bo in the house. Dr. Barton made it very clear how important it was to keep the wounds clean. I spoke up and asked Katie, "Do you suppose we could keep Bo in the Mex house?" I explained to her what the vet said about keeping the wounds clean.

"I don't see why that wouldn't be okay," she said, "but I'll ask Orville. He's checking on cattle in the north pasture. I can't imagine he would care."

I told her I'd be happy to clean up after him if necessary. When Orville returned to the house, he was on board with keeping Bo in the Mex house. I was also pleased that Orville and Katie both agreed with my suggestion of Donnie spending nights in the Mex house with me and Bo.

Katie put clean sheets on one of the cots for Donnie and she got some old blankets for Bo. We made him a comfortable bed on the floor up against the wall near Donnie's cot. Soon, Donnie and I were ready to turn out the lights. What a blessed day.

We were both lying in bed when Donnie said, "I'd like to tell God thank you for helping Bo come home."

"Okay, that would be great," I replied.

Donnie's prayer was simple, but came straight from the heart when he spoke these words:

"Dear God,
Thank you so much for helping get Bo home to me.
Please make Bo well soon. I promise I will be really, really
good, just like I said I would do if you could help Bo find
his way home to me. And please bless my new best friend,
Leon, for paying to get Bo all fixed up. Amen."

Donnie always found a way to warm my heart. I can assure you, we all dozed off to sleep with a much more peaceful feeling than we'd had for several nights.

CHAPTER 35

'I don't understand, why would I not have complete custody?
He is the one abusing these kids!'

Monday morning was soon upon us. Bo had been a trooper all night. Only waking us up one time to go out to pee and do his dirty business. The kids were soon on the bus. Orville and I were each on a tractor, pushing to get the soybean ground ready to plant.

At lunch, Katie mentioned to Orville she desperately needed groceries. They would normally go to town on Saturday afternoon. However, this past Saturday, fixing the cattle fence was way more important, so she hadn't gotten her groceries.

As we were finishing lunch, a neighbor drove into the driveway. Orville looked out the window, then said, "It's Frank Moore." He stepped out onto the porch and Frank explained to him the hydraulic lift on his tractor was not working. Orville told him he was sure it was an inner seal, and it would take a few hours to tear it down and replace the seal.

"You and I can fix it," Orville confidently said. "It'll just take some time."

Orville told Frank as soon as Donnie got in from school, he would have him drive his tractor and he would be over to help him.

When Frank drove off, Katie said, "What about the groceries? There are several things I'm totally out of." Katie added, "I also need to go by Bonnie's and make some last-minute changes on Alice's graduation dress."

Orville looked at me. "Would you mind taking Katie and the

girls to town this afternoon?"

I was over-the-top happy to do this but didn't want my enthusiasm to show. "Sure, whatever you need me to do."

The afternoon went by very quickly, and I saw the big yellow bus stopping at the Hopkins' house. I quickly got ready to take the women folk to town. Donnie climbed on the big tractor and headed to the field. He was such a good little worker.

In no time at all, I was behind the wheel of the Hopkins' family car, driving sweet Katie and those two cute girls to Malden. After Orville left to go work on Frank Moore's tractor, Katie told me she had called Bonnie. Bonnie's husband, Walter, had a dear friend, Lynn Hamby. Lynn was a prominent lawyer in Malden. He and Walter had been close friends since high school. They actually had gone to college together. Bonnie and Walter wanted Lynn to help Katie with her divorce. They thought this afternoon would be the perfect time for Lynn to drop by their house and meet with Katie.

I couldn't help but wonder how Orville was going to feel when it hit him that Katie and the kids were gone. He might very well realize that love can be like a gentle breeze, you don't notice it until the temperature outside turns cold.

While at the A & P Supermarket in Malden, the girls quickly helped Katie get the groceries. Then in just a few minutes, we were across town at Katie's dear friend, Bonnie's house. The last detail of Alice's dress was soon finished and Alice was ready to take it home.

It was nearly perfect timing. Walter and Lynn both drove into the drive at the same time.

Katie and Bonnie suggested the girls take a long walk.

Lynn didn't waste time making small talk. He went straight into the legal aspect of what Katie was facing, explaining the normal procedure and protocol she should expect. While Lynn methodically expressed how it takes overwhelming evidence, and proof, to deprive a natural parent of the right to visitation and partial custody rights. The chances with a trial judge completely depriving Orville visitation and custody rights were slim at best.

Lynn paused and looked at Katie. I'm sure he sensed the disappointment by her reactions to his comments. He said, "Katie, do you have any questions?"

Katie spoke up and said, "I don't understand. Why would I not have complete custody? He's the one who is abusing these kids."

Lynn explained, "I am going to be honest with you. For you to achieve an outcome whereas Orville doesn't have at least visitation privileges and partial custody will be almost impossible. The judges are very conservative in their family law decisions because they know they are going to be up for re-election."

I kept looking at Katie Jean while Lynn explained one legal possibility after another. I could tell Katie was somewhat confused. She also had a look of fright. I was convinced she wasn't expecting to hear the things Lynn threw her way. He kept repeating, "I am not trying to talk you out of this, Katie. I just want to be totally honest with you."

This obviously wasn't Lynn's first rodeo. He most certainly wasn't sugar coating a happy-ever-after conclusion. There was no doubt Katie had to do some soul searching. Lynn was very gracious and told Katie he would be there for her if and when she needed him.

It didn't take long to get everyone loaded up in the car. We said goodbye and headed back to the farm more perplexed than when we arrived.

Katie wasn't her usual cheerful self. She appeared deep in thought about what Lynn had laid out for her. When we got back to the house, Alice was excited about her new dress, and Katie was doing a good job hiding her feelings about what Lynn had dumped on her earlier.

I changed into my work clothes, checked on Bo to make sure he was doing okay, then proceeded to work on the chores. Donnie drove the tractor until dark as his dad had told him to do. I had all the chores done when he came in from the field.

Donnie and I explained to Orville how the afternoon went and told him we were going to the Mex house. He seemed pleased and said, "I'll see y'all in the morning."

Donnie spent some quality time petting and talking to Bo before going to bed.

CHAPTER 36

'It is much like someone giving you a green persimmon, telling you to eat it and pretend it is sweet. It is bitter and difficult to pretend that it isn't.'

Early Tuesday morning found everyone in a good mood, including Orville. Today was Alice's big day. Her 8th grade graduation would begin this morning at ten o'clock in the high school gymnasium. Everyone in the Hopkins' family would be there, including me. The seventh-grade class would be dismissed, and each student was expected to attend. Students in the other classes, who had a sibling graduating, were allowed to attend, so Mary Beth and Donnie would get to see their big sister graduate.

Orville and I were going to plow soybean ground until 9 o'clock. He waved for me to head to the house when it was time. I was so happy he was taking time to go.

I went straight to the Mex house and quickly showered and dressed in appropriate clothes. When I walked out of the Mex house, Alice was sitting on the front porch swing. I meandered across the yard and joined her on the porch. Alice was blessed to have inherited her mother's natural beauty. Seeing her sitting in that swing, with her new perm and that beautiful dress, was such a pretty sight.

I looked at her and said, "Who are you, beautiful lady? I don't think I have ever seen you before. I thought you were Alice, but you look way older than the Alice I know." Her smile turned into a warm glow. "Let me see that dress!"

Alice stood up from the swing. She did a cute little twirl, spinning several times, showing off her pretty new dress. Alice was a very confident young lady. Not cocky, but she had an air about her that fit her bubbly personality.

"You look absolutely gorgeous, Alice. I said, enjoy every minute of this day sweetheart, you have earned it." Katie Jean and Orville stepped out of the house.

Katie said, "We need to be in that car right now, we don't want to be late!"

The activity in front of the gymnasium was a buzz. Alice quickly got with her classmates. Orville, Katie, and I found our reserved seats with the help of Donnie and Mary Beth frantically waving, letting us know where we were to sit. Being at the graduation ceremony brought back memories of Larry and me, Mom and Dad.

Alice had been chosen to speak. I was amazed by her poise and maturity. She had already accepted the award for the 'best liked girl'. I looked over at Orville and Katie while Alice gave her speech. I could sense and feel their pride.

Unable to stop myself, I thought of Karen and me, which of course this day, for us as proud parents, would never be. I wish I could stop this kind of thinking. I told myself to take my mind somewhere else. It's much like someone giving you a green persimmon, telling you to eat it and pretend it is sweet. It is bitter and difficult to pretend that it isn't. And knowing I'll never experience this day with Karen and Randy, it's bitter, very bitter.

Soon the ceremony was over. Donnie and Mary Beth went back to their classes. We all took turns hugging Alice and telling her how proud we were of her.

Alice was going home with Julie, along with two other classmates. Bonnie was taking them to Malden for hamburgers and ice cream. They were going to an afternoon matinee at the movie theater. Later Bonnie would bring the girls to Katie's house and drop them off for a sleepover with Alice. The girls wanted to sleep out in the front yard under a tarp.

Orville and I quickly gobbled down a sandwich Kate had made for lunch and were soon back in the field plowing soybean ground. Work did not end until it was almost dark. Donnie had completed all the afternoon chores, including milking the cows. Katie had a supper fit for a king, including Alice's favorite coconut cake.

I was more than happy to help the girls set up their spacious outside sleeping room. We tied a tightrope between two trees and hung the large tarp over the rope. The girls carried cots from the Mex house. They ran a long electric extension cord from the Mex house to what they playfully referred to as the 'Paradise Hotel', their sleepover headquarters! The electric cord was for a small record player one of the girls had brought, along with some Elvis Presley records.

I can often do very dumb things, and setting up the Paradise Hotel as close to the Mex house was over the top dumb. I had very little trouble hearing the girls giggle, and giggle they did. I easily overheard their conversations and was entertained by how thirteen-year-old girls could find so much humor in a fart, but trust me, they did. There wasn't any way I was going to dampen their fun on this very special night. However, I more than once wanted to fling that darn record player across the road to the far side of the pig barn. After the one-hundredth time hearing Elvis sing, 'Everybody let's rock...Let's rock to the jailhouse rock,' I was about to scream.

I couldn't keep from feeling sorry for Alice when I overheard the girl's making fun of her wearing long P.J.'s on a warm night. Those girls just didn't understand. Alice was ashamed of the cuts and bruises on the back of her legs from the awful, unnecessary, whooping her daddy gave her a few days ago. Alice just let it slide, she seemed even more determined to giggle and laugh, and act as if the hard whooping never happened. I thought, *'even in a thick forest you can see sunlight filtering through the trees.'* Just as I had hoped, eventually they all surrendered to the sheer exhaustion from the eventful day. Finally, there was total silence at the Paradise Hotel. I, too, soon drifted off to sleep.

Orville woke up Donnie and me very early. He told us Katie had breakfast, and he and I were going straight to the field. He instructed Donnie to do all the morning chores by himself.

Orville said, "We are going to push the tractors hard this morning." He explained, "Donnie will be out of school at noon."

He continued, "I'm going to take the truck and go to Malden to pick up the soybean planting seeds and pick up Frank Moore's tractor hydraulic seal. He informed me as soon as he got home from town, he was going to Frank's to install the new seal."

It was a very pleasant morning. Orville and I were rapidly turning the black delta soil. I noticed the parents of the giggly girls were arriving to pick them up. The words to Elvis Presley's Jailhouse Rock repeated over and over in my brain. I believe in a songwriter's world, that is referred to as a hook. Trust me, I am totally hooked. I want to believe Alice enjoyed one of the most memorable times of her life. I sure hope so.

Soon it was noon, and we were going to the house for lunch. Katie had warmed up the leftovers from the big supper meal last night. The big yellow bus dropped Donnie off from school. Mary Beth was going home with Ola May, Bonnie's daughter. It was official now, school was out!

Orville rushed through his lunch, changed clothes, and headed to town. Katie and Bonnie were going to take the leftover material from the girls' graduation dresses, and some extra material Bonnie had from another project, and make the younger girls new dresses.

Donnie and I took some time to attend to Bo. Thank God Bo was on the mend. He should be able to travel with no problem come Monday when we all were supposed to make the long trip to Decatur. Donnie and I were soon back on the two John Deere tractors pulling disk plows. I finished the field I was working in and was headed to a field behind the drainage ditch. Before I left the field, I noticed Orville's truck pull into the driveway.

I dropped my disk when suddenly the tractor started to miss. Oh no, now what? This is all we need. The tractor stopped running and the engine went dead. I got off and surveyed the situation. I saw where fuel had run down the outside of the engine. I looked at the carburetor on the big G, a split fuel line. I looked at my fuel tank, completely empty. Only one thing to do, walk the quarter of a mile or so to the house. I was glad Orville had made it in from town. He'll no doubt have the fuel line fixed quickly.

When I made my way across the road to the edge of the yard, I heard Alice let out a frightened scream. I got closer to the house and heard her angrily yelling,

"No, no more, you hear me?" Her voice rose a notch, "No, no more!"

About that time the front door flew open and Alice sprinted out of the house. Surprised to see me standing only a few feet from the porch steps, she had a look of sheer fright and embarrassment. She bolted past me and ran toward the old bridge.

Orville quickly stomped out of the house, basically on Alice's heels. When he realized I stood at the steps he looked completely shocked. He had a look of surprise and guilt all rolled into one. Frozen, we stared into each other's eyes. Orville desperately tried to diffuse the scene. He blundered through his attempt to pretend nothing was alarming about what I just witnessed.

He asked, "What are you doing here?" I began to explain the fuel line issues. He gave me instructions to unload the soybean seeds. He said, "I'll change clothes and get some tools and a piece of rubber hose. We'll have the fuel line repaired in no time."

While I walked out to the equipment shed, I looked down the road to see if I could spot Alice. She was sitting on the edge of the bridge and appeared to be tossing rocks into the water below. I knew the best thing I could do was just keep my cool. Let it go, keep your cool, I kept telling myself. Orville quickly gathered up the tools he needed to get the fuel line repaired. He pointed to a five-gallon fuel can in the corner of the shed.

"We'll need to fill that can with fuel," he called out to me.

Before very long we had the fuel line repaired, and Donnie and I worked until dark. When we got to the house, Orville said he had the evening chores done and to go ahead and get ready for supper. I detected a hint of anger in Orville's voice when he said, "I am not sure when supper will be ready. Katie hasn't got her running-around ass back from Bonnie's."

I told Donnie to go ahead, get ready for supper, and I would look at Bo's wounds. Donnie took a minute to love Bo. Bonnie pulled into the driveway. The instant Katie stepped out of the car, Orville started blasting her right there in front of her friend. Bonnie quickly threw the car in reverse and backed out, throwing rocks as she sped off. Katie tried to explain why she was late.

"Orville," she said in a pleading voice, "we were getting into the car and starting home, when an old classmate pulled into Bonnie's drive." She continued, "It was Dorothy Thomas. Bonnie and I graduated from high school with her. She had moved to Illinois and we hadn't seen her since school. We got to visiting and time slipped away. I am sorry, Orville I don't know what else to say."

Orville blared out, "You best not say another damn word and get your ass in there and get supper on the table."

Katie stopped at the steps and turned toward Orville. She was getting ready to say something, but Orville rushed toward her, his arm stretched out and his index finger in her face. He said, "You best shut your smart-ass mouth and get through that door and in that kitchen before I knock your ass in there."

I was on my knees attending to Bo's wounds. I sprung to my feet and said to myself, 'you best not lay one hand on her, Orville Hopkins. That will be the bucket of water in my pond that would break the dam'. Katie turned and went into the house. Orville turned and started walking across the road to the pig barn.

He yelled at Katie through the screen door, "Call me when you get supper ready."

Katie didn't answer.

I took a deep breath. I didn't know how much more of this I could handle. I knew I couldn't be around Orville Hopkins right now. I didn't want to be the thread that comes unwound.

After Donnie cleaned up, I suggested that when supper was ready, we both fill a plate and eat in the Mex house. He was happy to do that, and I needed to keep my distance from both Orville and Katie Jean. We ate supper, made small talk, and went to bed.

Thank goodness tomorrow was Thursday, only five more days and I would be driving away from this farm and the two-faced Orville Hopkins. Like clockwork, the sound of the John Deere tractor engine once again awoke me. Donnie also crawled out of bed. It seemed Orville kept getting up earlier and earlier. He instructed Donnie and me to go to the house and eat breakfast. He was going to do all the morning chores and wanted Donnie and me to plow. He was going to Frank Moore's to work on his tractor.

Katie told me Orville doesn't charge any neighbor when he works on their equipment. However, this project with Frank Moore was a larger undertaking. Frank told Orville he was going to pay him cash, with money he received from the sale of a combine.

Katie commented how the cash would help them a lot on the trip to Bellville to the wedding. She also told me that Orville was going to pay me in cash for my labor. I was thrilled to hear that. Orville instructed Donnie and me to quit work a little early and do the afternoon chores.

He said, "I don't know how long I'll be at Frank's, but I know it'll probably be 'till after dark." We got the tractors to the house and split up doing chores, and were completely done in record time. Finally, we could take a little breather before supper.

Katie and the girls had the home place looking good. The yard was mowed and the garden was hoed. Mary Beth spoke up and said, "We're going to be all ready to go to the wedding Saturday. I'll get to see my favorite cousin, Carol!"

Katie pointed to the lawn chairs out under the big shade trees in the front yard. We both made our way over to the chairs and took a seat.

"Whoo, I am pooped," Katie said.

"Me too, it has been a long day," I replied.

Katie didn't waste any time letting me know why she wanted to talk. She said, "I don't know what to do."

With a perplexed look she said, "I'm really beginning to second guess myself about the divorce."

A part of me wanted to tell her that this was the perfect opportunity and she had to take advantage of it! Although, I knew I shouldn't say that. If I encouraged her against her will, and she lost custody of the kids, I would never forgive myself. Katie would never forgive herself either.

She said, "I know I need to make a decision by Saturday morning."

Alice and Donnie were walking from the backyard to the pasture behind the old equipment and my shower and toilet.

Katie said, "Well, I need to get in that kitchen."

I said, "Sweet lady, I'll be praying for you, and I'll support you whatever you choose."

"Thank you," she said. "You're such a gentleman."

While Katie made her way to the house, I walked to the Mex house. I abruptly heard Donnie's 22-rifle go off. 'Bang!' Then shortly there was another, 'Bang!' I was curious at what they were shooting at. I made my way past the shower and got behind an old corn picker. I didn't want them to know I was anywhere nearby.

Donnie was carefully explaining to Alice the proper way to hold the gun and how to aim down the barrel. It was apparent that Alice really wanted to understand how to load and operate the gun. Alice shot four or five rounds completely on her own. Donnie praised her for what a good job she did. He wrapped up his teaching session, I quickly got myself back to the Mex house before they saw me.

Alice returned to the house and Donnie came into the Mex house carrying his gun. I pretended as if I knew nothing about what he had been doing. I wanted to hear his explanation. He said, "Alice asked me yesterday to teach her how to shoot a gun. I promised her I'd teach her."

He added, "I don't know why she wants to learn how. She can't stand to even look at a rabbit or squirrel when I bring one into the house that I've killed. I just simply don't understand women, do you?"

I replied, "Well, they sure can be a mystery sometimes. But what would we do without them?"

Donnie shrugged his shoulders and said, "I don't know."

Donnie asked me, "Is it okay if I leave my gun in the Mex house?"

"Sure, I suppose."

"My Grandpa Davis gave me this gun. He's dead now. I sure wish you could have known him. He was a very good man. Momma sometimes cries because she misses him so much. I miss him a lot, too."

Donnie walked over to Bo. "Do you think it would be okay if I took Bo for a walk?"

"That's a great idea! I was actually going to suggest you do that."

Donnie and Bo exited the Mex house and started walking toward the old bridge. Actually, Bo was running, he seemed completely healed. I grabbed my towel and headed for the shower, all the while thinking about what Donnie said about his grandpa. I thought about how a grandpa can have a lasting impression on his grandkids, especially the grandsons. I simply admired my mom's dad, Grandpa Burns. He farmed and loved horses. He always had on an 'ol cowboy hat, and I never saw him without his old boots.

I pulled into his driveway one day. Even though he was getting up in his years and had lost much of his eyesight, there he was, working with a neighbor's horse. I thought to myself, he is a vanishing breed. Later on, the next day, I wrote this song.

VANISHING BREED

VERSE

He puts on that o'hat he has worn every day for years. If he lost those old boots, it would bring him to tears. He's got a watch in his pocket, but he can't see to tell time. He sees good in horses and people even though he is nearly blind.

CHORUS

It hurts me to see it, but he is a vanishing breed, the backbone of our country and a hero to me. But a man of his kind is almost extinct, it hurts me to see it, but he is a vanishing breed.

VERSE

He's a straight shooter, he won't throw you a curve, close any deal with a handshake and his word. He won't stand on a stump, and preach about his faith. It speaks loud by the way he lives each and every day.

CHORUS

It hurts me to see it, but he is a vanishing breed, the backbone of our country and a hero to me. But a man of his kind is almost extinct, it hurts me to see it but he is a vanishing breed.

Grandpa Burns was a simple man. He always felt people often put too much emphasis on material things. He was very content just going through life with the necessities. I have heard him more than once say, *'People can be so stupid, they buy things they don't need, with money they don't have, to impress people they don't even know.'*

I was also inspired to write another poem/song about Grandpa Burns. I overheard a conversation he was having with my mom. It was during an awful drought. Mom was stressing about their crops. Grandpa calmly said, "Doris, trust me, it will all work out." I remember him saying, *"Tough times don't last, tough people do."* I lay in bed that night and kept thinking about those words. I got up. It must have been way past midnight and I wrote this.

TOUGH TIMES DON'T LAST

"I can still see the sweat dripping from his brow. He must have walked a million miles behind a mule and a plow. I watched him kneel and pray down on humbled knees. I cling to every word he softly spoke to me. He said, "You are going to face some tough times down life's crooked road, there is one thing I feel you ought to know. Just some simple words but trust me they're true. Tough times don't last, tough people do. For when times get rough, tough people get tough. Buckle down and somehow make it through, because tough times don't last, tough people do."

CHAPTER 37

'His little lip started to quiver. Daddy got really, really mad at me and pushed my face into the dirt.'

K atie sent Mary Beth to summon us for supper. Katie told us that Darlene Moore had called and Orville was on his way home. When he arrived back at the farm, he acted exceptionally proud they had Frank's tractor lift working. He was in a good mood. However, the whole Hopkins bunch, including me, were extremely exhausted. Everyone turned in early. Donnie and Bo were sound asleep. I couldn't get my mind off the fact that Alice wanted to learn how to shoot Donnie's gun. I kept thinking about the words she screamed at her dad as she ran out of the house. "No! No, no more!"

I speculated as to what could have happened to make her say those words. I know what I witnessed with Orville and Donnie in the pig barn. So why not Alice? She was quickly becoming a young lady. Not only was her body changing, but her mental growth was also maturing. Most people have trouble understanding the mindset of someone like Orville. I know without a doubt, Katie could, and would do anything sexually to satisfy Orville's every need.

There was something Johnny Hooper told me. He was so confused as to why his dad chose to have him do things when he knew his mother, who was a very attractive woman, would have done anything to please his dad. He said he brought this up to one of the four therapists he had seen. The therapist said, "Oh Johnny, it has way more to do with control than the sexual aspect of it."

Johnny said he gave him an example. A rapist would pass up a 'lady of the night' if she offered the act for free, to go find someone he could control and rape. The therapist said that he didn't think his dad was a typical rapist or a pedophile, per se. He had an extreme need to control. Johnny said the therapists told him, "It is all about control."

Johnny's therapists explained his father's actions further. His dad had taken on the debt of the big farm near Jonesboro, Arkansas. He had two complete crop failures in a row. His life, as he knew it, had gone south. He could not control the rain. He could not control the banker who refused his loan. His personality gave him a need to control. He said his dad could never admit wrong, but the purchase of the big farm was a mistake. Then two extremely wet farming seasons left him in dire need to control.

Johnny fought back tears when he explained how the therapist reached out his hand to him and said, "Johnny, you were the scapegoat that your dad selfishly needed in his life at that time." I could not stop wondering what Donnie's life will be like when he becomes an adult. There is no doubt in my mind Donnie and the girls will have to cope with PTSD just as Johnny did.

The next morning Orville changed the oil on the family car to get ready to go to Bellville. I was extremely curious as to Katie's decision about the divorce. Only one more day to decide. It constantly lingered in the back of my mind. Her decision would change everything for me. I had a gut feeling she would not go through with it. If Katie backed out of the divorce, I knew I might cut my stay shorter and leave for Decatur once I finished my commitment of completing the chores through Sunday morning. I was concerned I might lose my composure and do something awful if I stayed, knowing what Orville was capable of.

Donnie and I plowed the ground till noon. After lunch Orville and Donnie put the four-row planter on the sixty John Deere. He helped Orville fill the seed hoppers with bean seeds. We worked in the field till sundown. I looked at Donnie and could tell he had been crying, no doubt from Orville's abuse. If not physically, most certainly mentally. I don't know how Donnie copes with a daily barrage of harsh negative criticism, without one word of praise, love, or comfort. Mental abuse can be devastating to a twelve-year old boy. I am so concerned PTSD in just over the horizon. Orville takes all his frustrations out on Donnie, the same as Johnny's dad. I felt helpless.

"God, where are you?"

Earlier I had noticed dirt caked in Donnie's hair and around his neck. On our way to the Mex house, I asked, "Did you fall down, Donnie?"

His little lip started to quiver. "I tripped and spilled the five-gallon-bucket of soybean seeds. Daddy got really, really mad at me and pushed my face into the dirt. He wouldn't let me up, I couldn't breathe. I thought I was going to die." Frankly, what I have learned about Orville's abuse staggered my imagination.

Donnie started to cry. His tears, mixed with the dirt on his face, became a light coat of mud. He looked so pitiful. It just wasn't fair. I was tormented as to what I should do.

I suggested to Donnie to take a shower and get ready for bed.

"Can I pull one of those mattresses over by Bo's bed?" he asked. I told him he could, then helped him move the mattress.

Hearing some quiet snoring, I looked over to see Donnie with his arm wrapped around Bo. I couldn't keep from speaking under my breath. "Thank you, Lord, thank you for bringing Bo home." Bo was more than a dog.

'He was the warm glow of light from the lantern that lit the darkened path Donnie too often was forced to travel.'

I made a decision at that moment. If Katie backed out of the divorce, I would build Bo an enclosed pen at the back of the house next to Donnie's window. I'll wait till Katie lets me know her decision in the morning.

I again looked over at Donnie with his arm around Bo. Both were sound asleep, creating a peaceful and tranquil sight. I thought about Donnie and his need to do silly things to make others laugh. I remember how Johnny's wife, Margaret, told me Johnny always had a need to make others laugh. I was concerned about where Donnie's life was headed. I vividly remember Johnny telling me when he was fourteen-years-old, he actually considered taking a gun and ending his dad's life.

I felt a need to write a poem about Donnie Roy. I felt my creative juices flowing. I knew I needed to get out of bed and write. An hour or so later I had finished this poem.

'DONNIE ROY'

Donnie Roy was a boy I knew quite well.
Donnie lived on the outskirts of hell.
Nobody would have believed it in our little town,
but bad things happened when nobody was around.
He became a clown just to hide his fears.
He cried out, but nobody would hear.
They caught his laughter, but they missed his tears.
Now Donnie Roy was a boy who was always confused
because no matter what road he chose, he was going to lose,
because Donnie was playing by another's rules.
He thought he could handle it, but there were too many scars,
and in the middle of the night a shot was fired.
Who could have done it? Nobody had a clue.
But I think Donnie might have changed the rules.
Oh, he cried out, but nobody would hear,
they caught his laughter, but they missed his tears.
Now Donnie Roy was a boy who became a man,
that family and friends wouldn't understand.
He would be judged, but they would be wrong,
for they had never gone where Donnie Roy had gone.
He cried out but nobody would hear,
they caught his laughter, but they missed his tears.

CHAPTER 38

'I have tried to hold my true feelings for you in check.
I never knew I could love someone the way I love you.'

Saturday morning found Orville knocking on the Mex house
door demanding Donnie get dressed and help him drive the
cattle from the pasture to the barn lot. He was going to round
up the three cows he would be taking to the sale barn early
Monday morning.

I no more than got dressed when I saw Katie coming toward the
Mex house. I sat back down and waited till she came in. She
looked as though she hadn't slept two hours all night. She sat down
on the bed across from the old chair I sat on. I felt the hurt in her
soul. I saw the pain in her eyes. She didn't make small talk. She
looked into my eyes, and with tears in hers, she began to speak.

"I can't. I just simply can't. I've fought this decision all night.
During these last few days, I've tried to hold my true feelings for
you in check. I knew it was best," she said. "I never knew I could
love someone the way I love you. But I just can't take a chance on
leaving these sweet, precious kids with their abusive daddy and me
not being here to help buffer some of that abuse. I know there will
be times when somebody will need to be here to pick up the pieces
of their shattered lives and comfort them with the love they need."

Katie stared at me with eyes that begged me to understand. I
studied Katie's face while she wiped away tears, and her words
were more than this tough Marine could handle. I again had a
mysterious warm thing running down my cheek. We both rose to
our feet and stepped toward each other. She laid her head on my

shoulder, her sniffles quickly changing into tears, desperately trying to sob away her grief. I was speechless, words wouldn't come, but she didn't need words. She needed an escape from this monster. But there wasn't an escape route. There wasn't a big white horse, there wasn't a knight in shining armor. Reality was hard to handle.

We could clearly hear Orville and Donnie herding the cattle into the barn lot. Katie quickly rushed to the back porch of the Mex house and washed her face in the old wash basin. She worked frantically to dry her eyes. I became sick to my stomach while I watched Katie walk back to the house. My heart felt her sadness. Her dreams had faded away.

I called out to Orville, "Do you need any help?"

"No," Orville loudly replied. "You'll only make the cows nervous."

I quickly walked back into the Mex house. I sat in the old recliner and thought about Katie.

Surely there was something someone could do. I felt helpless, I could not conjure up a solution. All I knew was a person should not be forced to have to live their life the way Katie and these kids had to live theirs.

"God where are you?"

Orville's yelling, screaming, and cursing at Donnie was more than I could handle. I had to make my final decision. I had to get away from this farm and Orville Hopkins. I decided to be off of this cotton farm and away from this poor excuse of a man by noon tomorrow.

Orville and Donnie soon had the three cows that Orville was going to sell cut away from the rest of the herd. Orville gave me instructions on the amount of feed to give them tonight and tomorrow morning.

Orville said, "We're going to help you with the morning chores before we eat breakfast." We all three jumped in and all the chores were done within a few minutes.

While we finished breakfast, I asked Orville and Katie if I could speak to them down at the Mex house, just the three of us. They both seemed puzzled but agreed. Katie told the three kids to start getting ready for their trip. I didn't waste any time revealing my reason to talk to them alone.

I began, "Last night's rain has made the fields too wet to plow today. I was hoping I could have your permission to build Bo a doghouse and an enclosed pen at the back of your house."

I told them I would pay for all the necessary materials. They seemed surprised, but after I explained my full plan as to how I would like to build a covered pen attached to the rear of the house with Bo's box up against. and level with Donnie's window, they agreed.

Orville actually spoke first and said, "I think that would be great."

I asked to take the farm truck and go into Malden this morning and purchase the rest of the materials I would need. Orville gave me permission then added, "I have some leftover woven wire from a roll over in the pig barn. Could you use that?"

"Yes," I replied. "I've seen that wire over there. I can attach one on top of the other and it will be tall enough." I went on, "I want it to be a surprise for Donnie when you guys return tomorrow afternoon."

Katie looked at me with that beautiful smile and said, "I think that is just super."

When Orville and Katie turned and walked away, a sickening feeling attacked the pit of my stomach. I knew within a few minutes they would get in their family car, drive out of the driveway, and head to Bellville, Illinois for the wedding. Little did they know, I would be long gone from this farm when they returned Sunday afternoon. A part of me felt sheepish, like a coward. I also knew it would be extremely hard on Donnie and Katie to say goodbye. I keep reminding myself this was for the best.

Donnie and Mary Beth were sitting on the front porch when I made my way across the yard. I purposely didn't go up on the porch, knowing I might get emotional talking to Donnie. I knew what was in store for him in the next few weeks, working everyday side by side with his abusive father. Alice walked out followed by Katie Jean. Orville had gone out through the back porch door and drove the car to the front of the house. Katie looked gorgeous as usual. We all said goodbye and I told everyone to have a good time. I made an effort to tell Orville not to worry about the chores.

I would take care of everything. I looked at Donnie and said, "I promise, I'll take good care of Mr. Bo."

They waved goodbye while they drove away from the farm. I choked back my emotions. I could have easily fallen apart. I didn't know when, or if, I would see them again. Knowing I had a long day of work ahead of me, I needed to change my focus.

I knew I wanted to get to the lumber yard in Malden as soon as possible. I purchased two pieces of half-inch 4x8 plywood and several 2x4's, and four sheets of corrugated sheet metal. I was ready to drive away from the lumber yard when I remembered I needed a combination lock for Bo's pen.

Orville had a nice workshop with all the tools I would need. I hurried back and built the big box first. It had a wooden floor and a wooden top. The top was the exact height of Donnie's window. Bo would have a nice warm bed inside the box during cold or rainy weather, and could lay at the window near Donnie's bed when the weather was nice. Donnie was going to love it. I built a nice swinging door, with a latch and a bracket to lock it with the combination padlock. The kennel would be eight-feet wide by ten-feet long, with corrugated metal sheets for the roof. I set the post and framed the sides and top. The whole project came together very quickly. The pen was complete, except for the roof.

I stopped construction knowing I needed to give myself time to get the evening chores done. When the chores were completed, I felt the day had been extremely productive. I could easily do the morning chores and finish the roof before noon tomorrow. I took my shower, tended to Bo, and once again thought how blessed we were to have him home.

Donnie at least had his rock back. Sitting in the old recliner with Bo at my side, I told him how proud I was of him and what a good boy he was. At times it seemed as though I was talking to my old friend Johnny Hooper. Bo and I soon laid in our beds and drifted off to sleep.

I was up before daybreak. I backed Ole Limpie up to the Mex house door and loaded her up for my upcoming trip to Decatur. I called Larry yesterday morning and told him not to expect me until he saw me, but I should be at his house late Sunday afternoon. Katie had made some big sweet rolls for me. I planned to be across the river and into Illinois before I would stop to eat a meal.

As soon as it became light enough to see, I began the chores and got everything done, including milking the two cows and gathering all the eggs. Katie's dear friend Bonnie and her husband, Walter, were coming over this morning to get the extra eggs and milk.

The roof on Bo's pen went up exceptionally fast. I placed Bo's water and feed pans in the new kennel. Bo sniffed around and explored every corner of his new motel room. He surprised me when he jumped on top of his new doghouse and looked into Donnie's room. Bo glanced at me, then laid down, as if he understood exactly what I had built it for. I looked at him and chuckled out loud. I fed Bo in his new living quarters and made sure he had plenty of clean drinking water.

Rushing back over to the Mex house, I retrieved my notepad and pen. I wanted to leave a letter for the family to read when they returned. I also wanted Katie to have a letter from me. When Bonnie and Walter came to pick up the eggs and milk, I planned to give the letter to Bonnie to hand to Katie at an appropriate time. I had trouble at first, finding the right words, while I wrote to Katie. Finally, I found myself able to say everything I wanted to convey to her. I knew I could trust Bonnie to keep it a secret.

I double checked everything in the Mex house, making sure I was totally packed and ready to leave. I was preparing to write my farewell note to the family when Bonnie and Walter pulled in the driveway.

The ole wagon was still backed up to the Mex house door. As soon as Bonnie got out of the car, she blared out, "What are you doing?"

I quickly asked her, "When was the last time you talked to Katie?"

"We talked Friday morning. Why are you asking me that, Leon?"

Before I could answer her, she said, "She's still going through with the divorce, isn't she?"

"No," I replied. "She told me this morning she just couldn't take a chance on possibly losing custody of the kids."

Bonnie immediately placed her hand over her mouth, and with a disgusted look let out a loud growl. She dropped her head and said, "No, dear God, no."

Bonnie looked toward my car backed up to the Mex house door.

She looked back at me. "You're not leaving, are you?"

By this time both of them had made their way close to me, and before I could answer her, Walter graciously extended his hand in my direction and said, "Good to see you."

We firmly shook hands. "Good to see you, too."

I looked back at Bonnie and said, "To answer your question, yes, I'll be leaving this farm in a matter of minutes."

Bonnie urgently said, "Please tell me she knows you are leaving."

I'm sure I had a guilty look of shame written on my face. "No, they don't have a clue. Please let me explain why I chose to do it this way." I paused for a moment. "I called my brother in Decatur yesterday morning. He informed me that a good position at the factory where he worked was open and that I would be qualified for it. The job has great possibilities for rapid advancement. The kicker to the whole thing is I need to be ready for an interview tomorrow."

I continued. "That's the number one reason. The number two reason is …" I looked over at Walter… "Walter, I think you can relate to this. As a man, it's impossible to stand back and watch the abuse this man is inflicting on his wife and these kids without interfering." I then added, "I know for a fact, if the right situation arose, and the right time presented itself, I am ready to come unwound."

"It could get very nasty for Katie and the kids to witness a physical altercation with Orville. Katie told me that if a fight occurred, it would only make it harder for her and the kids. That's why I've made a decision to get the heck off the farm today."

Walter spoke up and said, "I've witnessed Orville on a few occasions myself, and Bonnie has shared so many things about his abuse with me, and to tell you the truth, I honestly don't know how you have handled it the way you have for so long."

Bonnie said, "Well, as much as I wanted her divorced and away from Orville, I would say you are right. You leaving now is probably best."

I suggested we go to the house and get the eggs and milk.

When they were ready to leave, I spoke up and said, "Please come with me, I have something I want to show you."

They both followed me, and we made our way to the back of

the house. There was a look of total shock on their faces when they saw Bo's enclosed kennel. "This has been my project for the last couple of days."

Bonnie quickly asked, "Do Katie and Orville know you did this?"

I remarked, "Yes, they both were happy I was going to build it. However, Donnie and the girls don't know. It'll be a surprise for them!"

"Oh, how nice of you!" Bonnie said. She talked about how much Donnie loved that dog.

"You're right about that. Bo is Donnie's rock and his life raft in a sea of unnecessary abuse from his own father."

We walked to the front of the house where their car was parked. I then remembered Katie's note. "I'm leaving the family a farewell note. However, I have written Katie a personal note. I was hoping you could give it to her at an appropriate time, safe from the eyes of Orville."

Bonnie quickly spoke. "Oh, for sure! I would be happy to do that for you!"

I sprinted back to the Mex house and retrieved the note, then quickly returned. I looked straight at Bonnie. "The knowledge of this note needs to not go beyond the four of us, okay?"

Bonnie nodded, then said, "Absolutely! We've been best friends since we were in grade school. I'd never do anything to break that trust and friendship."

I graciously thanked her. I looked at Walter, then back to Bonnie, and said, "You don't know how thankful I am that Katie has a dear friend like you. I hope you understand, just as Bo is Donnie's rock, you are Katie's rock."

I gave Bonnie a big hug and Walter another firm handshake. I thanked them for being there for Katie Jean and the kids. I felt compelled to give Bonnie, Larry's phone number where I could be reached.

Most of what I related to Bonnie and Walter about my conversation with Larry was true. However, part of it was, as Mom would say, 'a little white lie.' I didn't have to be there Monday morning. It was best this way for everyone's sake, especially Katie's.

The note I left for the family said:

To: The Hopkins' Family   Sunday Morning

First off, let me say, I sadly regret that the circumstances since Saturday morning have led me to the conclusion that it's in my best interest that I should leave for Decatur today.

I placed a collect call to my brother, Larry, Saturday morning. The company Larry works for has an opening for a position he felt I would be well qualified to fill. He said the position should offer me a chance to rapidly advance in the company.

He strongly indicated it would be in my best interest to be ready to be interviewed early tomorrow morning. This is an opportunity I must take full advantage of. As much as I would like to have said my farewell in person, I am not going to be able to do that.

I feel so blessed to have had the opportunity to meet each and every one of you. Your gracious hospitality has been awesome. Alice and Mary Beth, what beautiful and wonderful young ladies you are. Donnie, I am amazed at what a grownup young man you are. I know your mom and dad are extremely proud of each of you.

Katie Jean, let me say, Orville should count his blessings every day to have such a life's companion. I promise I am going to miss your wonderful cooking. Orville, thank you for repairing my old station wagon. You truly are a good mechanic. Orville, I would also hope you would realize what a wonderful family God has blessed you with. Please don't take them for granted.

Hopefully our paths will cross again someday. My sincere prayer is that God will look over and bless each of you.

Your Friend,

Leon

P.S Donnie, I hope you like Bo's new pen. The combination to the lock is on a piece of paper lying on the bed in the Mex house. Also, Larry's telephone number is written down at the top of the calendar in the kitchen.

I made one more trip through the Mex house, making sure I had not left anything. Next, I wanted to say goodbye to Bo before I got into Ole Limpie.

While I walked up to Bo's pen, his tail started wagging. I dropped to my knees and patted him on the top of his head. When our eyes met, I had a fuzzy feeling run up my spine. I thought about how Bo had walked into Donnie's life at the exact time Johnny Hooper had committed suicide. It was as if I was staring into my old friend, Johnny's eyes. "Goodbye Bo," I said. "Take care of your bestest, bestest buddy, Donnie." I gave him one last pat on the head and turned and walked to the wagon.

The moment I reached the old bridge, I felt a need to stop and get out of the car. I looked across at the rows of fresh planted crops. I stared up at the homestead. What an unbelievable twenty-five days this had been. I crawled back in the old wagon and the Hopkins' farm was soon out of sight. Somehow, I felt I left a little bit of my heart on that damn old cotton farm. Perhaps more accurately, I left a big piece of my heart with three kids and a wonderful and special woman.

CHAPTER 39

'My philosophy has always been that it's much easier to train a dog that wants to please you, than desperately trying to make him obey you.'

In minutes I drove over the big Mississippi River bridge in Cairo, Illinois, then onto highway fifty-one north, which headed straight into Decatur. I stopped at a little café and consumed a couple of super-sized cheeseburgers. A part of me wanted to throw caution to the wind and push the old wagon hard. My better judgment told me, 'No, keep it easy.' For the last leg of my journey, I had a good back-up plan. Doyle Armstrong, a friend of Larry's, and the owner of the Oldsmobile dealership, loaned Larry a wrecker they use in his business. It was at Larry's house if we needed it.

Larry and Martha skipped church today to be home in case I called to notify them of a possible breakdown with Ole Limpie. Larry asked me to give him updates on the progress of my trip. He suggested I make my last call when I got to Pana, Illinois, which was about thirty miles or so from Decatur.

Even though it was Sunday, there were several tractors working in the fields. Cotton did not grow in this part of Illinois; however, corn and soybeans were abundant. There were acres and acres of freshly planted fields on both sides of the highway.

I noticed up ahead, on my right, there was a small lake. That's when I noticed a young man out with a beautiful chocolate lab. It was obvious he was putting the lab through a training session, throwing rubber retriever bumpers into the water. I thought of

Johnny Hooper. Johnny would talk about dogs for hours on end. One day I mentioned I heard more than one person refer to him as 'the dog whisperer.'

Johnny said, "I'm not a dog whisperer at all. I am a dog listener. When you slow down and give a dog a chance to bond and love you, they begin to speak to you. Not vocalizing of course, but rather speaking through their mannerisms and body language. The way they wag their tail, the way they look you in the eye, and their demeanor can all speak volumes. It is then you realize the trust and bond between the two of you has been enhanced and solidified."

"It is then, and only then, that the serious training should begin." Johnny said, "My philosophy has always been that it's much easier to train a dog that wants to please you than desperately trying to make him obey you. If you listen, he will tell you when he is comprehending, and likewise, he will tell you when he is confused. To be a successful dog trainer, you have to have the ability to let the dog speak, and then have the patience to listen. A dog is no different than we are. We all love compliments and so do dogs. It has always worked for me to hand out lots of praise."

Johnny continued. "It's a natural thing for puppies in a litter to establish a pecking order. What is amazing, once that order is established, they are just fine with their place. It's up to the trainer to be the alpha. This can be done without harsh treatment. Just be firm and show them love and respect, and they will accept your role as the boss. It is too bad God didn't give us humans some of the traits he gave to dogs."

Johnny rambled on and unveiled one positive characteristic after another about dogs and his feelings toward them. Later that night I wrote this poem, I titled it,

'OLE DOGS'

"I've had sunshine friends to drop me on a partly cloudy
    Day.
Had next of kin to turn and walk away.
But any ole dog I've ever had, stood steadfast beside me,
    Even when times were bad.
They will listen to your troubles never causing a fuss.,

The one thing in my life I could always trust.
Each time they come to greet you, it's always the same.
Walk a thousand miles beside you in a down-pouring rain.
If I should be so lucky that Heaven's my final home,
"I just pray the good Lord will let my Ole Dogs come along"

I also wrote Johnny's philosophy about training dogs in this creed.

OLD FRIEND— "MY OATH TO YOU"

"Just as I am positive you cannot read these words written on paper, I am just as sure you can read me like a well-educated scholar, my moods, mannerisms, likes and dislikes.

As we begin this journey together, here are a few rules, regulations and promises.

I will always be the boss. "No Exceptions." However, I will never control you to the point of breaking your spirit or that you don't enjoy being in my presence.

As I am not perfect, I will never expect perfection from you. I will demand respect, and in turn will always show you respect.

The ears and eyes of God or my nearest neighbor will never hear or see me abuse you. Your health, comfort and well-being are of the utmost importance to me. I will never knowingly put you in the hands of someone who does not hold these same concerns for you.

So 'Ole Friend' let the journey begin. Hold your head high, wag your tail often, let your inherited instinct and obtained knowledge soar like a high- flying eagle."

I gave both of them to him the next day. Johnny admired the poems so much he posted them on the walls of his kennel.

It was a little after five in the afternoon, and the next town was Pana. So far, so good, the old wagon ran like she was new. I very easily located a phone booth and made the call to Larry. I could tell by his voice he was anxious and pleased I would soon be in Decatur.

I had been to Larry's house before, but it has been a few years.

Larry said he and Danny would be on the highway at the edge of town and escort me to his house. They had a father and son relationship that I always admired. But I admit, for the last couple of years, there has been more jealousy and envy than admiration.

I saw a sign that read, Decatur 10 miles. I patted Ole Limpie's dashboard and said, "Don't fail me now ole gal, we are almost at the finish line." I was soon looking at what I had been hoping to see from the time I climbed out of bed this morning. A sign that read: Decatur, Illinois, Population 66,269. The sign was on the right side of the road, and so was Larry and Danny.

When I turned my right turn signal on, Larry and Danny hurried and got into their car. In just a few minutes we pulled into Larry's driveway. Larry's home was a fairly new ranch-style house that sat on fifteen acres. Everything was what you would expect from Larry and Martha, neat as a pin.

Larry and Danny waited 'til I parked Ole Limpie. Larry briskly walked toward me. We grabbed each other's hand, but the handshake was short-lived. We quickly gave each other a long-lasting hug. His voice broke when we looked at each other and he said, "So good to see you man!"

"It's good to see you too, big brother."

Martha and Joanne stepped out of the house. Martha and I hugged. I commented to both the kids on how much they had grown. We all visited briefly, then Martha announced that supper was on the table.

Shortly after supper, I mentioned to Larry that I would like to look at his new car. It was absolutely beautiful. I asked Larry, "Do you think your friend who owns the Oldsmobile dealership could possibly give me a good deal on one like yours?"

"Well," Larry said, "tomorrow after I get off work, we're going to meet my friend, Doyle Armstrong, at the dealership. He has a car he thinks you will love."

I smiled, "Have you seen it?"

Larry laughed. "Oh yes, and I think you'll love it." Larry continued. "However, I'm not going to say another word until tomorrow." He chuckled. "I will say, I think you'll like it better than Dad's old Ford wagon!"

Larry, Martha, and I talked well past their normal bed time. Martha insisted I sleep in Danny's room. I put my foot down and said, "Absolutely not." They had a hide-a-bed in their enclosed sunroom that would be perfect for me.

Larry had me up early and suggested I wear a white shirt with dark slacks. Luckily, I had both in my wardrobe.

CHAPTER 40

'She started to become more and more like the Brenda I knew. Her pleasant voice and those sweet little giggles warmed my heart.'

Larry had a nice office. It was apparent that all of his co-workers respected him. I spent most of my day filling out papers and trailing after him. I would be officially on the payroll beginning Wednesday and would train with Elbert Bratton for thirty days before I became an assembly line supervisor. I would have approximately fifteen to twenty men under my supervision. Larry said my two years of college and military background helped tremendously in me stepping into this role with the company. I'm sure Larry, and also Martha's uncle, had a great influence on personnel's decision to immediately place me in this position also.

Larry got off work at five o'clock in the afternoon, and I was very anxious to go to the car dealership. Larry introduced me to his friend, Doyle Armstrong. All three of us walked behind the dealership building. Doyle and Larry both had a big smile on their faces when Doyle looked at me and pointed to the most beautiful car, I had ever laid my eyes on. It was a 1959 Oldsmobile Super 88, Holiday Coupe, with rear fender skirts, and an eight-cylinder 394 engine. It was light blue, with tons of chrome trim and shining from chrome bumper to chrome bumper. My mouth must have dropped halfway to my waist.

"Well, what do you think?" Doyle asked.

"Oh my gosh," I said. "I love it, but I am afraid that is more car than I can afford."

Doyle shook his head. "Not so fast. My wife, Vera, has been driving it for the last seven months and put 5,100 miles on it. My dear friend, and your brother, has told me what a rough time you have had dealing with the loss of your wife and son. I want to offer it to you below wholesale."

I know I looked totally stunned.

"You'd be a fool not to buy this car for $1,700." He looked at me then toward the car. "The keys are in the ignition. Take it for a drive and park it in front of the building when you return."

I scooted onto the seat and under the steering wheel. I took a few seconds to just admire it. Larry and Doyle both smiled from ear to ear when I drove onto the highway. Oh my, I thought, it is way more than I had hoped for. I could not believe my luck. It drove like a dream, especially compared to the bumpy ride of Ole Limpie. It felt like I was floating on a cloud. I drove a few blocks and then returned.

Larry and Doyle hadn't lost their smiles, and I promise, they would take second place to the one I had on my face.

Doyle asked, "Well, what do you think?"

I looked him straight in his eyes, walked toward him, and stuck out my hand. "Mr. Armstrong, you just sold a car."

Doyle chuckled. "Guys, it's past closing time. Drive it home, you can stop in tomorrow and we will get all the paperwork done."

I thanked him, shook his hand, and just like that, I drove away in my new car.

I barely shut off the ignition at Larry's when Martha and the kids quickly ran out of the house and began to admire it. Larry stepped back and watched me glow with pride while I showed everyone one special gadget after another. I walked up to Larry, stuck out my hand, and he quickly grabbed it. "Thank you so much, big brother."

Larry smiled. "You're so very welcome. Trust me, I don't know of anybody who deserves that car more than you."

Shortly after we finished supper, they informed me they would be leaving on vacation early Friday morning. They asked if I would be okay with house sitting and taking care of the two dogs, the cat, and Danny's two 4-H calves.

I said, "Sure, absolutely."

They informed me they were going with Doyle and Vera.

Martha said, "They have two kids, a boy and a girl. They are the same age as Danny and Joanne and have all been best friends for a long time."

"How nice is that?"

"The eight of us are going to tour the Smoky Mountains," Martha said. "Then we'll go to Myrtle Beach in South Carolina. We'll be gone for ten days."

~ ~ ~ ~

I took off work at noon Tuesday and drove over to the car dealership. In less than an hour I had paid for my new car and was headed to the DMV to purchase my new license plates.

Thursday afternoon Larry, Martha and the kids needed to get their final packing done for their long trip. I felt the best thing for me to do was get completely out of their way. I also wanted to get my new car out on the highway. I drove about fifteen miles out of town. I felt like a kid at Christmas. I just couldn't believe this car was mine.

Everyone was up Friday morning bright and early. We were soon saying our goodbyes. I assured them not to worry about things in Decatur. The workday, if you could call it work, went very well and extremely fast. Martha, thoughtfully, left me supper in the fridge. I got Danny's 4-H calves fed, then fed Snowball, the kids' big white cat. I took a little time and played with Duke and Sadie, their two black labs.

It was great to be able to relax in a nice, big, roomy, clean house. The Hopkins didn't have a TV, so I truly enjoyed sitting in Larry's large recliner and watching TV while I ate popcorn and worked on my sixteen-ounce Pepsi. I had trouble going to sleep, just like the last several nights. I keep wondering what things were like at the Hopkins' farm. As much as I wanted to hope everything was okay, a part of me knew, all too well, that the whole bunch were catching pure hell from Orville.

I got up Saturday morning with one thing on my mind. A sweet lady in Lamar, Missouri. I had promised Brenda, I would call her when I got to Decatur. I was going to have a lot of explaining to do to convince her I had basically just arrived. I knew today was the day that a call needed to be made. I know the call, of course, will be long distance and cost a few bucks, so I'll tell Martha to let me know the amount when she gets the phone bill.

Brenda didn't have a phone. She said she didn't need the cost of a phone when she could use her folks for necessary calls, or Mary's phone at the café. I took out Mary's Café's phone number from my wallet. I was very anxious to hear Brenda's voice. I thought 'please dear Lord, let her be at work.' *Ring, ring.* I recognized Mary's voice when she answered the phone.

"Hey, Mary, I don't know if you will remember me are not. My name is Leon Wilson, the guy from Kansas who drove the old beat-up station wagon."

"Oh my, yes, I certainly do remember you," she said.

I quickly asked, "How are things going?"

"Good, how about you?" she said.

I replied, "Okay."

Mary knew the reason for my call was to talk to Brenda. She said, "Brenda is waiting on a table, but I will relieve her and let her take your call in my office."

"That's great, thank you so much," I said. In just a few seconds, I heard Brenda say, "Hello."

I said, "Hey beautiful, how are you?"

"I'm just fine," she replied.

Brenda seemed somewhat apprehensive. I feared she might have thought my feelings for her weren't as strong as they are. I knew I desperately needed to explain my reason for not getting in touch with her before now. She patiently listened while I told her about my car trouble, and how I felt the need to help the Hopkins family get their crops planted. I secretly prayed she would accept my apology for not reaching out to her sooner. In time her whole demeanor began to change. She started to become more and more like the Brenda I knew. Her pleasant voice and that sweet giggle warmed my heart.

We talked way longer than I intended. I knew I needed to let her get back to work, but she wanted to visit and asked Mary to cover for her. I promised I would call her in a few days. I could have spent the whole day talking.

CHAPTER 41

'So consumed in their self-centered song, their foolish pride will not let them admit wrong.'

I was up early enough Sunday morning to see a beautiful sunrise. The forecast was for a very nice, sunny day. I thought I would take a short road trip. It was hard for me to stay out of my car.

An hour or so after lunch, I was thirty to thirty-five miles north of Decatur. I drove past a well-kept cemetery when my eyes caught a freshly dug grave with a canopy set up for a burial. I probably didn't drive three miles when I saw an oncoming funeral procession. I pulled over to the shoulder of the road, stopped, and saw the sad eyes of the people in the car behind the hearse. It brought back memories of the day we buried Johnny Hooper.

I so vividly remember the conversation I had with Johnny only a few weeks before he took his life. He confided in me that he came very close, more than once, to doing the unthinkable. Looking back, I feel guilty for not being able to see the signs that Johnny no doubt expressed. I remember he said, "Leon, people don't understand PTSD and they don't want to understand someone who suffers from it. It is like 'out of sight, out of mind.'"

Johnny continued. "So many times, I feel as though I don't have a friend in the world. Sometimes I think it would be best for everyone if I would just exit this world."

"Me and Margaret aren't going to church," he said. "When I do pass away, I know my family is going to need someone to preach at my funeral. I don't want to put any more stress on them than necessary."

I felt the sad emotion in Johnny's voice while he continued telling me his story. "I have a cousin who is an Ordained Minister. I decided one night to call him and ask if he would officiate my funeral. I was not only shocked, but also hurt, when he said that he would not do it. He's not preaching any funerals now." Johnny shook his head. "I just sank lower. My gosh, I'm not worthy enough to get a family member to preach at my funeral."

Johnny hesitated for a few seconds, then continued. "I was raised on a farm. My mom would often have little baby chickens in a box with a towel over the box to keep them warm. When I was a little boy, I loved to raise the towel and peek in on those cute little baby chickens. One day when I raised the towel, I noticed one little chicken was off by itself. You could tell he was very weak, and several of the other baby chicks were just pecking him, one peck after another. I watched in total disbelief." Johnny said, "I hurried to my mother and explained what was going on. She told me that was just a natural thing. That it is nature's way of eliminating the weak."

He went on, "So many times in my life dealing with PTSD, I felt like that little chicken. Family and friends just pecking, one peck after another."

The day I got the news about Johnny's passing, I thought about that little chicken. I wondered if his death was just a natural thing. Was that God's way to eliminate the weak? Was God disappointed in those who failed Johnny? Those too consumed in their own lives to show him the real love and understanding he so desperately needed?

A few days after his funeral, I wrote this about Johnny's life.

"NO STRANGER TO THE PAIN"

Oh, little boy, oh little boy, what a price you paid.
But I ask oh Lord why must he still pay today?

He tried with all his might
Just to get it right,

But in his daddy's eyes he was always wrong.
He was the banker who refused his loan,

And who he was is the reason for who he became.
With each lash he cried out in grimacing pain.
He was the amount, too much or too little, he was the rain.

He became a man so misunderstood.
Some just didn't get it, though he felt they should.

So consumed in their self-centered song,
their foolish pride won't let them admit wrong.

Quick to judge they have done that all along,
but they have never been where little boy has gone.

With each deviant act, guilt flooded his soul.
He was the hired hand he could not control.

And who he was is the reason for who he became.
He is no stranger to the pain.

A promise was made to his closest blood kin.
You will never visit the cold dungeons where I have been.

Family and friends will have his back. Well, that's a joke.
They will drop him in a heartbeat if he rocks their boat.

It rips his heart, this silent ghost,
for this is the pain that hurts the most.

He was blessed in his twisted life.
God granted him this caring wife.

At times when his world seems so wrong,
there was always an ole' dog tagging along.

Was it by chance, or power from above?
Were these ole' dogs vessels delivering God's desperately
needed love?

So, laugh, little boy, laugh. That is what you have done all
along.
But now the laughter is also gone.

Only sunshine in Heaven, there won't be any rain,
and for the first time in years, he will feel no pain.

Perhaps he will return as an ole' dog, sent from above,
to walk beside some little boy, and deliver God's desperately
needed love.

While I returned to Decatur, I realized I had lost my bearings to where I was. I knew I needed to go south, southeast. It was obvious I had taken the wrong road to Larry's house. Then I recognized a landmark and knew I needed to take the next right. Just before I made my way out to the paved road that led to Larry's house, my eyes suddenly focused on a sign in the yard of a well-kept dwelling. The sign read in big large letters, *"Furnished Apartment for Rent Inquire at house"* and had a telephone number listed as well. I had already passed the house, and there was a car behind me.

My first thought was just drive on, then a little voice told me to circle the block and go back, and that is what I did. Although I didn't have any paper, I had a pen and planned to write the number on the palm of my hand. When I started to write the number, this somewhat heavy-set lady came from the side of the house and stared in my direction.

Since I was parked in her drive, I felt the right thing to do was to be kind enough to at least talk to her. I quickly got out of my car and walked in her direction. When I was in good ear range, I said, "Good afternoon, ma'am. How are you today?"

With a big warm smile she said, "I'm good, thank you. How are you, sir?"

I said, "I don't know how anybody could be anything but good on such a beautiful day as this."

Before I could ask about the apartment, she spoke up and said, "Are you interested in the apartment we have for rent?"

"Well, yes Ma'am. I might very well be." I knew I was going to need to get my own place as soon as Larry and Martha returned from their vacation.

Her home was rather large. I hoped perhaps she had turned two, maybe three rooms of her home into an apartment. This could be exactly what I was hoping for, somewhat out of town and very close to Larry. She pointed to a building I had not noticed.

She said, "The apartment is over there, would you care to look at it?"

"Sure," I replied.

We began to walk toward the small building, and she explained the reason why she had converted the building into an apartment.

She said, "This building was my husband's shop. He had a stroke a couple year's back. He is over at the house in a wheelchair. His right side is completely paralyzed, and he can't talk or walk. He always had a passion to build wood projects of all kinds. He'd spend hours in his workshop."

She kept giving me the full details of her reason for the apartment. "Otis, that is his name, retired after thirty years working for the Firestone Tire Co. Well, at least he got to enjoy a couple of retirement years before his stroke."

"We have two daughters, one lives in Rockford, the younger one lives in St. Louis, Missouri. A few months ago, the girls and their husbands came home, sold all his tools and lumber, and decided his shed would make a very nice apartment. They also knew me and Otis could use some extra income to supplement our Social Security."

We both stood outside the apartment door. She meticulously explained the situation. She said they fixed it up really nice. They insulated it and put up, new paneling and laid new linoleum. Just when I was sure the details of the apartment had reached its pinnacle, she continued telling me about the new bath and shower and the brand-new air conditioner. I took a deep breath and prepared myself for what I was sure would be another several minutes of apartment explanations-101. She stopped, looked at me, and started toward the door. "Wanna take a look at it?"

I had to work at not laughing out loud. Instead, I politely said, "Sure, I most certainly would."

We both stepped inside the apartment. She quickly placed her hand over her mouth and let out a large gasp. "Oh my!" she blared out. "I best get to the house and check on Otis, I left him on the commode, he had to poop. Look it over, I'll be back," she blared out while she rushed to the house.

I was amazed at how perfect the apartment was for me. The lean-to storage shed made a perfect carport, with a door directly into the small, but very adequate kitchen. There was a nice sitting area, a reasonable size closet in the bedroom, and a bathroom with a very nice shower and vanity.

All the furniture was second hand, but in like-new condition. There was a private drive from the street directly in front of the building. The building was a considerable distance from the main house. The large garage door opening had been completely closed in with a nice large window. I stood at the kitchen sink and looked through the window that viewed the house. I saw the sweet, bubbling Miss Landlord Lady walking toward me. I took another quick look around the apartment. Perfect, just absolutely perfect, I thought. Now I hoped the rent would be reasonable. The moment she opened the door, her mouth went back into full throttle, as though she had never left.

"Did you notice the large closet in the bedroom?" she quickly asked.

"Yes, ma'am, I sure did, it's very nice."

I realized while Miss Bubbly and I walked across the yard, we never introduced ourselves. I quickly spoke up, desperately hoping I could get a word in edgewise. "By the way, my name is Leon."

"Nice to meet you, Leon, my name is Ruth Ann, but you can just call me Ruthie, and you already know my husband's name is Otis." And without hesitation said, "We both have the very same last name, Martin."

I wasn't sure if she had a quick wit sense of humor, or whether she was a bit dingy. I just knew I liked her a lot, and I loved the apartment.

I asked, "How much does the apartment rent for, Miss Ruthie?"

"Well, that could be negotiable."

I was somewhat stunned.

"Straight out it would be $60.00 a month, and that includes the utilities. However, if you would be willing to help us around the place and mow the yard, we could drop the rent to $50.00 a month."

"Miss Ruthie, I would be happy to help you around the place and mow the lawn." Before I could continue, she spoke up and said, "I might want you to do some errands for me, like pick-up something at the market?"

I just smiled. "I think I am your guy, Miss Ruthie."

I knew I couldn't move in until Larry and his family returned from vacation. However, I also knew I didn't want to take a chance and not secure the perfect apartment for me. I explained to Ruthie my situation with my commitment to Larry.

I said, "However, if you can give me a receipt, I'll just pay my first month's rent today."

Miss Ruthie wrote me a receipt, retrieved the door key to the apartment and handed both to me. Immediately, and without hesitation, she said, "Our kids just mowed the lawn, but it will need to be mowed before you move in."

It was all I could do to keep from laughing. "I promise I'll get your lawn mowed whenever you wish."

While I was getting into my car, she briskly walked toward me, all the time pointing to the '*For Rent*' sign in the yard. "Could ya help me take down this sign?" she asked.

"You bet," I replied.

She smiled, "The kids put that sign up just before they left this morning, 'bout two hours ago."

I smiled back at her. "Well, I'm sure glad I drove down this street."

She gave me a big wave and said, "I'm glad you drove down this street, too."

CHAPTER 42

*'I recall that big ole southern moon, delta cotton, forbidden love,
both were in Full Bloom.'*

The following week flew by. It was already Friday afternoon. I was going to receive my first paycheck today. I almost felt guilty, it didn't seem like work at all. I liked all the guys on the assembly line and Elbert was just a super guy.

It had been very difficult this afternoon to keep my mind off Donnie. I felt so cowardly, knowing I didn't, and couldn't help him anymore. I keep recalling so many stories Johnny Hooper shared with me about things that happened when he was Donnie's age.

I get cold chills up my spine when I recall the time Johnny said he almost took his own life. He said his dad had been mad at the world for days. This particular day, he said his dad whooped him for something he did early in the morning. Later that afternoon, they were working on a piece of equipment. His dad told him to go to the tool shed and bring back a wrench and a large shop hammer.

Johnny said he got the hammer but forgot the wrench. His dad slapped him across his face and knocked him to the ground. When he got to his feet, his dad kicked him. The blow from his dad's large boot centered on his tailbone. I saw the pain on Johnny's face as he relived that day. He said, "Leon, for days when I sat down, I would have to sit on the side of my bottom. The pain was unbearable."

I was stunned as Johnny continued. He said later that evening he was instructed to go to the backside of their farm and drive some cows to the barn. Their farm actually boarded a seldom used country road. The abuse from that day and actually, the last several days, was just too much. He crawled over the fence and started to walk down the desolate old road. He had to get away from it all. He walked for several minutes and clearly remembered walking past a house, perhaps two. Then it hit him. He did not know where he was going, or what he was doing. He didn't have a penny, didn't have any food, and didn't have anybody to go to. He simply wanted away from that man and life as he knew it to be.

He quickly turned and ran back to the farm to drive the cows to the barn. Later that night, past midnight, he slipped out of bed, retrieved his dad's shotgun and walked out past the barn to a large patch of woods. He loaded the gun, positioned the stock to the base of a tree, and stuck the end of the barrel under his chin. Johnny continued. "The kid in me came out, I remember being more concerned about how bad it would hurt than the reality of ending my life. I just wanted to escape the hurtful and emotional pain from the abuse."

"I honestly don't know if it was an act of the divine, or my willing instinct to live, or perhaps I just didn't have the guts to pull the trigger. I sat there and became physically ill to the point I literally laid the gun down and puked. I eventually made my way back to the house and never shared this with anyone except you, Leon."

When I look back and recall all the things Johnny shared with me, I realize he wasn't able to escape the pain and anguish, even as he became an adult. He lived with those demons until he ended his own life. I thought how could so many have ignored his screams? How could they have been so consumed in their own lives they refused to hear his cries? How much louder did Johnny need to scream?

I have prayed so many times these last few days that Donnie will not go down that path. The reality is, I most certainly could see why he just might. "Please. Please, Lord, No! I beg of you."

I stopped at a little café close to Larry's house and took advantage of their Friday night special. As soon as I got home, I started working on a song I was writing. It was about Katie and our affair.

So many times, in my life, I will get an inspiration for a song or poem, from just one word or a short phrase. I vividly remember a

Sunday morning at the Hopkins' Church. The pastor had dismissed church, and everyone was visiting. I overheard a church member, who was also a cotton farmer, showing great enthusiasm while he told his listening audience he had secretly planted an extremely early plot of cotton at the back of his farm. He said he was lucky, and had missed the killing frost. You could tell most of his listeners had doubts when he proudly said, "I will have cotton in *'full bloom'* by the middle of June." At that exact moment Katie Jean walked past me, and I got a whiff of her sweet perfume. I immediately thought how our forbidden love was also very much in *'full bloom.'* I finished the last verse to my song and added a tag to it. This is the final version.

IN FULL BLOOM

Verse
"One summer I worked for a cotton farmer two shades shy downright mean. Never a kind word for his kids or his wife Katie Jean. Now I was hungry for a little affection, Katie was in need of a friend. Where we wound-up from where we started, was never in my plan."

Chorus
"Oh, I recall those hot summer nights and that big O' southern moon, Delta cotton, forbidden love both were 'in full bloom.' I have had a lady or two touch my heart, a few fulfill my needs, but I was never loved, like I was loved, by sweet Katie Jean."

Verse
"I can still smell her perfume, taste that first kiss. Remember how clumsy fingers unbuttoned that faded denim dress. Feel the heat of the passion that burned away the guilt. Setting a fire in my heart that is still blazing yet."

Chorus
"Oh, I recall those hot summer nights and that big O' southern moon, Delta cotton, forbidden love both were 'in full bloom.' I

have had a lady or two touch my heart, a few fulfill my needs, but I was never loved, like I was loved, by sweet Katie Jean."

Verse

"What she said to me early one morning didn't take me by surprise. I could feel the hurt in her soul, I could see the pain in her eyes. She said, I didn't know I could love someone like I love you, but there is more than us to think about, these kids need me too.

I drove out of that dusty driveway, leaving three kids and Katie Jean, and wondered why God in Heaven seems to have forgotten about sweet Katie Jean. She had a smile that could tame the Devil. An Angel without wings, and there will always be a special place in my heart for Sweet Katie Jean."

I was up early Saturday morning and wanted to take some things over to my new apartment. I unloaded my clothes and some other personal belongings that were still in Ole Limpie. I mowed the lawn and checked in with Miss Ruthie. She was thrilled and insisted I meet Otis. He couldn't talk, but he seemed so pleased that I had rented the apartment. He would just grunt and smile. What a shame I thought.

Larry called early Sunday morning to let me know they should be home around two pm that afternoon. At two-fifteen, Larry's big Olds pulled into the driveway. They all appeared very comical, having the look of a typical family returning from vacation. All four seemed exhausted, and a person might think they were going through a metamorphosis. The skin on their bodies was peeling from over exposure to direct sunlight. Despite the sunburns, it was apparent everyone had a wonderful time, each competing with the other for air time while they told me their favorite events of the trip. I patiently, and happily, listened to every detail of their adventure.

Eventually, I told them about my apartment. I felt it was best for everyone if I spent the night in my new pad. Getting prepared for my Monday workday in my new apartment gave me a measurable amount of contentment.

It was Tuesday, June 17th, Randy's Birthday. It would be a

tough one, it always was. I planned to spend today the same way I had done each year since his death. Just me alone, reminiscing of a better place and time.

The moment I was off work, I went by the bakery and purchased Randy a cake. I got to my apartment and removed Randy's photos from my photo album. I laid them all on the kitchen table, then went head tripping through 'Memory Ville.' Some memories danced across my heart, others crawled out of my eyes and ran down my face.

I lit the candles and let them burn for a while. Then I attempted to blow them out, but one candle refused. I backed up and simply let it slowly burn. The reflection of the warm glow of that one single candle, burning and flickering across the glossy prints of Randy's photos, was as though his spirit was in the room with me. The candle eventually burned out. I looked at Randy's cake and his photos and softly said, "Happy Birthday, buddy. Daddy loves and misses you so much."

CHAPTER 43

'The face of a child abuser is often not the face you might think or expect.'

Time flew by, days turned into weeks. Eventually it was Saturday, July 4th, Independence Day. Larry and Martha invited me to go to Martha's parent's house. Her family had a big cookout, made homemade ice cream, and shot off fireworks. Friends and family were all gathered and sitting in their big backyard after consuming all we could eat of the wonderful cookout food.

I drove my new car so I could leave if the situation warranted. The conversation led to Larry and me commenting on how conservative our dad was. He no doubt would turn over in his grave if he knew what I paid for that car. Martha spoke up and told of a comment she heard our mom make back when she and Dad were in good health. She said, "Your Mom actually told me, 'George Wilson is so tight with his money, if Jesus was selling tickets to heaven, and he had a terminal illness, he would tell me to wait a few months and see if he would possibly put them on sale'!" There was no question, Martha's story got the biggest laugh of the day.

Soon July was behind us. The hot days of summer repeated themselves, one scorcher after another. However, the much anticipated, cool front the weather man forecasted, finally arrived. Not any too soon, most would agree. Even though it was late August, there was a distinctive hint of fall in the air. I leaned back on one of the old chairs sitting on the concrete slab at the back of my apartment, and gazed at the starlit night. Curtains would soon fall on the chirping cricket choir that serenaded me. Summer was basically over. Most certainly, it had been a summer like no other I have ever experienced in my life.

I couldn't ask for a better job. The pay at Caterpillar was great, and the benefits were second to no other company. However, there was this constant pull at my heartstrings. I kept thinking of Johnny Hooper and, of course, Donnie Hopkins. I also knew there were so many others suffering from PTSD. Others that I very well could help. It kills me thinking of those kids that fall through the cracks in our society. It is especially disturbing when their abuser gets away with it, too easily, and way too often.

I distinctly remember Mr. Scott Morrison, my professor, who taught the class on childhood development. He more than once reminded us that the face of a child abuser isn't the face you might think, or expect.

I sometimes attended church with Larry and Martha. While I listened to the hymns, my mind would drift to the little church in Malden, and I would begin thinking about Donnie, Katie, and the girls.

Martha was determined I was going to date this lady who attended their church. Her name was Joyce, her husband was killed about a year ago in Korea. She was very attractive, intelligent, and didn't have any children. We went out a few times. She was everything a man could have asked for. There was no doubt, she was soon beginning to see me and her and a house with a white picket fence. But my heart wasn't in it. There is an old saying. *'You can lead a horse to water, but you can't make him drink. Well, you can also lead a heart to love, but you can't make it fall.'*

I was over at Larry's house after work one afternoon, and the kids were with some of their friends. The conversation between the three of us led off in the direction of Dad. We all three talked about what a wonderful, honest, hard-working man he was. Larry made some remarks about how he often wondered about Dad's soul. I suggested we go over to my apartment. "I might just be able to put that concern to bed for you."

He looked puzzled but agreed to go to my place.

We all three sat in the living area. I went into my bedroom and returned with a big box of poems, old letters, and a zillion lyrics to songs. After flipping through several papers, I finally found the writing I was searching for. I had discovered it in Mom's personal belongings a few months back. I laid it aside and began to tell them the story.

I began, "I too had wondered if Dad was in heaven. When Mom was in the hospital, just a couple of days before she passed, I sat by her bed and held her hand. I think you guys were probably in route to Wellington. She closed her eyes and softly spoke."

"She said, 'I am ready to go to heaven, son.' I felt her lightly squeeze my hand. She told me she knew it had been tough for me since my loss of Karen and Randy. Then she said, 'I know your heart, and I know someday you will once again follow the light'."

I looked at Larry. "Then she said this, 'I prayed and prayed for Larry, and now I know he walks in the Grace of God. We will all be in heaven someday son, including your dad'."

"Her eyes opened and moved slowly in my direction. I'm sure she wanted to see my reaction. She slowly turned her head and pointed to her Bible. She requested that I look in the Bible, and hand her the yellow piece of paper inside. I retrieved the paper, and she said, don't open it yet, she had a story to tell about it. I squeezed her skinny little hand and agreed."

"She said, 'I wanted your dad to go to church with me so bad. One Saturday I just hounded him all day long.' He finally said, 'Doris, I don't want to hear another word about going to church with you.' That night, we kissed and said good night, and both repeated, "I love you," a ritual we had practiced since we were married. The next morning when I got up, your dad was gone. There was a note on the kitchen table. You're holding that note. Please read it to me'."

I unfolded the piece of paper and began to read.

Dear Doris, I have gone to the river to go fishing. I have done all your chores, including gathering your eggs and feeding and watering your chickens. I will be home in the afternoon. You are a wonderful woman, Doris, and I consider myself a lucky man to have you for a wife. I hope you have a good and blessed day.
Love George

He had written this poem at the bottom of his note.

Don't think I don't know him.

"You won't find me on the front row of your church on Sunday Morning. I might be walking through some green peaceful valley or floating down some clear mountain river admiring His creation that astounds me and feeling His presence all around me. So don't think I don't know Him, you have never heard the talks we have had together. No, you have never heard me pray ever so humble. Saying Lord, I don't take this love you show me for granted and I know I am accountable for every bad seed I have planted. Perhaps you were not aware of the many times He held my hand and guided me through some mighty stormy weather. So don't think I don't know Him, you have never heard the talks we have had together. Go ahead and judge me if it makes you feel better. I will put a good word in for you the next time me and the good Lord have our talk together."

I glanced up from reading Dad's poem and made eye contact with both Larry and Martha. I continued telling them how Mom slowly turned her head, looked at me, then closed her eyes while a peaceful grin consumed her face. She said, "He will be there, Leon, trust me. He will be there."

I looked over at Larry. I witnessed something I haven't seen too many times in my life. Tears ran down his cheeks. He soon took control of his emotions, wiped his tears, and said, "Thank you so much for sharing that with us."

Martha looked toward the big box of poems and song lyrics that I had placed on the kitchen table.

She asked, "Do you have the poem you wrote for your mother's funeral?"

"Yes." I pointed to the box. "It's in this mess somewhere."

Martha said, "I just loved that poem so much. Would you read it to us?"

I thumbed through the large overstuffed box, finally locating it. I began to read.

Mama is the Brightest Rose

'Heaven knows she loves her family. She prays every day.
"Lord just let my children be a part of your bouquet."
For in our family garden where all her flowers grow
No matter how the others shine, Mama's still the brightest rose.'

In her darkest hour, like a candle through the storm
She always found a way to lift us up above the thorns.
Even tho' the years have turned, her petals white as snow
In my eyes, "Mama's still the brightest rose."'

I had no more than finished reading the poem when Martha began talking about a trip, she, Larry, and the kids had made back to Wellington. "It was Mother's Day. You were overseas with the Marine Corps, and Karen was staying with your mom."

Martha continued. "You had written the most beautiful poem to Karen for Mother's Day. She and I became very close during those years when you were not home. Karen was so proud of your poem. We went into her bedroom and she read it to me. I remember so vividly how we cried and hugged. I would love for you to read that one for us if you have it."

I fumbled through the box until I located it and began to read.

TO MY PRECIOUS WIFE,
THE LOVE AT THE BOTTOM OF MY HEART.

'You are the flowers in my life, you are the Rose I call my wife,
an Orchid I lean on, a bouquet in our home. You stood by me
through thick and thin, and through it all you have been my best
friend. Oh, it's a precious thing, a special love, in a special place,
blessed with God's love and grace. When I am forced down this
lonely road, there is a place that I go. I close my eyes and see your
smiling face. I feel your love in this special place, for it's a love
that won't be torn apart, it's the love at the bottom of my heart.'

I lifted my head up from reading and spoke directly to Martha. "Little did I realize when I wrote that poem for Karen that our love would be torn apart. Not by Karen or me, but it would come from the forceful hand of God."

I could tell Martha was searching hard for a comforting comment. She said, "Please don't blame God."

About that time Larry spoke up and said, "We just have to trust in God's will."

Larry and I stood and stared at one another. Martha quickly looked at Larry and said, "We need to be going, Larry."

After they left my apartment, I wanted to scream. Although they had good intentions, telling me to trust in God seemed so cheap. The two of them will tuck their kids in bed tonight and wake up in the morning, knowing they have one another. It doesn't work that way for me.

I walked over to my kitchen table, sat down and started searching through the massive numbers of songs I had accumulated over the past several years. I lifted one out of the big box that I wrote about Mom and Dad during my second year of college, before Karen and I married. I returned home from Wichita, and I pulled into the long drive that led to the house. There was a scene in front of me that day that I will never forget. Mom and Dad were sitting side by side in the swing on our front porch, holding hands. I thought about a quote I remembered reading inside a valentine card, *'Love is an endless bridge that connects two hearts.'* I slowed down and almost stopped. The big wave from the two of them spoke loudly, as if to say, "Welcome home, son, we are so proud of you and love you so very much."

Later the following week at college, I found myself trying to study, but the image of the two of them kept returning through the back fields of my mind. I thought what a strong love, and no matter what they faced, that strong love was the catalyst that carried them through. With pen and paper in hand I wrote this.

A LOVE THAT STRONG

"Two young hearts, love would bind,
bound together down the river of time.
They've seen some good times, made it through some bad,
through it all, gave it all they had.
Love and laughter made their house a home.
It comes so easy for a love that strong.
A love that strong was meant to lean on.
When the road gets rough it just keeps on.
Precious love can do no wrong,
and love's enough for a love that strong."

CHAPTER 44

'Had my screams not woke up my cousin, no one would have ever believed me.'

Caterpillar had an employee cafeteria. I always ate there; the meals are good and very reasonable. I made my way to the lunchroom one day and got a pleasant surprise. Larry was at the door to the cafeteria waiting on me.

He spoke up and said, "Would you let your big brother buy your lunch?" I quickly and gladly accepted. While we were going through the serving line, Larry began telling me the reason he wanted to talk. Our cousin Donna, and her husband Ronnie, who leased our family farm, informed Larry they were moving and wouldn't be renewing their lease next year. It seems they finally managed to purchase their long sought after dream, a four hundred twenty-acre farm that included a nice home. Larry informed me they would like to keep full possession of the farm until Ronnie could get all of his soybean crop harvested. Larry continued, informing me on the situation and filling me in on Ronnie's plans.

We finished our meal and were getting ready to go our separate ways. Larry didn't turn in my direction, but loudly blared out, "See you at church Sunday, bro." I just sort of grinned and kept walking in the opposite direction.

Larry called Sunday morning and practically begged me to go to church with him and his family. I declined the invitation. I didn't want to go to church. To tell you the truth, I have lately started to question my faith in God. How could a just and fair God have turned his back on Johnny Hooper, Katie and those kids?

Why would a caring God take my Karen and precious Randy? I know my brother meant well, but I have begun to regret making the move to Decatur. I wish I would have stayed in Kansas and never met Orville Hopkins, Katie, and the kids. Knowing their pain, and feeling so helpless has become a very heavy burden to carry.

Another weekend came and went, and another Monday workday was history. I couldn't wait to watch a little TV before I went to bed, only to toss and turn until I fell asleep. It was about the only time I could escape the misery and guilt from walking away from Katie and those kids. Thank goodness I don't like alcohol, because if I did, I would certainly be a drunk by now, just to help with this depressed state I found myself bogged down in.

I didn't want to disappoint Larry, but sometimes I wonder if I should just move back to Kansas. I could possibly spend a few days in Lamar, Missouri and see how things might go with Brenda, and eventually get the Hopkins' family out of my head. I used to turn to God and pray. However, it was difficult to pray when you question if He even exists. I would have never thought I would feel this way. How had things gotten so crazy?

I kept waking up in the middle of the night thinking about Johnny Hooper and all the things he shared with me. The more and more I became acquainted with Johnny, the more he began to open up to me, and he told absolutely horrifying stories. He would get so caught up in reminiscing about the abuse, he would become very emotional. It would seem as if it had happened only yesterday.

~ ~ ~ ~

Johnny told me most of the abuse occurred on the far side of the farm, or in the number of buildings on the farm. No one had a clue. However, there was one incident that he said happened when he was about twelve years old. His dad had taken him to a small lake on their farm. He tied him to a tree at the edge of the water with a rope around his midsection and his hands were tied behind his back. The water was up past his knees and he didn't have a shirt or shoes on. The event occurred after he and his dad were doing the late afternoon chores. Johnny was instructed by his dad to carry a large pail of milk to the house. He stumped his toe and spilled the full pail of milk, and it made his dad furious. He later told me the reason his dad chose to punish him by tying him up in the lake was because he had given Johnny a hard whooping the day before that left deep cut marks on his back and legs. Not wanting to reopen the wounds, his dad chose a different form of punishment.

Johnny described the incident occurring just at dusk, basically dark. After securing him to a tree in the small lake, his dad told him he would be back at daylight the next morning to untie him. The mosquitoes were horrible, and the lake was infested with large cottonmouth snakes. He told me it was a partial moon-lit night and his eyes had adjusted to the darkness. He could see snakes all around him. Then, what he was so concerned about, happened. One of the large snakes swam up to him and swam across his legs. The snake turned, and swam back, only inches from him. Then it just stared at him.

Johnny said he was so scared he almost passed out, and honestly, he said he didn't remember much after that. However, he must have screamed very loudly because a cousin, who lived in a house rather close to the lake, was sleeping by an open window and heard him. She woke her folks, Johnny's aunt and uncle, and they went to his parents' house and told them they heard someone screaming at the lake. Of course, word soon got out to the family, who said they just couldn't believe his dad had done that. Johnny said, "Had my screams not woken my cousin, no one would have ever believed me."

He continued. "I could tell many events like that, that absolutely happened, but I believed and feared most folks would not believe me. So, I have just kept them to myself."

There was always a gleam in Johnny's eyes when he would speak of his daughters.

He said, "I was honored on more than one occasion to have both my daughters attend therapy sessions with me. The therapist questioned the girls about my relationship with each of them. They both assured him, unequivocally, that I had never abused them physically or otherwise."

Johnny said he was so pleased when both girls told the therapist they couldn't have had a more loving father. The therapist turned toward him and said, "Johnny, no matter what you have accomplished in your life, I can assure you, that is your greatest accomplishment."

Then he looked toward the girls and said, "Consider yourselves very blessed, because that is not always the case."

So many people, when they hear PTSD, immediately associate it with our military, what has been referred to as battle fatigue, or shell shock. As real and devastating as it is in our military community, PTSD from childhood abuse can often be more severe.

Johnny shared his darkest secrets with very few people, one being a cousin who lived in Memphis, Tennessee. Only a few months after sharing his delicate secret of abuse, his mom told him that his cousin had mentioned that Johnny's dad was his favorite uncle. At that point, Johnny felt like he was on an island by himself.

Johnny once said, "I've told things that have happened, and my dad, of course, would lie and say it never happened. My mom, although she was a wonderful woman, would lie to help cover up the abuse." Johnny recalled one time when his older sister had invited a friend to come home with her after school, which made his dad very angry. Thankfully he didn't whoop her in front of her friend, but she was forced to take a tongue lashing in front of her. While Johnny stood nearby, feeling sorry for his sister, their father's anger turned toward him. His dad backhanded him and kicked him off the back porch. He knew he was hurt when he couldn't raise his right arm. His mom put a sling on his arm and told all the kids to tell everyone that he had been hurt helping his dad work cattle. And that's exactly what they all did.

I feel a need to learn and understand more about what makes a person like Johnny's dad and Orville Hopkins think and act the way they do. Their need to control. I so vividly remember Johnny telling me about his dad whipping his two older sisters. It was almost unbelievable. He said after his severe onset of PTSD, both his sisters shared with him, at different times, that their dad gave both of them an extremely hard whooping after each were out of high school. Not only were they out of high school, but both had engagement rings on their fingers and were only days away from their wedding.

Even though the whoopings, which were described more like beatings, occurred years apart, there were many similarities. Both girls were still living at home. They both explained, the whoopings were over a simple issue, nothing more than an opinion different from his. Each sister told Johnny that their dad said, "You still live under my roof and you will follow my rules!"

After Johnny shared this with one of the therapists he was seeing, the therapist said, "Your dad knew your sisters would soon be out of that house, and he would lose control over them. He had a need to control them as long as possible." I thought about Orville and his need to control Katie and the kids. Orville was like a beast in search of something to control. I know I am spending way too much of my awakened thoughts on Katie and those kids. The guilt of my driving away from them still eats at my very soul.

CHAPTER 45

'The scene that unfolded in my head that night was too graphic for me to describe to you'

I could not believe my life had gone in such a direction. If it was not for my passion to write, I honestly don't know what I would do. I had nightmares every week about Katie and the kids. One night I had this dream.

"Katie and the kids were in a small boat. They were all huddled down in this horrific storm. The boat was being thrown against these large waves. I was standing on the bank desperately wanting to help them, mercifully begging them to paddle toward me. Each one looked so frightened. Then this huge wave lifted their tiny boat. They capsized and each one disappeared under the water. I woke up from my own voice crying out for them."

The following week I had another dream.

"I was standing on this bridge. Katie and the kids were on the opposite side. They had their arms stretched out running toward me as I was desperately trying to get to them. Orville had the appearance of the Devil as he came closer and closer to them. We met almost in the middle of the bridge, when a large gap in the bridge suddenly broke and tumbled to the bottom of this huge deep canyon. I was desperately trying to reach out and pull them toward me. Orville made his way to them and pushed each one of them off the bridge into the deep canyon below. Each time he pushed one of them he would look at me and give this obnoxious laugh. I could only stare into their frightful faces as they plummeted to their death below."

The dream was so real I woke up with tears in my eyes.

Every time I wake up from a nightmare concerning Katie and the kids, I also think about Johnny. His wife Margaret told me during the time Johnny's PTSD was so severe, he would often wake her up yelling, and sometimes beating his pillow with his fist. They both agreed it would be best if they sleep in different beds.

I so clearly remember Johnny becoming very emotional one day while he re-lived a dream where his dad was chasing his daughters. All three were unclothed. Johnny's words became choked down when he said, "The scene that unfolded in my head that night was too graphic for me to describe to you." Johnny said he had awakened at three o'clock in the morning from similar nightmares involving his grandchildren several times, getting so angry and frustrated that he was unable to sleep the rest of the night.

Johnny said, "People are so quick to judge. They seem to think they know more than the trained and educated therapist." He would say with a hurtful heart, "I ask you, where is their diploma hanging?" He said one of the four therapists he had seen said, "Johnny, you could have a severely crushed leg that became infected to the point you couldn't walk without crutches, and most of your family and friends would have an enormous amount of sympathy for you."

"However, that same degree of wounds from someone dealing with mental health is often looked at with a whole different attitude. They would be striking the wound with a physical object, screaming at you and saying don't limp, walk! There is nothing wrong with you. Their minds twist and spin their uneducated opinions, working hard to justify their actions. So caught up in their own world, they fail to see the real hurt they often inflict on you. That is called secondary wounding, and it is often the pain that hurts the most." Johnny looked deep into my eyes and continued. "Secondary wounding from family and friends hurts deep, and most therapists will tell you it is a major cause of suicide." In hindsight, was Johnny screaming at my heart?

Johnny said, "I have a brother, and although there were, several years difference in our age, most of our adult life we have been fairly close. However, when I was diagnosed with PTSD, that all changed. All I did was become ill. It's like they all think I have a switch I can just turn on or turn off. But there is not a switch.

"During my darkest days, dealing with acute PTSD, I desperately wanted to get my life back to normal," Johnny remarked. "I was clinging to every word and suggestion my therapist was instructing me to do. He suggested I talk to a close friend or relative, perhaps, a person of deep faith. I thought of my nephew, he is a pastor of a church in North Arkansas."

Johnny said, "Not only was I shocked, but also hurt, when he said he would need some time to pray about it." I thought, "What is there to pray about?" He continued. "Leon, I more than once sent money to his mother, my sister, so they would have food in their stomachs. I can assure you I didn't have to pray about it. That didn't make me a hero, it was just the right thing to do."

"I almost gave up on the suggestion," Johnny said. "Then, I thought about my brother-in-law. He was my oldest sister's husband, a strong Christian man, a deacon in a church for over forty-years. I told him what my therapist had suggested. Even though he was several miles away from me, and extremely busy on his dairy farm, his reaction was remarkable.

"There wasn't one second hesitation before he said, 'When do you want me there? I can be there in two hours.' He didn't need to pray about it, Leon. I feel that is what God would expect from a good Christian."

CHAPTER 46

'There is not a book telling you how to handle this. You know what your precious mother would say! "Yes, son, there is, it's called the Holy Bible."'

A nother day has come and gone, another little piece of my soul has been lost in this mire of circumstances I found myself consumed in. I was so sure the move to Decatur would help me crawl out of this depressed state. I spent a large amount of my day replaying those images of Mary Beth in the garden, Donnie in the pig barn, Alice running out of the house, screaming at her dad, "No! No, no more!" In my mind, I can vividly see the bruises on Katie's body. Places no one else, except possibly Orville, had been privileged to see.

The whole thing had turned into a nightmare. The misery of it all consumed me. Things seemed to spin in all the wrong directions. Is this what my life had become? Did God have a purpose for sending me down this twisted road I am forced to travel? I found myself bogged down in envy and jealousy when watching and being around Larry, Martha and their two kids. I hate the fact I have erected walls around my heart. My zest for life was gone.

It seemed my longing for, and missing Karen and Randy, had become far worse instead of better. My grief most certainly had deepened. I really tried to get over their loss, but it is just something I must live with. It is a part of my life, a part I can't change. If I could go back and undo it, I would have done so immediately. Unfortunately, when someone you love so much dies, a part of you goes with them. You don't get over the grief, you only get used to the feeling. It becomes your new normal. Well, I hate this new normal. Life is too short to live like this.

It was Friday afternoon and I had just gotten to my apartment from a busy workday. I sat down to relax for a minute when the phone rang. It was Martha. She explained Larry was going to eat out with some guys at work and then go bowling. She said she had extra supper to share with me. I hesitated for a couple of seconds. I really didn't want to go, but I didn't want to seem ungrateful.

Martha spoke up and said, "I also need to talk to you. Just me and you, one on one." There was something in Martha's voice that concerned me. I politely accepted her invitation. She said, "Come on over, I'll have it on the table when you get here."

While I freshened up, I wondered what she wished to talk about. I knew it had nothing to do with her and Larry's marriage. I can assure you their marriage was as solid as any I have ever known. Could it be one of the kids? Was Larry having some type of health issues? Was it about me not going to church with her and Larry? The drive to their house only made me more and more curious about her statement. She had supper on the table just as she promised.

I no more than consumed my last bite of dessert, when she spoke up and said, "The kids are in their rooms. Can we visit now? I want this conversation to be just between the two of us."

My curiosity suddenly became even greater. She pointed to the sliding glass door that opened to their patio. She suggested we sit on the patio and I readily agreed. She turned her chair so she faced me. My view looked across their backyard. I sensed an uneasiness about her.

She began to blunder through her opening remarks. "I can tell you're very unhappy."

I can assure you she caught me totally off guard. She went on, "Larry and I have talked, and we both know you aren't happy here."

I looked at Martha. Goodness, I thought, is it that obvious? For some reason, perhaps it was the shame I felt. I had trouble looking Martha in the eye. I sat with my head bowed and stared at the floor.

Without looking up I said, "You're right. I've been struggling because I've cowardly abandoned three precious kids and a wonderful lady." I continued after an awkward pause. "It's the farm family I stayed and worked with in Malden, Missouri."

I began to unveil things I had never told the two of them before. I shared one thing after another about the abuse I witnessed at the Hopkins' farm. I could tell Martha was taken back with what I shared with her.

"I feel as though my hands are tied. There seems to be nothing I can do. I don't know of anyone to call. There isn't a book on how to handle this."

Martha, being the Godly woman she is, looked at me with a smirky grin and said, "You know what your precious mother would say? Yes son, there is, it's called the Holy Bible."

I nodded my head and somewhat agreed. She then politely said, "I want Larry to hear all of this also, not from me, but from you. He's off work tomorrow. How do you feel about Larry and me coming over to your place around nine in the morning to talk this over?" I quickly agreed.

I drove back to my apartment with many thoughts racing through my head. To be honest, I looked forward to sharing these things that I had always felt a need to keep to myself. Perhaps it would somehow help with the guilt I have wrestled with since the moment I drove away from Katie, Donnie, and the girls. Hopefully, tomorrow was a new day that would bring new hope.

~ ~ ~ ~

It was a beautiful Saturday morning. I made a fresh pot of coffee and patiently waited for the two of them to arrive. One minute till nine o'clock, their big Oldsmobile pulled into my driveway. Larry was very punctual. Without a doubt, he was Dad's son.

We didn't waste time on small talk. I began to tell the full chain of events that unfolded at the Hopkins' farm. I didn't leave out one detail, with the exception, of course, of revealing the sinful road Katie and I had traveled. Katie and I made a sacred oath we would never tell anyone. We both agreed we would take that secret to our grave.

For some reason, I also felt a need to tell them the amazing circumstances of how I met Johnny Hooper, how Johnny and I had become close friends, how he had suffered from PTSD and took his own life. I also shared how I strongly felt compelled to take a psychology class at Wichita State.

Our conversation went from a few minutes to over three hours. Larry intensely listened to me give one detail after another.

He boldly spoke up and said, "Those things you have shared are not, in any way, consequential or just circumstantial. It wasn't by chance you went to that baseball game and met Johnny, no more than it was just by chance the old wagon's water pump went out on that road at the exact time the little boy was riding his bicycle to the store. God is leading you in a direction, and I highly suggest you listen to Him. You've gained so much knowledge about mental health from Johnny and have seen first-hand the awful abuse from Orville. There isn't any book, in any college, that would have given you the insight to understand the effect of mental, physical, and sexual abuse as you have witnessed for yourself."

Martha readily agreed.

I have to admit, "My whole attitude about mental health has been drastically rearranged."

Larry, appearing shocked when he looked at his watch. "Oh my, Martha, I didn't have a clue it's so late. We've got to get home and get ready." Glancing in my direction, he began to explain that they were taking the kids and going to Martha's folks to spend the night.

"We're planning to go to church with them in the morning, then after church we celebrate Martha's mother's birthday." Larry smiled. "We'll be home late tomorrow afternoon."

I agreed to take care of their animals while they were gone.

While Larry got in the car, he looked at me and very seriously said, "God has another plan for you, and I hope you will follow his calling."

It still amazes me to this day how Larry had fallen into the graces of God. I remember so well how he was when we were growing up. He always seemed eager to exit off the straight and narrow road Mom tried so hard to send us down. Not only at times choosing a steep and crooked one, but sliding around every sharp curve.

~ ~ ~ ~

Sunday morning, I decided to go to Lake Decatur and walk around the park adjacent to the water. I saw a young mother playing with a little girl about Sheila's age. I thought about Brenda and Sheila. I remember Brenda saying that she always hoped Eddie Ray would mature, and their hearts would forever be bound together. I went back to my apartment and wrote this poem.

TWO HEARTS THAT BIND

Stumbling down life's mountain, she's desperately trying to climb.
Got to wake up that little one and get to work on time.
Fumbling with her laces, trying to tie her shoes.
She forces a smile for her, she can't afford to lose her cool.
Unanswered questions still haunt her twisted mind,
Why was I so dumb, how could I have been so blind?
What happened to my dreams of two hearts that bind?
She convinces her world everything is fine,
but those that really know her can read between the lines.
She tucks to bed this little one, and thanks the Lord on high
for giving her this little angel and these two hearts that bind.

CHAPTER 47

'Who knows, Lamar, Missouri just might be a really good place to fall in love.'

Monday morning, on my way to work, I kept thinking about the possibility of turning in my resignation. I was still somewhat on the fence with my decision. I knew I wanted to talk to Larry one more time.

While I was at lunch, Larry came by my work area and left me a note requesting I come by his house around 6:30 that evening. He said he had something to discuss with me. When I got there, he met me at the door and said that Martha and the kids were attending a school event.

In life there are talkers and there are doers. Larry most certainly was a doer. He informed me he had a co-worker that worked in management with him, who had a brother-n-law who worked for Social Services for the state of Illinois. He made some phone calls to the State of Missouri that morning and located someone in the Malden area who could possibly get some help for Katie and the kids. He said the person I should talk to worked out of the Poplar Bluff office. Larry gave me his phone number and his name, Glen Decker.

I felt Larry's heartfelt love and respect for me when he spoke. "Your happiness is the most important thing to me. As much as I would love for you to stay in Decatur, we both know your heart is not here. You know, as well as I do, that God is calling you in a different direction. My sincere advice to you is to give Caterpillar your two-week notice. I also think you need to get hold of Mr.

Decker in Poplar Bluff and set a date to meet. Those Hopkins kids need your help, and you aren't going to have peace until you know they have been helped."

That was the nudge I needed. I was totally on board.

"I think you're exactly right. I'm going to turn in my resignation tomorrow. Thank you for understanding."

Larry very confidently said, "It's not so much about me understanding. It's a simple fact that God has other plans for you."

I somewhat agreed.

Tuesday morning, I found myself in the office of Mr. Danny Sutterfield, the personnel officer for my area of the plant. I could tell Larry had already spoken to him. He was very gracious and wished me well.

The next day I found a note on my desk from Larry that said he had something to discuss with me and wanted to have lunch in the cafeteria again. I was halfway to the cafeteria when the noon time horn sounded. I was very anxious to learn what Larry wanted to discuss with me. He was usually at the cafeteria door waiting for me, but not so today. My eyes began to focus on who I was sure was Larry, briskly walking toward me at the far end of the long hall, no doubt in a hurry. He stopped in front of me, and in an almost panicked voice, said, "Hey, bro, I can't do lunch today. I have several fires I must get under control."

Before I could comment, he hurriedly said, "Martha is going to have supper for you tonight. Come over around six o'clock, I should be home."

"Okay, sounds like a plan." Larry gave me a fist bump and once again headed quickly back down the hall. The afternoon at work seemed to be in slow motion, and the time just dragged by. I was so curious at what Larry wanted to discuss with me. Perhaps Ronnie had someone he knew that wanted to lease the farm.

When I got to my apartment, I called Martha to see if I needed to pick something up. "No, just bring yourself," she said, and then added, "Be sure to clean out your ears. Larry has something to propose to you. I think you're going to like it."

I tried desperately to get her to tell me. As much as I tried, she would not utter one word about what was on Larry's mind.

All five of us had finished supper. Martha suggested the kids go to their rooms and get their homework done. I helped Martha clean off the table. I was prepared to help her wash the dishes, but she said she would do them later. Larry pointed to a chair at the kitchen table and instructed me to sit.

Martha and Larry joined me at the table. Larry opened up a notepad with what I could tell were prepared figures. He looked at me with a very serious look before proceeding.

"Martha and I have been thinking about something that could be beneficial for both of us." He paused for a few seconds then proceeded. "Please understand, we are totally okay with whatever your decision is, so please don't feel you have to go along with what we are proposing."

My anticipation level was rapidly rising. What the heck? I thought.

"How do you feel about Martha and me selling you our interest in the 120 acres including the homestead?"

I'm sure I looked stunned, and before I could answer, he quickly added, "Just to be clear, we are not proposing selling the 380 acres of crop ground."

I just replied with a long drawn out, "Well, I very well might be interested in that."

Larry said, "We want you to think about it for a couple days before you make your final decision. We could sell you our half-interest in that part of the farm and have enough money to pay off our home mortgage here."

Martha added, "We could, and would, set aside our present mortgage payment and put that money in a college fund for the kids."

"For this to be fair," Larry said, "I feel we need to get two or three appraisals." I agreed.

They had suggested I give myself a couple days before I gave them my decision. I told them I would think it over, but I didn't really need any extra time. I instantly knew this opportunity felt right. I was over the moon excited about the possibilities this could provide and had a smile on my face when I left their house. I always felt someday, I would reside on a small farm out in the country. However, the thought of waking up every morning on the ole' homeplace, with all its fond memories, simply warms my heart. After spending about an hour at home, I drove back over and told them I liked their proposal.

A few days after turning in my resignation, I arrived home from work, and in less than thirty-minutes, Larry called. He told me Martha and the kids were going to a pizza party with some of their friends from church, and he offered to buy my supper. I was shocked, pleased, and quickly agreed. He arrived at my apartment in less than five minutes. When I sat down in his car, a smirky smile came across his face.

"Remember when we were in high school, and the car-hops would skate around in roller skates?"

"Absolutely," I replied.

"Well, I know a place here in Decatur that still has car-hops on roller skates."

We drove to the drive-in eating joint. Sure enough, car-hops rolled around everywhere. We both ordered burgers, fries, and a milkshake and sat there shooting the breeze, reminiscing about our childhood. Soon, Larry just flat out asked me about my future plans.

"Well, I definitely plan to enroll in classes at Wichita State and earn my degree in Social Work. I've actually been wanting to run some things by you." I began to lay out my full plan. "I thought I might stay one night a week with Aunt Earlene. You know she still lives in Wichita by herself."

Larry chuckled and remarked, "Yes, and it would be like staying with our mom." He smiled, "That would make Aunt Earlene the happiest lady in Wichita!"

Aunt Earlene and Mom were sisters, and were so much alike, people would often get them mixed up. I continued to explain to Larry my plan. "I thought I would load up my classes for Wednesday and Thursday. I could drive back home Thursday night and have all the rest of the week at the farm."

The farmhouse was in good condition, but I explained how I wanted to paint and spruce up the place a little. I had already shared with them how I met Brenda. I am sure they could have seen a sparkle in my eyes when I spoke of her. Then I said, "You know Lamar, Missouri isn't that far from Wichita."

That brought a smirky grin to Larry's face, and he said, "Who knows, Lamar, Missouri just might be a really good place to fall in love."

I didn't comment. I just looked at Larry and sheepishly smiled.

CHAPTER 48

'Had Donnie done the unthinkable? Dear God no, please no.'

I kept looking at my watch, anticipating the sound of the loud bell that signaled the end of my shift. It was Tuesday. I only had three more days to work for Caterpillar. The instant that bell rang, I headed straight to my apartment. I had already informed Otis and Ruthie that I would be leaving on Saturday, October the 10th. They were very disappointed, but also understood. What wonderful people, I wished them the very best.

I wanted to have everything ready by Thursday night. I had already told Larry and Martha that I wanted to take them and the kids out for dinner Friday night.

My plan was to leave Saturday morning, fairly early, and drive to St. Louis to see my dear friend, Bill Johnson on my way to Poplar Bluff. I promised Bill and Wanda that I would spend the night and go to church with them Sunday morning. Then I would take my time to drive to Poplar Bluff. I planned to spend the night there, and be ready for my nine o'clock appointment with Mr. Glen Decker at the Department of Family Services office Monday morning. I finally felt empowered and was so hopeful to get Katie and the kids some much needed help from Orville's abuse. When my meeting with Mr. Decker was over, I planned to make tracks to Lamar, Missouri. I was quite anxious to see Brenda, and who knows, maybe play Roy Rogers and Dale Evans with Sheila.

~ ~ ~ ~

Martha asked me to stop at the little neighborhood market that was a couple blocks from their home. She needed milk and a couple more items. I was always glad to do small things for her and Larry. I was so blessed to have Larry for a brother. I've always looked up to him. When we were in college, I would have never believed I would admire him like I do today.

When I carried the requested items into the house, I made eye contact with Martha, and I immediately knew something was wrong. She had a totally different demeanor. I knew it wasn't the kids, both of them were in the living room. She didn't even speak.

"Martha! What's wrong?"

She said, "The pastor of the Hopkins' family church in Malden called this afternoon."

My stomach rolled.

"The pastor said Katie had asked him to call you. He asked me to tell you to call him as soon as possible. There's been a bad incident of some sort. He didn't offer any information, and I didn't feel at liberty to ask questions. It sounded urgent, Leon."

"Okay. I understand." Martha pointed to the piece of paper lying on a small end table next to the phone where she had written the pastor's phone number.

I walked to the phone and a thousand thoughts raced through my mind. I most certainly was nauseated, and had a weakness in my knees. There comes a breaking point with all of us. Had Donnie reached that point of no return and possibly done the unthinkable? I knew Johnny Hooper shared with me that when he was Donnie's age, he came close to taking his own life on more than one occasion. Dear God, no! Please no. I picked up the phone. I had a noticeable tremor in my hand while I dialed the number. A part of me wanted desperately to know, then another part of me didn't want to hear what I was so afraid I would be told. I dialed the last digit, busy, busy, busy, busy. I thought, oh no not now. I tried to use common sense and anticipated every scenario that crossed my mind. I knew Martha said that Brother Blackmore told her Katie knew I would want to know. So, I knew it wasn't Katie, but for God's sake, who?

If Orville had become extremely angry at Donnie, and Bo intervened, I could certainly see Orville killing Bo. I could also see Donnie killing his dad. What about Alice or Mary Beth? I thought about the day the fuel line on the tractor broke and Alice bolted out the front door. Those words Alice screamed at her dad, 'No! No, no more!' Her words just kept repeating in my mind. I also kept going back to the day Alice wanted Donnie to show her how to shoot the gun.

What if Donnie witnessed Orville sexually abusing one of the girls? I could see him losing it, and possibly taking a gun and ending Orville's life. Or what if Katie had witnessed Orville sexually abusing one of the kids? That, no doubt, would make a mother angry enough to pull a trigger.

I walked outside to try to calm down. I went back to the phone. Once again, I dialed the number. *Ring, ring.* Thank God, I thought, it's not busy. I heard Brother Blackmore answer. I cleared my throat trying hard to dislodge the lump that seemed stuck.

"Pastor," I said, "this is Leon Wilson."

"Leon, I'm so sorry to be the carrier of bad news." He took a deep breath. "Orville was tragically killed this morning in an awful tractor accident."

"Oh no," I replied. "How did it happen?"

Brother Blackmore explained. "Well, the way I understand it, he was preparing a piece of ground to sow some pasture grass. He was pulling a tumbling harrow behind the tractor. He turned too sharp, and one of the chains that was hooked to the draw bar caught on the large rear tire of the tractor and lifted the harrow on top of him. He rode the tractor, probably unconscious, across the field and it overturned in a drainage ditch. It landed on top of him."

Brother Blackmore said he wasn't sure about any funeral arrangements. I thanked him for the call and told him to tell Katie I would be there for the funeral.

Martha sat in the living room, anxious to know the full story. I told her what Brother Blackmore had said to me. Her feelings mimicked mine. Thank God it wasn't Donnie or Katie, or one of the girls. I was in total shock and sat there, my gaze fixed on the floor. Then I glanced up at Martha. We just stared at each other and both began shaking our heads in disbelief.

"This change's everything, Martha."

"Absolutely," she agreed.

Once the reality set in a bit, we both felt this was perhaps a blessing in disguise. I wouldn't have ever believed I would wish death on anyone, but honestly, this was absolutely the best scenario for Katie and the kids.

Martha and I were sitting in the living room, discussing my plans and where they might take me. Then we heard Larry's car pull into the garage. I think both of us were anxious to fill him in on the new turn of events. After giving Larry all the details, he said what I had already thought about.

"Thank goodness you have given your two weeks' notice several days ago."

Larry said that he would inform personnel at Caterpillar about my situation and pick up my last paycheck.

Martha had supper ready, but I didn't have an appetite.

"You guys go ahead and eat. I'm going back to my apartment to start loading my car."

My intentions were to leave early in the morning, drive straight to Malden and check into a motel. I would then go to the farm and see Katie and the kids.

I was up before the alarm clock went off. Larry and Martha suggested I come over for coffee and cinnamon rolls. As soon as I stepped into the kitchen, Martha handed me a cup of coffee.

"I hope you like driving in the rain," Larry said. "The weatherman predicted it would probably rain all morning." Before I could answer he added, "At least you'll have a good road most of the way down."

"Yeah, I'll be fine."

I wanted to get on the road and put some miles behind me. We all said our goodbyes. They wished me well, and we all agreed to keep each other informed.

CHAPTER 49

'O' he shines that big light that never seems to dim, but that bright light casts a shadow on the dark side of him.'

It's Wednesday morning. I predict, and actually hope, that Orville's service will be on Friday. My plan is to leave shortly after the funeral. I'll drive to Lamar, connect with Brenda, and just see where things go from there.

The rain finally ended and the sun is gradually gaining control of the cloudy skies. I am fascinated by all the acres of corn and soybean. Combines are working in fields on both sides of the highway.

I had trouble sleeping last night. I was wide awake around 2:30 and couldn't help wondering about Orville. Where was Orville, heaven or hell? In so many ways Orville was a good man, yet on the other hand he was this monster with his need to control and the unbelievable abuse he inflicted on his family especially Donnie.

A few weeks back I had written a song about Orville and his dark side that so many people never witnessed. About how fearful Donnie and the girls were of him and how wrong that was. About his need to shine a big light. The song goes like this......

Verse
"Little hands a trembling, choking back the tears,
a father should not be someone his own child would fear."

Chorus
"O' he shines that big light that never seems to dim,

but that bright light casts a shadow on
the dark side of him.
Yes, there was a dark side seldom ever seen,
except for three kids, Katie, Jesus and me."

I wanted the second verse of that song to be about Katie Jean. I worked on it from time to time, but nothing ever fell into place. Last night while I was awake and thinking about where Orville's soul was, the words quickly came to me for the last verse.

Verse
"I have often wondered come judgment day,
and he no longer controls everything his way.
And that big light he has been shining finally goes dim,
will the bright lights of Heaven shine on
the dark side of him?"

Chorus
"O' he shines that big light that never seems to dim.
But that bright light cast a shadow on the dark side of him.
Yes, there is a dark side seldom ever seen
except for three kids, Katie, Jesus, and me."

I sang the last verse a couple of times and was very pleased by the way it turned out. I thought about something Mom would often say, "The Lord has given you a calling, you need to follow that calling and write more." I remembered thinking about what she said. One day, while I plowed the ground to plant wheat, this little jingle kept repeating itself in my head.

"I don't hear voices calling me.
I don't see writing on the wall.
I don't know if it is my foolish pride or
from you, Lord, there's a call
I just know from time to time
there's a direction in my mind
That takes me to a place I have never been.
It is then I realize.
I don't write these words Lord, I just hold the pen."

I had made very good time in my new Oldsmobile. In the far distance, standing like a majestic castle, was the big bridge that crossed the mighty Mississippi River. In no time, I had quickly put Charleston, Missouri in my rear-view mirror.

The cotton and soybean fields that were on both sides of the road looked so different from just a few months ago when I was going to Decatur. I can so vividly remember how the season back home could change the way we visually saw our surroundings. The ugly naked trees and barren pastures in late winter, turned into rolling green fields of wheat. The big lawn trees, that surround farmers' homesteads, drooped like canopies, casting cool shadows on the lush grass beneath them. The sudden appearance of a wide variety of flowering plants, many *'in full bloom,'* added a finishing touch to mother nature's beautifully painted canvas.

The seasons of our lives are much the same. Things that seem so wrong, can suddenly change, and new and better things will appear. Times that seem to be mired in grief and sadness can again suddenly change and have gratifying solutions. I am desperately hoping I am headed in that direction.

I turned off Highway 60 at Dexter, Missouri and traveled straight south, only a few miles from Malden. The cotton fields were a sea of white as far as the eyes could see. What a sight! I had never seen anything quite like that in my life. Pickers, as they are called, were everywhere. Large groups of whites, Negros, and a sizeable number of Mexicans were in field after field. I wish Mom and Dad could have seen this.

I arrived at the motel in Malden, got my room, then freshened up a bit. I decided to go to a flower shop and buy Katie some flowers. With the flowers and a card setting beside me, I am on my way to see Katie and the kids.

I deliberately drove a little out of my way to go by the Hopkins' church. I slowed down while I drove by. So many things came rushing back to me. I could almost see Donnie at the little ballfield trying so hard to make someone laugh. The taste of that wonderful potluck Sunday dinner made my mouth water. I felt a bit of emotion reminiscing about the morning Donnie asked for prayers for Bo. Thank you, Lord, for answering that one.

I made the decision to turn on the next gravel road that would take me out to the little highway that I traveled the day the water pump went out. I thought how things could have been so different if the pump would have gone out a few miles down the highway. I couldn't help but ask myself, was it by chance, or power from above? I would have never met the Hopkins family. I can't imagine not knowing Katie Jean, the girls, and of course Donnie and his bestest, bestest friend Bo.

I approached the abandoned homestead where I first met Donnie. I recalled that day as though it were yesterday. I slowed down to a crawl when I reached the old bridge. I see the Hopkins' house up ahead of me. I once again remembered the night Donnie looked for Bo in that vicious thunderstorm. I look back to my left and across the field. Things were so different. The corn was brown, ready to pick. The soybeans and cotton fields were ready to harvest. I couldn't help but wonder what Katie would be like. I am excited, and nervous, to see everyone.

CHAPTER 50

'The only thing in life that is guaranteed, is the fact that nothing in life is guaranteed.'

There were several cars parked near the house. I saw people on the porch and several outside, either sitting in lawn chairs, or just standing and visiting. I parked my car out by the county road and began walking up to the house. I heard a sound as familiar as my own name, clop, clop. I knew exactly what it was, Donnie throwing that ball against the concrete garage. I stopped several feet from the porch and looked in his direction. Donnie drew back, ready to whizz the ball toward the garage. Then he saw me standing there, looking at him. It took him a couple of seconds to recognize me.

Donnie yelled out, "Leon, Leon!" He broke into a full run on his way to greet me. I instantly dropped to my knees and we both grabbed onto each other. I didn't realize how much strength a boy of Donnie's age had. He just about squeezed the poop out of me.

I backed up, never getting off my knees. I just wanted to look at him.

"Boy, it sure is good to see you, Donnie,"

"I am so proud you came," he said.

About that time something appeared in my peripheral vision, it was Mary Beth. I didn't get up, but just reached my arms in her direction. She hugged me almost as hard as Donnie did.

She said, "I think I am in love with you."

I said, "Well, I know I'm in love with you."

I looked toward the porch. Alice briskly walked toward us. I stood up and gave Alice a warm affection hug and said, "I didn't think you girls could get any prettier, but you both are absolutely beautiful."

That brought big smiles from both of them. She said, "Mama will be glad you came, and I am sure glad you are here."

"Well, it's good to see all of you, and I am so sorry about your dad."

While we walked to the house, all the people who were sitting on the porch smiled from the scene they just witnessed with me and the kids in the front yard. I spoke to two elderly men sitting in lawn chairs in the yard. I remember they were mainstays in the church.

Mary Beth flew up the steps and quickly went into the house, I was sure, to announce my arrival. I acknowledged and smiled at several people on the porch, then walked in with Donnie and Alice by my side. I felt my heart beat harder in anticipation of seeing Katie Jean. There she was, standing in the living room, her pure raw beauty shining through her swollen eyes, her hair ruffled, no doubt from the many hugs all the well-wishers gave her.

I worked to choke back emotional tears when we hugged each other. Katie didn't seem to want to let go. She patted me on the back and whispered, "Thank you for coming, Leon. Thank you so much."

Katie eventually released me from our hug. We stared at each other. I said, "I'm so sorry about Orville."

She looked at me and replied, "I'm still in shock. I feel like I'm moving in slow motion. I'm not sure what to do from minute to minute."

I didn't know if it was appropriate or not, but I said, "Hang in there, everything is going to be okay."

She had a pleasant smile and murmured, "Yes. I know it is, it's just hard right now."

I handed her the flowers and card. She smiled and thanked me. We hugged once again. I realized other people had stepped into the living room and were waiting to give their condolences, so I took her two hands and squeezed them and told her we would talk later. She once again thanked me for being there.

I noticed an empty chair in the far corner of the living room. I made my way through the crowd and sat down. I watched Katie

Jean greet each and every person. She shook their hands and hugged them. Everyone gave her their heartfelt condolences.

Watching Katie going through this hard time made me recall the times in my life I have been in Katie's shoes. The loss of Karen and Randy, my dad, and of course Mom. When you stop and think about it, you begin to realize something. The only thing in life that is guaranteed is the fact that nothing in life is guaranteed. Something you thought could never happen, can, in fact, happen, and your life will forever be changed.

I can't help but wonder what was truly going through Katie's mind. I wanted to think she had mixed feelings. Her husband of fifteen years, and father to her three children, was just tragically killed in an awful accident. I am sure not one of these people have a clue the kind of miserable life Katie had been living with this abusive man.

I decided to give my chair to an elderly lady that had entered the living room. I worked my way through the crowd and was able to exit the house.

CHAPTER 51

'I very clearly overheard their whispered conversation, "Looks like we have a nigger lover among us."'

I was about to walk off the porch when the sound of a very loud engine gradually came into focus from down the road. It was Katie and Orville's closest neighbors, Robert and Norvella Jones, B.J.'s mom and dad. Robert's old truck didn't have a muffler, so it was very loud.

Robert backed the old truck up the driveway a few feet. Miss Norvella jumped out of the truck and grabbed two sticks of firewood off the bed of the truck and secured the rear tires. She looked as if she wasn't sure what she should do next. I gave her a friendly wave. There was no doubt she recognized me and was happy to see me standing near the front of the house. She motioned for me to come to them. I quickly headed their way.

I walked down the hill toward her. She turned and retrieved a large, covered pot from the seat of the old truck. All of a sudden B.J. slid out of the truck. Donnie was at the far end of the house, saw B.J. and sprinted down the hill. His friend encouraged him to get his glove and play catch.

I greeted Norvella and Robert. Miss Norvella said, "Mr. Leon, would you be so kind as to take this fried chicken to Miss Katie Jean?" Before I could answer, she continued, "I fried three whole chickens. I wanted to bake them an apple cobbler, but we don't have any sugar, and frankly we just simply can't afford to buy any right now."

I replied, "Well, Miss Norvella, Katie will understand." Then I added, "My goodness, how nice of you to cook and bring the chicken."

She handed me the big pot and said, "Tell her we are so sorry about Orville."

"I know Katie would love to see you and Robert and thank you for the food."

Robert spoke up and said, "The battery in the truck is about gone. I'm gonna' need to keep the motor running."

"I'll carry the chicken to the house, but I want you to come with me, because I know Katie Jean will be disappointed if she doesn't get to see you. Just for a moment?"

"Well," she said, "I don't know how some of them white folks will feel about me being in that house."

I shook my head. "I don't know either, but I do know Katie Jean likes you folks and has a lot of respect for you. As far as those other people? Who cares? I'll be right there by your side. Katie will be delighted you came by."

She hesitated briefly, then glanced at Robert who just sat and didn't comment. She looked at me and said, "If you'll go with me, I guess that's what I'll do."

"That's great. Katie will be so happy."

While Miss Norvella and I walked up to the house, two men sitting in lawn chairs watched. One, I think, possibly both, were deacons at the Hopkins' church. I didn't know their last names, but I knew everyone called the one that was bald headed, Brother Bob, and the shorter of the two, Brother Charles.

We walked past them and started up the steps to the porch. I very clearly overheard their whispered conversation. Brother Charles said to Brother Bob, "Looks like we have a Nigger lover among us." Brother Bob said, "I think a lot of those Kansas people are Nigger lovers."

I don't know if they meant for us to hear them, or if they thought they were out of earshot. There wasn't a doubt in my mind about what I heard. I hoped Miss Norvella hadn't heard them. I didn't look in their direction and neither did Miss Norvella. We walked into the house, and I made sure Miss Norvella had Katie Jean's full attention. They both hugged. I looked towards them and held up the big pot of fried chicken.

"Look!" I said, "Miss Norvella fried three whole chickens for you all."

Katie Jean said, "Oh, bless you, Norvella, how nice. I've eaten your delicious fried chicken, and I promise, it will all be consumed."

I was thankful that most everyone in the house made eye contact with Miss Norvella and spoke to her with a warm friendly gesture. I took the chicken to the kitchen and poured myself a glass of iced tea. I tried hard to get those awful racial remarks out of my head. I thought about just walking out the back door to get away from everyone, but I knew Miss Norvella would appreciate me escorting her back to the truck. I went back to the living room, and as I thought, she was ready to leave. I walked Miss Norvella off the porch and across the yard. I didn't make eye contact with the two so-called Christians, Brother Bob and Brother Charles. I just gritted my teeth and walked straight past them to Robert, who waited in the truck.

Miss Norvella called out to B.J. playing in the yard with Donnie. The boys raced across the yard to the truck and began pleading with Miss Norvella to let B.J. stay and play with Donnie. She eventually caved in and said he could stay one hour but then needed to come home.

I spoke up and said, "I'll drive him home in about an hour, if that's okay."

She thought that was a great idea and thanked me. I removed the fire wood blocks from under the tires. Robert gunned the gas on the old truck, and in an almost deafening noise, they roared down the road toward home.

I turned and started to walk toward the house. I knew I would be walking very close to Brother Bob and Brother Charles. I kept telling myself to be careful and not let my emotions get the upper hand. A plan appeared to me, almost as if God had planted a seed of thought in my mind. I actually whispered out loud, "Yes, that is exactly what I am going to do."

~ ~ ~ ~

I walked straight over to the two men with a somewhat friendly smile and put my plan into action. A very fortuitous situation presented itself. A red fox squirrel was feeding under a tree on the far side of the large front yard.

I said, "You know, all the times I had the privilege to attend church with the Hopkins family, you two fellas were always there."

Brother Charles quickly spoke up, "You are sure right about that." Brother Bob quickly affirmed. "If the church doors are open, we will be there."

"Well, I'm sure you both know so much more about the Bible than I do. So do you think God made that red squirrel over there?" I pointed in the direction of the little creature.

"Oh yes, absolutely." Brother Charles replied, "God made everything."

I then pointed to Donnie and B.J. playing in the yard. "So do you think God made Donnie?"

A quick, "Of course. Absolutely," was once again their reply.

"So do you think God made B.J., the little black boy?"

There was somewhat of a hesitation. I could almost sense they had a feeling I was going somewhere with this they weren't expecting.

In a much lower tone, Brother Bob said, "Sure, God made everything."

"Okay then, let me ask you this, do you think God has made any mistakes?"

Both had a somewhat puzzled look on their faces. I patiently waited for their answer.

"No, God doesn't make, or never has made a mistake," both agreed. They not only took my bait, they swallowed it hook, line and sinker.

I said, "Please understand, I have limited knowledge of the Bible, however, if my memory serves me correctly, I do remember the Bible says in Genesis 1:31 'And God saw all that he had made, and behold, it was very good.' I continued, "It's my personal conviction that the Bible instructs us to believe that God, not only never makes a mistake, but God will never let anything, or anyone be forever lost, or to waste anything He has made."

Both men glared into my face while I continued. "I can't imagine how God would feel about someone degrading someone he has made."

I once again looked toward Donnie and B.J. and pointed in their direction. "Can you imagine how God would feel about someone calling Donnie a nigger lover, just because he is playing with B.J?" I continued. "I can only imagine how sad God must be at someone who would call anyone a nigger lover. But trust me, they are out there. God knows who they are. And I personally know two of them."

I glared into their stone-cold faces. Brother Bob was as white as a snowball and Brother Charles' face was as red as a ripe strawberry. I turned and walked away from them. After only a few steps, I slowly turned around, glared into their guilty eyes, and said with a nod, "You gentlemen have a nice day."

I walked toward the Mex house. I very much wanted to turn and look again into their stunned faces, but I kept walking.

CHAPTER 52

'Both B.J. and Donnie are the epitome of innocence, the epitome of honesty. Money, clothes or social status are meaningless. Wouldn't it be nice if we adults could think more like that!'

The door to the Mex house was never locked, so I just opened it and walked in.

Even though it had only been a few months, it was somewhat surreal. Everything was exactly the way I left it the day I drove out of the driveway. The bed where Katie and I had engaged in forbidden love ripped at my soul. The recurring feelings of pure pleasure were mixed with shameful guilt. I made my way out to the toilet and relieved myself of all the coffee and tea I had consumed today. I could hear Donnie and B.J. playing baseball in the pasture out past the toilet.

I opened the gate and walked toward them. They both began to beg me to knock them fly balls. I cheerfully agreed. They each took turns catching the baseball. We all three laughed and teased each other while I kept looking at my watch. I didn't want Miss Norvella to worry about B.J. What seemed like ten to fifteen minutes had swiftly turned into his allotted hour. I told B.J. it was time to get him home. Donnie and B.J. gave each other a high five.

"Are you going to come to my dad's service Friday?" Donnie asked.

B.J. paused for a few seconds, glanced over at me, then looked down at his shoes. He muttered, "This is the only pair of shoes I have. I don't have any dress shoes or clothes that don't have no holes or patches."

I looked at B.J.'s shoes. Robert had taken hog nose-rings and attached the soles of his shoes to the upper parts, and some of the upper seams were torn loose. I could tell Donnie was very disappointed. B.J. looked at Donnie and said, "I'm sorry Donnie, but Mama said that I best not go."

"I don't think that should make any difference," Donnie spoke in a low, but serious voice.

They both just looked at each other. My heart ripped right in two. B.J. was a very cheerful kid. He once again gave Donnie a big high five, and in a confident voice said, "Someday, when I am getting paid a lot of money to play baseball for the Cardinals, I won't have to wear these old shoes and clothes."

Listening to B.J. and Donnie comment that they didn't think clothes should matter, I thought about how they both were the epitome of innocence, the epitome of honesty. Money, clothes and social status were meaningless. Their friendship was far more than on the surface, it ran deep. I thought how nice it would be if we adults could think more like that.

While B.J. got in the car, he was all smiles and looked over every inch of my new Oldsmobile.

He said, "Mr. Leon, this must be the nicest car in the whole wide world." Before I could comment, he blared out, "I'm gonna' buy me a car just like this, 'cept I want it red, when I get big and play for the Cardinals." There was no doubt B.J. had big dreams. I glanced over at him and thought, thank God, B.J. can dream.

~ ~ ~ ~

Miss Norvella was out working in her garden when we pulled into the driveway. She saw us and walked in our direction. Chickens were everywhere. Big chickens, little chickens, and every size in between. She thanked me for bringing B.J. home, then asked me if I'd like a glass of tea. Before I could answer she said, "It's not sweet and somewhat weak, but it is tea, and you're sure welcome to a glass."

Quite frankly, I had no intention of accepting her offer, but I didn't want to seem as though her tea wasn't good enough for me. So, I graciously said, "I would love a glass of your tea."

We walked up to the porch. She pointed at an old chair and said,

"Sit down for a bit and relax, Mr. Leon."

She returned with the tea, and we both sat down. She said, "Robert is in the back field workin', he won't be in till dark. I appreciate him working so hard to keep us fed, but sometimes I wished we lived in town, so he didn't have to work so hard. Me and Robert both would like to leave this old farm and move to a city where things might be easier for us, and we could give B.J. a better life."

"Why don't you do just that?" I asked her while I looked into her eyes.

She gazed at me with sadness on her face. "Well, there are several reasons. We always seem to struggle to find enough courage to take that leap. We don't know where to go, we don't know anyone in the city that might help us find a place to live and help Robert find a job." Then she said, "And we owe Mr. Green, our landowner, so much money. We work hard, but never seem to get out of debt to him."

A bell went off in my head. Bill Johnson in St. Louis! I said, "Miss Norvella, I think I just might know someone who can help you." I began telling her all about Bill and Wanda Johnson, and how Bill worked for the Chrysler Corporation in St Louis.

"He was raised around Neelyville, much like you folks, and now he is a pastor of a church." Miss Norvella, I said, "I just know he will help you."

Her face had a bright smile when she said, "I can't wait to tell Robert."

I said, "Miss Norvella, I'm not trying to change the subject, but there is something I would like to talk to you about."

She seemed puzzled. "What's on your mind, son?"

I hesitated for a few seconds. I wanted to approach this right. I then realized there isn't a right or wrong way. So, I just flat out told her what I wanted to do. "Donnie sure does want B.J. to go to his dad's service with him."

Before I could utter another word, she said, "Oh Mr. Leon, B.J. don't have any clothes fit to go to no funeral."

"Well, I am pretty sure I have a plan to change that," I said.

I would have been okay buying B.J. some clothes, but I knew Miss Norvella and Robert were very proud folks, and most likely wouldn't want any type of handout. So, I began telling her about how my mom had left money for me and my brother to use to help good folks like her and Robert. She seemed intrigued.

I said, "The funeral is at 10:30 Friday morning. I could come back tomorrow morning and take you and B.J. into Malden, and we could get him some clothes and shoes. Then we could surprise Donnie. That would make Donnie so happy, and frankly, it would make me very happy."

She shook her head. "I just don't know what to say, Mr. Leon. That's so nice of you."

Before she could say another word, I spoke up and said, "Now you don't want to disappoint my mama, do you? She is looking down from heaven, and I can assure you, she would be thrilled to see B.J. sitting in that church, attending his best friend's dad's funeral service."

Her face lit up and was consumed in a beautiful smile. She looked straight at me. "Well, I sure don't think we wanna' disappoint your mama now, do we? What time do you want me and B.J. ready in the morning?"

"Can you be ready by 8:30?"

"Yes sir," she replied.

I got up out of my chair and walked off the porch. I was almost to my car when Miss Norvella called my name. I turned and looked in her direction. She said, "Mr. Leon, your mother sure did raise a mighty fine young man."

I graciously said, "Well thank you, I wish you could have known her. She was a very good, Godly woman."

"I know she was, and I want you to know how much we appreciate what you're doing for our B.J."

I answered, "You are welcome. I'll see you at 8:30 in the morning."

CHAPTER 53

'Stop and hear the laughter in a child at play, not so concerned about tomorrow they forget to live today. Happiness doesn't always go to the one with the highest bid. What's the matter, people, are we too dumb to learn something from a kid?'

I drove rather hard heading back into Malden. It was time for a good country style meal, and I was more than ready. Once I finished eating my fill, I went straight to the motel. I was exhausted. It had been a very hard day. After a long hot shower, I put on some lounge clothes and laid across the bed, thinking about all that had happened today. Suddenly my mind raced through the twisted memories of the last five months.

I thought about all the poems and songs I had written while I was in Decatur, mired down in the blues. One night Larry, Martha, and I were watching the news. A local TV station was doing a story about a Children's Research Hospital in Memphis that Danny Thomas had founded.

The short segment was very touching, showing the small, sick children with their parents in the hospital named St. Jude Children's Research Hospital. When I went to bed that night, I laid there, thinking about those kids and how they had big smiles on their faces. I also thought about how B.J. and Donnie could only play with each other on the weekends. How wrong was that? Once again, I was compelled to get my pen and paper out, and I wrote this.

STOP AND HEAR THE LAUGHTER

Verse
'Pushing and a shoving the world can be so rude,
but across town In Memphis, there is a place called St. Jude.
Though the pain is bitter lying there in bed,
a big smile on a little face, a card his Mama just read'.

Chorus
'Stop and hear the laughter in a child at play, not so
concerned about tomorrow, they forget to live today.
Happiness doesn't always go to the one with the highest bid.
What's the matter people are we too dumb
to learn something from a kid?'

Verse
'Donnie can't wait till the weekend he will play with his best
Friend, not concerned about the clothes he wears or
the color of his skin.
A child loves so easy, always willing to forgive.
Maybe, just maybe, that is how we all should live.'

Chorus
'Stop and hear the laughter in a child at play, not so
concerned about tomorrow, they forget to live today.
Happiness doesn't always go to the one with the highest bid.
What's the matter people are we to dumb
to learn something from a kid?'

I tossed and turned for a short time, then fell into a much-needed, long night's sleep. I was in a deep sleep when the alarm clock went off. Something I seldom ever do, I dressed and drove over to the little café I had eaten at last night, consumed a large breakfast, and headed to Miss Novella's. I deliberately drove the long way so as not to go by the Hopkins' farm. I no more than turned the ignition off when the door flew open. There was no question, B.J. and Miss Norvella were ready to go.

Our conversation going to Malden was mostly B.J. talking about how he and Donnie were going to play for the St. Louis Cardinals. I of course said, "I can see both of you doing that," knowing full well chances were slim to very slim.

Just as soon as we entered the clothing store, Miss Norvella was all business. She first went to the dress pants, then to the white dress shirts. A large shelf of Levi brand blue jeans and a rack of nice casual plaid shirts were nearby. It was very obvious to me, her common sense told her B.J. would get way more use out of blue jeans and a plaid shirt than the dress clothes. I wanted desperately to just stay out of it, but my better judgment was certainly pulling me in the direction of the blue jeans and plaid shirts.

I walked up to her and said, "Miss Norvella, my mom was a very smart and conservative lady. You choose whatever you wish for B.J. to wear. But I will say this, I think I hear my mama's voice saying be smart. B.J. will look just fine in a nice new shirt and a new pair of starched and ironed Levi blue jeans. He could wear them later to school."

Miss Norvella said, "I think your mama is right, and that's what I'm gonna do."

The decision on the shoes was much the same, and we both picked out a nice, rugged pair of casual-work shoes. B.J. tried everything on and Miss Norvella made sure they were slightly large. She said, "Trust me, I know he'll grow into them, possibly before we get home."

I love Miss Novella's bubbly personality. I had noticed a sign on the rack of the casual shirts where we got B.J.'s. It read, 'Buy one and get the second one half-price.' When we left the shoe area, I said, "Let's go back over to the shirts."

Neither one of them said a word, they just followed me. I turned and looked at B.J. "If I bought you another one of these shirts, do you think you could get me really good seats at a game in Sportsman Park when you're playing for the Cardinals?"

I don't know whose smile was the biggest, B.J.'s, Miss Norvella's, or mine. B.J. looked at me with a very no nonsense, look and said, "I'm gonna buy you tickets to all the games."

I immediately replied, "Boy! What a deal! Pick out another shirt!"

The store clerk bagged up B.J. 's clothes and shoes, then we all three loaded in the car. However, I had one more stop in mind. I remembered B.J. and Donnie talking about their birthdays being only days apart. I had bought Mary Beth and Alice a birthday present, the hula hoops. I knew I wanted to give Donnie something for his birthday. I also knew they both wanted baseball gloves alike. I drove up to the sporting goods store and parallel parked. I looked in the back seat and asked B.J. if he could keep a secret.

"Sure." "I am going to buy Donnie a new baseball glove for his birthday. Do you know which one he likes?"

"Yes sir! I know 'xactly which one."

"Would you care to go pick it out for me?"

"Sure!"

We made our way over to the large inventory of baseball gloves. He pointed to the one Donnie liked. I was lucky, they had two, both identical. I picked up both of them and started walking to the front counter of the store. B.J. didn't say a word, neither did I. Then I laid the two gloves on the counter, paid for both, and we walked back to the car. I laid the sack that held the gloves on the car seat between me and Miss Norvella.

She said, "Did you find it okay?"

I said, "Yes, as a matter of fact, I liked it so well I bought myself one just like it."

Miss Norvella had a thousand questions about my friends, Bill and Wanda Johnson in St. Louis.

She asked, "Do you have their address?"

"Yes, I most certainly do. I'll give it to you before I leave."

We had just about made it back to their house. I could hardly wait to spring the surprise on B.J. about this new glove. I couldn't help but wonder what was going through his mind. We pulled in the drive where Robert was out working on a piece of equipment. He waved and headed toward the house.

Miss Norvella had B.J.'s clothes in her hand and walked toward Robert. She was so excited to show him each piece of clothing and the new shoes.

I turned to B.J. and said, "Do you have a baseball?"

"Yeah," he replied.

"Go get it, let's try out these new gloves."

He sprinted into the house and returned in a flash. I tossed him one of the new gloves and I took the other one. We tossed the ball back and forth.

"What do you think about Donnie's glove?" I asked.

"Oh man, it's super nice."

I took the one I had on my hand and looked it over.

I said, "I don't care for this glove at all, it doesn't fit my hand, it's too small. I wish I hadn't bought it."

I was working very hard to keep a straight face. I said, "How does that one you have on fit you?"

"Ohhh man, it fits me perfectly!" he said.

I continued. "Well, how about you just keep that one, and I will give this one to Donnie?"

He was stunned, then he looked at his mom and dad, who both wore big smiles.

He looked back at me and I said, "Happy Birthday B.J. I've just been fooling with you."

"Oh gee, I think this is the best day of my life! Thank you so much!"

"You are so very welcome," I replied. I looked back over at Robert and Miss Norvella just in time to catch them both wiping tears.

We all made our way to the porch. Miss Norvella said, "I'm going to make some tea."

Just when she started into the house, Robert spoke in a very cheerful voice. He said, "Honey, come here, I've got some good news."

Before he could explain, Miss Norvella asked, "Did Mr. Carl come by?"

"Yes, he did."

"Did you get the money?" she asked.

"Yes and no," he answered.

Miss Norvella seemed puzzled.

He said, "He gave me one hundred dollars. He would have given me the two hundred I had asked for, but he wanted me to pay back the two hundred plus twenty dollars interest. I knew we could get by with just a hundred dollars right now, so I agreed to pay him $110.00 back. So now we can get a new battery for the truck and buy some sugar for the tea.

Miss Norvella laughed and said, "Yes, and I can bake us a cake."

"Mr. Carl Green is our landlord," Robert explained. "He won't pay us for our cotton until we get it all out and he takes his part. "We usually don't get out of debt to him, and I think he likes it that way. But this year should be different. I have put in a big lot of corn on some new ground. We have three sows that have twenty-two pigs. We will fatten them up and sell them. We have the best cotton crop we've ever had here. Our three milk cows all have big calves. We should have enough money to get out of debt and have enough money to perhaps move to St. Louis and start a new life." Before I could say a word, Robert added, "Leon, I'd like to get that friend of your's address."

"You got it! I'll get in touch with him, and I can assure you, he'll be helpful. I know Bill, and I promise, he will be able to help you folks."

We all sat on the porch and enjoyed our very weak, unsweet tea. B.J. sat next to me and was totally engrossed in his new glove, just squeezing it one way, then another, pounding his fist into the leather, forming what he perceived to be the perfect pocket.

I looked at Miss Norvella. "I want to surprise Donnie. I'm not going to tell him B.J. is going to the funeral. The funeral is at 10:30. I'll come down about 9:45 in the morning. Have B.J. ready. I'll have Donnie with me. He'll think I'm just taking him for a drive. I can't wait to see his face when he sees B.J. all dressed up and ready to go to his dad's funeral."

B.J. was giggling when he said, "That's going to be so much fun."

I finished my tea, said goodbye, then drove down to the Hopkins' farm.

CHAPTER 54

'His voice had a touch of doubt. "I guess I do, but I don't know how you could be so perfect to get into heaven."'

I hoped there wouldn't be anyone at the house. I wanted to have a few minutes to talk to Katie, just me and her. My wish soon faded, there were cars in the driveway. I parked, then walked to the house.

A young couple, probably in their early twenties, were on their way out of the house. We spoke to each other, and they soon drove away. I wanted to give Donnie his birthday present. I heard Katie visiting with a few other people. When I stepped up on the porch, Katie realized I was there and shouted for me to come in.

I entered the house and politely spoke to everyone. Katie quickly introduced me. They were neighbors I had never met. I didn't want to be rude, but I didn't want to stay in the house. I asked Katie if she knew where Donnie was. She said, "He's around here somewhere. I haven't seen him in a while."

I looked around the barn, no Donnie, no Bo. I looked in the Mex house with the same results. Then it hit me, the tater shed. Unlike before, I wouldn't be going to the back and peeping through a knot hole. I would go to the front door. I heard Donnie talking to Bo, I made sure he wasn't praying. It was obvious his words were for his bestest, bestest buddy in the world.

I eased the door open. There he was, sitting on a bale of hay with his arm around Bo.

Uninvited, I just walked in. "Do you mind if I sit down beside you?"

"Sure, I'd like that," he said. Donnie had his head down, staring at the floor. I wanted to grab him and give him a big hug. But Donnie was twelve-years-old, and very mature for his age. I knew I didn't want to make him feel uncomfortable, so I patted him on the back of the head. With his head down and his eyes glued to the floor, he softly spoke, "Do you think there is a heaven? I mean like a for-sure place where we all go when we die if we are good?"

I was rather sure I knew where Donnie's train of thought was. "Yes, I do, what do you think, Donnie?"

His voice had a touch of doubt. "I guess I do, but I don't know how you could be so perfect to get into heaven."

"Oh Donnie, I don't think God expects us to be perfect. As a matter of fact, I know God doesn't expect us to be perfect."

With his head still down and his eyes still staring at the floor, he asked, "Do you think Daddy is in heaven?"

It was a jolt to my soul. It was as though Donnie had written the last verse of my song. "Will the bright lights of Heaven shine on the dark side of him?" My mind raced in circles, and I desperately searched for an appropriate answer. The only thing I could think of was my old stand-by, answering with a question. "What do you think, Donnie?"

He hesitated for a minute. I most certainly wanted to know his answer. "I hope so, but I really don't know. Daddy was always helping people, and he always went to church. I know he was sometimes mean to me, Mama, Alice, and Mary Beth. He sometimes did really bad nasty stuff to me. When he got mad, he would curse really bad, like saying stuff with God's name in it. I don't want Daddy to be in hell. I don't know if it makes any difference to God about what he did to me, but I've been praying that God will not send him to hell for that."

It was like a big knot just wadded up inside my heart. To hear this young boy, who had suffered so much abuse from his own dad, confide in me that he actually prayed for his daddy's soul, and asked God not to send him to hell for the abuse he had inflicted upon him, was more than gut wrenching. Donnie still had his head down and began nervously kicking his heels against the hay bale.

I was shocked when he asked, "Do you think a person who tries to kill someone but fails, will go to hell?"

I answered him this way. "I suppose it depends on a lot of

different circumstances."

Donnie took a deep breath. "Well, I know no one took Bo out of our yard. About a month ago me and B.J. were playing baseball out in the cow pasture, and B.J. hit me a long fly ball. It went over my head. You know over by the old grown-up fence, where the old broken-down equipment is?"

"Sure, I've noticed that old rusty equipment over there."

"Well," he said, "the baseball rolled under that old corn picker. I crawled under it to get our ball, and hanging up a little way on a pulley, was Bo's collar. I took it down and looked at it. I knew it was Bo's, it's the same color and had his name and our phone number on it."

He hesitated for a few seconds. "Daddy tried to kill my Bo. I know it says in the Bible thou shalt not kill. I know Bo is not just like a normal dog, Bo is more like a person. So, I wonder if God will send Daddy to hell for trying to kill Bo."

I could tell this was ripping at his little heart. I most certainly was on the fence with this one. I thought about how extremely difficult it had been for Donnie the last few years. It was as though a voice said, 'Give him peace with this.'

"I believe our God is a fair God, and I believe He is going to remember all the good things about your dad. I, myself, believe your dad is not in hell, but is in heaven."

He raised his head for the first time since I walked in the tater shed. He looked at me and said, "That is what I am going to believe also. That Daddy is in heaven, not hell."

Donnie, as he often did, surprised me. He said, "I prayed God would forgive me for kinda' like, lying to Daddy." He continued. "You remember the combination lock you bought for the gate for Bo's pen?"

I nodded, not knowing where he was going with this.

"Daddy asked me to write the combination down on a piece of paper and put it in the glove box of the truck. After I saw Bo's collar, I was afraid Daddy would get Bo out and kill him when I wasn't around. So, I threw the first piece of paper away, and wrote a new combination."

I spoke with extreme confidence, and said, "Trust me, I can assure you, God has forgiven you for that. He knows you were just protecting your best friend."

I felt good about his assessment of the question he had asked, and I knew I didn't want to give it a chance to unravel. I quickly spoke up and said, "Hey! I have something out in my car for you. You want to go see what it is?"

His whole demeanor changed in seconds. "Sure! What is it?" he cheerfully asked.

"I am not going to tell you, but why don't we go see what it is?"

Donnie giggled. "Okay, let's go!"

While we walked toward my car, I noticed Katie's neighbors were standing on the front porch, giving her a hug. Donnie and I continued walking over to the car and opened the door.

"I bought you an early birthday gift, Donnie, and if you don't like it, you can exchange it for a hula hoop."

Donnie seemed quite anxious to look inside the big brown bag that held the baseball glove.

I told him, "I didn't wrap it up, is that okay?"

"Yep, that's okay, no problem," he said.

I held out the brown bag, looked at Donnie, and said, "I hope you like it. Happy birthday, buddy."

Donnie took the bag and quickly looked inside. He jerked that glove out of the bag in a flash. His eyes got wide, and his whole face exploded with pure excitement. "Oh man, are you kidding me?" he asked.

I honestly thought for a second, he was going to cry from just pure joy. He slipped the glove on and took his first pounding at the center of the glove.

I jokingly said, "Remember, if you don't like it, you can exchange it for a hula hoop."

Donnie looked at me, and with the wit he often exhibited said, "I might not be smart, but I'm not completely stupid. I want this glove, not no stupid hula hoop." He asked, "How did you know which one I wanted?"

"I just thought, if I were as good of a baseball player as you are, that would be the glove I would want." I smiled at him.

"Boy, you sure were right about the one I wanted. I didn't think in a million years I would get this one. Thank you so very much."

"You're very welcome."

He said, "Let's go try it out!"

"Okay sure, I would love that."

Donnie and I played catch out by the Mex house, as the neighbors that had been visiting with Katie were leaving. I looked toward Katie, she in turn, looked toward me. I suggested that Donnie toss the ball against the concrete garage and told him that I was going to visit with his mom. He nodded and thanked me again for the new glove.

CHAPTER 55

'Katie's eyebrows raised on her forehead she gave me a different look. I quickly said, "No I didn't in any way mention me and you."'

I walked toward Katie, and she pointed to the two lawn chairs in the front yard. We both reached the chairs at the same time. I turned my chair so I would be looking directly into her face. Katie looked exhausted, as would be expected.

I began, "I know it has been a hard couple of days Katie. My heart goes out to you."

"Thanks, and yes, it most definitely has been rough."

We made small talk for a few minutes. I had so many things I wanted to share with her, and I knew someone could be pulling in the drive at any time. A part of me wanted to just let the past go. I knew perhaps now was not the time to bring any of that up. However, I so much wanted to apologize for the way I cowardly tucked my tail and left. I kept pondering the discussion, then I just opened up and said it.

"Katie, I am so sorry for the way I left."

We continued to look deep into the other one's soul. Katie turned and looked across the yard, she looked back at me and said with a stern voice, "I understand, Leon, but I must admit, I hated you for a few days. It hurt so much. The girls were disappointed, but it just crushed Donnie. Orville was almost impossible to live with. He got up angry and went to bed angry. Poor little Donnie caught unbelievable hell every day."

She took a deep breath and in a softer voice said, "After several days, I was able to analyze the whole situation. I understand it really was the only way.

"However," she continued, "when you were here, there seemed to be a glimmer of hope. That simply vanished when you were no longer here."

I nodded. "Trust me, I visualized and considered every possible means to somehow help you and the kids. There just simply wasn't an answer. Any time I would visualize a scene as I said goodbye, I would get an image of a very ugly situation." I leaned forward, looked Katie straight in the eye, took her hand and gave it a gentle squeeze.

"These last four months I have thought of you and those kids a million times. I would wake up in the middle of the night thinking about Orville beating the dickens out of the kids, especially Donnie. I saw the many bruises on your body, and the extra make-up you would use to cover up a red mark on your face. It absolutely drove me crazy. My brother, Larry, and especially his wife, Martha, saw something was very wrong. I opened up to them one night and told them the whole story." Katie's eyebrows raised on her forehead, and she gave me a different look. I quickly said, "No, I didn't, in any way, mention me and you."

"Good," she quickly said. "I will go to my grave without ever telling anyone."

"After I shared with Larry and Martha, one incident after another about Orville, we all agreed I must do something. Larry worked with a gentleman who had a brother-n-law who was employed with the Division of Family Services in Illinois. Larry confided in him about your situation. He did some research and located the correct source of someone who could help in Poplar Bluff. I talked to him over the phone, and I actually had an appointment this coming Monday at 9:00 am to discuss your situation."

Katie looked at me, wiped a tear, smiled, and said, "Bless your heart." She took a deep breath. "Your intentions were wonderful and heartfelt. But I will say, I don't think there would have been any help from those people, and quite frankly, I believe they would have made things worse." She gave me a hard look. "That's just my true opinion."

Katie softly spoke my name. "Leon." There was a long pause. "Orville was the father to my three kids, and in some ways, he was a good, hard-working man. I shared my bed and my life with him for fifteen years. But Orville had this dark side, and those times made it very miserable for me and my kids." She took a deep breath then continued. "If this accident hadn't happened, I honestly believe that me or Donnie, or Alice, would have snapped. I feel one of us very well would have done something unspeakable. I'm sorry, but I am just being honest. I can say without reservation, and I might very well go to hell for feeling this way, but I think Orville's death is a blessing in disguise." Katie looked at me as if to be measuring my reaction. Before I could comment she said, "I know deep within my heart, this is actually how you feel also, am I not right?"

I responded, "I, too, might go to hell for feeling this way, but you're right, I do feel extremely relieved knowing you and the kids will no longer be abused."

I continued to tell her the whole story. "Caterpillar was a great company, and for a lot of people, it would have been a wonderful place to make a career. But after a lot of thought, some prayers, and some doors opening, I'm going a different direction in my life."

I was so grateful for this opportunity to tell her the full story. I explained that I had purchased Larry's half of the homestead. Larry and I were going to keep the 380 acres of crop ground and rent it out as we have been doing. I told her I was moving back to Wellington, and that my plan, at this time, was to enroll in classes at Wichita State. I wanted to tell her about my reason for going back to college, but we both heard a vehicle coming down the road.

"I'm leaving as soon as the funeral is over tomorrow." I took her hand, smiled at her and said, "Trust me, I'll call you in a few days and see how everything is going."

We looked up and saw not one, but three cars coming down the road. When all three cars pulled into the drive, Katie looked at me and said, "Don't leave now. Please come in and eat with us."

When I hesitated for just a second, Katie said, "Trust me, you don't want to miss out on Roger's BBQ ribs. You'll remember Roger, he's the song leader at church. BBQ ribs are his specialty, and he has been cooking all morning."

Roger and the rest of the group gathered their items and began walking our way, with several large trays of ribs. I looked at those unbelievable BBQ ribs, and just then I got a whiff of the aroma. I stuck my arm out toward Katie and said, "Twist my arm just a little bit."

Katie chuckled and said, "I promise, that's the best decision you have made today,"

Katie and I followed everyone to the kitchen. We all made small talk, mostly about the amount of food. There was food of all kinds. I quickly filled my plate, including a large portion of the wonderful ribs. I remember seeing a table that was set up on the front porch. I found a spot and had no more than set down when a couple of the men joined me. One of them was Buzz Overtree, the guy who we helped plant his crop on my first day at the Hopkins'. He remembered I helped and told me how much he appreciated my involvement in that day. He told me how much he had admired Orville, and how he was always one of the first to help his neighbors.

He said, "I feel it is now my duty to pay it forward. Come Monday, I have a large group, and I mean a very large group, of pickers, that will be descending on Katie's cotton fields. I have checked, and the weather should be good all next week. I've gotten in touch with several farmers with combines. They, too, will harvest all her soybeans and corn next week."

"Wow. How wonderful Buzz! Thank you so much."

Buzz replied in a somewhat emotional voice. "I just know Orville is looking down and is very happy we're doing this for Katie."

"Yes," I said. "I most certainly agree."

I excused myself from the table and remarked to Roger how wonderful the ribs were. I could have eaten another half-rack for sure, but I didn't want to pig out. I made my way back to the kitchen and looked for the dessert Katie had mentioned. Wilma, Katie's sister, realized what I wanted and whispered to me, "The desserts are on the back porch."

I thanked her and headed that way. To my surprise, Wilma followed me out on the porch. As I considered my many choices, she spoke up and said, "The coconut cream pie is in that old refrigerator."

I looked at her and smiled great big, and said, "Did you read my mind?"

She replied, "No, Katie told me that was your favorite." She continued, "Katie has told me so much about you, she simply adores you."

I felt my face blush with embarrassment. "I can assure you the feeling is mutual."

Wilma looked toward the kitchen door to make sure no one was in earshot. She whispered, "I also know you are aware of Orville's dark side."

"Yes, unfortunately I am." I shook my head.

Wilma continued to speak in that very low voice. "As far as I know, me, you and Katie's dear friend Bonnie are the only ones who know just how bad it really was."

I said, "Trust me, I saw enough to know how unbelievable it was."

"Yes, I know you did," she replied.

Wilma then said something that shocked me to the core. She said, "Chester and I think it was even worse than Katie Jean knew. I can't give you any details, but Chester witnessed something with Alice that he believes takes Orville's abuse to a whole other level."

Wilma looked straight into my eyes, seemingly waiting for my reaction. I just kept my cool. I don't know why Wilma felt a need to share this with me, but I kept silent.

She quickly changed the subject. "By the way, I know Katie has shared her and Orville's huge mortgage and farm debt with you." Before I could answer, or even figure out where she was going with this, she said with a very cheerful smile, "Katie told me this morning that Nathan Cooper, their banker, called her yesterday afternoon to give his condolences. During their conversation he told her that the bank had required Orville to purchase a life insurance policy, whereas their farm, and farm debt, would be paid in full in case of an accident, heart failure, or cancer. The premium was automatically added to their total payments annually." Her eyes just gleamed and danced when she said in a very excited voice, "Her farm and farm debt is totally clear of any mortgage. It's paid in full!" I felt a warmth of peace and joy fill my heart. I said, "Oh my, that is the best news I've heard in a while."

Just about the time Wilma was getting ready to cut the pie she had retrieved from the refrigerator, Katie walked out onto the porch. Wilma handed me the pie and said, "Enjoy."

I thanked her and she said, "I'm going to get me another one of those ribs." She walked back into the kitchen.

CHAPTER 56

'I could easily see how one could have a profound amount of respect for Orville, if you didn't have a clue about his dark side, and most didn't.'

I found a chair in the corner of the porch and sat down with my pie. I offered to retrieve another chair that was at the far end of the porch for Katie.

She said, "Oh no, that's okay. I need to go make a phone call. I just wanted to thank you again for being here for the funeral."

"Well, I have something I need to share with you Katie."

She looked at me with a question. "What would that be?"

"Yesterday afternoon, when I was playing baseball with B.J. and Donnie, Donnie asked B.J. if he was going to come to his dad's service. B.J. said he couldn't because he didn't have clothes that didn't have holes or patches."

Katie spoke up and said, "Yes, I know, Donnie told me. I would let him wear Donnie's clothes but B.J. is much bigger than Donnie."

"Well, don't tell Donnie, because I want to surprise him." Katie looked puzzled. I continued. "Miss Norvella, B.J. and I went to Malden this morning, and I bought B.J. some new clothes and a new pair of shoes."

Katie looked like she could cry. "Oh my gosh, that's so sweet of you!"

"Now listen, don't say a word to Donnie. I plan to pretend to take him on a ride in my car in the morning, just before the service, and pick-up B.J."

"You are just too good to be true."

"There's something else I want your approval of. I know Donnie wants B.J. to sit with him, how do you feel about that?"

Katie didn't hesitate. "I love that idea. As a matter of fact, I would love for you to sit with B.J and Donnie. Donnie obviously adores you." She smiled at me with one of those smiles that could tame the devil, then softly said, "So do I."

I finished my pie and told Katie I would see them in the morning. I was just beginning to back out of the drive when I heard Alice let out a loud yell. "Leon...wait!" I looked up toward the house and saw Alice running down the hill toward me. When she got to the car she gasped for air and said, "Thank goodness. I was afraid you'd be gone. Mama wanted me to tell you our church is serving a big meal tomorrow after the service. She told me to tell you to be sure and eat with us. There will be plenty of good food."

I had been wanting to talk to the kids, just me and the three of them alone. This would be a perfect opportunity to say goodbye to them. Alice, of course, was at the car, and I could see Donnie and Mary Beth over by the Mex house combing Bo's hair. I quickly asked Alice to stay there, and I called out to Mary Beth and Donnie, "Hey guys, can you come over here, please?"

I looked at each of them and said, "I know the loss of your dad has been tough. I'm so sorry you are going through this. Everything is going to be okay. It will just take a little time."

Each nodded in agreement. I took the time to compliment, each one of them, and let them know how proud I was to have met them. I told them that they would always be special to me, and that we would keep in touch. I also told them that I knew they were the type of kids that would step up and be there for their mother. Each assured me they would. I explained I was going to need to be on the road to Kansas just as soon as the service was over. All three seemed disappointed, but acknowledged they understood. I gave each of them a big hug, including Donnie. I looked at Alice, "tell your mom thanks for the invite for the meal at the church. Please let her know my plans to leave right after the service." She nodded. What great kids. I felt a mixture of love and relief, knowing the abuse was finally over.

~ ~ ~ ~

I drove back to the motel in Malden to relax. I laid across the bed and thought about Brenda, and how much fun it would be if I surprised her when I got to Lamar. I decided to call Mary's Café. Luckily Mary answered the phone. "Mary, how are things going? This is Leon."

"Leon! Brenda's not here, she's gone to take Shelia to the doctor."

"What's wrong? Hopefully nothing serious."

"She just has had a cold for several days and can't seem to get over it, so Brenda decided to take her to the doctor."

"Will Brenda be working tomorrow, late afternoon?" I explained, "I want to surprise her and drop in and eat supper at your place. I plan on staying at the Travelers Hotel there in Lamar tomorrow night and possibly even Saturday night, that is, unless Brenda runs me off."

Mary laughed. "You won't have to worry about that. I don't think there's been many days since you left that she hasn't spoken your name. You are going to make my little sister one very happy gal."

"Now, please, don't let her know I am going to be there, okay?"

"I won't say one word, but I am over the moon excited."

I drove across Malden to a gas station and filled up the car and got some snacks and Pepsi for my road trip tomorrow. I read all the newspapers I picked up at the station. The motel bed was a little short for my six-foot-three-inch body, but I managed to get to sleep fairly soon.

I woke up at three in the morning. I lay frozen in total shock from the dream I just had. I replayed the dream time and time again. I wanted to be able to remember every detail of this dream. It was like no other dream I had ever had before. I knew if I replayed it in my physical awakened state, I would be able to remember it. If I waited until morning, I would forget it. This most certainly was a dream I wanted to forever remember.

My anticipation for the day had me up early. After loading my car and checking out of the motel, I drove over to the café, and ate a nice country breakfast.

I arrived at the Hopkins' farm at about the perfect time. I knew this would be a rough day for everyone. I was excited, however, to surprise Donnie with having his best friend there. When I pulled in, several cars were parked in the driveway. It was as though Donnie had been waiting for me. He had on a pair of dress pants and what looked like a new white shirt. He started to walk toward me, and I felt a huge sense of relief lift off my shoulders. No more abuse, little man, no more abuse, was all I thought.

I commented, "Man, you sure do look nice, Donnie."

He smiled great big and said, "You look funny in that suit, Leon."

I thought oh, the innocence of a child. I always felt a measure of pride, knowing Donnie seemed so comfortable talking with me. I walked up to the house and spoke to everyone that was there. I briefly talked to Katie and told her I was going to take Donnie for a ride in my car. She smiled great big and gave me a wink. Donnie was out on the porch, so I suggested he come with me.

When we walked toward my car I said, "Hey, you haven't ridden in my new car. How would you like to take a quick spin?"

"Boy yea! That would be great," he cheerfully replied.

When Donnie sat down on the seat, his too-short dress pants scooted up halfway to his knees. He looked over at me and said, "My pants are too short, but Mama told me that there wouldn't be anybody looking at my pants anyway."

I had noticed they were a little short, but I just told him a little white lie about not noticing them at all. He seemed pleased with that. Then Donnie, as he often would do, just blurted out, "Me and Alice got into a fuss fight this morning."

"She insisted I wear a tie. I hate ties. And I told her I wasn't going to wear one. We were almost screaming at each other. Then Mama told Alice that it would be fine if I didn't wear it. So, ha, ha, Alice, I won."

Donnie was so involved in his story he hadn't noticed we were pulling into B.J.'s driveway. He immediately spoke up and shouted. "Oh, are we going to take B.J. for a ride too?"

About that time, in what almost seemed rehearsed, Robert and Miss Norvella stepped out on the porch. Both turned and looked toward the door. Then the star of the show walked out on stage. There B.J. was, looking like a million bucks. Miss Norvella had washed the new clothes and ironed creases that could cut you in both the shirt collar, sleeves, and down both pant legs. Donnie looked like a boy at a circus, eyes bugged out as big as half-dollars.

"Holy miracle!" he blurted. "B.J. got all new clothes!"

Donnie and I got out of the car and Robert invited us in. Donnie and B.J. glared into each other's eyes. Donnie broke the silence by saying, "B.J., you look plum handsome."

B.J. replied, "Donnie, I am going to your dad's funeral and sit beside you."

"Great!" Donnie answered.

About the time we got to the porch, B.J. bolted back into the house and quickly came out with his new glove.

B.J. looked at Donnie and said, "Look! I got a new glove for my birthday!"

Donnie quickly said, "You won't believe this, but I got one for my birthday just like it."

B.J. said, "I would believe it because I picked it out for you."

We all started laughing. You could see the light that came on when Donnie put it all together. I told the boys they best get in the car. We needed to get back to the Hopkins' house.

"Mr. Leon, when do you think you will have B.J. back home?" Miss Norvella asked.

I answered, "They're going to have dinner at the church after the service, but I don't plan on staying. I need to head back to Kansas this afternoon. I should have B.J. back by lunch time."

When we pulled up to the Hopkins' farm, people were beginning to load into cars. I told the boys to just stay in the car. We would follow everyone. We entered the church parking area, and the officials from the funeral home directed us to park near the side door. Shortly, we all entered the church and took our seats in the front rows on one side of the church. A part of me felt out of place. I most certainly wasn't family. However, it was Katie's call, more than anyone else, and Katie Jean very much wanted me there, along with B.J. for her precious little boy. So, I suppose, the heck with what anyone else thinks. I proudly sat on the very outside near the middle aisle. I made eye contact with a few who sat on the opposite side, including Brother Bob, the church deacon who referred to me as a nigger lover. Seeing him made me even more pleased that Katie wanted B.J. to sit with Donnie.

Orville's service was pretty much what you would expect. Traditional songs were sung, the eulogy was read, and positive remarks were made about what a good husband, father, strong Christian, and a helping neighbor Orville was. I could easily see how one could have a profound amount of respect for Orville. On the surface, he was all those things they were saying about him. Ninety-nine percent of the people attending his service had not seen his dark side. Just as soon as the service was over, I said goodbye to Katie Jean and the kids. I told Katie I would check on her in a few days.

CHAPTER 57

'I turned and walked away, only to turn and look back at Bo one more time. I felt my spirit was speaking directly with the spirit of an old friend. Thank you too, Johnny Hooper.'

B.J. and I made small talk while we traveled the road back to his house. In a few minutes we passed the Hopkins' home. I knew as soon as I dropped B.J. off, I wanted to go back to the Hopkins' homestead. I was sure everyone would be enjoying lunch at the church, so there shouldn't be anyone at the house. Just in case I never returned, I wanted to reminisce one more time. So many memories in such a short period of time, and I felt a need to say goodbye to a dear friend.

When we pulled into B.J.'s drive, I saw what I expected to see, Robert out working. B.J. spoke up and explained, "Daddy is building a new pig fence."

Robert waved and headed to the house. Just as B.J. and I got to the house, Miss Norvella came out onto the porch. They both asked about Orville's service. Miss Norvella instructed B.J. to go get his new clothes off and again graciously thanked me. They both had a few more questions about Bill Johnson in St. Louis. I gladly answered their questions, and assured them Bill and Wanda would help them.

I was in the process of saying goodbye to them when Miss Norvella spoke up. "I know you said you needed to get on the road, so I packed you a lunch to go."

"Oh, you didn't need to do that."

"I wanted you to have some of my fried chicken. I put in five pieces, two big biscuits, and a large piece of chocolate cake." She added, "I thought 'ya might wanna' stop on the way, at a picnic table."

I must have been staring at the handcrafted basket that held the chicken and cake. Miss Norvella noticed that and added, "The basket is yours to keep. Robert and I can't afford those store boughten gifts. But we are blessed to have a canebrake on the property we rent from Mr. Carl Green. Robert cuts the green cane and splits them and makes the basket while the cane is green. This one here he made for you is still green, but it will dry in a few days."

I smiled. "This is so nice of you guys. I'll cherish this for the rest of my life."

Miss Norvella grinned. "There's a reason we feel the need to make and give the baskets."

"You see, when Robert and I were at our lowest, the weeks after we learned we couldn't have children, we returned from church one Sunday, and sitting on the floor just inside the door, was a basket. Not only was the basket full of beautiful flowers, there also was a handwritten note. We don't have a clue to this day who left it. I rewrite the note, and we fill the baskets with flowers or food, and give, or leave them with people who we feel need cheering up. I believe God lets angels walk among us, and I also believe these angels also need a kind gesture from time to time."

She continued. "Your note is wrapped in some foil, and it's under your food. Mine and Robert's sincere prayer is God will bless you in all you choose to do."

I very humbly thanked her. I shook Robert's hand and gave both B.J. and Miss Norvella a big hug. I rolled down my car window and gave them a big farewell wave while I drove off.

There wasn't a soul at the Hopkins' house. I pulled into the drive and parked close to the house. I remember so very well that first day when Katie Jean walked out on the porch, and how I was amazed at her pure, natural beauty. I turned my head toward the yard to look at the long clothes line. My mind immediately went to the east end of the clothes line. I could still see those white towels hanging and gently blowing in the afternoon breeze.

I glanced up at the tater shed. The image of Donnie with his arm around Bo, his head down, eyes closed and praying, will forever be etched in my mind. I worked hard to erase the sounds I heard from Donnie, screaming from that awful beating across the road at the pig pens.

Little Mary Beth getting pounded for not planting the garden seed correctly still haunts me. I could be here till this time tomorrow if I attempted to recall all the abuse I heard and witnessed from Orville Hopkins.

It's hard for me, even now, not to become emotional. I can look down the road and see Bo wobbling when he desperately made his way home. His relentless, unwavering love for a little boy, gave him the strength to continue his journey back to Donnie.

Of course, there is the Mex house. So many sleepless nights found me writing songs and poems, and questioning what the heck I was doing. I could still vividly see Katie Jean's hungry eyes, while that big ole southern moon shone through the window the nights we engaged in forbidden love.

A quick glance at my watch alerted me I needed to be on the road. I also knew I wasn't leaving this farm until I said goodbye to a little boy's bestest, bestest buddy. I walked up towards Bo's pen and could tell Bo eagerly anticipated my visit. When I patted him on the top of his head, his tail rapidly wagged back and forth. I backed up so I could look into his face. Bo stared directly into my eyes. I felt he was thanking me for being there for his family. I wanted him to feel my heartfelt gratitude for him. I dropped down on my knees, and once again we stared into each other's eyes. I softly spoke, "Thank you, Bo, for walking beside Donnie and delivering God's much needed love." Bo's tail gently wagged a little faster. I said, "Goodbye Bo, take care of yourself, and take care of your best buddy in the world."

I turned and walked away, only to turn and look back at Bo one more time. I often wished Johnnie Hooper could have known Donnie. It then dawned on me again he just very well might. I felt my spirit speak directly with the spirit of an old friend. I whispered, "Thank you, Johnny Hooper."

I got back in my car, backed out of the driveway, then looked up toward the house one last time. All of a sudden, I had mixed feelings about what I was doing. I knew for a fact I could never find a better woman than Katie Jean. She was the full package. Very attractive, a proven hard worker, a loving woman. I most certainly knew my feelings for Katie could be real. How I would love to be the kind of daddy these kids needed and deserved.

Were my feelings for Katie Jean real love? Or had it all been my strong need to rescue her and the kids? Did Katie Jean truly love me? Or was I just her knight in shining armor on the big white horse that she needed to save her from the awful villain? If I stayed, could this be the first verse of a happy new song? Or should this be the last verse of a very twisted song?

Was I confusing true love with lust and sexual desire I enjoyed and craved? If I stayed, and there was true love, would she be willing to move to Kansas? We would have a nice home. All the kids could have their own room. Could there actually be a happy ever after? Then there is Brenda. Would I forever wonder, what if? Then it hit me. I know I must give this feeling for Brenda a chance. A real chance to either burn with a rage, or forever be extinguished.

CHAPTER 58

'Hold on to your faith, walk toward the light, and follow your heart.'

On my way toward Dexter, Missouri, I was amazed by the fields of white cotton. In no time, I was on the other side of Poplar Bluff, Missouri. My how quickly things changed. No more cotton fields, just mile-after-mile of cattle farms and forest land. I was beginning to think about Miss Norvella's chicken. I wondered how far it would be to a roadside park. My eyes were drawn to a big white church up ahead on the right. Darn. I had already driven past the long driveway to the church, so I turned my head far enough to see exactly what I needed. There was a covered pavilion at the rear of the church. I quickly made a U-turn on the highway and proceeded back to the church driveway.

It was actually more than I had hoped for. There were a number of large oak trees and several tall pine trees. I retrieved Miss Norvella's basket and my thermos, which I had filled with ice at the motel this morning. I sat down at one of the picnic tables under the covered pavilion. It was one of the most peaceful places I had been in my life. I began to eat, not able to believe how wonderful every piece of Miss Norvella's chicken was, plus the biscuits and cake were divine.

I finished my meal and was just relaxing. The sound of the wind whistling through the large pine trees mesmerized me. Then I noticed a very large, well maintained rose bush near the rear of the church. The blossoms were extremely dark red. I remember Karen had a rose bush very similar to this one. While I stared at the rose bush, a vivid memory appeared.

It was a few weeks after Karen and Randy's funeral, and I was consumed in total grief. Mom realized this and asked her church pastor, Brother Neal, to visit with me. I was carrying some trash out to the burn pit at the back of our house when Brother Neal, along with a male member of the church, pulled into our drive. We stood in the backyard and made small talk for a while.

The conversation led into Karen and Randy's death. Brother Neal said, "God had a need to call them home, Leon."

His statement just infuriated me. I made a statement, somewhat to the effect, that I had always been a Christian and had faith in God. I remember using a very harsh tone when I asked him, "You tell me how a just God could take my sweet Karen and my precious little boy?"

Brother Neal was stunned. He said, "Leon, I don't have a good answer for you." He pointed to the big, beautiful rose bush and said, "See that rose bush? A bad storm could come tonight. The wind could blow hard, heavy rain, and possibly hail could fall and damage that rose bush. Some of the beautiful blossoms could be torn away and lay wilting on the ground. Others might not be harmed at all. That is just part of nature and part of the Master's Plan. I think someday we will all clearly understand it."

Well, I didn't understand then, and I still don't understand it now.

Then almost out of nowhere, I had a clear vision of the dream I had experienced last night. I was so pleased that I took the time last night to recall and relive every image and event of my dream in an awakened state.

~ ~ ~ ~

I walked along the banks of a beautiful river and looked into the unbelievably clear, deep water. Every species of fish was so visible and extremely healthy. Every rock was so clean, and all the bushes and trees were extremely beautiful and lush.

I was admiring all the living things around me when out of nowhere, this big, magnificent bald eagle flew down and hovered a few feet over my head. It was as though I had zero gravity. I began to float, then I lifted straight upward. In an instant I became horizontal, the big beautiful eagle looked at me, and without verbalizing, let me know I was to follow.

We lifted upward and began to float above the river. I saw deep into the sparkling water. The clear water, at times, turned to an exceptional light blue. On both sides of the river were all types of animals. There were deer, bears, racoons, big cats, horses, cows and buffalo. There appeared to be every animal I had ever known about. Everything I saw was so beautiful and healthy.

They were all living in peaceful harmony, so content with each other. The eagle began to drift away from the river. We soared and glided across a lush green valley. We then climbed high and rose above a big marvelous mountain. When we reached the summit, I saw the whitest snow, then we smoothly glided downward.

We were rapidly approaching a long valley. Right in front of me was the most amazing thing I had ever witnessed in my entire life. It was a valley full of unbelievable, radiant flowers. Every type of flower known to mankind. Each one a perfect specimen, from roses of all colors to lilies. Some were very large, some extremely small and tiny, but every one, no matter the size, was bright and so radiant, glowing in every color you could possibly imagine, and they were all '*In Full Bloom.*' We gracefully glided down the valley, my breath at times was nearly taken away by the unbelievable beauty. We dropped lower and lower, no more than twenty-five to thirty feet above the valley floor.

I then saw dogs running through the flowers. Small dogs, big dogs, and mid-size dogs of every breed. All looked as though they had just walked out of the groomers. Their coats gleamed, and their faces spoke of happiness while they all played peacefully with each other.

There he was. Johnny Hooper. Sitting on a long bench, dogs sitting on each side of him and one sat on his lap. Johnny looked up at me and a big, warm smile consumed his face. He had a look of contentment and happiness like I had never seen before. I thought to myself, no more pain, no more being misunderstood, no more tears for Johnny. No more feeling the burden of making it difficult for family to love him. He slowly waved with a bright smile on his face while I glided past him.

Then a scene began to unfold in front of me, I assure you, I will never forget. Mom, Dad, Karen, and Randy, all clad in pristine white, all four with warm peaceful smiles. They were all so pleasantly happy. I desperately wanted to drop closer. I wanted to give each one a big hug. Instead, I began to rise, slowly, slowly moving away from them. I looked up and watched the big, beautiful eagle drift away from me. I, too, began to rapidly rise while I witnessed the eagle slowly vanish.

I suddenly woke up from the most fantastic, revealing dream I ever experienced.

~ ~ ~ ~

When I was done with my original dream, I quickly returned to my senses and realized I was reliving the dream. I sat on the picnic table bench and caught myself staring at the basket Robert had made and remembered Miss Novella's note. I unwrapped the foil from around the paper and began to read.

I was standing at the bottom,
had not been that low in all my years.

When a voice spoke softly,
and yet so very clear.

It said, I know about your troubles,
and I want you to know you are not alone,

I am offering you a shoulder
you are welcome to lean on.

When your troubles are too many,
you can't handle any more,

Put your troubles in this basket
and give the basket to the Lord.

Ask him for his guidance,
trust in his will.

He will hold your hand through the valley and
help you climb the highest hill.

I knew it was strictly symbolic, but I had an image of me placing my troubles in the basket, then the unthinkable happened. I literally pushed the basket to the far side of the picnic table. It was as though Jesus sat across from me.

Suddenly, the wind began to sway the tops of the big trees. I felt my eyes fill with tears. I was overwhelmed with sheer emotion. I dropped my head into my folded arms that lay on the table and began to weep. Tear after emotional tear flooded my eyes. As quickly as the tears had started, they stopped, they just simply stopped.

The wind quit blowing, and there was a calmness in the air. I sensed a light beginning to sparkle in the dark shadows of my heart. A peace came over me that I had not felt since my loss of Karen and Randy. A tranquil feeling of love consumed my entire body. A love like I have never felt before. A feeling I could easily forgive my greatest enemy.

In my attempt to understand the feeling I was experiencing, I wondered if this was the love God has for each of us? Was this possibly the abbreviated version of 'agape love' I have heard preachers speak on? I only know it was a feeling like no other feeling I had ever experienced.

I made sure I cleaned up around my table, then I made my way back to my car. It was a bright, beautiful sunny day, not a cloud in the sky. Just enough coolness in the autumn air to be comfortable with the window down. I made tracks toward Lamar, as the white highway divider lines swiftly zoomed past me. I was truly enjoying my afternoon.

~ ~ ~ ~

I found myself desperately trying to sort out the mixed feelings I still had about Katie and the kids. Just a few months ago, being romantically involved with a woman was the last thing on my mind. Now, I found myself being pulled between two. Somehow, I knew, regardless of what happened, Katie Jean and the kids would be just fine.

It is as though I clearly heard the voice of the Divine saying, 'Trust in God's will', and I knew that's what I needed to do.

~ ~ ~ ~

I drove up behind a slow-moving pick-up truck with a dog riding in the back. I thought of my dream and the vision I had of Johnny Hooper sitting with all those beautiful dogs. Then the thought occurred. Could the preacher that officiated Johnny's funeral been wrong? Perhaps Johnny had not trained his last dog.

Images of Brenda began to walk through the back pages of my mind. I was excited at the possibility of playing with a sweet little girl come nightfall. I couldn't wait to get there. Who knows, perhaps Larry could be right. Lamar, Missouri might be a good place to fall in love?

Suddenly a feeling of peace consumed my soul. I began to sing the ole hymn, *Amazing Grace.*

"Amazing grace, how sweet the sound, that saved a wretch like me, I once was lost, but now I'm found. Was blind, but now, I see."
Then out of nowhere, I heard voices singing the hymn with me. It was my family that I witnessed in my dream. They stopped singing and spoke to me. No, not physical voices, voices speaking to my heart. They all spoke in unison, in perfect harmony. Much like a well-rehearsed acapella choir, only they didn't sing. They spoke softly, yet so very clear.

Hold on to your faith, walk toward the light,
and follow your heart.
Hold on to your faith, walk toward the light,
and follow your heart.

That is exactly what I intend to do.

ABOUT THE AUTHOR

Jim Hooker was born in 1946, grew up on a cotton/cattle farm near Jonesboro, Arkansas. He attended elementary and high school in Bono, Arkansas until 1964, when his family moved to West Plains, Missouri. Jim graduated from West Plains High School with the class of 1965. He was owner/manager of a small Manufacturing Company for 38 years.

His love for dogs led him down a path to becoming a well-known professional dog trainer. Over the years he also raised different breeds of dogs including English Setters, American Brittanys, French Brittanys, English Pointers, and German

Shorthair Pointers. After his retirement in 2008, he continued to train dogs and established *Out and Back Kennel*, where he raised and trained quality registered Labrador Retrievers.

Jim and his wife, Marilynn, live on a small farm near West Plains, Missouri. They have two daughters who also graduated from WPHS, Tammie in 1988 and Andrea (Andi) in 1990. They both have college degrees and live in the Springfield, Missouri area.

A NOTE FROM THE AUTHOR

Unlike most paperback authors who use this page to promote future books and expose their past success, I will be honest with you, this is my first book and at age 77, most likely will be my last.

I have always enjoyed writing, mostly songs, poems, and short stories. I was encouraged by my high school English teacher to give writing a consideration as a career. In hindsight, perhaps I should have taken her advice. It is truly a passion for me.

The main reason for this book is to bring awareness to the devastating effects of mental health and the rough crooked road so many sufferers find themselves on, and also to bring awareness to the fact that *'the face of a childhood abuser is not the face you might think.'* Too many young children suffer from abuse that goes unnoticed. I was diagnosed several years ago with acute, complex PTSD, not as most would assume from Military duty, but from early childhood abuse.

As a young boy, like the character in this book, I had a black dog that was my rock. Without a doubt, my experience with him played a big role in my lifetime love of dogs.

I hope you enjoy IN FULL BLOOM and perhaps gain some insight for the purpose of its existence.

THE AUTHOR'S PERSONAL
EXPERIENCE WITH PTSD

The emotional roller coaster I found myself on was becoming worse. I was having difficulty sleeping, having what I now know were anxiety attacks, and outbursts of anger. I was driving down a highway and suddenly started to cry for no reason. There was a noticeable tremble in my hands. I was determined not to let anyone know about my condition, including my wife.

I had always had a 'tough man, don't-tread-on-me' persona. I was 8 feet tall and bulletproof. The guy who never cried at a sad movie. Suddenly I found myself getting emotional at the slightest thing, at times, with an outburst of uncontrollable tears. I thought, am I going crazy? A few weeks prior to my emotional problems, I had been diagnosed with Rocky Mountain Spotted tick fever. I had become extremely ill and spent several days in the hospital. I was questioning if my problem could be a reaction from the tick bite.

The tick fever had affected my urinary tract. I was sitting in the examining room at my urologist's office, when a nurse noticed something was wrong with me. She point-blank asked, "Mr. Hooker, are you okay?"

I replied, "No, I am not okay," and I broke down with tears running down my face. In hindsight, it was what I now know to be a trigger. The prostate exam the doctor would soon perform was a flashback.

I was sent immediately to my primary care doctor. My wife was called and my well-kept secret was revealed. The doctor sent me to a neurologist. The next few weeks, I went through a series of physical tests. My family's concern was possibly a brain tumor. All tests came back negative. The neurologist sent a jolt down my spine. Would you consider seeing a psychiatrist? What? I have a mental problem? I desperately wanted my normal life back and readily agreed to seek help.

On my second visit, the therapist asked me what I had done in Vietnam. I told her I was never in the service. She began to question me about my childhood. She first asked about my mother. I told her I had a wonderful and loving mother. She then asked about my dad. As I began to reveal things about my dad, she began to dig deeper into my relationship with him. She soon diagnosed me with acute complex PTSD. That was over 20 years ago.

Over these years, I have struggled with this mental illness and its devastating effects. I have sought help from three different behavioral health therapists. There has not been one day since my diagnosis that I haven't felt the hurt from my past. When it was assumed, my condition was physical, family and friends had an enormous amount of sympathy and concern. However, when it became known that my diagnosis was mental, things quickly began to change. I was pretty much on this island by myself.

PTSD–BASICS

Post traumatic stress disorder (PTDS) is a mental health problem caused by experiencing or witnessing a stressful event, or events over a period of time, that are life-threatening, scary, and/or traumatic.

Anyone can develop PTSD at any age. Factors that increase the chance of having PTSD are not under that person's control. For example, having a very intense or long-lasting traumatic event or getting injured during the event can make it more likely that a person will develop PTSD. It is also more common after certain types of trauma-such as combat, sexual assault, and childhood physical and sexual abuse.

SYMPTOMS

The symptoms usually start soon after the traumatic event, but may not appear until months, or years later. Memories of the event can come back at any time. They can feel very real and scary. A reaction can occur, brought on by hearing, seeing, or smelling something (a trigger) that is a reminder of the traumatic event, causing an intense feeling of reliving the event (a flashback). Nightmares are often another symptom.

Negative changes in thinking and mood may include:

    Negative thoughts about yourself, or others.

    Hopelessness about the future.

    Memory problems.

    Difficulty maintaining close relationships.

    Feeling detached from family and friends.

    Avoidance of crowds.

Other symptoms may include: feeling numb—unable to have positive or loving feelings toward other people—a loss of interest in things that used to be enjoyable—feeling of guilt or shame about the event–irritability–anger-outburst or aggressive behavior. Suicidal thoughts may occur when dealing with Acute Complex PTSD. Sadly, many sufferers have taken their own lives.

If you are having suicidal thoughts, reach out to a close friend or loved one. Contact a minister, a spiritual leader, or someone in your faith community.

To contact a suicide hot line in the U.S. Call or text 988 to reach the 988 Suicide and Crisis lifeline.

PTSD–SECONDARY WOUNDING

"They will have your back, well that is a joke, they will drop you in a heartbeat if you rock their boat. So consumed in their self-centered song, their foolish pride won't let them admit wrong. It rips his heart, this silent ghost, for that is the pain that hurts the most."

(Lines from a poem the Author wrote about Secondary Wounding)

Most professionals would agree, secondary wounding is a major contributing factor for those who chose to take their own life.

Below are quotes from a book, I CAN'T GET OVER IT

by author, Aphrodite Matsakis Ph. D.

"Secondary wounding occurs when others judge the victim negatively for normal reactions to a traumatic event, or from any long-term symptoms he or she may suffer. "It happened years ago, so get over it." Showing no sympathy for the victim, or the impact on the victim's life."

"As important to the healing process as other people are, it's an unfortunate truth that often people do more harm than good."

"Ignorance and insensitivity can take many forms…it is their effects that are often most devastating."

"Strangers who don't understand your situation can be unintentionally cruel, but so can those who should know better, family and friends."

"In essence, secondary wounding occurs because people who have never been hurt sometimes have difficulty understanding and being patient with people dealing with mental health. In addition, some people are simply not strong enough to accept the negatives in life. They prefer to ignore the fact that sadness, injustice, and loss are just as much a part of life as joy and goodness. When such individuals confront a trauma survivor, they may reject him or her, because that individual represents the parts of life they have chosen to deny."

"I Can't Get Over It" by Author Aphrodite Matsakis, Ph. D. (1996)

"Family and Friends" who will....

Come to your
B.B.Q

Visit you in
the Hospital

Go to your
Kids Wedding

Help you
Move

Stay beside you
When you have
a mental
problem

ACKNOWLEDGEMENTS

I want to thank all the wonderful people who lifted my spirits with words of encouragement to complete this book.

My behavioral health therapist, Mr. Tom Nixon, you were right, finishing the last chapter was very therapeutic, and added some closure.

Thank you to my critique readers, my dear friend, Jay Padgett, and my old West Plains high school classmates and dear friends, Jim and Juanita (Henry) Walker, Kenny and Sandy (Henderson) Joplin, and Janice (LeFevers) Bowden. Everyone's honest feedback was greatly appreciated. A very special thank you to classmate Linda (Gleason) Calhoun, your expertise and knowledge helped so much.

A big thank you to a fine young man, Mr. Judge Dixon and Kenny Joplin's beautiful black Labrador retriever for the cover photo, and T.M. Photography, your professional work was exceptional.

Sharon Kizziah-Holmes, with Paperback Press and my Publishing Coordinator, your talent and patience walking this old inexperienced writer through the legal and necessary protocol to complete a book, has been remarkable.

To my sweet daughter Tammie, thank you so much for being there, from day one to the very end. Your tech savvy computer skills were a blessing.

Last and most importantly, my wonderful wife and the love of my life, Marilynn. The truth is, this book would have never been completed without you. At times when I wanted to give up, you kept encouraging me to keep on pushing on. From the first day of my diagnosis of PTSD and to the present, like a peaceful tranquil island in the seas of life's stormy waters, you have been there. Thank you for everything you are.

Made in the USA
Monee, IL
23 March 2024

54981300R00187